'Jill Mansell just
gets better and better'
***** *Heat*

'A fab,
feel-good read'
Prima

PRAISE FOR

this could
change
everything

'Mansell is another writer whose
easy, breezy and uncomplicated
books have won her tons of fans . . .
feel-good escapism'
Daily Mail

'Feel-good'
Bella

'A page-turner'
Look

'Should be prescribed reading
for anyone feeling down
in the dumps'
Veronica Henry

'Achingly romantic . . .
we loved it!'
Heat

'A glorious, heartwarming
romantic read'
Woman & Home

THE JOY OF
Jill Mansell

'A lovely
uplifting read'
Good Housekeeping

'Jill Mansell is the
queen of witty,
heartwarming,
feel-good love stories'
Red

'A heartwarming treat
from one of my favourite
writers'
Katie Fforde

'Curl up with this hilarious
tale that's as heartwarming
as they come'
Sunday Mirror

Jill Mansell

is the author of over twenty *Sunday Times* bestsellers including THE ONE YOU REALLY WANT, TO THE MOON AND BACK and MEET ME AT BEACHCOMBER BAY. TAKE A CHANCE ON ME won the RNA's Romantic Comedy Prize, and in 2015 the RNA presented Jill with an outstanding achievement award.

Jill's personal favourite amongst her novels is THREE AMAZING THINGS ABOUT YOU, which is about cystic fibrosis and organ donation; to her great delight, many people have joined the organ donor register as a direct result of reading this novel.

Jill started writing fiction while working in the NHS, after she read a magazine article that inspired her to join a local creative writing class. Since she was first published in 1991, over ten million copies of her books have been sold worldwide. She is one of the few who still write their books by hand, like a leftover from the dark ages. She lives in Bristol with her family.

Jill Mansell

this could change everything

REVIEW

Copyright © 2018 Jill Mansell

The right of Jill Mansell to be identified as the Author of
the Work has been asserted by her in accordance with the
Copyright, Designs and Patents Act 1988.

First published in Great Britain in 2018 by
HEADLINE REVIEW
An imprint of HEADLINE PUBLISHING GROUP

First published in paperback in 2018 by
HEADLINE REVIEW

1

Apart from any use permitted under UK copyright law, this
publication may only be reproduced, stored, or transmitted, in
any form, or by any means, with prior permission in writing of
the publishers or, in the case of reprographic production, in
accordance with the terms of licences issued by the
Copyright Licensing Agency.

All characters in this publication are fictitious and any resemblance to
real persons, living or dead, is purely coincidental.

Cataloguing in Publication Data is available from the British Library

ISBN 978 1 4722 5199 2 (A-Format)
ISBN 978 1 4722 0898 9 (B-Format)

Map illustration by Laura Hall

Typeset in Bembo Std by Palimpsest Book Production Limited, Falkirk, Stirlingshire

Printed and bound in Great Britain by CPI Group (UK) Ltd, Croydon, CR0 4YY

MIX
Paper from
responsible sources
FSC® C104740

Headline's policy is to use papers that are natural, renewable and
recyclable products and made from wood grown in well-managed
forests and other controlled sources. The logging and manufacturing
processes are expected to conform to the environmental
regulations of the country of origin.

HEADLINE PUBLISHING GROUP
An Hachette UK Company
Carmelite House
50 Victoria Embankment
London EC4Y 0DZ

www.headline.co.uk
www.hachette.co.uk

For Lizzie Neath

With grateful thanks for her wonderfully generous
donation in aid of the victims of the
Grenfell Tower disaster.

Percival Square

Essie's attic flat

Zillah's house

Lucas's flat

the Red House

Chapter 1

What could be more glorious than sitting at a pavement café on a sunny afternoon in June, wearing a marvellous new hat and witnessing an imminent crime?

Zillah Walsh adjusted the brim of her red fedora and sat back, observing the scene unfold before her with fascination. The boy was definitely intent on shoplifting.

How exciting.

OK, it hadn't happened yet, but he was clearly in shop-lifting mode. You could tell by his body language: the hesitation, the air of elaborate casualness, the repeated glances over his left shoulder at the elderly customer behind him.

It was also pretty apparent that he wasn't the most accomplished of criminals, seeing as he hadn't noticed that he was being closely observed through the window by the owner of the shop.

Oh poor boy. What he was doing was wrong, of course it was, but Zillah couldn't help herself. Her heart went out to him. He'd picked up the item now, was pretending to examine it whilst stealthily inching it towards the pocket of his grey hoody.

Meanwhile the shop owner had moved closer to the door and was preparing to make a grab for him . . .

Oh no, she couldn't let it happen.

'Darling, I've changed my mind!' Zillah waved her arm in the air to attract the boy's attention and called across in her most carrying voice, 'Can you get me some of those too? Come here, you'll need more money.' She beckoned him over and watched as he belatedly spotted the shop owner waiting to pounce.

The boy replaced the about-to-be-stolen item on the display stand outside the shop and crossed the narrow street. Zillah took a five-pound note out of her purse. 'Buy a big bag of them, then come back and sit down with me. If he asks, tell him I'm your grandmother.'

He feigned innocence. 'Why would he ask?'

'Don't kid a kidder. Because I've just saved you from getting arrested.'

The boy cocked a cheeky eyebrow at her. 'OK. But I'm telling you now, you're *way* older than my grandmother.'

Zillah smiled as he turned away. She briefly wondered if he'd take the fiver and make a run for it, but no. He returned to the greengrocer and was now choosing fruit from the display.

The shop owner cast a suspicious glance in Zillah's direction and she nodded back at him charmingly. Oh yes, there were times when being a well-spoken, stylish octogenarian definitely came in useful.

'Here you go.' The boy was back, handing her a bulging bag of Pink Lady apples.

'Thank you. You may keep two for yourself. And I didn't know if you drank coffee,' said Zillah as he dropped the change into her hand, 'so I've ordered you an orange juice instead.' She pointed to the empty chair opposite. 'Sit.'

The boy sat down. 'Why are you doing this?'

'Honestly? I was intrigued. Aren't teenage boys these days more likely to shoplift cans of energy drink or strong cider? It isn't often you hear of them going for apples.'

He had a thin face, spiky dark hair and watchful eyes. 'I like apples. We don't get them at home.'

His clothes were cheap and a bit scruffy. Zillah said, 'I like apples too. But they're not worth getting a criminal record for.'

'I thought they wouldn't bother. It'd be more trouble than it was worth.'

'Maybe, but you don't know that for sure. How old are you?'

The orange juice arrived and he took a series of thirsty gulps. 'Thanks. I'm sixteen. How about you?'

'I'm eighty-three.'

'Wow, that's ancient. You look pretty good, though. For your age, I mean.'

'Thank you,' Zillah replied gravely. 'I do my best.'

'You look . . . rich.' His tone was matter-of-fact.

'I wear make-up. I buy myself nice clothes. I prefer bright outfits to dull ones.' She indicated her peacock-blue silk jacket, the vivid beads around her neck, then tilted her head and tweaked the brim of her scarlet fedora. 'I'm also very fond of a hat.'

He broke into a grin that lit up his thin face. 'I tell you what, you're *nothing* like my grandmother.'

His name was Ben, she discovered, and he was bunking off school. But it didn't matter because it was only citizenship, which was boring and didn't count.

3

'How do you know it doesn't count,' said Zillah, 'if you aren't there to learn about it?'

'That's the kind of thing teachers say. I've been often enough to know it's boring.' Ben nodded at her left hand, the back of which was covered with a large dressing. 'What happened there, then?'

'I was at the hospital this morning. It's just minor surgery.'

'What for?'

'I had a tattoo removed.' Zillah sipped her coffee.

'*Seriously?* . . . Oh, you're joking.' He looked disappointed. 'What was it really?'

'A synovial cyst.'

'Is that cancer?'

She shook her head. 'No, it's nothing nasty. They just drained fluid from it.'

Ben said, 'Well that's good. But what would you have done if it had been cancer? I always think about stuff like that, don't you? Would you write a bucket list?'

Zillah spluttered with laughter and put down her cup. 'A what?'

'Come on, you must have heard of them. People do them when they find out they're going to die. One of my cousins lives in Swindon and his next-door neighbour had cancer. He wrote a bucket list of things to do and went up in a hot-air balloon, which was pretty good, but then he pegged it before he could do any of the other stuff. Like, he wanted to meet Mick Jagger, but it didn't happen. Everyone was doing fund-raising things to send him to see the Rolling Stones in concert, but they ended up using the money to pay for the funeral instead.'

4

'I have heard of bucket lists.' Zillah nodded, because he was still looking quizzically at her.

'If you ever find out you're going to die, you should do one.'

'Darling, I'm eighty-three. Either way, I don't have many years left in me. I don't think people do bucket lists at my age.'

Ben shook his head. 'It must be weird, being so old.'

Zillah was enjoying herself immensely, all the more so because the owner of the greengrocer's shop was still watching them, trying to work out if they really were related. 'You kind of get used to it. So tell me, what would you put on your bucket list?'

'Good question.' He pointed at her approvingly. 'OK, what would I have? I'd go out for the night with Miley Cyrus. D'you know who she is?'

'Singer. Doesn't wear many clothes. Has been known to twerk. That the one?'

'Yeah. And I'd go swimming with dolphins. And definitely visit Disney World. And I'd get annual membership at the zoo.'

'In Disney World?'

'No, *here*.' Ben gestured over his shoulder and she realised he was pointing in the general direction of Bristol Zoo, roughly half a mile behind them. 'Don't tell me you've never been? It's wicked. Costs loads to get in, but if you buy a year's membership you can go in for free as often as you like. Every day, if you want.'

Now he'd really perked up. Zillah said, 'Which are your favourite animals there?'

'Oh no, don't make me choose. That's where I want to

work when I leave school next year.' His eyes were shining. 'It's like the best place in the world.'

When they'd finished their drinks, Zillah paid the bill and Ben said, 'Yeah, well. Thanks.'

'My pleasure. You could do me a favour in return, if you like.'

He rolled his eyes slightly. 'What's this, lecture time? No more shoplifting?'

'You don't need me to tell you that. Actually, I was wondering if you'd help me carry this little lot back to my car. What with my hand hurting a bit.' She indicated the dressing on the back of it. 'And me being so ancient.'

Zillah wasn't stupid; she knew there was a slim chance that when you passed your belongings to a stranger, including your handbag, they might run off with them. But she wanted to take the risk, and that meant really hoping this wouldn't happen.

It was an uphill walk past Clifton Suspension Bridge and across the broad stretch of grass separating the shops from the hospital where this morning's minor surgery had been carried out. Clifton being the parking nightmare it always was, she'd left her car in the hospital car park.

When they finally reached it fifteen minutes later, Ben placed the various shopping bags in the boot and gave her back the large leather handbag.

'Thank you,' said Zillah. 'I'm very grateful.'

'Nice car.' He ran a hand lightly over the Mercedes' gleaming navy-blue paintwork.

'I know. I can give you a lift home if you like.'

He gave a snort of laughter. 'You don't know where I live. Try driving down our road in this thing and you'd get hijacked. They'd have it off you and leave you lying in the gutter.'

6

'Well, if you're sure.' Opening her purse, Zillah belatedly realised that paying the bill in the café had left her without any change. She shook her head. 'Oh look, I was going to give you a couple of pounds, but I don't have anything. Sorry.'

Ben's face fell; he'd clearly been hoping for a tip. 'It's OK,' he said, attempting indifference. 'Doesn't matter.'

'Here, write down your address for me and I'll post it to you instead.' She found a pen and an old receipt in the bottom of her bag. Ben hesitated for a second, then did as she asked. Returning them to her, he said, 'You don't need to.'

'If I post it, will it reach you?'

'What, two pound coins in an envelope?' He shrugged. 'I suppose miracles do happen.'

'Take the apples as well.' Zillah smiled as she handed them over. 'They're yours.'

That evening, back home in Bath, she addressed an envelope to Ben, slipped a ten-pound note inside and added a brief note saying: *I enjoyed meeting you!*

An hour later, having looked at Bristol Zoo's website and purchased online a year's membership in his name, she printed off the confirmation and added it to the contents of the envelope.

Then she sealed the envelope and poured herself an ice-cold gin and tonic, raising it by way of silent celebration.

Would he use the membership?

Would he sell it for a bit of ready cash?

Who knew? She certainly didn't.

Ah well, here's to Ben, the inept apple thief. Cheers!

Chapter 2

It was five o'clock and the Christmas lights were on, illuminating the busy shopping street below, whilst flakes of snow tumbled from an ink-black sky. Through the third-floor window of Georgian building, Conor McCauley gazed down at Bath's bustling shoppers, took in the festive atmosphere and listened to the distant sound of Mariah Carey singing about all she wanted for Christmas. Closer to hand, he could also hear the strains of a violin being played. The music was familiar and hauntingly melodic, and he pushed open the heavy sash window in order to be able to hear it more clearly.

There was the violinist, tall and long-haired, standing in the centre of the street that had been closed to traffic for the evening. As he played, the folds of his full-length Sirius Black style coat swayed around his thin denim-clad legs. There was a hat on the ground in front of him, containing a handful of coins. Few people were stopping to listen – they were too busy and too cold – but he carried on anyway, his bow darting and dipping as he played, lost in the beauty of the music . . .

8

The next moment Conor did a double-take, because the violinist was no longer alone. A girl had appeared from nowhere and launched into a series of ballet steps that caused his breath to catch in his throat. She was wearing a white bobble hat, a Puffa jacket and jeans, and a long knitted scarf that swung out as she spun and danced and leapt like a gazelle into the air. Her feet were enclosed in plain white trainers but that didn't hold her back. He glimpsed the girl's broad smile as she raised her arms, freestyled elegantly once more around the violinist like a will-o'-the-wisp, then executed a graceful leap into the air followed by a stunningly beautiful series of pirouettes.

Within two minutes, it was over. Despite the falling snow, a group of around thirty people had stopped to watch. They broke into enthusiastic applause and threw money into the violinist's hat. Aware of the pound coins in his own jeans pocket, Conor was tempted to throw them down too, but maybe not; if he hit someone on the head he might kill them stone dead.

Which wouldn't be a good look.

As he continued to watch, entranced by the unexpectedness and the charm of the impromptu scenario, the girl in the white bobble hat briefly waved her gloved fingers at the violinist before retrieving the bag of shopping she'd left at the kerbside and melting away into the crowd of Christmas shoppers, who'd been oblivious to the display.

For a moment all Conor wanted to do was race downstairs and chase after the disappearing girl. He longed to tell her how delightful her brief performance had been, and to find out who she was and what had made her do it. If this were one of those romantic films girls were often so crazy about,

9

it would be a matter of love at first sight; their snowy chance encounter in the street would change their lives forever and lead to—

The door behind him opened and a middle-aged woman carrying a camera and a mince pie appeared in the room.

'Sorry to keep you, dear – Arthur couldn't remember where he'd put it! His memory's not what it used to be, bless him. Still, at least he still knows how to repair broken cameras. There you go, all fixed now. And he says you must have a mince pie to make up for having to wait so long.'

By the time Conor had paid and left the tiny workshop on the third floor of the building, the girl in the white bobble hat was long gone, and the long-haired violinist had departed too. Even the snow had stopped falling.

It was like Brigadoon, as if the entire magical scenario he'd witnessed had never existed.

Unaccountably disappointed, Conor did the only thing he could do and took a consolatory bite of his mince pie.

Oh well.

Chapter 3

'Oh Essie, will you look at this place? It's like you're an actual proper grown-up now!'

'I know. Isn't it weird?' Essie still marvelled at the ways in which her life had changed in the last twelve months. At twenty-five, she and Scarlett had been sharing a shabby, cluttered flat with lavish amounts of mould on the ceilings, posters covering the cracks in the walls, noisy neighbours above and below, and the kind of furniture that looked as if it had been stolen from a skip. Which, knowing their landlord, was most likely where it had come from.

Then she'd met Paul, almost exactly a year ago, and by some miracle he'd liked her as much as she'd liked him. Better still, after eleven months together, the grasping landlord had announced that he was raising the rent and Paul had said, 'For that dump? What a nerve he has. Tell him to get lost.'

'Great idea,' Essie had jokingly replied. 'I'll do that, and move into a five-star hotel instead.'

That was when Paul had taken her hands in his and looked deep into her eyes. 'I mean it, Ess. I love you. It's going to happen sooner or later, so why don't you move in with me?'

Well, who in their right mind would want to turn down an offer like that? Paul was the type of perfect boyfriend most girls could only dream of. He was kind, he was thoughtful, he was good-looking and he always emptied the kitchen bin before it was too full.

Scarlett called him Prince Charming.

Now she gazed around the cottage in admiration. 'You've done well for yourself, Cinderella.'

'I know it's lovely, but that's not why I'm here,' said Essie.

'Oh of course I know that! You'd be happy living in a tent if it meant being with Paul. I'm just saying that the fact he has this place is a bit of a bonus.'

Essie grinned and opened the bottle of wine she'd taken out of the fridge. 'I suppose it doesn't do any harm.'

'I can't get over everything being so perfect. The glasses are a full set . . . those kitchen blinds are exactly the same shade as the floor tiles . . . even the tea towels match the toaster!'

'Nothing wrong with a bit of coordination.' Pouring the wine, Essie said, 'Paul likes his home to look good, and now so do I. I'm growing up. Cheers!'

'Cheers. I'm not having a go at him, by the way. You know I love Paul. I'm just jealous . . . I mean, look at that.' Scarlett pointed gleefully. 'Completely empty! You don't even have any dirty dishes soaking in the sink!'

'That's because he only left this afternoon.' Since Scarlett knew what she was like, Essie didn't have to pretend to be a domestic goddess. 'He's away for two days, so I'll have to make sure all the washing-up's done before he gets back.'

An hour later, their gossipy catch-up was interrupted by a call from Essie's brother, Jay.

'My favourite sister! Hellooo!'

'What a racket,' said Essie, barely able to hear him over the background noise of voices and music. 'Where are you?'

'I'm in a library. OK, maybe that's not true. I'm here in Bath. I drove over for a party.'

'And did you find one?'

'Believe it or not, I did. Hang on, let me move somewhere quieter. OK, the thing is, if the party'd been rubbish I was going to drive home. But it isn't rubbish, it's great, so now I'll be heading back tomorrow. Which means . . .'

His voice had trailed off. Essie knew what this meant. She said, 'You're spending the night in your car? It's cold out there, mind. You'll want to borrow a blanket.'

'Did I happen to mention you're my favourite sister?'

She was his only sister. Essie said, 'You may have done, once or twice.'

'Ess. Lovely Ess. Can I crash at yours?'

Her brother lived twenty miles away, in Bristol, and had old uni friends in Bath. Three weeks ago, he'd come over and spent the night in the spare room, before heading home the next morning.

'OK,' said Essie. 'Paul isn't here, but that doesn't matter.' She knew Paul wouldn't mind. 'What time will you get here?'

'Who knows? But it'll be late. Don't worry about waiting up – just leave a key somewhere and I'll let myself in.'

'Fine. I'll hide one under the blue plant pot by the front door. But don't make any noise, all right? Because a kick down the stairs often offends.'

'I'll be silent! As silent as the grave,' Jay promised. 'And I'll bring you up a coffee in the morning. Thanks, Ess. You're a star.'

13

While Essie was on the phone, Scarlett had been inspecting the Christmas cards lined up on the mantelpiece. Now she said, 'There's no glitter on any of these cards.'

'I know.' Essie had already noticed this; she was partial to a bit of glitter.

'And no Father Christmas either. They're all so . . . boring.'

This thought had crossed Essie's mind too. 'The word is tasteful.'

'Who *are* these people?'

'Family friends. Of Marcia, mainly.'

Marcia was Paul's mother. Scarlett pulled a sympathetic face, then picked up a folded sheet of paper that had been tucked behind one of the cards. 'What's this, a secret love letter? Don't tell me Paul leaves romantic notes for you to find when he's away . . . Oh bum.' She looked disappointed. 'It isn't a love letter.'

'It's a round robin,' said Essie. This one, written by one of Paul's aunts, had arrived yesterday. She'd read it and started to laugh, and Paul had warned her that there would be more to come. His family, he explained, were very keen on the tradition of sending out round robins; they all did it and would be disappointed if she and Paul didn't write one too.

'I've heard of them, but I've never seen a real one before . . . Oh my God this is brilliant, Hyacinth Bouquet as I live and breathe!' Letting out a shriek, Scarlett adopted a Hyacinth voice and began to read aloud:

'"Jonathan managed not to disgrace himself and scraped through his GCSEs with eleven A stars and one A! Such a shame to have missed out on a full house – we've told him he must work *much* harder in future! Meanwhile, Hugo has been promoted yet again and is now leading a team of seventy – apparently the youngest person ever to hold such a senior position within the company!'" Doubled up with laughter, Scarlett began skimming in order to pick out the best bits. "'Arabella's violin lessons continue apace . . . she has been inundated with offers to play at prestigious events" . . . oh, and "Letitia's stay at the yoga retreat in Arizona proved marvellously calming and relaxing after the pressure of her dazzling career in the banking world . . . Our holiday this year was a wonderful month in a villa on the banks of Lake Como, where we became quite accustomed to bumping into a certain world-famous film star on an almost daily basis. Jeffrey grew quite jealous of the attention he paid me on one occasion when I accidentally dropped my sunglasses next to his car!"'

'How can I write one of those things?' Essie cringed at the idea and pulled a face. 'Just the *thought* of trying to put one together makes me want to die of embarrassment.'

'Oh, this is better than brilliant.' Pointing to the final paragraph, Scarlett cackled with delight. "'We can't wait for the hordes to descend this Christmas for a week of merriment and good cheer! Our children and extended family do *so* look forward to coming to us so we can all celebrate the festive season together in the traditional way!"' She snorted. 'Ha, of course they do. I can imagine how much they look forward to it.'

'Well according to Paul, Letitia's so-called yoga retreat was actually a rehab clinic,' Essie confided. 'Jonathan's an insufferable know-it-all who likes to shoot at birds from his bedroom window with his BB gun. And Arabella's a slutty minx whose favourite hobby is sleeping with other women's husbands.'

15

'See? That's the trouble with these things.' Scarlett waved the round robin triumphantly. 'Why do people always have to pretend their lives are perfect? All it does is make other people feel like failures. Why can't they be honest about what's going on?'

'Exactly.' Essie nodded vigorously in agreement. 'Because then we'd like them *more*. It just makes so much sense!'

'Right, that's it. What were we saying earlier about not knowing what to get each other for Christmas?' Scarlett spread her hands. 'Well, problem solved, we'll do this instead. I'll write a completely honest round robin to you, and you can write one to me. And no one else will ever see them, they'll be our secret. How about that?'

Entertained by the idea, Essie divided the last of the wine between their glasses. 'Hundred per cent honest?'

'No holds barred. Let it all out. It'll be like therapy, only cheaper.'

'And it's just between us?' she double-checked.

'Of course. Million per cent.'

'OK, let's do it.' Scarlett trusted her and she in turn trusted Scarlett. 'It'll be fun. And cheap!' Essie held up her glass. 'The truth, the whole truth, and nothing but the truth. Cheers!'

And since there was no time like the present, as soon as Scarlett had left the cottage to catch the last bus home, Essie decided to make a start. Sitting with her laptop balanced on her knees and her mind bursting with ideas, she began to type.

How time flew. The words, helped along by the bottle of Sauvignon Blanc they'd demolished earlier, came tumbling out. Gosh, this was fun. And so cathartic! Seriously, though, wouldn't the world be a happier place if everyone could just relax, let go of their inhibitions and write one of these things? Ooh, it was probably like in the olden days when people kept diaries, except this was way more fun because Scarlett would soon be reading it, shrieking with laughter at the funny bits and appreciating every last—

God, what was that noise? Was there a *dolphin* in the kitchen?

Essie pushed the laptop to one side and leapt off the sofa, because the unearthly sound was so high-pitched it was hurting her ears. The next moment she yelped and jumped back onto the sofa as Ursula burst into the living room with a panicking, terrified crow in her mouth.

'No!' Essie let out a howl of horror because the crow's eyes were wide open and it was making a terrible squawking noise. Much like herself. It was also flapping its wings wildly in an effort to escape.

Oh God, this was *so* gross. In the few weeks Essie had been living here, Ursula had brought her the odd present in the form of mice and voles, but they'd all been completely dead.

That had been gruesome enough, but this was worse. Essie yelled, '*Drop it, DROP IT!*' then realised this would mean having to pick up the crow herself. Urgh, and the high-pitched noise emanating from its gaping beak was getting louder. Launching herself off the sofa cushions, she clapped her hands and attempted to shoo the murderous cat back into the kitchen.

'*Kikkikki!*' shrieked the petrified crow, both wings flailing as Ursula ducked and dived around the living room with its body hanging out of her mouth.

17

'OUT!' bellowed Essie, grabbing a cushion and brandishing it at Ursula. Oh no, and now there were drops of blood landing on the carpet. In desperation, she flung open the window and chased the cat around the living room a couple more times. It was like one of those frenetic Benny Hill sketches her grandfather had loved to watch on TV years ago, except this was less of a comedy romp, more of a nightmare.

Finally Ursula released her grip on the crow. She gave Essie a malevolent look as if to say, 'This is all the thanks I get?' before turning and exiting the kitchen via the cat flap in the back door.

Evidently relieved, the crow flew up in the air, circled the living room and did a series of victory poos by way of celebrating having escaped with its life.

'No, *don't*,' Essie wailed, ducking as it swooped back towards her, just missing her head. Her heart was clattering with panic; she hated seeing any living creature in pain, but the frantically flapping wings were making her feel sick.

Moments later, as suddenly as it had arrived, the crow found the open window and flew out through it, disappearing with an upwards swoosh into the cold night sky.

Thank goodness. At last.

Essie listened to the blessed silence and clutched her still-pounding chest with relief. Then she hastily closed the window before the bird could come blundering back in, and turned to survey the scene.

It was carnage. There were feathers scattered everywhere, and tiny spatters of blood that wouldn't have shown up if Paul had only chosen a dark patterned carpet rather than a plain cream one. But he hadn't, which meant they were all

18

too visible. And there were splodges of black-and-white crow poo too. What more could you want at eleven thirty at night?

Essie exhaled slowly. There was nothing else for it; she was going to have to do her best to clear up the mess before it dried in. The carpet had been expensive. If Paul had been here, he'd be doing it himself, but seeing as he was up in London on business, the task fell to her.

Forty minutes later, the cat flap rattled and the would-be murderer strolled back in to sit on the sofa and observe the clean-up operation unblinkingly.

'Thanks, Ursula.' As she scrubbed away at the carpet, Essie noted how cosily the cat's front paws were tucked beneath her. 'No, really. Thanks so much. You're a great help.'

It was twenty to one in the morning before she finished the job, having worked on the stains until her arms and shoulders ached. Ursula, who'd been sleeping, opened a laconic eye as Essie carried the cleaning equipment through to the kitchen and gave her hands one last wash. Finally, she left the spare front door key under the plant pot next to the porch so that Jay could let himself in when he turned up.

Right, all done.

Shattered now.

Bed.

Chapter 4

Seven hours later, Essie was dragged out of sleep by the sound of her mobile ringing on the bedside table. Fumbling for it with her eyes still closed, she pressed Answer and murmured, 'Yes?'

'Oh my God, Ess! What did you do? What *happened* after I left you last night?'

Just reaching across for her phone and holding it to her ear had exacerbated the ache in her shoulder from all the scrubbing. Essie rolled onto her back. 'Don't remind me. What a complete nightmare! Ursula brought a live crow in through the cat flap and raced around the cottage with it in her mouth, then she let it go and it was flapping its wings and *pooing* everywhere and there were spatters of blood on the carpet . . . It's the most hideous thing that's happened to me in years—'

'Whoa, whoa,' Scarlett interrupted. 'I'm not talking about Ursula. This is about the email.'

'What email?'

'The one you *sent*. The round-robin thing! Ess, did you open another bottle of wine after I left?'

'What?' Essie frowned. Had she? No, there'd been no

more wine, just plenty of Cif and scrubbing sponges and hot soapy water and stain remover. 'I didn't send any email. One hundred per cent definitely didn't do it.'

'Well someone did! OK, did you write a round robin?'

'Yes, but I didn't send it to you.'

'You're right, you didn't send it to *me*.' Scarlett sighed. 'OK, brace yourself. You sent it to everyone in your address book.'

'No . . . I haven't sent anything to anyone.' Essie's stomach began to clench with fear, cottoning on faster than her just-woken brain. 'I wrote it, but that's all. What do you mean, it's gone to everyone in my address book? It can't have done . . . that's impossible. Are you joking?' As she said it, she threw back the duvet and jumped out of bed.

'I wish I was. This isn't a joke. Ess, I don't understand, it's right here on my phone, I'm looking at it now. It's been sent out to over two hundred email addresses . . .'

Oh fuck. *Fuck*. Now Essie had never been more awake in her life. Swallowing a wave of nausea, she wrenched open her bedroom door and heard the telltale burble of the TV playing downstairs.

So much for having made up the bed in the spare room. After a good night out, Jay had always preferred to collapse on the sofa and fall asleep with the TV on. And yes, there he was, out for the count and with his shoes kicked off, but otherwise fully clothed.

And there was her laptop, sitting on the marble coffee table. Where had she left it before going to bed? On the sofa with the lid up. Now the lid was closed. Essie's knees were trembling as she descended the stairs, opened the computer and saw what she already knew she'd see.

But viewing the evidence in black and white brought her to a whole new level of panic and despair, as the enormity of what it signified began to sink in. There was no other conceivable way it could have happened, no way at all.

'Oh my God, you *stupid* . . .' It was no good; words simply failed her. Nothing was bad enough. Essie shook her brother's shoulder, which elicited no response, then gave him an almighty shove so that he rolled off the sofa and landed on the floor with a thud.

'*Ow*,' Jay complained, jolted awake and gazing up at her in wounded disbelief. He blinked blearily. 'What was that for?'

'The email you sent. It was you, wasn't it? I can't believe you did it.' She aimed a barefoot kick at his leg and was so angry she managed to miss it completely. 'I let you sleep here and that's how you repay me? How could you even *think* it would be a good idea?'

'What . . . ?' He screwed his face up in apparent confusion.

'Don't even try to wriggle out of this. I left my laptop open, you saw what I'd written and you'd had enough to drink that you thought it'd be hilarious to send it out to everyone I know. Jay, I actually want to kill you. Because guess what? It isn't funny. What you've done is going to cause me a whole world of trouble. This could wreck everything, don't you get it? *Everything.* You sent it to Paul, you sent it to his *mother* . . . I can't even bear to think about what's going to happen when they see it, and it's *all your fault.*'

'OK, look . . . I didn't do anything. I know what's happened,' Jay said suddenly. 'It was the cat. She walked across your keyboard. I bet that's what it was. You know what cats are like.'

Essie stared at him. 'Are you seriously saying that's how the email got sent out?'

'Yes!'

Her voice rose. 'And you're actually expecting me to believe it?'

'That's what cats do! They walk over things!' Still on the floor, Jay made cat's paws out of his hands and mimed them padding along.

'So you reckon Ursula pressed All and *then* she pressed Send. Of course she did. Oh God, Paul's going to dump me, his mother's going to sack me, my life is going to be over and I'm never, *ever* going to forgive you for this . . . Aaargh!' Essie let out an even louder shriek of alarm as behind her, someone cleared their throat. She spun round wildly. 'What's going on? Who the hell are *you*?'

'I'm Lucas. I'm sorry. I did it. It was me.'

'You *what*?' Essie stared at the stranger in the living room, then back at her brother on the floor. 'Who is he? What's he doing here?' It was like the worst kind of dream, except she wasn't dreaming. That would be far too easy.

Jay shrugged. 'His name's Lucas. I met him at the party last night. He'd lost his jacket with his wallet and keys in it and couldn't get home. And it was, like, four in the morning, so I said he could stay here. I knew you wouldn't mind.'

'You're telling me a complete stranger spent the night in our spare room, even though he could have been anyone. And you didn't even think to ask me if it was OK?'

'Oh come on,' Jay protested. 'At four o'clock in the

23

morning? You told me not to wake you up! Anyway, if I had asked you earlier, you know you'd have said yes.'

'I offered to sleep on the sofa,' said Lucas, 'but your brother insisted I took the bed.'

'But first you sent my letter to everyone?' Essie could scarcely bear to look at him; she was shaking. 'Why? Why would you do that?'

'I'm sorry. I'm so sorry. It was such a bad idea.' He shook his head helplessly. 'We'd been to a great party, we'd had some drinks . . . well, quite a few drinks . . . then we came back here in a taxi. Jay picked up your laptop to move it somewhere safe, and that was when all the stuff you'd been writing appeared on the screen. So we read it, and we thought it was hilarious, then Jay went off to the bathroom and I just . . . you know, kind of . . . sent it.'

'Because?'

He shrugged. 'I guess we'd thought it was funny, so why not give more people a laugh? It was one of those stupid, spur-of-the-moment decisions. The next thing I knew, I was pressing Send to All, then I closed the laptop and headed up to bed. It wasn't your brother's fault. He didn't know I'd done anything. It was all me.'

Through gritted teeth, Essie said, 'Great.'

'Again, sorry. I'm an idiot.'

'I wrote some awful things about my boyfriend's mother. It was a private joke between my best friend and me. No one else was ever going to see it, let alone the people I'd written about. But now you've sent it to them.' There was a dull ache in Essie's chest. She knew she was in shock; her brain was doing its best to protect her by shutting out the worst of the panicky thoughts that were ricocheting around it.

24

'Is there any way we can delete the email? There must be,' said Jay.

'There isn't.' Essie shook her head. 'Not once it's been sent.'

'Well there should be.' Jay frowned. 'Someone needs to invent an app for that. They'd make themselves a fortune.'

Lucas looked at him for a long moment, his jaw taut. Then he turned back to Essie. 'OK, I've got it. You tell them it was nothing to do with you. I'll say I wrote the whole thing. They can't blame you for that, can they? Not if I go and see them and confess.'

Essie considered this option, willing it to be possible but already aware that it wasn't. The details she'd included in the letter had clearly come from her. No one else would have been able to invent them.

'It's no good, it wouldn't work. They'd know it was me.' Tears of frustration sprang into her eyes as she realised there was no way out. No amount of grovelling would ever make up for this.

'I'm sorry,' Lucas repeated.

'You keep saying it, but it doesn't help. You have no idea what you've done. You've ruined my life, quite literally *ruined it*.' The words caught in Essie's throat as she took a shuddery breath. 'I don't even know you, but I despise you.' She hated crying, but it was happening anyway; the tears were sliding down her cheeks and dripping off her chin. 'And I never, ever want to see you again. Go, please. Just leave.' She looked at him and pointed to the front door. 'You've done enough.'

Breaking the ensuing deathly silence, Jay said, 'What about me? Do you want me to stay?'

Essie shook her head. 'No point. There's nothing you can do.'

'OK.' He glanced at Lucas. 'Come on, let's go. I'll call a cab.'

Once the two of them had left, Essie sat down and wrote out a long explanatory email to send to everyone who'd received a copy of the round robin. It hadn't been genuine; it had been a joke, of course it had. Someone had played a trick on her, writing and sending it on her behalf, and it went without saying that none of it was true.

Which would take care of most of the recipients, those who didn't actually know her that well. They would read the round robin, have a good laugh about it, hopefully sympathise with her over the embarrassment that had been caused, then promptly forget it.

Unlike those closer to home. Who definitely wouldn't.

But it had to be done. Trembling and feeling sicker than ever, Essie brought the round robin up on the screen and forced herself to reread the words she'd written.

Oh God . . .

Chapter 5

Hi, Essie here!

Well, the festive season is fast approaching and – surprise – all my wonderful plans to spend the last year improving myself crashed and burned. I still hate lettuce, didn't manage to get past page eight of Anna Karenina and I never did join that evening class in conversational Spanish. As for those sixty sit-ups a day . . . what was I thinking of? Not a chance!

Other than that, the year got off to a very happy start when I met Paul. He's the love of my life and we're now living together, which is brilliant, even if he thinks he doesn't snore. And he's so tidy, too, which has been a bit of a shock to the system. Never mind, I'm sure as time goes by I'll get used to our Sunday-morning vacuuming sessions with his top-of-the-range Gtech.

I have a new job, too! And what could be lovelier than working for your boyfriend's mother? Well, it might be lovely if she weren't a complete nightmare, but it was Paul's idea, so I had to go along with it. They needed a new receptionist at the dental surgery and he insisted I'd be perfect for the job. Everyone else there is nice, though; it's only his mum we have to watch out for. She's so bossy! Which is fair enough, I suppose, seeing as she *is* my boss, but oh, does she have to be such a dragon?!

Which is why I'm dreading Christmas Day SO much. Ten whole hours at her house – just the thought of it makes me want to run away and hide. The last time we were there for lunch she asked me to lay the dining table, then told me off for using one of the best Sunday table-cloths instead of a weekday one. And when I offered to do the dishes afterwards, she got cross because I washed the cutlery before the pudding bowls. Oh, and I gave her a really pretty purse for her birthday, and she asked me where it was from. When I said I'd bought it from a stall at the Guildhall Market, she gave me one of those sneery, shuddery looks of hers and went, 'Hmm, yes, thought so.'

So my best possible Christmas present this year would be *not* having to spend the day with Paul's mother. But I do have to, so wish me luck. What a shame I can't wave a magic wand and swap her for someone nice!

Anyway, that's my news – it's been a swings-and-round-abouts kind of year, as you can see. On the upside, I now have unlimited access to dental floss!

A very happy Christmas to you all.

Much love,

Essie xxx

'I'm so sorry,' Scarlett said miserably when Essie called her back. 'I feel like it's my fault. If I hadn't had the idea of us sending each other a round robin, none of this would have happened.'

'You could say it was my fault for writing it. Or Ursula's fault for bringing that crow into the cottage . . . or Jay's fault for inviting that idiot friend of his back here . . .'

'He's the main one,' Scarlett agreed. 'He was the one who sent it. That was pure evil.'

Essie felt sick all over again. 'I know.' Although to be fair, he hadn't been evil. Just brainless.

'Have you heard from, you know, anyone else yet?'

She meant Paul and his mother. 'Not yet. Still have that to look forward to.'

'Oh God.' She could practically hear Scarlett wincing with sympathy down the phone. 'Good luck.'

The sound of his front-door key turning in the lock two hours later caused Essie to jump a mile. Paul had left his very important weekend business conference in Dulwich and driven home down the M4.

One look at the expression on his face told her all she needed to know.

Not that she hadn't been expecting it, seeing as he hadn't replied to any of her voicemail messages or texts.

He surveyed her now. 'I don't know what you thought you were doing,' he said stonily, 'but I hope you're happy with the result.'

'Of course I'm not happy! It was an *accident*.' Essie spread her hands. 'A terrible mistake. It was meant to be a joke and your mum was never supposed to see it!'

'She always said I deserved better. Turns out she was right.'

Marcia had actually said that? *Ouch*. Then again, hadn't Essie always known, deep down, that her own rather modest upbringing hadn't met Marcia's high standards?

'The fact that we saw it isn't the point,' said Paul. 'It's that you wrote it. My mother gave you that job at the clinic and this is how you repay her. And it's how you repay me for suggesting you for the position in the first place.'

He was furious, and understandably so; there was no sign of his usual friendly manner and easy smile. Essie said, 'I know. It was a horrible thing, but—'

'Anyway, you've managed to solve your problem,' he continued. 'No need to dread spending Christmas at Mum's house, because you're no longer invited. So that must come as a relief, mustn't it?'

'I'm sorry. I honestly never meant for it to happen.'

'And you won't have to listen to my snoring any more, either. Even though I don't snore.'

There was a permafrost edge to his voice now. Essie couldn't speak.

'It's like looking at a stranger.' Paul shook his head. 'You're not the girl I thought you were. I feel as if I don't know you at all.'

Essie swallowed; she was officially a terrible person. What else was there to say?

'And what's *that*?' He was now pointing down at the carpet, where, in the harsh light of day, it was apparent that the spots of blood hadn't been completely eradicated after all. He raised his gaze. 'What's been going on here?'

'Ursula brought a crow in through the cat flap. It was still alive and spraying blood. I did my best to clean it up.'

'Did you now? How caring of you, how thoughtful.' He paused, raised a sceptical eyebrow. 'Or have you had that noisy friend of yours over here, hmm? Might the stains actually be red wine?'

'It wasn't wine! It was *blood*,' Essie protested. She'd already done one very bad thing and been found out. Being accused of something else and this time being innocent was just unfair.

'You used the carpet cleaner that contains bleach. That's for white carpet only.' Paul pointed. 'Look at the faded patches. This one's a Berber and it cost over two thousand pounds.' He shook his head in disbelief. 'You can't even clean a carpet properly.'

It was hard to believe that just two days ago they'd been dancing together in the kitchen because her favourite song by Adele had started playing on the radio, and as they'd sung along to the track Paul had broken off to say, 'God, I'm so lucky to have you.' She'd grinned and replied playfully, 'Yes, you are.' Then mid-dance she'd kicked Ursula's water bowl, sending it skittering across the floor, and they'd both burst out laughing . . .

There had been so many happy memories like that.

Well, clearly Paul wasn't feeling quite so lucky to have her now.

Essie looked over at Ursula, who was sitting on the windowsill slowly swishing her tail as she observed their tense exchange. She was perfectly well aware that Ursula had never liked her either.

'You do know we're over, don't you?' said Paul.

'Yes.' What a way for it to end.

'Are you going to kick up a fuss?'

'No.'

'Well I suppose that's something to be grateful for.' As he spoke, he took out his phone and rapidly fired off a text. Thirty seconds later, Essie blanched as her own phone began to ring.

'That's my mum. She'd like to speak to you now.'

It wasn't one of the high points of her life. But it had to be done. Her mouth as dry as the Sahara, Essie said, 'Hello?'

'Estelle, thank you for letting me know what you think of me. I'm sure we'll both enjoy Christmas all the more for not having to tolerate each other's company.'

Zing-zing-*zinggggg* went the poisoned arrows aimed directly at Essie's chest. She swallowed with difficulty. 'Look, can I just say how—'

'I don't think we need to bother with any of that, Estelle. I already know everything I need to know, and I shall accept your resignation from the surgery with immediate effect. If I could have that in writing by the end of the day, it would be appreciated.'

'Oh, but—'

'And that's better than you deserve, young lady. You can thank your lucky stars that I'm not dismissing you on the spot.'

A click, followed by silence. Marcia had hung up.

Through the living-room window, Essie saw that outside it had begun to rain heavily.

'You'd better get your things together.' Paul's tone was dismissive. 'You're not staying here.'

That was it. All over. Essie nodded, because how could she even begin to argue? She'd insulted his mother and it was what she deserved.

Happy Christmas to me.

Chapter 6

Sleeping on a pink inflatable lilo wasn't remotely luxurious, but it was better – just – than bare floorboards.

Not that Essie was asleep anyway. Having dozed off an hour earlier, she was now wide awake once more, all the better to endure the awful dull, empty sensation that was radiating from her chest.

Unhappiness.

Hopelessness.

Failure.

To the outside world she'd been doing a pretty good job of appearing to be OK, but inside she was devastated. Seeing Paul so furious had come as a shock; it was a side of him she'd never encountered before. They'd been very happy, despite their many differences. Yes, he was tidy and house-proud, but he was entitled to be proud of his home. And when she'd teased him about his high standards, he'd always taken it in good part. They'd had fun together; he was kind and thoughtful, ambitious and hard-working. When he'd suggested her for the receptionist's job at his mother's busy dental practice, it was because he'd wanted to help her into the next phase of her career.

Which was good of him, even if working at the surgery hadn't exactly been her ideal job. Deep down, Essie suspected that Paul might have been happier telling people his girl-friend was a dental receptionist rather than having to say she was a waitress.

And of course she'd been grateful at the time, what with the restaurant she'd been working in having gone out of business. But if she was being honest – and now she could be honest – sitting behind a desk dealing with patients who were there for dental treatment wasn't the jolliest of occupations.

Because nobody really looked forward to going to the dentist, did they? Most of them were either dreading it or completely terrified, or downright furious that having some-thing horrible done to their teeth was costing them so damn much.

Whereas working in the hospitality industry was way more fun. Bars and restaurants were where Essie liked to be, in an atmosphere that was warm and relaxed, and with customers who were happy to be out enjoying themselves. As a young carer for her mother, she'd missed a lot of schooling during the crucial exam years, and her GCSEs had suffered as a result. This had meant future career options were limited.

Thankfully, the work she'd fallen into out of necessity after her mum's death had turned out to be right up her street. Taking a job in a busy local pub with a restaurant attached, she'd discovered that a quick brain, a cheerful smile and a capacity for hard work was all that was needed, and the more effort you put into each day, the more you got back.

And OK, maybe it wasn't up there, career-wise, with nuclear physics, but luckily the world needed more than just nuclear physicists, and even they sometimes needed somewhere to eat and drink.

Well, presumably. Come to think of it, she'd never actually met one.

Maybe they preferred their own sandwiches, and stewed tea in a Thermos.

Essie blinked up at the ceiling, realising that she was doing her best to distract herself from the Paul situation, but it wasn't working. The ache of sadness was still there in her chest. It had all happened on Saturday morning and she'd moved out of the cottage that afternoon. If it hadn't happened, she and Paul would still be a couple, and twelve months from now – who knows? – they could have been getting married. And in years to come, they might have had babies together, beautiful babies with a magical mixture of Paul's ice-blue eyes and her own over-wide smile . . .

Except none of that was going to materialise now; those babies had been summarily deleted from existence.

That particular future had gone for good.

And now it was up to Essie to find a new one.

Something insecty crawled across her hand and she made an involuntary *eurgh* sound in her throat as she jerked her arm to dislodge it. The plastic lilo squeaked beneath her and she heard Scarlett turn over in bed.

'You OK?' Scarlett murmured into the darkness.

'I'm fine. Sorry, I think it was just a spider.' In this flat, you'd think she'd have grown used to them by now.

'Oh Ess, why don't you share my bed? I really don't mind.'

'It's OK.' Scarlett's bed was smaller than standard double size, which wasn't ideal when you were trying to share it with someone you weren't romantically involved with. Essie, grateful for the lilo, was determined not to be any more of a nuisance than she was being already.

But they'd been friends for years. Scarlett, evidently reading her mind, reached down and gave her shoulder a clumsy reassuring squeeze. 'You can stay as long as you like, Ess. You know that.'

Essie reached for her hand and murmured, 'Thanks,' because she knew Scarlett meant it. Although once their landlord found out she was back, he'd kick her out in no time flat.

It was Tuesday night. Tomorrow she definitely needed to find somewhere to live.

The further into December they moved, the busier the shops became. On Wednesday afternoon, Zillah threaded her way through the crowds and paused to watch as the Salvation Army band played carols in the shadow of the towering abbey.

The air was crisp and cold. Bath's annual Christmas market was buzzing and Zillah was wearing her most recent acquisition. The amethyst trilby suited her, she knew, and had already attracted compliments. The baby boy being carried on the shoulders of the man to her left was gazing at it in fascination. Zillah smiled as he leaned over to touch it and the father, apologising, moved him out of reach.

'It doesn't matter at all. How old is he?'

The man said with pride, 'Ten and a half months.'

'So this will be his first Christmas. How wonderful.' Zillah let the baby clasp her finger and smiled. Would this be her last Christmas? Who knew?

Fifteen minutes later, she arrived at the glass-fronted offices of Haye and Payne, and climbed the front steps to the entrance. Having spotted her through the window, Malcolm Payne was already opening the door in order to usher her inside.

Bless him, he was such an old woman. Entertained by this observation – Malcolm was thirty years younger than herself – Zillah wondered if she was the letting agent's least favourite client. She suspected she might be.

The good news was, it didn't bother her one bit.

'Mrs Walsh, come along inside, how wonderful to see you again. And looking so well, too! Here, please take a seat. May I offer you a drink?'

'Thank you, how kind. I'll have a large vodka and tonic.'

'Oh, but—' Malcolm looked startled, then realised she was teasing him. 'Ah, you got me there, Mrs Walsh. Now, tea or coffee?'

'Coffee would be lovely,' said Zillah, even though this was a big lie; their coffee was pretty diabolical.

Malcolm signalled for his son Jonathan to bring out a cup of coffee and a biscuit.

'Could I have two biscuits?' Zillah beamed at him. 'Actually, three?'

'Why not? It's almost Christmas! So, how did yesterday's interviews go, Mrs Walsh? Well, I hope? My fingers are crossed!'

They were. He was crossing them now. He had soft white hands that reminded her off-puttingly of bratwurst sausages.

It occurred to Zillah that if anyone with fingers like that applied to become one of her tenants, she would have to turn them down.

She wouldn't tell Malcolm that, obviously. But she could think it.

'Thank you so much.' She nodded as Jonathan placed the coffee and biscuits in front of her before attending to a new customer. 'I'm afraid none of them were suitable, Malcolm.'

Malcolm's face fell. 'Oh dear. Really?'

'Sorry.' *Not sorry.*

'But we did check them out very thoroughly before sending them over to see you, Mrs Walsh. I can assure you their credentials are impeccable.'

'Do you have any owners fussier than me?' said Zillah.

Malcolm sighed. 'No, Mrs Walsh. Since you ask. No, we don't, but I do understand your situation . . .'

'Exactly. I'm not an absentee landlord. It's my house, my *home*, and I care about who's going to be sharing it with me.'

'Of course you do, but are you sure you aren't being a bit hasty? I did meet all three applicants and they seemed perfectly decent to me.'

Decent. What a deadly dull way to describe someone. It was on a par with a girl meeting a potential boyfriend and telling her friends afterwards that he'd been *sweet*.

Talk about the kiss of death.

'OK, the first one had a twitchy eyebrow. I couldn't stop looking at it.'

'Twitchy eyebrow.' Malcolm wrote it down on his notepad.

'The second one, Amelia, was wearing horrible shoes. And horrible tights. Well, horrible everything.' Zillah shuddered at the memory.

38

'Horrible everything.' This was accompanied by a hint of eye-roll.

'And the third one, the chap who works as a geologist, gave me a *very* disapproving look when I swore.'

'You swore at him?'

'Of course not,' Zillah exclaimed. 'I'm not an animal. The smoke alarm went off because I'd left my lunch in the oven, so I said, "Oh *fuck*." I mean, who wouldn't?'

'Right,' Malcolm murmured, noting it down on his pad.

'The way you flinched just then? That's exactly what he did.'

'Well, it was a bit loud.' He inclined his head discreetly in the direction of the other potential client, who was sitting across the office with Jonathan.

'He also smelled of mustard,' said Zillah. 'I mean, *mustard*. I couldn't put up with that.'

'So you're rejecting all three candidates.'

'I want to share my home with someone I like. Is that too much to ask?'

'They also have to like *you*,' Malcolm replied pointedly. 'We can keep trying, but you have to understand that at this time of year there's going to be a lull.'

'Rather a lull than someone who smells of mustard.'

He reached for his ringing phone. 'Excuse me while I just get this . . .'

It was a boring conversation about a leaking roof. Zillah's attention wandered to the exchange taking place on the other side of the office, where Jonathan was sucking air in through his teeth, studying a list on his computer screen and shaking his head. 'I'm sorry, but we just don't have anything in that price range.'

'Nothing at all?' The girl had been offered neither coffee nor biscuits. She was leaning forward on her chair, looking faintly desperate.

Jonathan shrugged. 'This is Bath.'

'I know.' The girl's shoulders drooped in defeat. 'Can I leave you my details? If anything does come in, could you let me know?'

Zillah took a sip of the disgusting coffee, her practised eye taking in the girl's shoulder-length wavy blonde hair, the purple and gold scarf around her neck, the dark blue sweater and jeans worn with purple ankle boots.

'Of course.' Jonathan brought up a fresh page on the computer screen. 'Fire away. Name?'

'Essie Phillips.'

He paused and looked at her. 'You're kidding. Really?'

The girl flushed and nodded.

'Ha, I *knew* I recognised your face! I saw that thing about you in the paper the other day. I can't believe it's you,' he exclaimed. 'So that's why you're so desperate for somewhere to live.'

She kept her voice steady. 'Shall I give you the rest of my details?'

'Oh. Sorry. Yes, go ahead.'

When he'd finished, the girl rose to her feet and swung her tan leather bag over her shoulder.

Since Malcolm was still busy on the phone, Zillah said to her, 'Now I'm intrigued. What happened to make you famous?'

Essie pulled a face. 'Not famous,' she said wryly. 'More like infamous. I did a bad thing and got caught out.'

'Out of interest, did you hear me say *fuck* just now?'

'Yes, I did.'

Zillah noticed that her eyes were green. 'And did it shock you?'

The girl looked amused. 'When you're a glamorous seventy-something wearing a fabulous hat, I reckon you can carry it off.'

Once the door had closed behind the girl, Zillah said, 'Was she in prison?'

'What?' Jonathan looked startled. 'God, no, nothing like that.'

'Name?'

'Erm . . .' He hesitated, then pointed to the name tag on his chest. 'Jonathan.'

'*Her* name,' said Zillah.

'Oh.' He watched, abashed, as she whipped out her phone. 'Sorry. Essie Phillips.'

Chapter 7

It was a grim, narrow bedsit with a mottled carpet the colour
of raw liver and cloudy windows that evidently hadn't been
cleaned this side of the millennium. The view from the main
window was a close-up of the wall comprising next door's
extension. As she gazed down into the tiny yard below, Essie
saw a large dog yowling and heard a female voice screech,
'If one of you kids don't take that fucking animal for a walk,
I'm chucking the telly out the window.'

Which just went to show that some people could carry
off a bit of profanity with style, and some people couldn't.

She turned back to look at the room once more. It was
awful, grim beyond belief, but it was pretty much all she
could afford right now.

'Well?' The landlord was leaning against the doorway, lazily
scratching his vast stomach.

Should I take it? Oh God, I think I'm going to have to.

Her phone began to ring and Essie flinched because it
was an unknown number, which might mean it was another
journalist. Oh well, she could always hang up. She pressed
Answer and said cautiously, 'Hello?'

42

'Essie? This is Zillah Walsh. I saw you an hour ago in Haye and Payne. I was the one in the hat.'

'Oh!' Of all the people she hadn't been expecting to take a call from. 'Hi!'

'I persuaded that young lad to give me your number. He's not terribly bright, is he? Anyway, he told me you'd gone viral.'

'On the internet,' said Essie. Did old people understand what going viral meant?

'I know, darling. I'm not completely decrepit.' Amused, the woman continued, 'I googled you, read all about it. Got yourself into a bit of a pickle by the sound of things.'

'You could say that. Obviously it was never meant to be seen, but it was my own fault,' said Essie. Because, essentially, the buck did stop with her.

'And are you still looking for somewhere to live?'

'Well . . .'

'Ahem.' Behind her, the landlord cleared his throat impatiently.

'You lazy little bastards,' bellowed the woman next door.

'Yes I am,' Essie said with feeling into the phone.

'OK, come and have a chat with me. Number twenty-three, Percival Square. No guarantees, but I may have something for you.'

'When, now?'

'If it's convenient for you, that'd be great. I'm here now, so you can turn up as soon as you'd like.'

Percival Square was one of the most elegant addresses in the city. Most of the trees that grew in the square were twisty and bare, but a fir tree had been installed on a plinth and strung with coloured lights and stars. Tourists were gathered around, taking photographs of themselves and their friends in front of it. As Essie made her way past them, an American tourist gestured expansively to his wife and said, 'Oh honey, imagine *living* somewhere like this.'

The glossy deep purple front door of number 23 was adorned with a dark green and gold Christmas wreath. Essie rang the bell and waited. She wasn't getting her hopes up. The old woman was clearly a favoured client at Haye and Payne and a wealthy one at that; she presumably owned a number of rental properties, the kind that they let out to students and managed on her behalf.

Fingers crossed she had a tiny one going extra cheap.

Then the door opened and Zillah Walsh appeared in front of her, now minus her hat and coat but still stylish in a topaz jersey dress, with several strings of amber beads looped around her neck.

'Hello again. Come inside.' She beckoned for Essie to follow her. 'Now, can you remember what you said about me earlier?'

The old woman's eyes were dark and bright. Her brown hair was fastened back in a bun. She had excellent cheekbones and her crimson lipstick was still as perfect as it had been over an hour ago. Which was a feat Essie herself had never been able to achieve.

'Erm . . . I said your hat was great?'

'You did. And?'

'I didn't mind you swearing?'

Zillah Walsh nodded in agreement. 'You also said that seeing as I was seventy-something, I could get away with it. *Seventy*-something,' she repeated.

'Oh no, God, I'm so sorry.' Essie clapped a hand over her mouth. 'This is why my life is such a disaster – I'm always putting my foot in it. And I don't even know why I said that – you look fantastic. Not a day over sixty!'

'Darling, don't be alarmed. I was charmed by what you said.' Zillah Walsh's large silver earrings jangled as she reassured her. 'I'm actually eighty-three.'

In the kitchen, Zillah made a pot of tea then carried it on a tray through to the rather grand sitting room, where bottle-green walls were hung with an eclectic assortment of framed artwork, and heavy scarlet silk curtains clashed wonderfully with a burnt-orange velvet sofa and wing chairs.

'Help yourself to crisps and biscuits.' Zillah handed her a plate. 'No need to be polite. Take as many as you like. What do you think of this room?'

'It's perfect. I love the colours.'

'So do I.'

'That's incredible.' Essie pointed to one of the paintings in an alcove. 'It's you!'

'When I was twenty-one.' Zillah turned to look at it. 'Back when my skin was smooth and I couldn't imagine what it would be like to have wrinkles.'

'OK, I *want* to say that I bet you turn even more heads now than you did back then. But I don't want you thinking I'm only saying it to flatter you.'

'If it's true,' Zillah replied with a brief smile, 'it's more than likely due to me having outlived most of the opposition. Anyway, enough about me. Tell me about you.'

Over the course of the next forty minutes, Essie realised she was being expertly interviewed. It felt like a friendly chat, but there was clearly far more to it than that. Finally,

Zillah said, 'So, I do have a place I can offer you. It's very small, I'm afraid, but it's clean and well maintained. Would you be interested?'

'Yes! I'd be so interested you wouldn't believe it. Of course I would,' said Essie. 'If I can afford it, that is. I mean, Scarlett's letting me sleep on her bedroom floor at the moment, which is lovely of her, but I can't carry on doing that. Where is this place? Is it in Bath?'

'It's right here, on the top floor.' Zillah's diamond rings glittered in the lamplight as she raised a hand and pointed at the ceiling.

'Here in this house?' In *Percival Square*? Essie's eyes widened. 'Are you serious? Oh no.' She shook her head. 'I can't afford it then.' So much for having got her hopes up; apart from meeting a strikingly attractive eighty-three-year-old, the afternoon had been a failure after all. Back to square one.

'Darling girl, have a bit of faith in me. I did ask them at the office what your budget was. And I had a little idea. As you know, I'm not as young as I was. It would be nice to think I could ask for the occasional favour . . . running errands, popping to the shops, that kind of thing. So if you'd be up for helping me out every now and again, I'd be happy to accept the amount you can afford. How does that sound to you?'

And *breathe* . . .

'Really?'

'Why not? This is my home. I like you and I think we'd get on.' Zillah's mouth twitched. 'You have no idea how many people there are out there whom I *wouldn't* want living in my house. I've chosen well so far, haven't landed myself with any duds. And you don't seem like a dud to me.'

'I don't know what to say.' Essie blinked, because leaping up onto the coffee table and punching the air probably wouldn't be appropriate. 'Thanks so much.'

'No need to thank me. You need somewhere to live, and I could do with the occasional helping hand. Plus, I'd far rather have you upstairs than someone who can afford to pay more but who bores me to tears or eats like a chimpanzee.'

'So that's why you served biscuits and crisps.'

'Too right. Can't stand a chomper. Or a tea-slurper. You passed those tests with flying colours.'

'Thank goodness for that.'

Zillah smiled. 'You haven't even seen the flat yet.'

'If it's just a bathtub inside a cupboard, I'd still want it.'

'Come along then.' The older woman rose to her feet. 'Let me give you the full guided tour.'

The flat, up on the third floor, was indeed tiny. But it was perfectly formed.

'My husband died nine years ago,' Zillah explained. 'I loved living here and didn't want to move, but the house just felt far too big for me on my own. I was rattling around in it like a bean. A friend suggested I had the two top floors converted into flats, and it's been great. A bit of extra company for me, nice people to interact with, and some extra income too.'

'Perfect.' Essie gazed around the living room, with its clean pale yellow walls and curtains to match. They were up in the attic, half of which had been converted into a self-contained one-bedroom apartment with a compact bathroom and a kitchen area that was part of the main room.

'I've had Maria here for the last three years,' Zillah

continued. 'She was lovely. But her boyfriend was offered a job in New Zealand and he selfishly went and asked her to marry him. So she moved out six weeks ago and they're living in Auckland now. Whereas I've spent the last six weeks interviewing potential new tenants, but not one of them has felt right.' She paused. 'Until you came along. So, do we have a deal?'

'Yes please.'

'And how soon would you like to move in?'

'As soon as possible. Tomorrow? Tonight?'

'Let's do it. Hooray, I've found someone at last.' Zillah's dark eyes flashed with mischief. 'Thank fuck for that!'

Chapter 8

Later that evening, once her belongings had been shifted out of Scarlett's overcrowded room and installed in her new attic flat, Essie headed back out into the frosty night in search of some form of job.

One, preferably, that didn't require glowing references from her most recent employer.

This close to Christmas, everywhere was busy. A couple of bars and restaurants said they might have something for her in the new year. Regardless, Essie gave them her details and said if they ever needed anyone to please give her a call. Would they? Who knew? All she could do was keep going – and remain outwardly cheerful – until someone eventually gave in and said yes.

Because she had some money, but not much. The small amount of savings she'd managed to put away was better than no savings at all, but it wouldn't last long.

The first place she'd tried had been the Red House, a buzzy-looking bar less than two hundred metres from her new home, situated on the south-east corner of Percival Square. Zillah had suggested she should try there, but a raucous office party had been in progress and the staff were clearly rushed off their feet.

Now, two hours later, she paid a return visit as the last members of the party were trickling out. Hopefully someone would be available to speak to her now.

People were clearing up after what had evidently been a hectic night. Essie approached the tall brunette who was hanging clean glasses behind the bar and explained that she was looking for work.

'We've got everyone we need just now.' The brunette was sympathetic but unable to oblige. 'Sorry.'

That was a real shame; a two-minute commute would have been perfect. Essie said, 'OK, but can I leave you my number? I'm living right here on the square now, so if you're ever short-staffed and desperate for help, you could just give me a call and I'd be happy to step in. I've done plenty of bar work before, and waitressing too.'

The brunette said good-naturedly, 'Haven't we all? OK, give me your details and I'll leave them in the office . . . Oh, thanks, very efficient.' She took Essie's card, then glanced down at it and did a barely perceptible double-take. 'Your name. Where have I heard it before? It's definitely familiar.'

'If you're thinking of something to do with a round robin,' Essie said ruefully, 'that was me.'

'That's it, yes! I saw all the stuff about it on Facebook. Poor you!'

'Thanks. Hopefully the novelty will wear off soon and it'll be someone else's turn to have the mickey taken out of them.'

'Your boyfriend really did kick you out, then. Nightmare.'

'Yes.'

'You must be devastated.'

There really was nothing like finding yourself an object of fascination. Essie said, 'Well, it hasn't been the best week of my life.'

'I promise you,' the brunette told her earnestly, 'if we need someone, we'll be in touch.'

Sixteen hours later, miraculously, Essie answered her phone and heard a female voice say, 'Hi, it's Jude from the Red House. One of our bar staff has just called in sick, so if you're able to cover his evening shift that'd be brilliant. Could you be here by six so I can talk you through the till and show you where everything is?'

Hooray! Be lovely, smile at everyone, work hard and win them over! This could be the break she'd been waiting for. Metaphorically crossing her fingers, Essie said, 'Thank you so much. I'll be there before six.'

At ten o'clock that evening, the absent member of staff left a second message on Jude's phone to let her know that he wouldn't be in work tomorrow either. Unfortunately he was more ill that he'd first thought.

Jude called him back. 'Except you aren't ill, Henry, are you? Because your friends were in here earlier and I heard them saying you'd caught the Megabus up to Newcastle with Cal to go to his cousin's twenty-first, because apparently it was going to be the party of the century and there was no way in the world you were going to miss it.' As she spoke, she rolled her eyes. 'So I hope the party was worth it, because you've just used up your last life with us.'

Essie, pouring wine, did her best not to look too over-the-moon. Because this was thrilling news and just about the best thing that could possibly happen *ever*.

Well, apart from the Chris Hemsworth fantasy, obviously. If that happened, it would be way better.

'No, don't even try,' Jude continued bluntly. 'You can't behave like that and expect to get away with it. You messed us around, Henry, now you pay the price. Because let me tell you, you might not be bothered about this job, but there are other people who are. So you have a great Christmas now, OK? Bye!'

Hooray.

Jude put the phone back in her trouser pocket with a flourish and turned to Essie. 'Did you hear all that?'

'Well,' said Essie, 'I do have ears.'

Jude smiled. 'You do. And I've been watching you this evening. You're good. So I'm going to make an executive decision and offer you the job.'

'Wow.'

'Is that a yes?'

For a moment Essie couldn't speak. She'd been doing her utmost to put on a brave face and come to terms with everything that had happened in the past week, but the last few days had been tough. Really tough. There'd been a lot to take in and not much time in which to assimilate it. Then yesterday she'd met Zillah Walsh, which had seemed like the most amazing and fortuitous stroke of luck.

And now this. Not just any job, but one she knew she'd love. Everyone here at the Red House had been so nice tonight, warm and welcoming. The atmosphere was convivial. Plus, it was so close to home. What could be better than that?

Talk about serendipity.

'I'd love to.' She nodded at Jude. 'It's a million times yes.'

Forty minutes later, possibly to pay her back for feeling so smug, the door to the Red House swung open and in walked the architect of all her recent misfortunes.

Essie, busy wiping down empty tables and piling glasses onto a tray, stared in disbelief as he made his way to the bar. It was him, no doubt about it. And wasn't he looking just . . . *fine*.

Then again, why wouldn't he be fine? There was no reason why he shouldn't be cheerful and relaxed, was there? She was the one who'd borne the brunt of last week's disastrous sequence of events, whilst he'd got away with it scot-free.

His name was Lucas, but that was as much as she'd learned about him because it was all her brother had known. Jay had met him at a party, drinks had been downed and they'd bonded in that particular way men had a habit of doing when alcohol was involved.

Which was how they'd ended up, at four in the morning, back at her place. Well, Paul's place. Whereupon havoc had been caused, following which her own life had disastrously imploded.

And now here he was, which meant she had the opportunity to give him a piece of her mind, if she could just figure out how to do it in a way that wouldn't mean losing her brand-new job.

By hiring a hit man, maybe.

A discreet one.

Needing time to gather herself, Essie concentrated on rearranging the collected glasses on her tray. His back was to her now, but she could remember exactly what he looked like. Dark hair and darker eyes that signalled amusement even when the situation was the polar opposite of funny. He was tall, olive-skinned and wearing a dark suit. He was also the kind of good-looking that went hand-in-hand with untrustworthiness. If it suited men like him to do something, they simply regarded it as their right to go ahead and do it. Other people, so far as they were concerned, only existed for their entertainment.

Now he'd walked into the Red House and their paths were about to cross for the second time. Which, in a relatively small city like Bath, wasn't the most unlikely of situations.

But the sight of him still caused Essie's skin to prickle with suppressed anger and her breathing to quicken.

Was he even aware that thanks to his actions she'd become a public laughing stock?

The next moment the door to the kitchen was pushed open and Jude emerged, her face lighting up when she saw the new arrival, who was currently busy messaging someone on his phone whilst he stood waiting at the bar.

'Hello, you're back! I didn't think we were going to see you tonight.'

Which meant he was a regular here, the kind who spent every evening drinking and socialising. From a distance, Essie's lip curled with disdain; because of course he did. Par for the course.

God, though, what a pain to see him here. She'd have her work cut out being polite to him. With a bit of luck, his conscience might kick in and send him off to haunt another bar.

If he even had a conscience.

Ugh, and now Jude was actually giving him a welcoming hug. But that was the thing about men who looked like he did: when you were that physically attractive, there'd always be women more than happy to overlook your faults.

The next moment, glancing over once more, Essie saw that Jude was now murmuring something in his ear, and it struck her that they could be a couple. Oh no, that would be too much to bear.

Then they moved apart and Jude went behind the bar to pour a measure of cognac from the optics. She handed it to Lucas and said something else to him, then turned and beckoned to Essie.

Possibly to chastise her for being the world's slowest glass-collector.

Essie picked up the loaded tray and made her way over, the little hairs on her arms lifting like iron filings on a magnet.

'By the way,' Jude was telling him, 'Hopeless Henry let us down for the last time, so I gave him the push earlier. But we've got a replacement and she's going to be brilliant, I promise.'

One of the glasses on the tray contained an abandoned half-pint of lager. If Lucas recognised her and started laughing, Essie knew she'd be compelled to throw the contents straight in his face.

Even a smirk would be enough.

But when he turned to look at her, she saw only genuine shock in his eyes, swiftly followed by growing suspicion. He inclined his head and said evenly, 'Hi.'

Jude was beaming. 'Lucas, this is Essie. Essie, this is your new boss!'

Essie stared at him. Oh for crying out loud.

Not that.

Anything but that.

Somehow she managed to say, 'Hello.'

'And if you're wondering why she looks familiar,' Jude rattled on, 'it's because her photo was in the papers last week . . . Essie's the one who got caught out by that embarrassing round robin about her boyfriend's mother!'

'Right. Yes.' Lucas nodded and took a sip of cognac. His expression was utterly unreadable.

As Essie put down the tray and began offloading glasses, Jude said to Lucas, 'You don't mind that I hired her without asking you first, do you? She's so much better than Hopeless Henry. I just thought, why wait?'

'It's fine. I wasn't expecting to come in and find . . . someone new, that's all.' He pushed his fingers through his hair, raking it back from his forehead. 'Maybe I'll take her up to the office, get everything sorted.'

'Are you sure?' Jude looked surprised. 'I can take care of that tomorrow.'

He rested his hand briefly on her arm. 'I'll do it now. It's fine.'

Having ushered Essie upstairs and into the tiny office at the end of the corridor, Lucas signalled for her to sit down at the desk. Still holding the drink he'd brought through with him, he demanded without preamble, 'Go on then, what's this about?'

For all the world as if *she* were the one at fault. Essie bristled. 'Excuse me?'

'I'm simply asking you to tell me what you're doing here.'

'I think you could probably work out the answer to that, couldn't you? I lost my job, which meant I had to find another one. That's generally the way these things work, isn't it?'

'And as far as you're concerned, I owe you a job?'

'Are you serious? Is that what you think?'

'I don't know. That's why I'm asking. Either that or you're here to cause some kind of trouble, to somehow pay me back by making things difficult . . .'

'So you think I tracked you down and came here on purpose?' Essie was outraged. 'I had no idea this was your bar! Believe me, if I'd known, I wouldn't have applied to work here . . . It's the last place I'd have come crawling to!' She could feel the heat in her cheeks, because he was scrutinising her so intently.

'Right.' Lucas was clearly sceptical.

'You still don't believe me? My God. OK, just pop out tomorrow and ask every bar in the city if I dropped in yesterday asking for work,' she said furiously. 'If anyone else had offered me a job, I wouldn't be here now.'

He looked at her. 'So what you're saying is this is just an embarrassing coincidence?'

Was he being sarcastic? Essie shook her head. 'It's worse than embarrassing. Everything's ruined now. I was so happy this evening . . . I loved every minute here, until you turned up. And now this has happened, which means I'm back to square one all over again. Because there's no way I can work for you.'

He leaned back against the wall, loosened his tie and

unfastened the top button of his white shirt. 'Could you stop glaring at me like that?'

'I think I'm allowed to glare. You've lost me two jobs in one week. How would you feel if it happened to you?'

'OK, OK.' He made calm-down gestures with his hands. 'But you haven't actually lost the second job. I'm not the one who's said you can't work here.'

'So basically you still have no idea what you've done to me.'

'I've apologised. How many more times can I say sorry? It was a lapse of judgement, a stupid mistake. I didn't know what was going to happen,' said Lucas. 'When your brother read out what you'd written, I wasn't even listening properly—'

'You must be feeling guilty,' Essie cut in, because it had only just occurred to her. 'Jude knows all about what happened to me, but you didn't tell her you were the one responsible.'

Lucas inclined his head. 'No, I didn't.'

'So you have to be a bit ashamed of what you did.'

'What are you saying?' He raised an eyebrow. 'You're going to tell everyone here that it was my fault?'

Essie's brain whirred, because this scenario hadn't even occurred to her. Of course it would be tempting, in one way, to embarrass Lucas. It might make her feel better and would serve him right.

Then again, she'd never been a vindictive person. OK, his ridiculous thoughtless actions had had unforeseen consequences, but how would she feel if her tit-for-tat retaliation did too?

No, it wasn't the kind of thing she'd ever do.

Just call me St Essie.

She said, 'Luckily for you, I would never do something so mean.'

For a couple of seconds he gazed directly at her. Then he put down his almost empty brandy glass. 'Well, thanks. I appreciate that.'

'So you should.'

After another pause, Lucas said, 'You can carry on working here if you want.'

She shook her head. 'No, I couldn't.'

'Because you can't stand the sight of me?'

'Because I can't stand what you did.' Was he unable to comprehend what she'd been through, thanks to him?

'Well, that's a shame.' Lucas shrugged. 'Jude's going to wonder why you changed your mind.'

This was true. Essie thought about it. 'It has to be something personal.'

'We met a year ago, I asked you out on a date, I stood you up.' There was a glimmer of amusement in his dark eyes. 'You never got over it and it would just be too awkward, us working together.'

'How about I was the one who stood *you* up?' said Essie.

'OK, I suppose the least I can do is let you be the stander-upper.' Lucas nodded in agreement. 'Deal.'

He paid her for the evening's work, collected her coat from the staff cupboard and let her out through the side entrance so they would be spared the inevitable awkward encounter with Jude and the other members of staff.

'Sorry again.'

Essie wound her scarf around her neck. 'Yes.'

'Just think, if you hadn't stood me up that time last year, we could have been married by now.'

'I'm glad you think my situation's amusing,' said Essie. 'But guess what? I don't.'

What a day.

And now, what an evening.

From his office window on the first floor, Lucas Brook drained the last drops of cognac and watched as the girl made her way diagonally across the square. Beneath the glow of light from the street lamps, her red coat showed up vividly and her blonde hair gleamed. Against his better judgement, there was just something about her that was getting to him. It would be easier – God, *so* much easier – to simply let her go and put the whole mess out of his mind. But now his conscience appeared to be hell-bent on kicking in.

Great.

Maybe he'd leave it for tonight, at least.

Then again, maybe not.

The card bearing Essie Phillips' name and contact number was still lying on the desk where Jude had left it. Lucas pressed the numbers into his phone and seconds later saw her stop dead in her tracks, just as she reached the huge lit-up Christmas tree. After a bit of scrabbling in her bag, she answered.

'Who's this?'

Time to adopt a strong West Country accent. 'All right, my love? You left a card here in our pub with your number on it. Still looking for work, are you?'

'Oh! Yes, I am!' The note of hope in her voice was almost heartbreaking.

He dropped the accent and said, 'Well stay where you are. Don't move.'

He saw her stiffen as she recognised his voice. She swung round, searched the windows above the Red House and spotted him at once.

'For God's sake. What is this, some kind of game to you?'

'Not a game,' said Lucas evenly. 'Just hear me out. Please.'

It was frosty outside. His breath puffed out in front of him and the grass crunched beneath his feet as he made his way towards her. The multicoloured lights on the tree illuminated her face.

'Hurry up.' Essie's tone was brisk. 'My feet are cold.'

'Look, you need a job. I can offer you one. I know you can't stand me now, but—'

'I'm not planning on changing my mind about that.'

'OK, but I'm just saying, don't make things harder for yourself than they already are. If you think there's even a one per cent chance that you might wake up tomorrow morning and regret saying you couldn't work for me . . . well, you've got my number.' He raised a hand. 'Don't say anything now. If you change your mind, give me a call before midday. If I haven't heard from you by then, I'll find someone else.'

Essie looked at him. 'I won't change my mind.'

So stubborn. 'OK, but the offer's still there. Just so you know.'

'I'm never going to forgive you for what you did.' She thrust her hands into her coat pockets. 'Just so *you* know.'

Touché. Lucas said, 'Come on, I'll walk you home. What number are you?'

'I thought you knew my address?'

'The card's upstairs on my desk.'

'Twenty-three.'

'Ah. Is that Zillah's place?'

'You know her?'

'I do.' Lucas nodded. 'Everyone knows Zillah. She's a character.' He paused, then said, 'How's your brother?'

'Fine, as far as I know. He's skiing in Austria at the moment with friends.'

'You're OK with him, though?'

'You mean after he brought you back to the cottage with him? I wish he hadn't,' said Essie, 'but that's Jay for you: he doesn't stop to think about things like that. He thought he was doing you a favour. And it's not his fault, is it? He didn't know you were going to do something so completely idiotic.'

'Neither did I.' Lucas heaved a sigh. 'But I've learned my lesson. I won't do it again, I promise.'

Essie had gone to bed at midnight. A couple of hours later, her mobile rang again. By a stroke of luck, she'd had far too much on her mind to be able to get to sleep anyway.

She rolled over in bed and answered. From the level of background noise it was pretty obvious her brother was in a bar.

'Hey, you!' said Jay. 'What's up?'

Essie squinted at the clock. 'Well, it's almost two in the morning. So not much really.'

'Oh God, were you asleep? I've just seen your text. You said to call you.'

'I did, but I sent it twelve hours ago.' She'd wanted to hear a friendly voice and had planned on asking Jay if he happened to know of any jobs going locally. 'Maybe the signal's bad in the mountains.'

'No, it's my fault. I ran out of battery at lunchtime. Someone just lent me their charger. I'm only up to three per cent, though, so it won't last long. How are you doing, anyway? Everything OK?'

'You mean apart from losing my boyfriend and my home and my job? Couldn't be better.'

'Oh yes, sorry. But you've found somewhere else to live, haven't you? When you messaged me yesterday, you said you had.'

'I have,' Essie agreed. 'And tonight I was offered a job in a brilliant bar . . .'

'Well, that's great news!'

'It was great until the guy who owns the place turned up, and guess who it was?'

'Donald Trump,' Jay said promptly. 'Nigel Farage. Or, hang on, that comedian you can't stand, the one with the tattoo of a—'

'*No.*' Essie marvelled at the way his brain worked. 'It was Lucas.'

'Who?' He sounded genuinely baffled.

'The guy you brought home from the party, the one who'd lost his keys. The drunk one who thought it was funny to send my letter to everyone in my address book. *That* guy,' said Essie.

'Oh, right.' Jay's tone grew sombre. 'Him.'

'I know. What are the odds?'

'And what did he have to say?'

'Sorry, mainly. He's still apologising. But I told him there was no way I could work for him.'

63

'No? Well, it's probably for the best. And you'll find another job,' said Jay. 'Who wouldn't want to employ you?'

Essie said wryly, 'Well, there's Paul's mother . . .'

'Apart from her. Anyway, don't worry about this Lucas guy. You don't want to be working for an idiot like that.'

'I know. It's such a shame, though – if it wasn't for him, I'd have been really happy there. Anyway.' Essie changed the subject. 'How's your holiday?'

'The best. You should see the snow. Skiing conditions are perfect.'

'The après-ski doesn't sound bad either.' She could still hear the sound of clinking glasses, music and riotous laughter in the background.

'It's bearable, I suppose.' From the amusement in his voice she guessed he'd already chosen the girl he'd be spending the next few nights with.

'Have fun,' she said.

'Don't worry, I will. Down to one per cent battery now, going to have to go. Good luck with the job hunt, Ess. Keep me up to date, OK? Right, I'm—'

The phone cut out. He'd gone. Essie smiled to herself. Jay was incorrigible and he drove her nuts sometimes.

But he was her brother and she loved him to bits.

It was now just gone two in the morning and the square was silent, apart from the sound of a car being parked nearby. Hearing the murmur of voices, followed by the closing of car doors, Essie hopped out of bed and drew back the curtain in order to peer nosily down at what must be, at a guess, her new neighbours.

But they weren't neighbours; they were moving away from a gleaming dark Mercedes and making their way towards her house. Moreover, one of the people was Zillah. The other, younger and taller, with broad shoulders and tousled fair hair, held out a supporting arm to help her up the steps. As the front door opened, Essie wondered if this was Conor McCauley, who lived in the flat below hers.

And where had they been, to be coming home at this hour? Zillah had definitely said that she was looking forward to an early night.

Oh well, she'd probably find out soon enough.

Time for bed.

Chapter 9

Conor McCauley was able to point to the exact minute his life had changed so dramatically, four years ago.

Up until then, he'd always done what had been expected of him. As a teenager he'd worked hard at school, gaining good grades in his exams because his father was a solicitor who wanted his son to follow in his footsteps.

Then there'd been university, the inevitable law degree this time, and another excellent result. His father, attending his graduation, had been visibly proud of him and Conor had in turn been proud of himself. A position as a solicitor was a fine thing, everybody said so. How fantastic to have a career so well paid, so varied, so interesting.

Fast-forward five years. On the day in question, Conor's third client of the morning was a wealthy man who had married at twenty-five and was now in his fifties. He had left his wife six months ago for a very much younger model, who was currently sitting in the waiting room wearing a Barbie-sized Lycra dress, chewing gum and chatting on her mobile to her friends.

Her new fiancé fixed his gaze on Conor and said, 'Look,

I know I can't get away with giving my ex-wife nothing, but you have to make sure she only gets the bare minimum. It's not my fault that I lost interest in her. She let herself go, big-time. I mean, seriously, what a state.' He leaned across the desk, scrolling through the photos on his iPhone until he found what he was looking for. 'See? There she is! Who'd want to stay married to something like that?'

Conor had glanced at the photo on the screen, of a plump, anxious-looking woman with short hair and a shy smile. She was standing in a garden wearing a blue shift dress and gardening gloves, and clutching a spade.

'You get the picture?' The woman's husband was triumphant. 'Is it any wonder I'd rather spend the rest of my life with Stacey-Louise? I mean, Christ alive, who wouldn't?'

Conor hoped with all his heart that the reason his client's wife was holding a spade in the photo was because she was busy digging a husband-sized grave in a tucked-away corner of their garden. Now that would be a story with a happy ending.

'Does your wife have a career, Mr Benson?'

'A career? You're joking, aren't you? Bloody woman hasn't done a day's work in the last twenty years.'

'Although she has looked after your five children,' Conor replied evenly.

'Yeah, but she's never had a proper job since the first one came along. Anyway, my mate Jezzer Kane recommended you, said you'd get me a cracking result. So just make sure you do, OK? No way is that lazy cow going to walk off with my hard-earned cash.'

What an absolute charmer. Conor said, 'I don't recall the name . . .'

'No, your boss Margaret looked after him, but she was too booked up to take my case. Still, you work for her, yeah? So I'm sure she's taught you a few tricks of the trade. Know what I mean, ha ha.' As he spoke, the man drew a fat fore-finger across his even fatter neck and roared with laughter. 'Get the message, lad? Whatever it takes!'

Margaret Kale was the head of the firm. A terrifying and ruthless woman in her sixties, she made Rosa Klebb look like a playful squirrel. Eyeing the man across the desk with disdain and loathing him with every fibre of his being, Conor murmured, 'We'll do our best.'

His fourth client of the day was a thirty-three-year-old woman called Jessica Brown. He'd known in advance that she'd made the appointment in order to discuss writing her will, but it wasn't until he called her through to his office that Conor realised the urgency of the situation. Her skin was tinted yellow and she moved slowly with the aid of a walking stick. Underneath her loose pink dress, her stomach was distended, and there were dark grey shadows beneath her eyes. But despite the shadows, the clear evidence of weight loss and the jaundice, she was still visibly herself, with elongated blue eyes and strikingly long lashes. When she smiled, her face lit up. She also had a beautifully shaped mouth.

As soon as the niceties were out of the way, Jessica Brown said, 'Well as you can see, I need to get things sorted out. Better late than never, eh?'

'I'm so sorry.' Conor's heart went out to her; what must it feel like to face death at such a young age?

'Thanks. It's not as if I have much . . . you know, *stuff* to leave in a will. There's no house, nothing like that. But I do

68

have my daughter, and she's only twelve . . .' Having tried so hard to maintain control – she'd been practising the words, Conor could tell – her voice now cracked with emotion and she held up a thin hand by way of silent apology.

'Don't worry, take as much time as you like.' He spoke reassuringly. There was a box of tissues in his drawer and he took it out, placed it on the desk.

After twenty seconds or so, Jessica Brown managed to visibly swallow the lump in her throat and speak again. With a faint smile, she murmured, 'Only a solicitor could say something as daft as that. You charge by the minute, don't you? I can't afford to take as much time as I'd like.'

'Apologies. But the first thirty minutes are free.'

'Then I'd better not waste them.' And this time she managed a brief laugh, accompanied by a rueful shake of her head. 'Bizarre, isn't it? Most of the time I'm fine, in control; I can even crack jokes about it when I'm talking to other people. It's only when I think about Evie that it really gets me. You'll just have to put up with it, I'm afraid. And maybe stock up on tissues.'

'Take as many as you want,' said Conor.

Jessica talked and he took copious notes as she did so. The cancer that had metastasised throughout her body had begun to make itself felt less than a year ago, but its march had been relentless and her hospital consultant was now reluctantly predicting that she had six months to live.

If she was lucky.

'And luck's been pretty thin on the ground lately, so I'm not holding out too much hope.' She pushed a strand of blonde hair behind her left ear. 'Ironic, isn't it? After Evie was born, I was so happy it scared me witless. I felt like the luckiest girl in the world and kept thinking something had to go wrong, to balance out all the joy. Because she was just so perfect, you know? And beautiful. And such a *good* baby . . . Sorry, here I go again . . .'

The father, Conor learned, had done a near-instantaneous bunk and Jessica had been too proud to chase after him. Instead, she'd raised Evie alone and, if she said so herself, had made a pretty good job of it. Amid tears and smiles, she showed Conor photos of her beloved daughter, with her huge eyes, dimples and white-blonde curls. And she explained to him the plans she'd made for Evie's future.

'My sister's going to have her. Thank goodness. Evie loves her and I'm so grateful for that. Mum will be around to help too. It's not as if she'll be left on her own.' The tears were still sliding down her thin cheeks. 'So really, we're lucky, it could be a lot worse. I just wish I didn't have to leave her behind. I'm going to miss her so much.'

And now Conor was the one who found himself unable to speak. He couldn't break down, *he mustn't*. But for several seconds he had to duck his head and pretend to be busy writing things on his notepad so she wasn't able to see his face.

Then a single giveaway tear plopped onto the notepad and Jessica reached across the desk to pull yet another tissue from the box. As she handed it to him, she said, 'Sorry to be putting you through this. I'm a right laugh a minute, aren't I?'

They worked on through Conor's lunch break and got the preliminary paperwork planned out, because Jessica was keen to complete it as soon as possible. By two o'clock they'd done as much as they could, and his next client was waiting outside in reception.

'Thank you so much. You made it easier than I thought it would be.' She reached for her pink canvas handbag and took out a small denim purse. 'Now, how much do I owe you so far?'

Conor had already decided not to charge her for the work he'd done during his lunch break. In fact, he planned to carry out the rest of the paperwork in his own time too. As long as he squared the situation with Margaret and reimbursed her for lost business, that would be OK, surely? He shook his head. 'Oh no, there's no need for any of that.'

'I'd rather pay it now, though.' Jessica was taking out notes, counting them under her breath. 'Please, I want to get it out of the way. I've always hated owing money, but now it's even more important to make sure everything's sorted. Just tell me how much, please. I couldn't bear it if anything happened before . . . Well, you know what I mean. I'm not going to land someone else with my debts.'

He knew exactly how much – or rather how little – Jessica had in the bank; they'd just been over her finances in detail. He saw the look of utter determination on her face as she waited to hand over the amount she owed.

'Look,' he said, 'there isn't going to be any invoice.'

'What?' Jessica was confused. 'Why not?'

And that was the clincher: she genuinely didn't think she deserved to be treated any differently. But how, given the situation, could he possibly take her money? Sometimes you encountered someone – for just a few minutes, or maybe a couple of hours – and knew you'd remember them for the rest of your life.

Jessica Brown had touched his heart and he wouldn't forget her.

He also knew that she had plenty of pride.

'OK, now don't go telling everyone about this, but here at Kale and Grey we have a private . . . arrangement. Each of us in turn is allowed to waive the fee for a client who deserves a break. Well, this week it's my turn.' He shrugged. 'And I'd like it to be you.'

'Oh! Are you serious?' She looked pleased but also surprised, bordering on suspicious.

'Completely. If you refuse, I'll just have to choose someone else. And I'd rather not.' He grimaced at the imaginary prospect. 'They could be some awful person who'd just splurge the money down the bookie's instead.'

Jessica's blue eyes were fixed on his. Then she reached for her walking stick and rose carefully to her feet. 'In that case, it would be crazy of me not to accept. Thanks so much.' She broke into a grin. 'That's incredibly kind of you, and it's going to be a real help.'

'That's good.' Conor wanted to give her a hug, but couldn't. He was the solicitor and she was the client. Instead, they shook hands and he explained that the paperwork would be sent to her to be signed and returned. As he was showing her out of the office, he said, 'Evie has a mother to be proud of.'

Jessica turned to look at him. 'Thank you, but if you knew her you'd understand why I'm the one who's proud.'

The next client, impatiently pacing in reception and speaking on her mobile, rolled her eyes as Jessica made her way carefully past with the aid of her walking stick.

'Mrs Barker?' Conor turned politely to address her once Jessica had left. 'Hello, I'm—'

'I know who you are, your photo's on the website.'

72

Without pausing, Yasmin Barker continued to speak into her phone. 'OK, babe, I'm being seen, *finally*. Shall we meet for drinks later? I'll catch you up with all the goss, ha ha. Champers on me if all goes to plan! Call you in a bit . . . *Ciao, ciao* . . .'

With the passing of every minute in the company of Yasmin Barker, Conor despised her more. She was a twenty-six-year-old with a trout pout that made her look much older. Her top was cut so low that if the cosmetic surgeon who'd installed the breast implants had signed his work in the lower right-hand corner, the signature would've been visible. She wore tight pink PVC shorts and five-inch plat-form boots. She had two-inch false eyelashes. She was also hell-bent on divorcing her husband.

'I call him Three B,' she explained with a cackle of laughter. 'He thinks it stands for Beautiful Babe Brian, but it's really Boring Bald Bastard, ha ha!'

She was utterly poisonous. Conor marvelled at her open-ness, but then that was what happened when people engaged you as their solicitor: they felt able to tell you everything. You were working for them, therefore no pretence was necessary. Yasmin had married Brian for his money, and now that enough time had passed – 'Two and a half years, and every day felt like a month!' – she was ready to stake her claim on everything he owned. 'Because I've bloody earned it, haven't I? God, all that man ever does is moan at me for going out with my mates and complain about how much I spend on clothes. Ha, wait until I tell him I'm off! Then he'll find out how much I can cost him when I put my mind to it. Serve the stupid bastard right.'

★　★　★

Yasmin had sashayed out of the building two hours later. Conor had discovered that sometimes you could meet people, loathe every single thing about them, then put them out of your mind once they were gone and carry on perfectly happily with your day, as if the encounter had never taken place.

But that day it wasn't happening. He felt as if the two awful clients had infected him with their poisonous attitudes, and the urge to somehow scrub away their vitriol was overwhelming.

And in between them, there'd been Jessica Brown. He wanted to introduce her to them and explain to them how lucky they were not to be in her appalling situation. He longed to give them a shake and tell them to get a grip.

But he couldn't do any of that, because he was their solicitor. Essentially, it didn't matter how despicable and selfish they were. It was his job to enable them to leave their respective marriages with as much of their spouse's money as was humanly possible.

Oh God, what was this place turning him into? When you looked at it that way, he was no better than they were.

At five thirty, as he was closing down his computer, Margaret Kale materialised beside his desk.

'Conor. I've just taken a look at your billing timesheet for the day. You were with Jessica Brown for one and a half hours but you haven't charged her for the meeting.'

He took a breath. 'I was helping her to write her will. She only has a few weeks left to live.'

'And?'

'One of those hours was my lunch break,' said Conor. 'I'll reimburse you for the company's share of the invoice, so you won't lose out. I'm not going to be charging her for my services.'

'This isn't a charity, for God's sake.'

'I'm aware of that.' He'd been lying, of course, when he'd told Jessica Brown that the company occasionally saw deserving cases for free. 'I thought it might be a nice gesture.'

Margaret's pencilled eyebrows rose in disbelief. 'Sounds like an idiotic gesture to me. Once you start falling for the sob stories, it's a slippery slope.'

'As I've already said, it won't cost you a penny. You can send me the invoice, if you want. Or just take it out of my salary. Whichever's easiest for you.' The *easiest* came out with an audible edge to it; dislike for his boss was surging into his throat like nausea.

'Fine, I shall.' Her gimlet stare was unflinching. 'But I wonder if you'd have said that if I hadn't queried the issue. I imagine you were hoping it would slip by unnoticed.'

She wasn't the only one capable of not flinching. This was the moment Conor knew for sure what he had to do. He was seized with certainty and knew no fear.

'Nothing slips by you, Margaret. It's not in your nature to allow a small amount of potential profit to go astray.' As he spoke, he rose to his feet. 'I'd say it's been nice working for you, but that would be a big lie.'

'You're leaving? Excellent.' A chilly smile lifted the corners of her thin lips. 'Shall I tell you something, Conor? You were never cut out for this firm. You tried to fit in, but you're just too soft.'

This was exhilarating; he should have done it long ago. He smiled too, in a non-chilly way, and said, 'Thank you. I'll count that as a compliment.'

'It wasn't meant as one,' said Margaret. 'Off you go.'

And he had. It had been one of the very best days of his life. For years he'd toed the line and done the sensible thing.

Now the time had come to do what felt right.

He was also aware that he was fortunate. Following the death of his father, he had inherited the family home in Keynsham and moved into it two years ago. The house was too large for him but he'd been happy living there. Losing his job meant he needed some form of income, and renting the place out had been the answer.

In the meantime, Zillah had just finished having her own home in Percival Square converted into apartments. As she and his father had been long-standing platonic friends, Conor had known Zillah for years and it had been his idea that she should do this. Now, in turn, it was Zillah's idea to offer him the flat directly above her own.

When it came to a new career, Conor had asked himself whom he most envied. And whilst he'd been at home one morning pondering this question, he had glanced out of the living room window and seen the answer. Next door, the gardeners had arrived and were engaged in tidying up his neighbour's spacious garden. They'd been his father's gardeners too, and following his dad's death Conor had felt terrible about dispensing with their services. He'd apologised and explained that since he enjoyed gardening so much, he'd really like to take over the job himself.

To his relief, they hadn't been upset at all. Roddy, whose family company it was, explained that they had plenty of work to keep them busy and frequently had to turn down jobs, so he needn't feel guilty.

Watching as Roddy and his son got busy with secateurs

and a hedge-trimmer, chatting away easily to each other as they worked, Conor knew that this was the career he'd enjoy the most. You worked on gardens, made everything look better, and got paid at the end of the day by people who appreciated what you'd done for them.

What could be more rewarding than that?

Chapter 10

Now, facing Essie across the broad scrubbed-oak table in Zillah's kitchen, Conor shrugged and said, 'That was four years ago. I learned about gardening as I went along, and it turned out to be the best thing I could have done. I haven't regretted it for a minute.'

'Apart from the time that rat was hiding in one of your wellington boots,' Zillah chimed in, 'and when you tried to put it on, the rat bit you on the toe.'

'Apart from that time.' Conor looked rueful. 'Yes.'

'I love that story,' Zillah said happily. 'Makes me laugh every time I think of it.'

'If anything traumatic ever happens to you,' Conor told Essie, 'she'll probably find that funny too.'

'But in a kindly way.' Zillah's dark eyes glinted with mischief. 'And Essie's already had her share of trauma, don't you think?'

'True,' said Conor. Essie had already relayed the story of how she'd come to be here. 'Anyway, I thought I'd tell you what happened to me, just so you know that these things can sometimes turn out well.'

Essie said, 'Thanks, good to hear. Let's hope everything works out for me too.'

'Exactly what I thought.' Zillah poured herself another cup of tea. 'The two of you have that in common, both of you leaving your jobs a bit more speedily than most people. It's a bonding experience.'

Amused, Conor shook his head. Zillah's modus operandi was one he'd grown to recognise. It meant she was wondering if there could be a match to be made here, if maybe the two of them might hit it off in the romantic sense. He adored Zillah, but she was like a singularly pushy fairy godmother, always keen for him to find the right girl and settle down.

They'd been chatting now for over twenty minutes and he already knew he liked Essie Phillips. She was funny and forthright and undoubtedly attractive, but he also knew that the essential spark that needed to exist between two people was lacking, on her side as well as his. It was either there or it wasn't; you couldn't click your fingers and magic it out of thin air.

Basically, he and Essie weren't each other's types.

'By the way,' Essie said suddenly, 'I saw the two of you coming home late last night. Well, this morning really. Did you go somewhere nice?'

And now it was Zillah's turn, when Conor glanced across at her, to discreetly shake her head and mouth, *Not now*. Because it wasn't that it was a secret, but to explain what they'd been doing took time. It wasn't something you could rush, and Zillah was on her way out to meet up with members of her book group.

'I spent the evening at a friend's house. Conor picked me

up and gave me a lift home.' She finished her cup of tea. 'I'm going to head off now; it's almost midday and Audrey will roll her eyes at me if I'm late for—'

'Oh God, *midday*?' Essie stared in horror at her watch and leapt to her feet. 'I had no idea it was that late. I need to go too.'

Essie hurried across Percival Square, weaving her way ninja-style through an obstacle course of prams, pushchairs and children's trikes. Like Cinderella in reverse, she reached the Red House just as the bells of Bath Abbey began to chime twelve in the distance. Having raced up the stone steps and in through the glass doors, she saw Jude serving behind the bar and waved to catch her attention. 'Is Lucas here?'

'Hi! He's in the office. Do you want to go on up?'

'Thanks.' Essie made her way along the corridor to the staircase. At the top, she knocked on the closed office door and waited, catching her breath.

She heard Lucas call out absently, 'I'll be with you in a minute.'

After ninety seconds, she knocked again. This time he opened the door and raised his eyebrows when he saw her. 'Oh. Hello.'

'I've changed my mind.' She still despised him for what he'd done, but refusing to work here would definitely be cutting off her nose to spite her face. And her ears and mouth too. 'I'd like the job.'

'Ah. You had until midday to let me know.' Lucas glanced at his watch. 'It's now two minutes past.'

'That's because I've been waiting out here for you to answer the door.'

'Sorry, I was busy on the phone to the Job Shop, asking them to send over their best applicants.' But as he said it, his expression was playful.

'Were you really?' Essie surveyed him steadily. 'Or were you standing at the window, watching me head over here across the square?'

'I suppose that's another possibility. You looked as if you were in a bit of a hurry. I thought you were going to trip over that little kid on the scooter.'

'I thought I was too. If they're going to ride those things, they should learn how to do hand signals. So, is the job mine?'

He dropped the pretence. 'Of course. I told you that last night.'

Phew. Essie nodded. 'Did you think I'd be back?'

'I hoped you would be. Can you start straight away?'

'Yes. Busy here this afternoon?'

'It will be. There are a couple of office parties booked in.' He paused. 'Any news on the boyfriend front?'

'You mean have I found myself a new one? No, not yet.'

'I meant have you heard from the old one?'

'I haven't,' said Essie.

'Well, if there's anything I can do . . .'

At least he was feeling guilty. *As he should be.* But it was one of those polite but meaningless offers. After a moment, she shook her head. 'No. I'm the one who wrote those things. It's me he can't forgive.' If anything, Paul might be grateful to Lucas for having revealed her true feelings towards his mother. Up until then, he'd had no idea.

'Do you miss him?'

A memory instantly began to play in her brain, of the

81

morning of her last birthday, when she had sat up in bed and Paul had brought her all the foods she loved best, even though he categorically disapproved of hot chocolate, a Greggs sausage roll and two cream doughnuts for breakfast. He'd done it because he loved her. He'd even stuck lighted candles in the doughnuts.

And there were so many other happy memories like that. You couldn't help replaying the good ones, could you?

Essie looked at Lucas. What a stupid question. 'Of course I miss him.'

'Well, you never know, maybe he'll change his mind. Give it a few more days and he might realise he overreacted.'

Did he genuinely believe this? Essie said, 'I doubt it. Shall I go downstairs and start work?'

Lucas was looking at her intently, as if there was something else he wanted to say to her.

She waited. The moment passed. Finally he nodded. 'That'd be great.'

Chapter 11

'My goodness!' Zillah exclaimed, fanning herself with her gloved hands. 'So many people. Are you managing OK?'

It was the following morning, the last Sunday before Christmas, and the countdown was now happening in earnest. From behind armfuls of shopping Essie said, 'I'm fine. How about you?'

'Darling, you're the one having to carry everything. I feel like the Queen. Shall we get a coffee before heading back? Give our feet a rest?'

'If you like.' Essie, in her flat pirate boots, was impressed by Zillah's choice of navy patent leather court shoes with three-inch heels.

In one of the independent cafés hidden away down a narrow side street they found a free table and ordered cappuccinos and cakes from the waitress.

'You don't miss a thing, do you?' Amused, Essie noted the way Zillah shrugged off her coat, adjusted her sunset-hued scarf and gazed intently around the room at each of the other customers in turn.

'I'm interested in people. I just love to watch them.

Everyone's fascinating in their own way, aren't they?' Zillah thanked the waitress who'd brought over their drinks. 'I'm curious about other people's lives. Or plain nosy. One of the two.'

'Maybe that's what keeps you young,' said Essie.

'Ha, yes, could be! I can't possibly pop my clogs yet.' Zillah was busy adding sugar to her coffee. 'Not while there are still so many people to watch and listen to and wonder about.' She leaned closer and whispered, 'See those two women sitting over there by the window? They're pretending to be friends but they can't stand each other!'

'You can tell just by looking at them?' Essie was wildly impressed.

'I'm not Derren Brown.' Zillah burst out laughing. 'The skinny one's my doctor's ex-wife, and the blonde one's his current one.'

'Oof.'

'He's a good GP but he's always been a bit of a one for the ladies. It makes visits to the surgery great fun,' said Zillah. 'OK, how about those two men next to the door?'

They speculated happily about several of the other customers before moving on to cover last-minute presents, the purple velvet beret Zillah had been tempted to buy in Jolly's, and the merits of salted caramel versus peanut butter Magnums.

Twenty minutes later, coffee and cakes finished, Zillah beckoned the waitress over to ask for the bill.

'And could I also pay for whatever the lady in the corner is having?' She'd lowered her voice. 'The one in the grey raincoat.'

'Oh!' The waitress sounded surprised. 'She ordered a

pot of tea and a slice of lemon drizzle cake. Is that OK?'

Zillah nodded. 'Absolutely. But when she asks for her bill, please don't tell her who took care of it.'

Essie looked over at the woman, who was, at a guess, in her early seventies. Her hair was short and silver-grey, she was wearing brown shoes with worn-down heels, and her mac appeared to be a few years old too. Between sips of tea, she was either gazing out of the window or turning the pages of the magazine on the table in front of her.

Once they'd left the café, Essie said to Zillah, 'Did you know her?'

'No, darling. I just thought she looked a bit sad.'

Essie nodded. 'She did.'

'There was a wedding ring on her left hand, but it was too big for her, as if she'd lost weight but couldn't bear to stop wearing it. Maybe her husband recently died and this is her first Christmas without him.'

'And that's why you paid her bill?'

'Why not? It might brighten her day, just a tiny bit.' Zillah flashed a smile. 'It certainly brightens mine.'

'Do you do this all the time?'

'No, just when the mood takes me. It's fun. Once you get to my age, it's nice to have a hobby.' Her tone grew mischievous. 'For the sake of a few pounds I can cheer someone up with my ill-gotten gains! Who wouldn't want to do that?'

The noise of a bus trundling past had all but drowned out her words, but Essie was almost sure she'd just said 'ill-gotten gains'. Opening her mouth to ask the next question, she was cut off by Zillah coming to a dramatic halt in the street. 'It's no good: if someone else grabs it, I'll never forgive myself – I *have* to buy that velvet beret! Is it OK if we just pop back to Jolly's?'

'No problem,' said Essie.

Ill-gotten gains. Hmm, intriguing. And now Zillah was desperate for a beret . . . very Bonnie and Clyde.

Maybe she had once robbed a bank.

Then the seemingly endless run-up was over and it was Christmas Day at last. At nine in the morning, Essie and Conor both joined Zillah in her kitchen for a celebratory breakfast of smoked salmon, orange juice and chilled Prosecco. The three of them were heading in different directions – Conor was visiting his cousins in Cirencester, Zillah was spending the day with old friends at the Francis Hotel, and Essie was heading over to Scarlett's mum's house.

At ten o'clock, Essie's phone rang while she was in the shower. Her heart did a weird little leap and she was out in an instant, shampoo pouring down her face and into her eyes as she skidded across the bathroom floor to reach her mobile. Because she'd watched enough Richard Curtis films in her time, and it was Christmas morning, after all. What if it was Paul?

It wasn't, though.

'Ho ho ho,' Scarlett bellowed over the sound of carols playing in the background. 'Happy Christmas! Mum says you can come over whenever you like but lunch is going to be served at two thirty. Oh, and she's making that stuffing again, the one with the apple and sultanas, because she knows it's your favourite.'

'And that's why I love her,' Essie said fondly. 'I'll be over in a bit.'

Forty minutes later, dressed in a festive red dress and black lacy tights, she was putting the finishing touches to her make-up when the doorbell rang downstairs.

Her heart, like an ever-optimistic puppy, did yet another foolish leap.

Because what if Paul had woken up this morning and realised that he couldn't stand being without her for a moment longer, that life had become meaningless and he had to let her know how he felt? What if he was standing on the doorstep right now, clutching a huge bunch of flowers, ready to tell her that he still loved her, and to beg her to forgive him for overreacting to something that had been a complete accident?

What if her life was about to turn into the last scene of one of those movies that made you want to cry with happiness because it was about to end in the most perfect way imaginable, with snowflakes tumbling down, Christmas music playing in the background and Paul's Santa hat tilting jauntily over one eye as he drew her into his arms?

OK, scratch that. Paul might be fond of a romantic gesture, but he would *never* wear a Santa hat.

Essie put down her lipstick and did her best to breathe normally. Yes, she was perfectly capable of being single, but she did miss being one half of a couple. Downstairs, the front door was being pulled open. She deliberately hadn't run to the window because that would jinx the fantasy instantly. For the same reason now, she remained where she was and stared at herself in the mirror.

Is it Paul?

Then she heard Conor call up the stairs, 'Essie? It's for you!'

It's him, it is him, it's actually happening.

The things you do when something completely unexpected catches you by surprise. Still gazing at her reflection, the first thought whooshing through Essie's brain was the one reminding her that she was wearing red lipstick and Paul didn't like her wearing red lipstick. Her hand grabbed a tissue from the box on the dressing table and she hastily scrubbed off as much of it as she could.

At the top of the stairs – *please don't fall down them* – she called out in a casual yet festive manner, 'Coming!'

OK, hold onto the banister, cue that end-of-the-movie music and appear completely surprised when you see him.

Oh, and look adorable too.

'Hi,' said Lucas. 'Happy Christmas.'

The end-of-the-movie music skittered to a halt. The look of surprise was spot-on. As their eyes met, humiliatingly, Essie realised that she'd not only failed to conceal her disappointment, but that Lucas knew exactly why she was disappointed.

'Sorry, it's only me.' He was wearing black jeans and a pale grey V-neck sweater with the sleeves pushed up. 'Look, I'm a bit stuck so I have to ask, but it's OK to say you can't do it. Jude was going to help me with the lunchtime shift but she's gone down with a bug. It's not one of Hopeless Henry's excuses; she's properly ill. You wouldn't be able to step in, would you? We're only open from twelve until two. But like I said, if you can't manage it, that's fine.'

He stopped, waited. It clearly wasn't fine, but nor was it a matter of life and death. The Red House was a bar, not an operating theatre.

'If I say no, is there anyone else who can help out?'

'Not really. I've already tried everyone else and they're busy with family. I left you till last.'

'Right.'

'Only because I assumed you'd turn me down.'

'Hmm.' It was an understandable assumption.

'Double pay,' said Lucas.

Essie wrapped her arms around her torso as a cold breeze made itself felt. 'I'm supposed to be going over to my friend's house for the day. Her mum's serving lunch at two thirty.'

'Where's the house?'

'Bradford on Avon.' It was a small market town seven or eight miles from the centre of Bath.

Lucas was clearly considering his options. 'How about if we're out of the Red House by two fifteen and I'll drive you straight over there afterwards? You'll be there in time for lunch.'

Double pay.

And no taxi fare to Scarlett's mum's house.

Plus she'd get good tips from the jovial Christmas Day lunchtime crowd.

'Go on then, I'll do it,' said Essie. 'I'll be over at twelve.'

'Thanks. You're a star,' said Lucas, visibly relieved.

'I know.'

Chapter 12

'Well?' said the taxi driver bringing her home twelve hours later. 'Had a good day?'

'Fantastic, thanks.' Essie smothered a yawn, because it had been a great day but a tiring one. The Red House had been jam-packed with happy punters wearing festive sweaters, with lengths of tinsel looped around their necks. Then Lucas, as promised, had given her a lift over to Bradford on Avon and she'd arrived at Scarlett's mum's house in time to join the riotous table of ten for lunch. Having eaten her own body weight in turkey, stuffing, stupendous roast potatoes and every vegetable known to man, she had spent the rest of the afternoon and evening playing energetic games with Scarlett's hyperactive nephews and nieces.

Now, at almost eleven o'clock at night, she was still full of food but had been packed off by Scarlett's mum, Kim, with a selection of plastic containers containing everything from mince pies to half a smoked ham and a whole Camembert, because 'You might get a bit peckish and need something to keep you going later.'

The taxi pulled up outside number 23 and Essie was

cheered to see light behind the curtains of Zillah's living room. After just a week the house already felt like home, and she was looking forward to hearing about Zillah's day.

Letting herself in through the front door, she saw that Conor was back too. He helped her in with her bags. 'Come on through, we're in the kitchen. Can you manage a mince pie? Between us, we've been sent home with twenty.'

Essie held up one of the plastic containers. 'Make that thirty.'

'Hello, darling!' Zillah was boiling the kettle. 'What do you fancy? Glass of champagne or a cup of tea? Sit down and help yourself to cheese; we're never going to get through this lot.'

Neither Zillah nor Conor was drinking champagne, so Essie settled for tea too. They exchanged stories about their days, but there appeared to be an undercurrent of . . . well, unrelaxedness was the only way she could describe it. As if they were expecting something to happen or for someone else to appear.

Twenty minutes later, Zillah's mobile rang and she and Conor both jumped. Essie realised that this was what they'd been waiting for. Having been about to make her excuses and head on up to bed, she stayed where she was.

'Yes?' Zillah glanced across at Conor as she answered the phone and listened to the voice at the other end. 'Right. Thanks, we'll see you in a bit.' She nodded to Conor and broke into a smile, but it was a get-the-job-done kind of smile rather than a joyous one. 'Yes, we'll be there by then.'

She ended the call and rose to her feet. 'It's going ahead.'

'Good,' said Conor. 'I'll get my things, then we'll leave.'

And Essie realised that whatever was about to happen was important to both of them. She looked at Zillah. 'Am I allowed to ask what this is about? Or is it none of my business? Sorry, forget I said that. I'll leave you to it.' Belatedly she realised that this was connected to the goings-on the other night when she'd spotted them arriving home together in the very small hours.

'Darling, it's not a huge secret. Now, are you shattered and ready for bed or would you like to come with us?' Leaning across the kitchen table, Zillah was blowing out the candles and squeezing the still-smoking wicks with her fingertips to ensure they were completely extinguished. 'Entirely up to you.'

'It depends. If you're off to run a midnight marathon, I'll leave you to it. But I don't know where you're going.' As Essie spoke, Conor returned to the kitchen wearing a warm jacket and with a Nikon camera slung around his neck.

'OK,' said Zillah. 'You know when we were in the café the other morning, and we saw the woman sitting at that table in the corner?'

Essie was completely mystified. 'Yes.'

Zillah continued winding a soft pink scarf around her shoulders, checking that her gloves were in her bag. She straightened up. 'Well, it's not exactly the same, but it's kind of like that.'

The roads, at this late hour on Christmas night, were about as empty as they'd ever be. A light frost sparkled in the headlights as they left the city behind them and made their way along the twisting narrow lanes. Having complained that Zillah drove too fast at night, Conor was behind the wheel of her Mercedes. Zillah, sitting in the back seat alongside Essie, was explaining the purpose of their expedition.

'I was visiting an old friend last year in Amsterdam,' she said. 'Over dinner one evening, she told me about a charity they have there called the Ambulance Wish Foundation. It was started in 2006 by a paramedic who was driving someone very ill from one hospital to another. When the second hospital said they couldn't admit him for a couple of hours, the paramedic asked if there was anything he'd like to do. And the patient said he'd love to visit Rotterdam Harbour to say goodbye to it. So that's what they did,' said Zillah, 'and the man was so happy to see it one last time, because he'd worked there all his life.'

'That's amazing,' said Essie.

'Isn't it? The paramedic was so moved, he arranged for the man to be taken back there a couple of days later, lifted on his stretcher onto one of the boats and taken for a last trip around the harbour. It was a small gesture with a huge impact. It meant so much. And when my friend told me this story, I was deeply touched by it. Because there are lots of charities granting bigger wishes for younger people . . . and that's fantastic, of course it is. They and their families go on trips to Disneyland and have a holiday to remember. But what this paramedic discovered was that when you're bedbound and very close to death, your final wishes can be very small indeed.'

'I've never even thought about it,' said Essie.

'I know, I hadn't either. But it struck such a chord with me. The charity really took off in the Netherlands. Now they have hundreds of volunteers and several ambulances, and they've fulfilled thousands of wishes. I'm eighty-three,' Zillah went on. 'I can't set up anything like that at my age. But when my darling husband was dying, it would have been lovely if there'd been something nice we could have done for him. So in the smallest way I decided to arrange for a few last wishes to be granted. And that's the story,' she concluded with a shrug. 'This is what we're on our way to do now. The only reason I didn't mention it before was because I didn't want you to feel obliged to join us, especially on Christmas night.'

They reached St Mark's Hospice ten minutes later. It was a modern single-storey building in well-tended grounds. Essie knew of it – they had several charity shops dotted around the area – but had never been here before.

There was a private ambulance already waiting at the top of the driveway, and signs of activity in the dimly lit reception area. As they climbed out of the car, Essie said, 'Will they mind me being here?'

Zillah shook her head. 'Not if you're with us.'

But Essie hung back all the same and waited beneath the covered entrance as Zillah warmly greeted a very old man beside the reception desk. He had slicked-back grey hair and an Errol Flynn moustache, and was bundled up in a long dark winter coat.

'Is that him?' she murmured to Conor, beside her. 'I thought he'd be iller than that.'

The next moment she mentally kicked herself, because a set of double doors had swung open and two uniformed paramedics appeared, pushing a stretcher on wheels. A curvy middle-aged woman walked alongside them and Essie saw that the patient was a parchment-pale elderly lady who couldn't weigh more than five stone.

'I'm such an idiot,' she murmured.

'Don't worry about it.' Conor held open the main door so everyone could make their way down the ramp. The sick woman was wearing an oxygen mask and there was a drip

94

running into her left arm, but she was smiling and murmuring a few words to her husband as they passed by.

Finally, loaded up, the ambulance moved off. Flowers were brought out and placed in the boot of Zillah's Mercedes, and Conor resumed his place behind the wheel so they could set off in pursuit.

This time the journey took thirty minutes. When they finally arrived in the small Cotswold village of Alton Tarville, Conor followed the ambulance into the narrow driveway that led up to the church.

The vicar was waiting for them. As Essie and Conor carried the flowers into the simple, twelfth-century church, Essie marvelled at the sight of the stained-glass windows lit up from below by rows of glowing ivory candles. There were more candles flanking the altar, and trails of holly and ivy had been arranged around the choir stalls. The heating was on and the air smelled of must and dust, of ancient stone and beeswax polish.

Quickly they placed the arrangements of flowers for maximum effect. The organist took up position. At a signal from the vicar, he pumped the pedals and began to play, and the familiar opening bars of Wagner's Bridal Chorus filled the church.

The heavy oak door opened and through it came the middle-aged woman, whom Essie now knew to be an off-duty doctor. She guided the front of the wheeled stretcher between the pews and greeted the rest of them with a nod and a smile to reassure them that all was well.

John, the man with the Errol Flynn moustache, had removed his coat to reveal a smart grey suit with a white rose in his buttonhole. He held the hand of his wife of fifty-six years as the two of them headed together up the aisle. The two bearded paramedics, in their green uniforms, solemnly brought up the rear like oversized bridesmaids.

The music soared to the rafters and Essie saw the look of joy on the face of John's wife Elizabeth as he lovingly clutched her hand.

When the organist had finished, the vicar spoke about John and Elizabeth's long-ago wedding in this church and their happy marriage. Elizabeth didn't take her eyes off her beloved husband whilst they renewed their vows, and when it was over, John bent to kiss her with infinite tenderness.

Everyone present in the tiny church, including the burly paramedics, was wiping their eyes. Then the organist launched into Mendelssohn's glorious Wedding March. Conor, who had discreetly taken several photographs during the renewal of the vows, moved forward and took more. Essie knew now that he always did this. Tonight's visit here had been brought forward by Elizabeth's physician because her health was failing fast; she wasn't expected to see in the new year. But it had been her dearest wish to come to St Mary's church one last time and renew her wedding vows with the husband she'd adored for so long.

And for John, Conor's photographs would provide a precious reminder of this night in the months and years to come.

They gathered beside the heavy oak door and John and Elizabeth insisted upon thanking each of them in turn.

'You're angels, every one of you.' Her voice wavering, Elizabeth reached for Essie's hand. 'You can't imagine what this means to us.'

And Essie was able to reply with complete honesty, 'I wouldn't have missed it for the world.'

Chapter 13

The thing about Scarlett was you never knew when the next crush might be about to strike, or whom it might involve. She didn't go for a recognisable type.

Watching her, Essie thought back to the boyfriends Scarlett had acquired and discarded during the last couple of years. The variety was endless.

Most people, offered a tin of Quality Street, went for the same ones each time. The Brazil nut one in the irresistible purple wrapper was Essie's own personal favourite.

But if you were to offer Scarlett a full tin every day for a fortnight, she'd choose a different one every time. And she was exactly the same with men. The last boyfriend, Pete, had worked in a motorbike repair shop and had worn his waist-length dark hair in a plait. Pablo, the one before that, had been a sleekly besuited accountant.

And now she was clearly interested in adding Conor to the metaphorical notches on her bedpost.

The question was, would Conor be similarly entranced?

It was the fourth of January, a freezing Monday lunchtime, and Lucas had left for a meeting two hours earlier, instructing his staff to take down all the Christmas decorations. Once they'd been bagged up and the tree had been hauled outside to shed the rest of its needles in the back yard, Essie had wailed, 'Oh no, I don't like it like this! The walls look so empty now. They're all naked and sad.'

Whereupon Jude had replied, 'Not to worry. They'll soon liven up.'

And Scarlett, who'd dropped in to warm her hands and feet, said, 'If you want a bit of Banksy-style graffiti, I'm handy with a can of spray paint.'

Thirty minutes later, Conor had strolled into the bar and Essie, surprised to see him, had said, 'Oh, it's Conor. Hello!'

Behind her, in an ooh-I-say way, Scarlett had murmured, 'He*llo*.'

Conor was carrying an artist's portfolio, which he laid out on one of the empty tables. As he unzipped it, Scarlett bounced over. 'Hi, Conor! We meet at last! I'm Scarlett!'

Cartoon hearts weren't *quite* emanating from her eyes, but it was a close thing. Amused, Essie turned her attention to the contents of the portfolio.

'Where did these come from? Are they yours?'

'No, I just found them on a park bench. Yes,' said Conor, 'they're mine.'

She'd seen the colour photographs he'd taken of Elizabeth and John during the renewal of their vows on Christmas night. She knew photography was his hobby, but had assumed he simply took photographs of scenic views and maybe the occasional garden.

These, though, were eye-catching portraits, black and white and taken on the streets of Bath. More than that, they were great.

'You're a street photographer,' Scarlett exclaimed. 'Essie didn't tell me that. Cool!'

'Essie didn't know,' said Essie.

'I'm a modest chap.' Conor shrugged. 'I just enjoy taking photos of people. I'm a big fan of faces.'

'Oh, you must take some pictures of me!' Scarlett sucked in her cheeks and did a selfie pout. 'I love having my photo taken!'

'I'd never have guessed,' Conor said good-naturedly.

Jude had disappeared to the storage room. Now, returning with an armful of frames, she announced, 'Essie was worried about the walls looking bare. I told her not to panic, they'd soon be sorted out. Some of the regulars have been asking when your photos would be going back up.'

Essie was impressed. 'These were on the walls before Christmas?'

'The previous lot were. This is the new collection. I took these over the last fortnight.'

They were wonderful portraits of people he'd randomly encountered around the city. Some were gazing directly into the camera lens, creating an up-close connection that had incredible impact. Others looked elsewhere, enabling you to take in every detail of them. Some were quirky; others were calm and classical. Each and every one of them had the effect of making you long to know more about the characters of the people themselves.

'You're good at this,' said Essie. 'I mean, really good.'

'Thanks. I started doing it at university. It's been my hobby for years.' Lifting out an A4-sized photo of an unrepentantly grinning woman in her sixties, Conor said, 'What does this one say to you?'

'She looks naughty.'

'She was just on her way to the shops to return the horrible slippers her sister-in-law gave her for Christmas. She's going to get the money back and buy herself a bottle of gin instead.'

It was a simple job to slide the photographs into the plain Perspex frames. There were twelve in all, and once they'd been hung around the bar, the walls no longer looked bare. They were popular with the customers, who looked forward to seeing each new set. And every other Sunday evening, Essie learned, everyone featured in the photographs was invited along to meet and chat with the other people there. Not all of them could make it, of course, but those who did always enjoyed themselves and were given their portrait to take home at the end of the night. The following Monday morning, the replacements went up.

Having explained the system, Jude said, 'It's been really successful. To begin with, it was just a way to keep the walls interesting. Then it grew more and more popular, especially among the singles set. Because twice a month they could turn up and meet other single people, and the new photos meant there was always something to talk about. So completely by accident, it turned into an event everyone really enjoyed coming along to.'

Essie said, 'That's brilliant.'

'Well I'm single,' said Scarlett. 'And I'm definitely going to come along from now on.' She beamed at Conor. 'I meant what I said earlier, you know. I'd love you to photograph me so I can hang on one of these walls.'

'I'm happy to take a few pictures if that's what you want,' said Conor. 'But the ones I choose to put on show do tend to be of the kind of people who wouldn't ask to have their photo taken.'

'You mean ugly people.' Put out, Scarlett pointed to one of the framed shots of an ancient man with a face full of wrinkles and a lopsided grin revealing one missing tooth and one gold one.

'Nobody's ugly,' Conor said mildly. 'I like faces that are interesting.'

'What, and mine isn't?'

'Strike a pose.'

Scarlett instantly sucked in her cheeks once more, tilted her head back and did the pouty thing with her mouth.

'What about you?' He pointed to Essie, who promptly puffed out her cheeks and crossed her eyes.

Conor laughed. 'See? That says so much more about a person.'

'It says Essie doesn't mind making herself look like a prat,' said Scarlett.

He took out his phone and held it in front of her. 'Go on, now it's your turn.'

'And let you take a photo of me looking like that? No way!'

'Shame.' Amused, Conor put the phone away. 'I'd have put it on display. Ah well, never mind.'

'God, he's annoying,' huffed Scarlett when Conor had left.

'I thought you fancied him.'

'I do! That's why it's so annoying that he's annoying!'

Essie gave her shoulder a consoling pat. 'You mean he didn't fall under your spell.'

'He hasn't fallen under my spell *yet*,' Scarlett corrected her. 'But he will. Sometimes they just need a bit of time.'

'And a nudge in the right direction.'

'And that's where you come in. You can put in a good word for me.' Having finished her Coke, Scarlett wriggled her fingers back into her multicoloured fingerless gloves. 'OK, I need to get back to work. Don't forget, will you? Just keep telling him how fabulous I am.'

Essie smiled, because Scarlett's endless optimism was what she loved most about her. 'I'll drop it into every conversation, I promise.'

'And I'm definitely coming here on Sunday evening. What can I do to make him like me more? Ooh, I know!'

'Give me a clue.'

'He's a gardener,' Scarlett exclaimed. 'I can dye my hair green! He'll love that!'

'You're new,' said the girl who'd come into the bar.

Essie nodded and said, 'I am.'

'Can I just try something? I'm good at this. Look into my eyes . . . good . . . OK, I'm going to guess that your name begins with an E. Am I right?'

Essie smiled politely; she could guess where this was going. 'You are.'

'E . . . s . . . s . . . i . . . e.' The girl looked expectant. 'Did I get it? Is that your name?'

'It is. Well done.' The unwanted recognition following the round-robin fiasco had begun to wear off during the last week, but people did still occasionally look at her and make the connection.

'I cheated,' said the girl. 'Lucas told me he'd taken on someone new. I'm Giselle.'

'Ah yes. Hi.' Essie relaxed, because Giselle was Lucas's girlfriend. A nurse working here in Bath, she'd spent the last two weeks over Christmas and New Year with her family up on the Isle of Skye. And now she was back. Goodness, she was pretty, with huge amber eyes, a flawless porcelain complexion and a mass of deep auburn curls tied up with a tangerine scarf.

'Is he here?'

'Sorry, no, not back yet. But he won't be long.' She was so friendly and warm, and her soft Scottish accent was just wonderful to hear. 'Is there anything I can get you?'

'It's OK, I'm fine.' Glancing around to make sure no one else was listening, Giselle said, 'He told me all about that round-robin thingy. Poor you, what a nightmare.'

'Thanks. Yes, it was.' Essie hesitated, wondering just how much Lucas had told her.

Evidently reading her mind, Giselle said, 'Hey, I know nobody else knows, but I'm his girlfriend. I've heard the whole story. He was an idiot and he did a daft thing. That's boys for you, isn't it? They just don't think these things through. But you're here now and he says you've settled right in. So that's great!'

And this time Essie had to force herself to smile, because Giselle was blithely excusing Lucas, defending him, almost dismissing his actions as nothing at all. Which she was bound to do, really, but it hadn't been nothing, had it? Didn't it bother her, even slightly, that her boyfriend had done something so thoughtless?

'Actually, I think I will have a drink. Could you do me a little rum and Coke?' Patting her chest, Giselle confided, 'It's been two weeks since I last saw Lucas, and I've got butterflies! How crazy is that? It's like being sixteen all over again.'

Moments later, Jude returned from her break and greeted Lucas's girlfriend with genuine affection. Essie, who already knew how popular Giselle was with the staff, marvelled at Lucas's ability to attract such a lovely girl.

For the next few minutes Jude caught Giselle up on the gossip she'd missed over the last fortnight. In return, Giselle took out her phone and showed them photos of all the snow they'd had in Kinlara, and the ceilidhs she'd been to with her family. Then the door to the Red House swung open and there was Lucas, his face lighting up at the sight of her. And Giselle, in turn gazing at him with sheer joy in her eyes, said, 'Hello, what's your name? You look nice.'

Lucas grinned. 'God, I've missed you.'

'Not nearly as much as I've missed you.' Clearly unable to tear her eyes from his face, Giselle said, 'If I run towards you and swallow-dive into your arms like in *Dirty Dancing*, will you promise to catch me?'

'After you've just spent the last two weeks eating Christmas food? We'd better not risk it.'

And Giselle, who was skinny enough for it not to be an insult, said, 'Oh Lucas, come here. Two weeks is too long to not see you.'

Then they were hugging each other, and it was actually quite lovely; Essie felt as if she were watching one of those films with the ultimate happy ending. The kiss was heartfelt without making onlookers cringe. Lucas's hand was curled around the back of Giselle's neck and she was touching his face with her fingers, smiling as she murmured something only he was able to hear.

Lucas smiled too and it didn't take a genius to work it out. His arm slid around Giselle's waist and he gave her a squeeze.

'OK, we're not busy,' he told Jude, 'so I'm going to leave you in charge. See you later, kids.'

'Can't imagine what they'll be getting up to,' said Jude as Lucas and Giselle left the bar and headed upstairs to his flat.

One of the regulars seated at a nearby table said, 'Reckon it's time for Lucas to unwrap his Christmas present.'

Chapter 14

After the first-week-of-January lull, Sunday evening at the Red House caught everyone by surprise. By eight o'clock the place was packed and Conor found himself queuing to be served at the bar. The stand-out stars of the show tonight were turning out to be Mary the slipper-returner and Jethro the gold-toothed nonagenarian. Loving their moment in the spotlight, they were greeting visitors and relaying scurrilous stories about their lives.

Jethro had asked for a pint of Guinness and Mary had requested a brandy and Babycham because it was what she'd drunk as a teenager and she thought it might make her feel young again.

Was Babycham even still sold in bars?

Conor shifted from one foot to the other and wished the customer in front of him would get a move on. In her late thirties, she had bleached hair and an overloud voice. Her perfume was strong and heady, she was wearing a slightly too-tight stripy dress that made her look like a giant wasp, and the heavy make-up on her face was noticeably more orange than her neck.

Most annoying of all, though, was the fact that she'd already been served with her drinks yet was *still* standing there talking loudly to Lucas, who was helping out behind the bar.

'. . . I can't believe how busy this place is,' she was saying now. 'We've never been here before, but a friend said it was good fun so we came over to try it out. Those photos are a great idea to get the punters in through the door.'

Conor heaved a sigh, because the woman was yet to pay for the two glasses of wine. The next moment she whipped her head round and snapped, 'Ugh, would you mind not doing that?'

Conor said evenly, 'I was breathing.'

'On the back of my *neck*.'

'That's because I'm standing behind you, waiting to be served.'

'Well there's no need to sigh like that. Have some manners, Mr Stroppy.'

Mr Stroppy?

'Thank you for that suggestion,' Conor replied. 'Now how about you open that purse and pay for your drinks? Then we can all move on with our lives.' It wasn't like him to retaliate, but sometimes the situation demanded it.

'Wow, you're a bundle of laughs, aren't you? Ever thought of chilling out and having a bit of fun instead? No, clearly not. I tell you what, I feel sorry for whoever you spent Christmas with. They must have had a whale of a time with you.'

Behind the bar, Lucas was finding the exchange hilarious. Evidently far more interested in discovering what might happen next than in calming the situation, he said, 'Now this is what I call love at first sight.'

God, the thought of it. Just imagine. Conor said to the loud woman, 'And I wonder how *your* Christmas Day companions enjoyed themselves? Were they by any chance wearing earplugs?'

The woman gave him an up-close killer stare. 'I *needed* to raise my voice to be heard over the sound of your *sighing*.'

Conor looked over at Lucas, who was spluttering with laughter. 'When you're ready, could I have a pint of Guinness and a brandy and Babycham?'

Which was, of course, the very worst thing he could have said. The loud woman threw back her head and gave an ear-splitting screech like a parrot. 'Ha ha, of course that's what he drinks! Why am I not surprised?'

Ignoring her, Conor addressed Lucas. 'It's for Mary. I wasn't sure if you sold Babycham, but I said I'd ask.'

'We don't, but I can do a mixture of brandy, lemonade and Prosecco. Might do the trick. Thanks,' Lucas said as the intolerable woman in the waspy dress finally paid for her glasses of wine.

'My pleasure.' She leaned against the marble-topped bar and surveyed Lucas with open appreciation. 'Can I just ask, are you single by any chance?'

She was doing it deliberately now, Conor thought, just to keep him waiting. 'No, he isn't single. And if he were, I don't imagine—' No, *no*. He stopped himself in the nick of time, didn't utter the words that had been on the brink of tumbling out. What was happening to him? He was a good person, he had standards, and he wasn't going to let his irritation with wasp woman get the better of him.

'Wise decision.' She raised her glass in an ironic toast.

'Seeing as a drink chucked in the face often offends. Bye, Mr Stroppy.'

She squeezed past Conor and headed over to the other end of the room. Which, with a bit of luck, was where she would stay.

The good news was that Mary greatly approved of her Babycham substitute.

'Mmm, takes me back, that does.' She smacked her lips together and took another glug. 'I'm having such a good time, love. Haven't had this much fun since my first husband's funeral.'

Which caused Zillah, next to Conor, to splutter into her drink. 'My first husband's funeral was like that too.'

'Get the worst one out of the way first, that's my motto.' Mary pulled a face. 'I mean, I know we shouldn't speak ill of the dead, but I reckon we get special dispensation when they really deserve it. How many times have you been married, my love? I've done it twice.'

'Three times for me,' said Zillah.

'Amateurs.' Jethro's gold tooth glinted as he took another swallow of Guinness. 'I've had four wives.'

Essie, weaving between them as she collected empty glasses, exchanged a look with Conor. 'I feel like such an underachiever.'

'Stick with me, darlin',' said Jethro. 'Play yer cards right and you could be number five.'

A couple of hours later, Conor was talking to Zillah when he felt a gust of warm breath on the back of his neck, followed by a noisy sigh.

Seriously, was this woman for real? Ignoring her, he

continued his conversation until she tapped him on the shoulder.

Quite hard.

He turned. 'Yes?'

'OK, stop trying to think of smart comebacks and just listen to me for a moment. We're off now. But before we go, I need to tell you that I'm actually not a complete monster. I asked the good-looking guy behind the bar if you're single and he told me you are. So I wanted to ask if you'd—'

'Look, I'm sorry,' Conor blurted out before she could say it, 'but no. Really, no.' God, what a nightmare; he couldn't believe this was happening. 'Sometimes you just know when something wouldn't work out, and this is one of those times.'

Urgh, not a chance in hell.

'Ha, you seriously think I meant *me*? You thought I was asking you out? No way, Mr Stroppy, not in a million years! Listen to me, and this time try not to jump to barking-mad conclusions.' The loud woman held up her hand like a traffic cop. 'You might not be my idea of a hot date, but I have a friend who I think might be perfect for you. She goes for your type. And I reckon she'd be your type too. Believe me, I'm good at this,' she continued before Conor had a chance to react. 'I've done it before. You live here in Bath, yeah?'

'Yes, but—'

'I'll bring her along next week. Can't do Sunday, so it'll have to be Saturday. Make sure you're here by eight, OK? And don't be late.'

Conor stared at her. 'What makes you think I'd even want to do that?'

'Because you'd be an idiot not to.' The woman was utterly

confident. 'Just go with it. You might not like me, but you can trust me. I know what I'm doing and I'm always right.'

And with that, she flicked up the collar of her emerald-green leather jacket. 'Don't forget, eight o'clock. *Ciao*.'

'Well.' Zillah arched an eyebrow when the woman had left. 'Interesting.'

'Nightmare,' said Conor.

'Aren't you going to do it?'

'Not a chance.'

'Oh darling, why not?'

He looked at her, aghast. 'Are you serious? She's a horror. I mean, it's not often I take against someone from the word go, but for that one I'll make an exception.'

'OK, so you didn't hit it off with her. But she's talking about introducing you to her friend.' Zillah gestured with the exuberance of someone onto her third Negroni. 'Her friend could be perfect in every way!'

'Once a matchmaker, always a matchmaker.' Conor shook his head good-naturedly, because Zillah never gave up. 'And no, I don't think her friend would be perfect in every way. If she was, she'd have better taste than to have a friend like *that*.'

'So you're not even tempted to meet her? In case you're wrong?'

'I'll take that chance. And don't look at me like that,' said Conor. 'I'm quite happy being single.'

'You're not as young as you used to be.'

'I'm only thirty-two!'

'Hmm,' said Zillah. 'I call that knocking on a bit. By the time I was thirty-two I'd been married, widowed and married again long enough to realise I'd made yet another dreadful mistake.'

'You make it sound so tempting.'

'But I learned from my mistakes, darling boy. That's the whole point.'

Entertained, Conor said, 'Well maybe I'd rather wait and get it right first time.'

Chapter 15

'You really want to hear the whole story?' said Zillah. Having left the Red House and made their way across the square, she'd invited them into her flat for a nightcap. Conor had declined; he had to be up early in the morning. But Essie, who could never fall asleep straight after finishing work, had been happy to join her.

'Only if you want to tell me. Don't worry if you'd rather not.' Essie, who was busy spreading Cambozola on water biscuits, looked apologetic. 'Sorry, I overheard you and Mary and Jethro talking earlier about how many times you'd been married, and I wondered how it all came about, but I'm just being nosy . . .'

'Darling, I'm more than happy to tell you. It's a cautionary tale, if nothing else.' Having kicked off her shoes and made herself comfortable on the orange velvet sofa, Zillah took a sip of coffee. 'Actually, it all started with that.' She nodded at the portrait hanging on the wall in the alcove.

'I love that picture of you,' said Essie. 'How did it start everything off?'

'My father decided to have my likeness painted for my

twenty-first birthday, by a society portrait artist. I went along to his studio for sittings. But of course I wasn't his only client, which meant he had several other commissioned paintings on the go. And one of the other sitters was Richard. Well, he saw my portrait progressing each week and decided he liked what he was seeing on the canvas. So the following week he turned up at the studio while I was there, to decide whether real-life me matched up to the painting.'

'And you did,' said Essie. 'That's actually quite romantic.'

'Oh, it was. And who doesn't love a bit of romance? I was flattered and impressed. Richard Haig was quite a catch. Here . . .' Zillah reached for her iPad and found the folder of photographs she'd stored on it, brightened-up digital copies of old black-and-white snaps that had been kept for years in heavy leather albums. 'That's Richard there. My friends were so jealous of me. He was incredibly handsome.'

'Blimey.' Essie's eyes widened. 'You're not kidding. He looks like a film star.'

'Of course he was also incredibly self-centred, incredibly good at lying and incredibly unfaithful. Not that I discovered that until after the wedding.' Zillah shook her head at the memory. 'He took great care to hide all his less attractive qualities before we were married. From then on, he just grew more and more relaxed about it.'

'That must have been so horrible for you,' said Essie.

'It was, but once I realised what he was really like, I suppose I stopped loving him. I felt stupid, though. And gullible, and ashamed. Because why wasn't I enough for him? Why did he need to have affairs with other women? It was a bit of a blow to the ego, I have to say. And divorce wasn't as easy back then as it is now.' Zillah shrugged. 'Everyone told me I'd be crazy to leave him. Back then, you were expected to tolerate that kind of behaviour. When I told my mother I wanted to end the marriage she was horrified and begged me to stay with him.'

Essie pulled a sympathetic face. 'You poor thing.'

'Except we weren't poor,' Zillah said wryly. 'Richard's family were hugely wealthy, and he'd inherited a fortune from his great-uncle. So we were financially secure, but I was still miserable. Then one day I came home early and caught him in bed with his latest mistress. I told him I was leaving him and he laughed in my face. He said I'd never do it, and that was when I had to.'

'Good for you,' said Essie.

'I told him I was going to visit an old school friend in Brighton for a couple of days, and that's what I did. She said I was welcome to stay with her for as long as I wanted. So forty-eight hours later I caught the train back to London to collect some of my things and tell Richard I was moving out for good. I can't describe how relieved I felt that I was finally doing something . . . I was really looking forward to it.' Even now, Zillah could recall every moment of that train journey, fuelled by adrenalin and determination. 'Except when I got back to the house, it was empty, and an hour later two police constables arrived on the doorstep to tell me Richard was dead. He'd been driving like a complete maniac as usual, and had skidded going round a corner and smashed into a bridge. It turned out he'd been on his way to meet up with yet another of his floozies. Well, he didn't make it, was killed outright. The funeral was interesting,' she said drily. 'There was practically a girlfriend in every pew,

115

all weeping and wailing and doing their best to convince themselves they were the one Richard had liked best.'

'God, and what was that like for you?' Essie's green eyes were like saucers. 'How did it make you feel?'

'Me? Confused, guilty, relieved. I'd loved him to begin with. But he'd turned out to be not the nicest man after all. And now I was the grieving widow. The very wealthy grieving widow,' Zillah added. 'You'd think that would make me happier, wouldn't you? But it actually made me feel worse. The guilt was just awful. I was twenty-four years old and no longer needed to go through a tricky divorce. Oh, and I was also a millionaire.'

Essie nodded at the portrait hanging on the wall. 'You were beautiful, too.'

'I was,' Zillah said simply. 'The next couple of years were pretty scary. I was having to fend off any number of advances from charming young men, because now it was my turn to be a catch.'

It was late, but neither of them was remotely tired. Zillah poured them both another drink and Essie helped herself to more Cambozola from the fridge.

'Go on then,' Essie prompted when she sat back down. 'Tell me about husband number two. How did you meet him?'

'OK, I'm a bit ashamed of this one.' But she'd decided to tell the whole story, so Zillah put down her glass and prepared to be honest. 'You know how sometimes you see a beautiful dress in a shop window and you set your heart on it because you've managed to convince yourself that this is the dress that will make you happy?'

'I know that feeling,' said Essie.

'Then you *finally* buy it and carry it home and try it on and look at yourself in the mirror.' Zillah paused. 'And you feel your heart sink a bit, because it doesn't look as fantastic as you thought it might.'

'Oh.' Essie nodded sympathetically.

'But the thing is, you can't take it back to the shop. You have to wear it all the time, for years and years, even though it's now your least favourite dress.' Zillah reached across for her glass and took a sip of cognac. 'Well, that was Matthew.'

Poor Matthew.

'But it wasn't your fault,' Essie protested. 'You thought you liked him at first. Otherwise you wouldn't have married him. That's nothing to be ashamed of!'

'I know. Sadly, that wasn't it. The shameful part is that he had a sweet girlfriend before I came along and decided he was the one for me.'

'Oh.' Essie sat up, enthralled. 'Wow. What happened?'

'I don't feel good about it. When I think back, I kind of despise myself. Have you ever seen *Gone with the Wind*?'

'Are you serious? I *love* that film.'

'Well the best way I can describe what happened is by saying I was self-centred Scarlett O'Hara and lovely Alice was Melanie Wilkes. Everyone adored her. She was kind and thoughtful and always helping other people. Like an angel. Whereas I was struggling to trust anyone at all. I wanted to be happy again, but I knew I couldn't let myself get involved with someone like Richard. I needed to find a man I could trust, who would support me and never make me miserable. So I looked around at everyone I knew, and decided to find myself someone as kind and genuine and trustworthy as

Matthew Carter. I wanted a man who would adore me as much as he adored Alice. But the months passed and no one else matched up to him. And the more I watched Matthew and Alice together, the more I found myself being drawn to him. In my mind, he became my perfect man.' Zillah stopped and shook her head, disparaging herself. 'Well, Alice was called away to York to look after an aunt who was poorly, and I invited Matthew to go along with me to a country-house party. Poor man, he had no chance. By then, I'd made up my mind. I told him how I felt about him and it blew his world apart.'

'He could have turned you down,' said Essie.

'He did try. But it was one of those nights. I seduced him, and after that there was no going back. He'd betrayed Alice and there was a good chance she'd get to hear about it. Not from me,' Zillah said hastily. 'But a couple of other people at the party saw him leaving my room the following morning, and that was the kind of gossip no one could resist passing on. Poor Alice, I can't imagine how devastated she must have been. Matthew ended their relationship and told her he was in love with me.'

'What did she do? Did you see her after that?'

Zillah shook her head. 'No, we never saw her again. She returned to York and stayed there. And I married Matthew six months later, convinced that this time everything would be fine.' She pulled a face. 'Be careful what you wish for. It didn't take me long to realise I'd made another terrible mistake.'

'What was wrong?' Essie was clearly engrossed in the story.

'I'd thought I wanted someone nice. Matthew turned out to be too nice. Within a year I was bored to tears. I'd broken Alice's heart, and for what? Nothing!'

Essie said, 'Did Matthew know how you felt?'

'Not at first. But eventually he did. He begged me not to leave him, said we had to stick it out. He promised that things would get better and I felt so guilty that I stayed. For ten long years. I tried my best to make it work, I really did, because I so desperately wanted everything to be OK. But in the end we just couldn't carry on any longer. A single friend told me one day how lucky I was to have Matthew, because he was the most wonderful man she'd ever met. So I told her we were on the verge of breaking up and said if she wanted him, she had my blessing to go ahead. Then I told Matthew what a good couple they'd make. And at last it felt as if I'd done something right, because Matthew and I divorced and a few months later they were married.'

'You're kidding. How brilliant. That's a happy ending!'

'Well, happy for them. Less so for Alice, poor thing.' Zillah scrolled through the photos on her iPad. 'Here they are, Matthew and Christina. I took this photo of them at their wedding.'

'You were invited?'

'Darling, I was the guest of honour! Matthew publicly thanked me for getting them together. And a year later, Christina gave birth to twin sons.' Zillah smiled at the memory. 'After all the misery and carnage, finally something good happened. Their marriage was a huge success. Christina died five years ago, but Matthew's still alive.'

'Ooh.' Essie's eyes widened. 'So you're single and he's single . . . Aren't you tempted to give things another go?'

'Give things another go with the man who never stops talking about his eleven wonderful grandchildren?' Zillah fanned her hand in mock horror. 'You must be joking. Bless his heart, he's even more boring now!'

She showed Essie the rest of the photos from that extended period when she'd been single once more. Then they came to the first ones of her and William together, and Zillah felt her heart expand with love, as it always did when she remembered how incredibly lucky she'd been to find him.

'So it was quite a while before you met William,' said Essie.

'Oh yes. I was thirty-six when I left Matthew, fifty years old when William and I found each other. After two disastrous marriages I thought I should give being single a real go. And that's what I did for fourteen years. It was fine,' said Zillah. 'I worked, I travelled, I socialised with friends. There were lots of adventures. Then I met William and that was it, everything changed.'

'How did it happen?' Essie sat forward, enthralled. 'Was it fantastically romantic?'

Zillah thought back to their fateful encounter. 'Actually, we didn't get off to the best of starts.'

She'd spent a couple of days up in London, attending the christening of a friend's daughter and taking a trip to the theatre. Now, heading back home to Bath, she found herself on Paddington station with forty minutes to kill before the train departed.

In the shop, she picked up a packet of Polos and a newspaper for the journey, then wandered across to the shelves of books to see if any of her favourite authors had a new novel out.

After a couple of minutes of searching, she became aware

of a fellow traveller standing several feet away. He was holding a paperback in each hand, studying the blurbs on the back covers, clearly struggling to decide which one to buy.

'If it helps,' said Zillah, 'I found that one pretty disappointing.' She pointed to the book in his left hand, then indicated the one in his right. 'But that one's brilliant. Her best yet.'

The man looked up and she saw that he had merry grey eyes that creased at the corners. He held up the book in his right hand. 'Let me guess. You wrote this one?'

'I didn't. I wish I had. But I can really recommend it.'

'And the other one? Why was it disappointing?'

'The murderer turned out to be the hero's psychotic identical twin. Twins are just cheating.'

The man nodded slowly. 'Indeed. Well, many thanks.'

'Happy reading.' Zillah turned away, pleased to have been able to help. There was nothing else on the shelves that particularly caught her eye; she'd make do with her newspaper instead.

Thirty minutes later, she boarded the waiting train. As she made her way along the carriage, she spotted the same man ahead of her, occupying a window seat and already completely engrossed in his paperback.

Smiling to herself, she waited until she was almost level with him before opening her mouth to say cheerfully, 'Didn't I tell you it was good?'

Well, that was what she *would* have said, if at that moment he hadn't glanced at his wristwatch, affording her a brief glimpse of the book's cover.

'*What?*' Zillah stopped dead in her tracks. 'You bought the one I told you not to buy?'

The man raised his head. 'Oh, hello!'

121

'Never mind hello.' In disbelief, Zillah gestured at the paperback. 'Why would you do that? *Why?*'

'Honestly? I prefer this author's books. I like the way he writes.'

Her voice rose. 'But you know how it ends. I told you the big twist!'

'I know you did. But sometimes I quite enjoy being in on the secret. It gives you a different perspective.'

A voice behind Zillah said, 'Excuse me, I wonder if we could get to our seats . . .'

'It ruins a book,' Zillah told the infuriating man. 'What's the point of reading a mystery thriller when it isn't thrilling or remotely mysterious? I can't believe I recommended a book and you completely ignored my advice!'

'Actually, I—'

'That's just so *rude*.'

'No it isn't,' the man protested. 'If I'd asked for your advice, I would have taken it. But I didn't ask, did I? You volunteered your opinion.' He shrugged easily. 'Doesn't mean I have to do what you say.'

'Ahem, excuse me again, but there's quite a queue behind you . . .'

'You're welcome to sit beside me if you'd like to.' Her adversary patted the vacant seat next to him.

'No thank you.' Still offended, Zillah said, 'The book I recommended is fifty times better than that one.'

'Is it really?' Bending down, he reached into the bag at his feet and drew out the other book. 'Then I look forward to reading it next.'

Zillah felt her blood pressure fall. She shook her head and laughed. 'Touché.'

The man patted the empty seat once more. 'Will you join me now?'

'Yes,' sighed the woman still stuck in the aisle behind her. 'She'd love to join you now.'

Thirty-three years on from that meeting, Zillah looked at Essie. 'And that was it, that was how we met. I sat down next to him and we talked about books for the next hour. What we liked and didn't like about different genres and styles of writing. We argued too, because I didn't agree with some of his choices and he said I wasn't allowed to criticise any author whose work I'd never properly read. We had about ten arguments in the space of an hour. But I knew.' As she said it, she patted her chest. 'In here, I knew something amazing was happening. Or I was hoping it would. He was wearing Givenchy cologne and a gold signet ring. He was funny and he wasn't afraid to tell me when I was wrong. And when he laughed . . . oh, he had the best laugh. I just wanted to listen to it forever. He was travelling on to Bristol so I was getting off the train first. As we reached Bath, he asked me if I'd like to see him again.' Zillah shook her head at the memory, still crystal clear in her mind. 'I told him I would, and he took my phone number. Then he said he'd give me a call at the weekend and if I could prove that I'd read a book by Jeffrey Archer, he'd come over and take me out to dinner.'

'Why?'

'Because I'd said something rude earlier about Jeffrey Archer's books without having read any of them. And he thought that was unfair. Of course, I told him there was no way on earth I'd be obeying his petty rules,' said Zillah. 'Who did he think he was? It was a ridiculous thing to ask me to do. And then we pulled into Bath station and I jumped off the train.'

'I love this story,' Essie declared. 'What happened next?'

'Well, I left the station and headed straight for the nearest bookshop. I chose the thinnest of the Jeffrey Archers and took it over to the counter. Then, just as I was about to pay, a voice in my ear said, 'That one's good, but *Kane and Abel* is much better.'

Essie clapped her hands in delight. 'He got off the train!'

'He'd got off the train,' Zillah agreed happily. 'And followed me. When he saw that I was going into the bookshop, he said that was it, that was the moment he knew he wanted to marry me.'

'And did you buy *Kane and Abel*?'

'I did. I read it, too, from cover to cover. And he was right,' Zillah said with a fond smile. 'Annoyingly. It might not be classed as great literature, but that book was a damn good read.'

Chapter 16

At six o'clock on Saturday evening, a howling gale was battering the city of Bath. Rain was sweeping across Percival Square in relentless waves and the trees were swaying like diehard fans at a Michael Bublé concert.

Inside the Red House, even more chaos reigned. Everyone was standing on chairs. Lucas, tempted to whip out his phone and take a photo of the scene, marvelled at the infinite variety his job entailed.

OK, first things first, find the culprit before his eardrums imploded.

'Right, everyone calm down,' he yelled. 'It's not going to hurt you.'

But he was no match for the hen party, who knew better.

'I saw it! It's an actual tarantula! Swear to God, it's bigger than my *foot*,' shrieked one of the girls.

Her friend, squealing with horror, took a leap up from the chair she'd been teetering on and landed on the table next to it. Presumably in case the spider had superpowers and springs in its legs. Her high heel knocked against a half-empty pint glass and Essie, swooping to the rescue, caught it in her left hand before it could crash to the floor.

'Well held,' said Lucas, although she wouldn't be able to hear him above all the screaming. The hen party had arrived in a convoy of taxis an hour ago and were due to depart at eight for a bar in Bristol. But if he wasn't able to locate and remove the spider that was currently freaking them out, they'd be leaving a lot sooner, which wasn't ideal under the—

'Got it,' shouted Essie, only her bottom visible as she knelt under one of the tables.

'Aaaarrrgh,' screeched one of the girls wavering on top of the nearest chair.

'It's OK, panic over. I've got him.' Having wriggled out backwards with her hands cupped around the spider, Essie got carefully to her feet. 'Ooh, his legs are all tickly! Can someone open the door for me so I can put him outside?'

Lucas led the way and she walked behind him, to a chorus of screams and groans of relief. One of the girls who'd originally seen the spider scuttling along the wall yelled out, 'Oh God, how can you *do* that? Is it the biggest one you've ever seen in your life?'

'It's pretty huge.' Essie nodded in agreement as Lucas held the door wide open for her.

Outside, as the wind whipped her blonde hair into her eyes, he said, 'Well done. I'm impressed.'

Essie uncupped her hands to show him they'd been empty all along.

'Now I'm even more impressed. What if it shows up again?'

'After all the racket that lot have been making, I think the poor spider will probably stay out of sight for the rest of the night. If he does turn up again later, hopefully it'll happen after they've left. Anyway, I'm off duty soon, so it'll be your problem, not mine.'

Lucas smiled. It seemed like every time he saw Essie he encountered a new side to her. She had repartee, a quick mind, and an air of trustworthiness that meant the hen party wouldn't doubt for a second that she'd caught and disposed of the monstrous galloping spider.

Whereas in reality she was probably as terrified of it as they were.

'What?' she said suspiciously, because he'd been looking at her without saying anything.

'Nothing.' Except there was something. Lucas said, 'I'm glad you came to work here.'

For a second, Essie didn't reply. She held his gaze and he couldn't begin to work out what was going through her mind. Then she said, 'I should think you are. I'm indispensable.'

At that moment an almighty crashing sound came from inside the bar. Lucas said drily, 'The fun never stops. I suppose we'd better see what's going on.'

There was a lot of shrieking, that was for sure.

Essie said, 'Maybe the spider's back.'

But when they headed inside once more, it was to a messy sight. The hen, whose name was Lauren, had attempted to clamber down from her table onto the padded velvet seat of a stool. Losing her balance, she'd grabbed hold of her friend's arm and tumbled to the ground, taking her friend with her.

It might have been less disastrous if the friend hadn't been holding a cocktail at the time, which from the look of it had been the one containing Chambord and cassis.

127

'Oh noooo,' Lauren wailed, scrambling to her feet and surveying the damage with dismay. 'My skirt! What am I going to doooo? It's completely *wrecked*.'

She wasn't kidding. What a mess. Her hen-night outfit was a crystal-studded long-sleeved black top teamed with a short white skirt and black-and-white high heels. Up until a couple of minutes ago she'd looked fabulous. Now she was on the verge of tears and her friend was mortified, dabbing helplessly at the purple-stained skirt with a shredded tissue.

'Well that's it, we may as well cancel the taxis right now.' Lauren welled up. 'I can't go to a club looking like this. No way, I just can't.'

'Hey, don't panic, we can sort this out.' Essie held Lauren's forearms and twizzled her round, taking a good look at her waist and hips. 'We're the same size. I have a white skirt that'll fit you and I live just across the square. Wait here, OK? I'm going to go and get it now.'

In no time she was back, wet and windswept, clutching a supermarket carrier bag. Two minutes later, when Lauren emerged from the ladies' loo wearing Essie's skirt, everyone in the bar applauded.

'It fits me!' Lauren did a triumphant twirl, then hugged Essie. 'You saved my hen night. I'll bring it back in the week, is that all right? And I'll try my best not to spill anything on it!'

When Essie's shift ended and she went to fetch her bag and coat, Lucas said, 'That was a nice thing you did, with the skirt. What if it gets wrecked?'

'Doesn't matter. I bought it from a charity shop. Hi.' Essie turned to greet Giselle, who'd just arrived.

'Hey! What are you doing tonight? Out somewhere nice?'

'Scarlett and I are off to a birthday party at a friend's flat, down by the river. It's going to be fun. Actually, you could do me a favour.' Essie brightened. 'Conor's meant to be meeting a blind date here at eight. He swore he wasn't going to turn up, but I bet he does. So if you see him in here with someone, don't say anything, but if you could take a sneaky photo of the two of them together, that'd be brilliant. Then send it to me and I'll have won my bet.' Her eyes glinting with mischief, she added, 'I'll really be able to take the mickey out of him after that!'

And Lucas, watching the way Essie's face lit up as she smiled conspiratorially at Giselle, wondered what it would take before she could relax enough to smile like that at him.

Then he jumped, because directly behind her, a huge, thuggish-looking spider was crawling up the wall. Suppressing a shudder, he murmured, 'Jesus, it's back.'

Whereupon Essie turned, deftly scooped the spider into her left hand and covered it with her right.

'It does tickle,' she confirmed as a couple of furiously waggling black legs poked out through the gaps in her fingers. 'Don't worry, I've got him this time. I'll drop him somewhere safe on the way out.'

Rain was rattling like handfuls of gravel against the sash windows of Conor's flat. It was looking and sounding horrendous out there.

Essie would have finished work by now and was off to some party or other with her friend Scarlett. Zillah had gone out too. Conor, alone in the house, was more than happy to contemplate an evening in front of the TV catching up with a favourite box set.

And yet, and yet . . . His brain kept giving him a nudge, reminding him about the blind date who could be waiting for him over at the Red House.

It wasn't that he wanted to go. As he'd told Essie, any friend of that dreadful pushy female in the green pleather jacket had to be the kind of woman any sane person would go out of their way to avoid.

But two things continued to bother him. Firstly, what if she wasn't?

And secondly, the weather out there was horrendous. Could he really allow her to come out tonight expecting to meet someone, and deliberately not turn up?

That would be downright cruel, and he wasn't a cruel person. Ironically, if there hadn't been a violent storm, he might have been more likely to stay at home. But now he wasn't sure he could ignore his conscience and be that mean.

He heaved a sigh and realised he was going to have to go over to the Red House. It was seven fifteen, which gave him plenty of time to shower, shave and change into something casual but decent. He would head across the square at eight, and with any luck they wouldn't turn up, which meant he could be back here by half past at the latest.

Ditto if they were there and the blind date turned out to be as catastrophic as expected.

Either way, at least his conscience would be clear.

As he stood under the steaming shower, it occurred to Conor that there was a very slight chance she might turn up and exceed his expectations.

He towel-dried his hair, chose the turquoise shirt that apparently suited his colouring, and found himself splashing on some of the aftershave he'd been given for Christmas. By Dior, no less. Well, couldn't do any harm, could it?

At seven forty-five, his mobile rang as he was trying to decide between his tan leather jacket and the dark blue Barbour. 'Hello?'

'Conor, is that you? Oh thank goodness! It's Geraldine Marsh here, and I need your help.'

'Geraldine, hi. What's the problem?' Geraldine was a regular client, an elderly lady with a quavery voice at the best of times. Conor glanced at his reflection in the mirror, pleased to note that his hair was looking good tonight. Furthermore, Essie had been right: this shirt really did bring out the colour of his eyes. OK, pay attention to Geraldine; she was probably wanting some advice about her spring planting programme, which she liked to map out in great detail . . .

'It's the oak tree in my back garden. It's come down in the storm and flattened next door's fencing. And they're not happy about it, because it means they can't let their dogs out. They've told me I have to get the tree sorted before the new fencing can go up. And if I can't, I'll be the one responsible when their dogs escape and go on the rampage and kill someone . . . Oh God, I can't bear it, Conor, I'm a nervous wreck; those dogs are terrifying! Please can you come over and deal with the tree? I'm *desperate.*'

Conor looked again at his reflection in the mirror. All modesty aside, he'd never looked better. He should probably wear turquoise more often.

Ah well, his blind date wasn't likely to be turning up tonight anyway. If she had any sense at all, she'd be staying at home in the warm.

It was just a shame you couldn't scrape designer aftershave

off your clean skin and decant it back into the bottle, especially when it cost more than diamonds.

'Don't worry, Geraldine, I'm on my way over now. We'll get your tree sorted out.'

Overheated and out of breath from dancing, Scarlett made her escape from the crowded living room and headed up to the bathroom on the second floor. It had turned out to be an excellent party. She'd spent an hour earlier chatting to a lovely man called Dale who ran a limo service and who had regaled her with stories of celebrities behaving badly in the backs of his cars. As well as being highly entertaining, Dale had made it clear that he was interested in her and had already offered to take her out in his vintage Rolls, but sadly she hadn't experienced that *zing* of attraction in return.

It was annoying, but that was how single life went. Having washed her hands, Scarlett now studied her face in the mirror and blotted her shiny forehead with a tissue. It was all about the imbalance of interest between people, wasn't it? Tonight Dale had been a two out of ten in her eyes, but he'd regarded her as an eight. Whereas last Sunday, meeting Conor McCauley for the first time, she'd instantly been drawn to him. Out of ten, he was easily a nine. Conor, on the other hand, had taken one look at her and been singularly underwhelmed. It wasn't his fault, nor was it hers; it was just one of those things that happened and over which you had absolutely no control. Some people loved Marmite, others couldn't stand to have it in the same room as them. When your body made up its mind at a cellular level, you couldn't do a thing about it.

Oh well, couldn't be helped. Scarlett blew herself a kiss in the mirror, because *she* still liked herself, and luckily there were plenty of men who didn't shrink away in horror at the sight of her. She was popular, she was lively and the fact that she loved having her photo taken wasn't as much of a massive turn-off for them as it evidently had been for Conor.

Pfft, his loss. She ran her fingers through her purple hair to spike up the ends and left the bathroom. On her way along the landing, she paused at the window overlooking the back of the house. Earlier this evening there'd been plenty of noise and activity out there and now, at close to midnight, it was still going on.

Peering out, Scarlett saw that the storm was still going strong too, as was the chainsaw. Two doors along, a huge tree had been blown down, demolishing a wooden fence. In the darkness, a small figure in an oversized coat stood clutching an umbrella in one hand and a torch in the other. The torch lit up a larger figure, who was wielding the chainsaw, methodically carving through a mountain of branches, stopping every so often to gather them up and pile them at the far end of the garden.

Scarlett watched as rain and sawdust swirled in clouds around the larger figure. What a task, and what a rotten way to spend a Saturday night. For a moment she wondered whether to take them out a couple of mugs of hot chocolate with a splash of cognac to warm them up. Except it was probably a bit frowned upon to give alcohol to people in charge of a chainsaw.

'Hi, what are you looking at?' Carrie, whose party it was, came up the stairs and joined her at the window. 'Are they still out there chopping up that tree? You know, we only have to breathe a bit loudly in this house and Geraldine's on the doorstep lecturing us about noise pollution.' She pointed. 'That's her, under the umbrella. I can't wait to complain about the racket they're making. That woman might seem meek and mild on the outside, but on the inside she's a witch.'

'You can't help feeling sorry for them, though.' Scarlett winced as a particularly vicious gust of wind almost turned Geraldine's umbrella inside out. 'I was wondering whether to make some hot chocolate and take it out to them.'

'Hmm, can I tell you something? After we moved in here last year, I invited Geraldine over for tea one afternoon. Just to show her I was a nice neighbour.' Carrie pulled a face at the memory. 'She complained that I didn't have any almond milk, then went through my entire fridge and gave me a thirty-minute lecture because I'd bought things that weren't organic. If you made her a mug of hot chocolate, she'd tip it away.'

'Oh,' said Scarlett.

'Come on.' Carrie gave her a friendly nudge. 'Don't waste your time feeling sorry for that old bat. Let's go back downstairs and have another dance instead.'

Chapter 17

The following Saturday was a whole lot better, at least as far as the weather was concerned. Having spent the afternoon exploring Bath and photographing people in the street, Conor arrived back at Percival Square to see that a beautiful handwritten letter had arrived in the post from John, whose beloved wife Elizabeth had died on 28 December. He wanted to thank them for making their last Christmas together so special, and to let them know that his favourite of the photos Conor had sent him of their vows being renewed had taken pride of place at Elizabeth's funeral service.

Poor John. Conor hoped he'd be all right during the difficult months that lay ahead; his wife had clearly meant the world to him. How lucky they'd been to find each other all those years ago.

At seven forty-five, Conor found himself casually making his way across the square because he felt he deserved a drink. It wasn't anything to do with the thought that maybe his blind date hadn't turned up last Saturday because the weather had been so dreadful, but she could, just possibly, be there tonight instead.

Definitely nothing to do with that.

Which was just as well, seeing as there was no sign of the bossy woman who was her friend. Nor was there anyone in the bar who could be her.

Conor had one more drink and waited until nine, just to be completely sure she wasn't turning up. Of course she didn't; why would she?

Then he waved goodbye to Essie, working behind the bar, and headed back home.

At least he'd tried.

Essie was in the cellar changing one of the barrels when she felt her phone buzz in her back pocket.

Since she wasn't in front of customers, and seeing as the call was from her brother, she answered it.

'Ess, I'm in Bath! Where are you? Want to meet up for a drink?'

'Well I'm working, but you can come over to the Red House and see me anyway. We can chat between customers.'

'Oh, right. Is your boss there? Luke?'

'Lucas. Sorry, no, he's out for the evening. But I'm here,' said Essie, 'so that's even better.'

'Of course it is. OK, I'll be over in a bit. And try not to gasp with amazement when you see me,' Jay warned, 'because I'm telling you now, I've got even better-looking.'

Essie smiled, because he was her brother and she loved him. 'Not to mention even more modest.'

'I'm just saying, so you can warn the other barmaids in advance.'

Twenty minutes later, the doors opened and Jay made his entrance. Typically, Essie saw at once that he'd been right: his fortnight in Austria had left him with the kind of spectacular tan that was so much more noticeable in January when hardly anyone else had one. His teeth and the whites of his eyes were dazzling by comparison. Plus, he was a strikingly handsome man in his prime who'd always exuded charm and bonhomie. No wonder he and Lucas had hit it off so well at that party back in early December. They were kindred spirits.

Of course that had also been the night they'd drunk far too much, with disastrous consequences for *her* . . .

Jude, next to her, raised an eyebrow. 'He's new.'

'Actually, he isn't. He's old,' said Essie as Jay approached them.

'I am.' Jay grinned. 'I'm ancient. Just very well preserved for seventy-five.'

'He's my brother,' Essie told her, 'and he's twenty-nine.'

'That's not my name, by the way.' Having given Essie a hug, he said, 'I'm Jay.'

'Jude,' said Jude.

'Ah, yes.' Jay nodded sagely. 'Essie's told me all about you.'

This was a lie. She hadn't. But Jude was smiling at him. 'Really? What's she said?'

'She told me you were a fantastic person, and I think she's right. Hi.' He reached for Jude's hand and gave it a formal shake, which always intrigued the girls he encountered. 'It's so good to meet you at last.'

Essie rolled her eyes slightly. Over the years she'd heard her brother's chat-up lines a thousand times. Then again, they generally had the desired effect, so why wouldn't he carry on using them?

'Nice to meet you too.' Jude sounded amused. 'You're very smooth, aren't you?'

137

Jay's shrug was self-deprecating. 'I try my best, then more often than not I muck it up. If I do that tonight, just pretend you haven't noticed, OK? Humour me.'

Then the door opened behind him and Jude, distracted by the new arrivals, called out, 'Wait, what are you two doing here?'

Essie glimpsed the unamused expression in Jay's eyes as he turned and recognised Lucas, who was heading towards them with Giselle at his side. She hoped he wasn't about to do his protective-older-brother thing and make some scathing comment about the round robin. Not because Lucas didn't deserve it, but because it was simply easier all round if Jude and the rest of the staff didn't know. Essie liked working here too much to want to create an awkward atmosphere.

'The lead singer fell off the stage,' said Lucas. 'Broke his leg.'

They'd gone to Moles, a local club, to see a band who'd played a dazzling set at Glastonbury last summer. Everyone had promptly become enthralled by them in general and the handsome lead singer in particular, and the tickets for tonight's show had sold out in record time.

'Oh no.' Jude was sympathetic. 'You were so looking forward to seeing them.'

'We were. Hi.' Lucas nodded at Jay, then briefly introduced him to Giselle. 'But they'll reschedule. And Gi got her chance to rush to the rescue, which made her day. She looked after him until the paramedics turned up.'

'It was brilliant.' Giselle grinned broadly. 'I was up for giving him mouth-to-mouth, but he said he didn't need it. I got to hold his hand, though. And use my soothing voice. I'm pretty sure he won't forget me now.'

Lucas said, 'There was a bit of brow-soothing, too. You pretty much saved his life.'

Which made everyone else laugh, although Essie did her usual trick of pretending to be otherwise occupied with putting away glasses, because relaxing too much in Lucas's presence might make him think she'd forgiven him.

And there was no way that was going to happen.

The rest of the evening went well, though. One of the regulars, a friend of Lucas's, was a magician who specialised in close-up magic tricks that enthralled everyone who witnessed them. Rounds of drinks were bought. Between serving customers, Jude continued to chat to Jay. Someone else produced a guitar and began to play songs, with others enthusiastically joining in. To Essie's surprise, Lucas turned out to have a really good singing voice. Pretending not to have noticed, she carried on working, keeping the place running smoothly.

A few minutes later, Giselle joined her at the bar, leaning across and saying in a conspiratorial whisper, 'Looks like your brother's weaving a magic spell of his own on Jude.'

Essie nodded. 'He's woven quite a few in his time.'

'Ah. Bit of a player, is he?'

'He doesn't mean to be. He just likes women, and they like him back. He's nearly thirty,' she said. 'I keep waiting for him to meet the right girl and settle down, but it hasn't happened yet.'

'Who knows? Maybe we're watching it happen right now.' Giselle did mystical movements with her hands as they observed Jude and Jay together. 'I mean, look at them. This could be the night everything changes!'

Lucas, coming up behind her, slid an arm around her waist and said easily, 'Why's this the night everything could change?'

Essie swallowed. What was it that caused her to feel that little twist of unwanted emotion inside her chest? Was it the casual way his fingers were resting on Giselle's hip? Or the smile they exchanged as she leaned against him?

Shutting down both her own feelings and the conversation, she said, 'I need to serve those guys over there from the rugby club,' and moved away to the far end of the bar.

As Essie slowly woke from sleep, time appeared to have slipped into reverse. She was lying in bed with her eyes closed, breathing in the scent of freshly ground coffee, which made no sense at all. It was something that had happened last year whenever she'd stayed over at Paul's cottage. As the proud owner of a top-of-the-range coffee machine, he had always brought her a perfectly made cappuccino in bed before leaving for work. Even if, secretly, she would have preferred a mug of tea.

Her fuzzy brain swam into focus. OK, time *hadn't* reversed itself. It was also unlikely that Paul had gained entry to her flat and brought his beloved coffee machine along with him.

She opened her eyes, tilted her head to one side and saw the takeaway coffee cup standing on her bedside table.

Then she turned the other way, and there was her brother leaning against the door jamb in the open doorway.

Jay grinned. 'Thought that'd wake you up. Morning.'

He'd stayed last night, sleeping in the living room on the sofa. And seeing as they'd had a fair amount to drink, he was looking unfairly good.

'Morning. You didn't need to go out to the coffee shop.' Essie gestured vaguely in the direction of the kitchen. 'There's a jar of Gold Blend next to the kettle.'

See? Gold Blend. *Posh.*

'But real coffee's nicer. And you deserve the best. So I thought I'd treat you.'

'Why? What have you done?'

Jay gave her a wounded look. 'I'm being nice! I'd planned on taking you out to lunch later too, but if you're going to be all mean and suspicious, I won't bother.'

Lunch. On a Sunday. Sunday lunch was one of her favourite things in the world. Essie sat up. 'Where?'

'Oh, just the place that won a gold medal for serving the best Sunday lunch in the south-west. But don't worry, I can cancel it.' He waggled his phone at her. 'Shame, though. They're pretty booked up. When I called them this morning, I only just managed to grab the last table.'

Essie smiled. This was an offer she couldn't possibly refuse. Shooing him away, she said, 'I'd better jump in the shower then. Be a shame to waste the last table.'

Three hours later, over plates of rare beef, buttery crunchy roast potatoes and masses of vegetables, Jay said, 'So how are you getting on, working for Lucas?'

'I cope.' Essie reached for the jug of gravy and poured it lavishly over her Yorkshire pudding. 'I'm impressed that you're calling him by his actual name at last.'

'Yes, well. I was watching you last night. You only speak to him when you have to.'

'It's called being polite. I still don't like him.'

'Everyone else seems to.'

'Maybe because he didn't do to them what he did to me.'

Jay put down his knife and fork. 'Ess, I'm sorry. He didn't do it to you; I did. It was me.'

141

Chapter 18

Essie had just taken a mouthful of roast beef and gravy. Her heart began to thud like a drum in her chest. She stopped dead in her tracks and stared at Jay, chewing her food until it was safe to be swallowed.

When it was once more possible to speak, she said, 'Really?'

He nodded. 'Really.'

'Why did you do it?'

'Because I'm an idiot and sometimes I do idiotic things without thinking. I'd had loads of vodka and it just seemed funny at the time. And for some reason I thought I was just sending it to your friends . . . It didn't actually occur to me that Paul and his mother would see it too.' He winced as he said it. 'I'm so sorry, that sounds ridiculous now. But you know what I'm like.'

She did know. Jay had always been impulsive, particularly where drink was involved. He'd once woken up the morning after a party with no memory whatsoever of having booked a holiday to Las Vegas. It was why she hadn't believed him when he'd initially denied all knowledge of having sent the round robin to everyone in her email address book.

'So you said you hadn't done it, but you had.' Her heart was still bumping chaotically against her ribcage as the implications sank in.

'I know. You'd just woken me up. You were yelling at me and I was confused . . .'

'And then Lucas appeared and said it was him.'

'Exactly!' Jay spread his hands. 'He did!'

'But *why*? Why would he say that when it wasn't true?'

'I have no idea. I couldn't believe it either.'

'You must have asked him, though. Once you'd left the cottage.'

'I did, but he just shrugged it off. Said it was easier that way, seeing as you didn't even know him. Then he changed the subject. I tried to thank him but he just shook his head. He really didn't want to talk about it.'

'That happened seven weeks ago,' said Essie. 'Why are you only telling me now?'

'OK. To begin with, I thought he was right. I'd done something spectacularly stupid, he'd taken the blame and I was grateful. It *was* easier that way. When you ran into him again, that just seemed like bad luck, but he didn't tell you the truth. Then you decided to take the job at the Red House and he *still* kept it up. I suppose I thought you'd stop hating him and pretty much forget about it.' Jay paused for a second to take a drink. 'But last night I saw the way you acted around each other . . . the way things were between the two of you . . . and I just felt terrible, because it doesn't need to be like that. It *shouldn't* be like that. All I had to do was man up and come clean.' He exhaled slowly. 'So that's why I brought you here. And it's what I'm doing now.'

'Right.' Essie was still trying to get her head around the change of circumstances.

'You don't have to hate him any more.'

'No.'

'He isn't a dick. He's actually a good guy.'

'Yes.'

'I'm the one who was the dick. And I really am sorry about you and Paul.'

'And my job at the dental surgery,' said Essie.

Jay shrugged, accepting his culpability. 'That too. Although . . . well, I know I never met his mother, but she always sounded like a complete witch.'

This might have been true, but it was for her to say, not Jay. Taking advantage of the moment, Essie reached across with her fork and pinched a small but extra-perfect roast potato from his plate. 'I still can't believe you did something so stupid.' It made slightly more sense, though, than Lucas having done it. Especially when, since getting to know him, she'd come to realise he really wasn't the type.

'I'll never do anything bad again,' Jay promised. 'When I'm ninety years old and someone asks me on my deathbed what the biggest regret of my life was, I'll tell them it was this.'

'Not putting me in a cardboard box when I was five and pushing me down the stairs?' Essie raised an eyebrow; that wasn't something she was ever going to let him forget. She'd tobogganed excitedly to the bottom, gone *splat* into the wall opposite and lost two front teeth in the process. One of them hadn't even been loose.

'That's my second biggest regret,' said Jay.

'Mainly because Mum confiscated your bike for a week.'

144

'God, yes, I remember that.' He looked rueful. 'Devastating. I cried even more than you did.'

The stolen roast potato, golden and irresistible on the end of her fork, was now mere inches from her mouth. Essie smiled. 'Served you right.'

Essie woke late on Monday morning and pulled back her bedroom curtains. The sun was out, the sky was a clear ice blue, and a glistening white hoar frost covered Percival Square.

Such a beautiful sight mirrored her mood; since discovering the truth yesterday, she'd gone to bed feeling so much better, lighter, less conflicted. It had simply never been in her nature to actively dislike someone as much as she'd been actively disliking Lucas Brook.

And now all the ill feeling had dissolved, dissipated, floated away like a helium balloon disappearing into the cloudless sky.

Leaning her elbows on the windowsill, Essie watched as a tall elderly man threw a red ball for his labradoodle. The dog chased after it, grabbed it in its mouth, and did a lolloping victory lap around the square.

Then, behind him, Essie saw the door of the Red House open from the inside and Giselle emerge carrying a blue canvas overnight bag. Turning, she paused to kiss Lucas on the mouth before skipping down the steps and heading off in the direction of Milsom Street with a cheerful backwards wave. At a guess, she'd catch the bus from there and make her way to the hospital to start her shift. And she'd known the truth about the round robin all along, Essie realised. That explained why she'd been so unbothered by what Lucas had supposedly done.

Having watched his girlfriend leave, Lucas raked his fingers through his unbrushed dark hair, called out a greeting to the owner of the labradoodle, then disappeared back inside.

Essie headed to the bathroom; time for a shower.

And an apology.

Forty minutes later, she rapped on the door of the Red House, then let herself in. Maeve the cleaner was energetically vacuuming the carpeted area and singing along to something on her headphones that might have been Barry Manilow's 'Copacabana'. Lucas, in the process of shrugging his way into a brown leather jacket, was reaching for his car keys when he turned and saw Essie.

'Oh, hi.' He looked surprised, which was fair enough really, seeing as she wasn't due to start work until five. 'What's up?'

'I just wondered if I could have a word?' Essie felt her pulse begin to quicken.

'Whoops-a-daisy, mind your feet, love!' Maeve flicked the electrical lead, wielding it like a whip in order to get it around one of the tables. 'Or you'll find yourself trussed up like a cow at a rodeo!'

'Sorry.' Essie stepped out of the way and mouthed to Lucas, 'In private?'

'I was just on my way out to the wholesaler. I'll be back in an hour.' He paused, sensing that this wasn't what she'd wanted to hear. 'Unless you'd like to join me.'

She couldn't wait, not now. She nodded. 'I'll come with you.'

'OK.' Lucas signalled to Maeve that they were off. 'Let's go.'

The traffic was heavy as they crawled eastwards along

Upper Bristol Road in Lucas's slate-grey BMW, then approached the left turn onto Windsor Bridge Road. Essie waited until the traffic lights had turned to red, then said, 'It wasn't you.'

He turned the heating down a notch. 'What does that mean?'

'God, you'd make a good secret agent.' She'd been watching him closely, and not by so much as a flicker had he indicated that he knew what she was on about. 'Jay told me yesterday. You took the rap for him. He was the one who sent that round robin, not you.'

'And?' said Lucas.

'And what?'

'After he told you, what did you say to him?'

'I called him an idiot, because he *is* one. I probably called him a couple more names,' said Essie, 'but I can't remember now.'

'Are you still talking to him?' Lucas glanced sideways at her.

'Yes, of course I am. He took me out for lunch. He's my brother. He drives me nuts . . .' She spread her hands, then let them fall back onto her lap. 'That goes without saying. But he's still my brother.'

Lucas nodded slowly. The lights changed to green and he turned left. 'Well, that's good then.'

'All these weeks I've been horrible to you. Well, not *horrible*,' Essie amended. 'But you've known what I was thinking about you this whole time. And you didn't say a word; you just let me carry on thinking it.'

'Seemed like a good idea at the time.'

'But *why*?'

'Look, swans.' As they crossed the bridge over the River Avon, Lucas pointed them out.

'It's almost as if you're changing the subject.' Essie looked at him.

'Hey, it's done now. You know what happened and you're still OK with your brother, that's the important thing. The other important thing is that we can be friends. You don't have to glower at me any more.' With a glimmer of amusement he added, 'Working together's about to become a whole lot easier. For you and me both.'

'It is.' She nodded. 'That's what Jay told me. He saw the way things were between us on Saturday night.'

'It's all going to be different from now on,' said Lucas.

'So different.' The sense of relief was huge.

'You might even start laughing at my jokes.'

'Ooh, steady on, I wouldn't go that far.'

'Did you hear about the albino fruit salad?' He raised an innocent eyebrow. 'It had no melon in.'

Melanin.

'And that's why I won't be laughing,' said Essie, but only for a second or two was she able to maintain a straight face.

Then the sign for the cash-and-carry wholesaler appeared ahead of them and Lucas, indicating right, swung into the car park.

It only took forty minutes to load the trolley with all the stock they needed. The difference between them was already tangible. As they'd made their way up and down the aisles, it had felt completely natural to chat about the Red House, the other members of staff and their regular customers. Before, Essie had always found things out about Lucas via some third party, but now the barrier between them had come down. It was as if it had never existed. She could talk about anything she wanted, ask him any question she liked. In all honesty, it was what she'd been longing to do for weeks, but it hadn't been possible then because she hadn't been speaking to him.

'Here, catch.' He threw a box of crimson paper napkins over to her, to put in the trolley.

'I still don't know why you didn't tell me the truth once I'd started working for you,' said Essie.

He paused and looked at her for a moment. 'I'll tell you. Not here, though. Let's get this out of the way first.'

Once he'd paid, they loaded everything into the car and drove off. But instead of heading to the Red House, Lucas changed direction, finally pulling up outside Royal Victoria Park.

They walked for a few minutes along the winding path that led past the duck pond, then climbed a slope, turned to the left and reached a small clearing ringed by shrubs and trees.

Lucas stopped walking and Essie wondered what kind of a story she was about to hear.

Chapter 19

'I've been to this park so many times,' said Essie, 'but I've never seen this part of it before. I had no idea it was here.'

'I found it by accident back in the autumn. It's my favourite place to visit. And before you make fun of me,' said Lucas, 'I *know* that makes me sound ninety years old. But I don't care, OK? Sometimes you just find a place and it feels right.'

There was a wooden bench in the centre of the clearing. Other visitors had occupied it earlier; Essie could tell, because the frost that still clung to the leaves and branches all around them was absent from the seat of the bench itself.

'Shall we sit down?' said Lucas.

There was a brass plaque fixed to the backrest. Essie touched it. 'Barbara and James. I love it when you see people's names on benches. It makes you wonder who they were and what their lives were like.'

Lucas said, 'James was my dad's name.'

'Really? *This* James?' She pointed to the plaque. 'Is this your dad?'

He smiled slightly, shook his head. 'No, it's just a coincidence. So, you think it was a pretty weird thing I did, that morning at your boyfriend's cottage? I suppose it was weird. Which is why I'm feeling the need to explain everything to you now.' The humorous glint in his dark eyes had disappeared; he was sitting back with his legs stretched out before him, crossed at the ankle. His fingers were loosely clasped across his torso. The expression on his face gave nothing away.

'You don't have to.'

'No, I think you deserve to be told. It's not something most people get to know about, though. Giselle does, obviously. But . . . well, I'd rather you didn't write it down and send it to everyone in your contacts list.'

Essie, glad that she'd come out wearing her warm Puffa jacket, pulled out her Christmas pudding knitted gloves and put them on. 'I won't tell anyone, I promise.'

What could she be about to hear? She watched as a robin flew down in front of them, hopping about on the frost-encrusted grass in search of stray breadcrumbs left by the previous occupant of the bench.

'When I was seven,' Lucas began, 'we went down to Cornwall for a weekend. Me and my mum and dad. We spent Saturday afternoon on the beach, playing games and having a picnic. And we went swimming, too. Then, after we'd eaten, I carried on paddling in the water. Just skimming pebbles, collecting crabs in a bucket, that kind of stuff. I knew I wasn't allowed to swim on my own, but that was OK, I was happy just messing around in the shallows. Until a freak wave came along and knocked me off my feet.'

They were both still watching the robin, but Essie heard Lucas's breath catch in his throat.

'The sea dragged me away from the shore, and I was

panicking and yelling . . . and my dad raced in to rescue me. He swam out and managed to grab hold of me, then he passed me back to Mum, who'd followed him into the water. She got me back to shore. But there was a strong rip tide and Dad got caught up in it.' Lucas took another audible breath, then slowly exhaled, the fingers of his left hand tapping rapidly against his right. 'The thing about rip tides is they don't look dangerous on the surface. But underneath, they can be lethal. And this one dragged my father under . . . it carried him off before the lifeguards could get to the beach, because it was the first week of October and the summer season was over. I mean, they came as fast as they could, but by then it was too late. He was dead.'

'That's just awful. *Awful.*' The words caught in Essie's throat. It was difficult enough having to hear Lucas describe what had happened; she couldn't imagine what it must have been like for him to witness the tragedy.

He nodded slowly. 'Yes.'

The robin flew away.

'I'm so sorry,' said Essie. If it had been anyone else, she'd have reached for them, clutching their hand or their arm and giving it a sympathetic squeeze. But she couldn't do that with Lucas.

Oh, but how traumatised must he have been? A seven-year-old boy watching his father drown after racing into the sea to save him.

'I know.' Lucas shifted on his side of the bench. 'And we haven't got to the relevant part of the story yet.'

There was more? Wasn't that enough?

'Only if you want to tell me,' Essie murmured. Although if he decided not to, she'd really regret having said it.

152

'My dad had a younger brother,' Lucas continued. 'Max. There was only eighteen months between them, and he lived close by so we saw him all the time. He was the best kind of uncle, brilliant with kids, always up for a game of cricket or football. Everyone loved him. Just before we went to Cornwall, he and my dad had a falling-out about something and stopped talking to each other. It wasn't the first time, apparently. But we had the weekend break booked, so we went down to stay in the holiday cottage, just the three of us. Normally Uncle Max would have come along too – sometimes he'd bring a friend or a girlfriend – but of course this time he wasn't there.' Lucas paused. 'If he had been, Dad would probably still be alive. Uncle Max was a much stronger swimmer.'

Essie shook her head. What could she possibly say?

'Are you freezing?' said Lucas.

'No.' Not true, but never mind.

'So anyway, Uncle Max wasn't there to save Dad's life, and he never forgave himself for that. And of course they didn't get the chance to make up after their argument either. He blamed himself for that too.'

'Did you find out what it was they'd argued about?'

'Not for years. I remember realising that it had happened after Uncle Max took me to the park and put me on the monkey bars. I lost my grip and fell, and landed badly on my ankle. It was OK, but for a couple of minutes it hurt like crazy and he was worried I'd broken it. Which would have messed up our weekend in Cornwall. So for a while I thought that might have been what caused the falling-out.'

'Oh, but—'

'It's OK.' Lucas saw the expression on her face and intervened. 'I kind of figured out eventually that it must have been something a bit more important than my twisted ankle. I asked my mother when I was eighteen and she told me it was to do with Uncle Max's girlfriend. Apparently my dad wasn't crazy about her, didn't trust her, and would have been happier if she hadn't been coming down to Cornwall with Max. That was what caused all the upset.'

'What was she like?' said Essie. 'Did you like her?'

'I was seven.' Lucas shrugged. 'Her name was Teresa and she was very pretty, that's about all I remember. She seemed OK to me.'

'And what happened to her?'

'Uncle Max took her off to Vegas and married her a year later, just the two of them there, no other family invited. Then a year after that they split up. He was never at home, always out at the pub. He didn't play cricket or football with me any more . . . the drinking took over his life. He lost his job, lost his home, moved away. I think he just couldn't cope with the guilt. The last I heard, he was living in Spain, selling souvenirs to tourists on the beach.'

It was all so unbearably sad; Essie's heart went out to him. 'And your mum? Did she ever remarry?'

'No.'

'Where does she live?'

'In the north of England.'

'Do you get the chance to see her often?'

'I see her when I can.' Having given as much detail as he evidently wanted to give, Lucas sat up straighter. 'So anyway, that's the story of my family.' He turned to look at her. 'And now you know why I told you that it was me who sent

154

out the round robin. I didn't know you; all I heard was you being absolutely furious with your brother. And that wasn't something I could cope with, because what if the two of you had ended up not speaking to each other, and then something terrible happened and one of you died?'

Essie saw the residual guilt and pain in his dark eyes. She said, 'Well thank you for doing it. I wouldn't have stopped speaking to him for long. Maybe a day or two. But that's the trouble, isn't it? We never know when the bad stuff's going to happen. You did a kind thing for a good reason. And I'm sorry I've given you such a hard time since then.'

'That's OK. You didn't know.'

He was half smiling now, and Essie was struck by just how much she hadn't known about him and how many erroneous assumptions she'd made. Everyone did it, though, didn't they? When people came to the Red House and met Lucas for the first time, they were instantly charmed by his easy-going, cheerful persona. It was a huge advantage in this kind of business; knowing he'd be there was what made them want to come back again and again. He was extrovert and funny, the perfect host, exuding charisma and bonhomie.

To look at him, who would ever guess that his childhood – and undoubtedly his subsequent life – had been blighted by tragedy?

Because he'd changed the subject, she wasn't about to press him on it now, but there was definitely something else about his mother that he hadn't told her. For a start, he hadn't been to visit her over Christmas, nor had she travelled down to Bath to see him.

'Oh *no*,' wailed a high-pitched voice, and they both looked to the left, where a small boy in a Spiderman anorak had skidded to a halt at the edge of the clearing. 'Grandpa, there's *people* on our special bench! What are we going to do *now*?'

His expression was so outraged that Essie and Lucas both burst out laughing, which caused the boy to glare at them with even more vehemence.

'That's it, I'm scared,' Lucas murmured. Then, rising to his feet, he said to the small boy, 'It's OK, we're leaving now. You can have your special seat.'

'There, isn't that kind of them? Say thank you,' prompted the boy's grandfather.

The boy surveyed Lucas with disdain. 'No. I want them to go away.'

Back at the car, Lucas switched on the engine and turned the heat up to maximum. As they waited for the windscreen to de-mist, he said, 'That's the first time I've told a member of staff.'

Essie nodded. 'You can trust me.'

'I know. Like I said before, it's not some huge secret. It's just easier all round if it isn't common knowledge at work. I don't want people feeling sorry for me, or feeling as if they have to watch what they say. It's my job to relax them, make sure they have a good time.'

'And you do a great job of it.'

'Of course I do. I'm brilliant.' The corners of Lucas's mouth twitched. 'Anyway, I'm glad I told you. And . . . thanks.' He lifted his hand, as if to rest it on hers, then stopped himself and replaced it on the steering wheel instead.

And at that moment Essie realised she was holding her breath, had wanted him to make that physical contact. Because right now, the connection between them was almost palpable. She wanted him to know that she was unequivocally on his side.

But no, Lucas had stopped himself and was right to have done so. He was her boss; they'd only just started speaking to each other like normal people. Furthermore, he was Giselle's boyfriend, which meant it would also be deeply inappropriate.

OK, it had only been a potential hand-clasp, but right now, the way the adrenalin was fizzing through Essie's body, it would have felt like so much more.

She forced herself to relax. They were friends and she wanted them to stay friends.

A car had pulled up alongside them, winking its indicator and ready to move into their parking space. Twisting round in her seat, she said in as casual a voice as she could manage, 'All clear behind us. Let's go.'

Chapter 20

It had been a busy Monday at the Red House. Conor's latest set of street portraits had gone up and he'd been asked to come over tonight to meet a visiting group of enthusiasts from a photography club. Once they'd left, Essie had said, 'Have you ever taken any pictures of Lucas? You should have one of him on display.' And Conor, realising that he hadn't, and that it was a good idea, had gone back to his flat and collected his favourite camera.

Now, as Essie and Jude cleared up after last orders, Lucas was sitting on a stool enduring having his photograph taken.

'Lean forward a bit more,' Essie called across to him. 'Come on, show off that cleavage.'

Without looking at her, Lucas grinned and raised a middle finger in her direction. Essie laughed. 'Oh well, there's always Photoshop.'

She opened the glass-washing machine, which had just finished its cycle, and was enveloped in a cloud of escaping steam.

Jude said, 'This is so much nicer, you know.'

'What is?'

'You and Lucas. I don't know what's changed, but something has. You're talking to him like you talk to the rest of us. It's like a big wall's come down.' The steam evaporated and Jude's face appeared, her eyes bright. 'I suppose I'm just curious as to what's happened to make such a difference.'

Essie began unloading and hanging up the hot, squeaky-clean glasses. 'We'd had a misunderstanding before. Now it's sorted out, that's all.'

'A misunderstanding? What kind of misunderstanding? Now I'm really interested!'

Essie looked over at Lucas, who shrugged. 'If we don't tell her now, she's going to think we're having a wild affair.'

'I'm already starting to think it,' said Jude.

Essie flicked a tea towel at her. 'Well don't!'

'Hey,' Lucas called over. 'Remember the round robin that lost Essie her last job? She thought I was the one who sent it.'

'Which is why I've been secretly furious with him,' Essie chimed in, 'ever since the day I discovered he was my new boss. But yesterday I found out it wasn't him.'

'So now she's decided I'm not so terrible after all.'

'Wow.' Jude widened her eyes. 'How did you find out?'

'The real culprit came clean,' said Essie.

'And Essie felt bad because she'd been blaming the wrong person all this time,' Lucas continued as Conor snapped away. 'But now we're friends and all is—'

'Hang on, though.' Jude was frowning, puzzled. 'It was done by someone who stayed at Essie's cottage.'

'True. I stayed there that night, which was why she thought it was me. But it wasn't.'

Jude looked at Essie. 'So that means it was your brother.'

159

Oh.

'That's right,' said Lucas. 'It was.'

'Jay,' Jude double-checked.

'Yes.' Lucas nodded.

'Well I'm sorry,' said Jude, 'but what a plank.'

Ah.

'Seriously, though.' She turned back to Essie. 'If I'd known you thought it was Lucas, I could have told you he'd never do anything like that. He just wouldn't.'

'Well I know that now,' said Essie.

'Honestly, though, when I met your brother the other night, I thought he was good fun. I can't believe he did something so idiotic.' Jude gave a huff of annoyance. 'I'm actually really disappointed.'

Oh dear, poor Jay. Essie found herself defending her brother. 'We all do stupid things sometimes.'

'Maybe, but not *that* stupid,' said Jude.

Yesterday evening, snow had begun to fall and settle on the roads and pavements of Bath. Now Percival Square had been transformed into a Disney-style winter wonderland. Small children were charging around in a state of high excitement, flinging handfuls of powdery snow into the air, chasing each other and building tiny lopsided snowmen that were promptly knocked down by even more overexcited dogs.

'I recognise you,' a blonde mother said to Conor. 'You're the one who displays your photos over in the Red House. I'd love it if you'd take one of my boys.'

And Conor, who generally preferred to choose whom he photographed, pointed and said, 'These two? Of course I can.' Because they were twins, three or four years old, bright-eyed and pink-cheeked in matching snowsuits, and screaming with laughter as they lay flat on their backs making snow angels on the ground.

He fired off fifteen or twenty shots, then a dozen or so more when they leapt up and began racing in circles around their mother. One of the boys, scooping up a handful of snow, tried to throw it at his brother and missed. His twin shrieked with delight. 'Mummy, I want it to snow for all time!'

'Wait till you grow up,' his mother said drily. 'You'll soon change your mind.'

Amused, Conor told her that one of the photos would be included in next week's display at the Red House if they wanted to see it *in situ*. He handed her his card, then waved goodbye and headed over to Milsom Street and down towards the busiest section of the shopping area.

Ten minutes later, he spotted a familiar figure standing outside the entrance to Bath Abbey. The snow had stopped falling but the air temperature was still bitterly cold. She was bundled up against the weather in a bright yellow coat, black jeans and red boots. Oblivious to his presence just a few metres away, all her attention was concentrated on the phone in her ungloved hands. Amused, Conor moved close and removed his camera's lens cap. Was she texting someone? Catching up on social media? Playing Pokémon Go?

Whichever, she still had no clue he was there. He took a couple of photos, then said, 'Hi, Scarlett, you OK?'

She looked up at him, saw the camera in his hands and broke into a huge smile. 'Conor, hello! Are you going to take my photo? Hang on, you'll have to give me two minutes to sort myself out. I'm a mess . . .' As she spoke, she was already reaching into her shoulder bag, pulling out a powder compact and lipstick.

'No need. Already done.' He waggled the Nikon playfully. 'While you were engrossed in your phone.'

Scarlett's delight turned to dismay. 'But that's not fair! I look horrible!'

'You don't look horrible at all.'

'Show me.'

She came to stand beside him and Conor brought the two photos up on the screen so she could see them. Scarlett wailed. 'Oh God, I look like a moose! And my nose is all *red*.'

'It's not red, it's pink. Which makes sense, seeing as you're surrounded by snow.' It drove him nuts when people were so critical of their own appearance. 'See the contrast of you on your phone with the abbey behind you? Those colours are great and the composition works really well.'

'But I could look so much better. Seriously. Let me just put on a bit of lipstick and we'll do it again.'

'No.' Conor shook his head. 'It wouldn't be the same. You'll do that thing with your mouth. Can I put one of these up in the Red House?'

'No *way*,' yelped Scarlett.

'Fine.' He deleted them both. 'There, gone.'

'Did anyone ever tell you how annoying you are?'

Conor smiled. 'Only neurotic narcissists find me annoying. What are you doing here anyway?'

'Waiting for my group to turn up. They're due to meet me here in five minutes.' Opening her compact, Scarlett deftly toned down her nose, then applied over-bright fuchsia-pink lipstick, smacked her lips together and blew him an ironic kiss. 'A family of ten from New York have booked a two-hour city tour.'

He knew from Essie that Scarlett worked as a guide for visiting tourists. She also ran a stall at the vintage market on Sundays, selling artwork and jewellery, and spent a couple of afternoons a week doing something else over in Bristol. He indicated her shiny emperor-purple hair and said, 'What's your natural colour?'

'Who knows? Who cares? I like to dye it. And my tourists appreciate it.' She nodded and waved at a cluster of people who were hesitantly approaching her. 'Means they don't lose me in crowded places.'

'Is that them? I'll leave you to do your thing,' said Conor.

'Sure you don't want to take a nice photo of me before you go?' She was teasing him but also kind of meaning it; his previous refusals clearly still rankled.

Conor said good-naturedly, 'Maybe one day.'

From a distance, he stood and watched as Scarlett greeted her charges cheerfully, then led them off in the direction of Pulteney Bridge, gesticulating as she addressed them along the way.

He turned and headed back past the Roman Baths, turning left down Stall Street. His attention was caught by an old man standing beside a wall, clutching the remains of a takeaway burger. He was carefully shredding the bun and throwing the crumbs onto the snow in front of him, and birds were flying down to grab them in their beaks. What the man didn't know was that on the wall just behind him a black cat was crouched, light green eyes gleaming and tail slowly swishing . . .

Reaching for his camera, Conor said, 'Hello, sir, would you mind if I take a photo of you?'

'Yes I would mind,' said the elderly man. 'Very much. Bugger off.'

Right.

Conor hid a smile. Fair enough; some people didn't want to cooperate and that was entirely their decision. He turned away, his gaze skimming over the snowy street populated by shoppers and workers, as well as visitors who'd travelled from all over the world in order to experience the magical city of Bath . . .

That was when he saw her.

What?

It couldn't possibly be her, though. He knew that.

But it was.

She wasn't dead. She was here.

Chapter 21

Conor felt the blood thundering through his body as his brain attempted to process something that made no sense. It was like finding yourself dropped into the middle of a movie with no warning at all.

Oh, but this wasn't a movie, it was real life. And a medical miracle had clearly occurred. Because she looked so *well*.

It had been four years, but Conor had never forgotten Jessica Brown. How could he? She'd had a huge impact on his life. Unwittingly she'd shone a light on his chosen career and shown him just how unsuited to it he was. The day he'd met Jessica and heard her heartbreaking story was the day he'd had his showdown with his old boss Margaret Kale and left the company. The following morning, realising that he'd also left Jessica in an awkward situation, he'd emailed Margaret and instructed her to retain any money she owed him in order to settle Jessica Brown's account.

And that had been that.

Until now.

The next moment, as if suddenly realising she was being

stared at, Jessica Brown turned and looked in his direction. Their eyes met and Conor felt his stomach disappear.

'What the *hell*?' yelled the old man as the cat launched itself from the high wall and the birds flew up into the air in a panicky cloud. The cat leapt after the slowest of them and missed, the bird let out a triumphant squawk and the man dropped his burger on the ground, whereupon it was promptly seized by the cat.

'Bloody thing, get yourself out of here.' He flapped his arms furiously at the cat. 'Go on, sod off.' Then, noticing a group of children pointing and laughing, he snarled, 'And you lot can clear off too.'

To spare his feelings, Conor edged away and glanced over again at Jessica. She was smiling as well. Then she met his gaze once more and he found himself moving towards her.

Because how could he not?

Now she was looking at him quizzically, and he realised that she didn't recognise him. It had only been one meeting, after all, and she'd had rather more important things on her mind than paying attention to what her solicitor looked like.

'Hi,' said Conor.

'Hi,' said Jessica.

'You don't remember me.'

'Sorry, no, I don't.'

'Not to worry, it's fine. It was four years ago. A lot's changed since then.' Conor nodded. 'Well, for both of us. But for you more than me.'

She nodded. 'Yes, it has.'

'You look fantastic.'

'Thank you. Sorry, this is getting a bit embarrassing now.

166

I really wish I could remember you, but I can't. Could you give me a clue?'

'Conor McCauley. I used to work at Kale and Grey,' said Conor. 'Solicitors. You came to see me, we had an appointment . . . you needed to make a will . . .' As the words trailed away, he realised his own mistake and simultaneously saw the light of recognition finally dawn in the woman's blue eyes.

Because she wasn't Jessica Brown, was she? Of course she wasn't.

'Well that explains the confusion,' she said. 'You thought I was Jess. I'm her sister, Belinda.'

'Oh God, I'm so sorry. What an idiot I am.' Conor shook his head.

'It's OK, it's fine.'

'Did Jessica . . . ?'

'Die? Yes, she did.'

Of course she had died. Her condition back then had been diagnosed as terminal, and she'd known she hadn't had more than a few months left to live. Still mortified by his error, he said, 'I can't believe I thought you were her. But you look exactly alike. I mean, you don't, but only because she was so ill when I met her. You look exactly as she would have looked if she'd been well.'

'I know. We were always alike. But I was four years younger than Jess, so it's only now that I've caught up with her, age-wise. No wonder you were confused.' Belinda smiled. 'I remember her telling me about you now. She said you were really kind to her, and that you'd chosen her to have the will drawn up for free. That was such a lovely gesture for the company to make.'

Conor nodded, remembering paying the invoice; he still regarded it as the best money he'd ever spent.

Belinda continued, 'Then the next time she went up there, to sign the final documents, some woman dealt with her instead. She told Jess you'd left the company.'

Of course neither of them knew what had prompted his abrupt departure. Conor said, 'I did, yes,' then hesitated. Was it weird that he so clearly recalled the name of Jessica's daughter?

'She died three months after making the will.' Evidently thinking that this was what he'd been on the verge of asking, Belinda added, 'It wasn't too awful at the end. For her, I mean. We still miss her every day, obviously. Poor Jess.'

'And what happened to . . . Evie?'

'You remember her name!' Belinda sounded pleased.'Evie's doing well, all things considered. She's a fantastic girl.'

'And where does she live? Is she with you?'

'Yes. It was a bit of a steep learning curve at the beginning, but we've got used to each other now. And I love her to bits.' She shrugged modestly. 'We're muddling through.'

'Well that's good to hear. Good news.' Conor nodded and shifted from one foot to the other. He'd just said the word 'good' twice, which probably signalled that they were reaching the end of the conversation. Not that he wanted it to end, but there came a point when a chance meeting in the street between two strangers drew to a natural conclusion. It simply wouldn't be normal to keep talking, asking more and more intrusive questions about people he'd never met in his life. He cleared his throat. 'I'm glad things are going well . . . well, as well as can be expected.'

Oh God, listen to me; now I've said 'well' three times . . .

'Thanks. We're not doing too badly.' Belinda shook back her blonde hair and smiled. 'Could be a lot worse, considering all the—'

'Oh my God, are you *kidding* me? Look who's crawled out of the woodwork!'

Conor felt the hairs on the back of his neck rise in revulsion. The voice behind him had the effect of nails on a blackboard, and he recognised it instantly.

Seriously, was he doomed to be haunted by this hideous woman, and why did it have to be happening now? Did she not understand that her butting into two people's private conversation might not be welcome?

'It *is* you,' the voice continued as he turned to look at her. 'Ha, I don't believe it! How about that?'

'It really isn't that much of a coincidence,' Conor replied coolly. 'I live here, after all.'

Last time, she'd been wearing the turquoise pleather biker jacket and far too much shiny make-up. Today it was a fake-fur leopard-print coat and even more shiny make-up, because her spirit animal was clearly Bet Lynch.

'Couldn't be bothered to turn up at the Red House the night I told you to be there, though, could you? No manners, that's your trouble.'

'Did I ever say I'd be there?' Conor retorted. 'It was your idea, not mine. And if you don't mind, you're interrupting a private conversation.'

Which caused the dreadful woman to rock backwards on her cream patent heels and let out a screech of laughter that had heads turning from all directions to discover what was happening.

'Blimey,' said the old man who'd been throwing crumbs

to the birds. 'Tape up the windows. A racket like that'll shatter glass.'

Ignoring the bird man, she raised her eyebrows at Conor. 'A private conversation, is it? About what, exactly?'

'Are you for real?' Conor stared at her in disbelief. 'What on earth makes you think I'd answer that question?' He turned to Belinda. 'Look, I'm really sorry about this. I don't even know who she is.'

'Don't you? She seems to know you.' Belinda sounded amused.

This was getting uncomfortable now. 'OK, she accosted me the other week and ordered me to turn up for a blind date with her friend. I mean, seriously, who in their right mind would do that and expect it to happen?'

'Stop it,' Belinda said to the awful woman, who'd started cackling with laughter again like a helium-filled witch. Then she looked back at Conor. 'Well I suppose I did, otherwise I wouldn't have gone out and got my hair completely wrecked in that storm.'

As the words slowly sank in, Conor realised that leopard-print woman hadn't joined them because she'd recognised him. She was here because Belinda was her friend.

The friend.

Unbelievable though it seemed.

Actually, unbelievable was an understatement.

'It was you?' He needed to double-check.

'It was me,' Belinda agreed.

'Sorry.'

'So you should be,' leopard-print woman chimed in. She frowned. 'So how come you two were talking to each other anyway?'

'He knew Jess,' Belinda said simply. 'He thought I was her.'

'Ah, right. God love her.' She gave Conor a challenging look. 'What happened, did you stand Jess up too?'

'No,' said Conor. Although in a will-writing way, he kind of had.

'So anyway, here she is. My friend Belinda.' Leopard-print woman made lavish presenting gestures with her hands, like a TV game-show hostess. 'I said she'd be a good match for you, and I was right. Regretting standing her up now, you ungrateful bastard?'

Which, in the realm of awkward questions, had to be up there with the best of them.

'Leave him alone, Caz. You're a nightmare sometimes.' Belinda shook her head.

'You don't say,' Conor murmured, earning himself a scornful glance from Caz.

'Why don't you give us ten minutes?' Belinda looked encouragingly at her friend. 'I'll meet up with you in Aqua and we'll have a nice lunch, yes?'

'Fine,' said Caz.

When she'd left them, Conor said, 'Quite a character.'

'Caz? Oh yes.'

'Is she your . . . *best* friend?'

'I know what you're thinking.' Belinda's smile was dry. 'She's loud, she's over the top and she says it like it is. If something's on her mind, she comes out with it, for better or for worse.'

'I'd noticed.'

'But she's also one of the kindest people you'll ever meet. Seriously, she has a heart of gold. Caz lives next door to me

171

and Evie, and I couldn't have coped without her. She's always there to lend a hand, cheer me up when I'm feeling down, help me out if I need anything at all.'

'I'll take your word for it.' Conor changed the subject. 'OK, can I just say, I felt guilty about deciding to stand you up, especially in that weather. So I got myself ready to come over after all. Then at the last minute someone called me in need of help. I didn't want to go, but I had to. They were desperate.'

'Really?'

'I promise, hand on heart. I ended up spending the next six hours clearing up a fallen tree with a chainsaw. In the rain.'

'Karma,' said Belinda, 'for not wanting to meet me in the first place.'

Could he say it out loud? Conor paused, gathering his courage. 'If I'd known it was you, I'd have wanted to meet you.'

'Oh.' She smiled.

'I thought Caz would be setting me up with someone just like her.'

'Well, I did once own a pair of leopard-print slippers.'

'And I went over to the Red House at eight o'clock the following Saturday,' he added. 'In case you'd decided to give me another chance.'

'I did think about it,' Belinda admitted. 'But then I decided that only a complete loser would give herself the opportunity to be stood up two weeks running.'

He exhaled. 'I still can't believe it was you.'

'I've just realised something else.' She indicated the camera slung around his neck. 'Those photos on display in the Red

House . . . We were looking at them while we were there, and someone mentioned the photographer's name. They're yours!'

Conor nodded. 'They are.'

'I loved them.'

'Thank you.'

'My favourite was the guy with the dreadlocks pushing his daughter on the swing in the park. Their faces were just perfect.'

'They were great.' Since she was eyeing the camera once more, Conor said, 'Would you like me to take one of you?'

Belinda wrinkled her nose. 'Am I allowed to say no? I don't really like having my photo taken.'

'It's fine.' He was glad.

'Caz does, though. She'd love to pose for you.'

He smiled briefly, because that wasn't going to happen. 'When Caz decided to set us up, she said she can always tell when two people will get on well together.'

'She can,' Belinda agreed. 'She matched up her nephew's maths teacher with her dog's vet. They got married last year.'

Conor was taken aback. 'Wow.'

'Oh, sorry. Now I've scared you. You don't have to marry me, I promise!'

'Right.'

Belinda checked her watch. 'Anyway, she's waiting for me. I'd better get over to Aqua.' She paused. 'But it's been really nice to meet you. Maybe we'll bump into each other again.'

'That would be great.' As always, the more interested in someone Conor was, the shyer he became. He nodded vigorously, wondering why his confidence always turned tail and deserted him just when he needed it most.

'They said at the Red House that you have new photos going up every couple of weeks. Maybe Caz and I should pop in again soon . . .'

OK, it's now or never.

'Or to make up for messing you around before, I could take you out to dinner sometime.' The words tumbled out in a rush. 'This week, maybe, if you're free. But if you're busy, it doesn't matter . . .'

'I'd love to.' Belinda beamed and fanned herself. 'I thought you'd never ask.'

Oh, thank God. 'Great. Well, name the evening.'

'Friday?'

'Friday it is.' Conor took out his phone and handed it to her. 'If you key in your number, I'll text you later.'

When she'd done it and returned the phone to him, she said, 'This dinner invitation. I should check. Is it just me, or is Caz invited too?'

She was teasing him. Conor mimed alarm. 'Just you.'

'OK. I'm looking forward to it.'

'So am I.' And now it was his turn to exhale with relief. 'Phew!'

Chapter 22

Barry clearly didn't have long left on this earth. His skin was the colour of church candles and his breathing was laboured. But when he was lifted out of the ambulance, his whole face lit up.

'Daddy!' His two girls raced across the tarmac, reaching up on tiptoe to give him a kiss on each cheek. 'You're here . . . We've been waiting for you!'

Watching them from a discreet distance, Essie had a stern word with herself, because whatever happened, she mustn't cry. This was her afternoon off work, and when Zillah had asked if she'd like to help, she had jumped at the chance. Together they'd driven in Zillah's car to collect Barry's wife and children from their family home in Midsomer Norton. When Barry had been asked what his wish might be, he hadn't hesitated for a second. His favourite place in the world, he'd told Zillah, was the one that held the happiest memories for both himself and his family.

Tamsyn, his wife, was now saying to her daughters, 'We're going to have one last lovely visit, and then we'll remember it forever, won't we?'

If Tamsyn could say it without breaking down in tears, there was no excuse for the rest of them.

For the next hour they toured the dogs' home where Barry and Tamsyn had first met whilst working as voluntary walkers, visiting all the dogs in their separate glass-fronted cubicles and choosing which ones they'd like to take out for a walk. Essie helped the older daughter with a bouncy, waggy-tailed mongrel called Bernard. Together the motley group made their way along a winding path. Conor, who'd been delayed at work, arrived with his Nikon to take photos of the family. There were happy squeals, there was chatter and laughter and there was a volley of barking when the dogs spotted a squirrel racing up a tree.

'He's running away,' the older girl told Essie, pointing as the squirrel disappeared into the highest branches. 'He's going all the way to heaven!'

'Woof woof woof.' Bernard was desperately scrabbling his front paws against the tree's gnarled trunk.

'Don't be silly, Bernard. You can't climb up there. You're a dog.'

The younger daughter was peering up with interest. 'Mummy, are there squirrels in heaven?'

'Ooh, I should think so,' said Tamsyn.

'What about dogs?'

Tamsyn nodded and stroked her daughter's blonde head. 'Oh sweetie, definitely. Heaven is full of lovely dogs.'

'That's good. Will you be able to take them for walks, Daddy? When you're in heaven?'

Barry managed a smile. 'I will. Every single day.'

And Essie had to turn away, because the look he was

giving his younger daughter was so heartbreakingly full of love.

Essie was working the following evening when Conor arrived, carrying his portfolio case.

'I know it's not Monday,' he told Lucas, 'but I thought I'd bring over your photo. It's not as if it's only going to be on show for a week, is it? Seeing as this is your place, you should keep it on permanent display.'

'Hmm, not sure about that.' Lucas sounded doubtful. 'I'll decide after I've had a look at it.'

Essie said, 'Come on, let's see! Does he look really ugly?'

'Watch it,' Lucas warned.

She grinned. 'Are we allowed to laugh? I won't, I promise. Probably.'

Lucas said, 'If you laugh, you're sacked.'

Conor unfastened the portfolio and took out the photo, already framed in its clear Perspex case. 'Here you go. I'm pleased with it, anyway.'

Everyone else gathered around to look. Essie, hanging back, was glad all the attention was on the portrait, because the effect it was having on her was visceral. A burst of adrenalin had galvanised her heart and set it racing, purely because Lucas's gaze, as captured by the camera, was so intense.

There he was, in his open-necked white cotton shirt and his narrow black trousers, casually perched on the stool with one elbow resting on the high table next to him. The portrait was in black and white too, carving shadows beneath his eyes and cheekbones as he sat with his head turned slightly to the left but his eyes looking directly into the camera lens. The very faintest of smiles lifted the corners of his mouth, and there was a spark of humour combined with impatience in those dark eyes. A lock of hair had fallen over his forehead, as if he'd just shaken his head because someone had said something he couldn't quite believe.

Next to Lucas, Jude said, 'That's the exact look you gave me during the Christmas quiz when the other team thought *Pride and Prejudice* had been written by Jane Eyre.'

'Well I think it's fantastic.' Sharon, one of their unshy regulars, fanned herself and mimed being overcome with lust. 'You look hot.'

'I'm pleased with the composition,' said Conor. 'It works well.'

Lucas turned his head and Essie accidentally caught his eye. He raised an eyebrow. 'What do you think? You haven't said anything yet.'

Essie swallowed, because there was no way she could announce what she was really thinking. Instead, studying the portrait, she said, 'The eyes follow you around the room. It'll stop the bar staff trying to slip their friends free drinks.'

Lucas laughed. 'In that case we'd better make sure we hang it up where everyone can see it from behind the bar.'

It was three o'clock in the morning and Lucas woke with a start, confused for a moment to find himself in a cool darkened room. In his dream he'd been strolling along a white sandy beach in blazing sunshine, watching as flying fish leapt out of the turquoise sea. In his right hand he was carrying a straw hat. His left arm was curled around Essie Phillips' waist.

Right. Wake up properly now.

He opened his eyes and stared at the ceiling. OK, you couldn't help who you dreamed about, but it was somewhat concerning that for the third time this week his dreams had featured Essie.

Even worse, it had happened while he was lying in bed next to his girlfriend, who, still fast asleep, had no idea he'd been dreaming about walking along a tropical beach with his arm around another girl.

Lucas tilted his head sideways and looked at Giselle for a moment. Then he slid silently out of bed, reached for his white towelling dressing gown and let himself out of the bedroom.

Downstairs, he switched on the lights in the bar, made himself a coffee and added a splash of cognac. From its position on the wall opposite the bar where Jude had earlier decided it should be hung, his portrait regarded him with what was beginning to feel like mocking amusement.

Shit, what was happening to him, and what was he meant to do about it? Life had been so much easier when Essie had still believed him to be the idiot who'd sent the round robin and ruined her life. He almost wished her brother hadn't felt guilty enough about it to confess all.

Lucas looked away from the portrait. He probably shouldn't have told Essie about his own family history either. At the time he'd wanted to, had *needed* to do it, but it had only served to deepen the unspoken connection between them. His attraction towards Essie was growing at a rate of knots, but there was no way he could act upon it. He had Giselle, who was everyone's idea of a perfect girlfriend, and he couldn't believe the situation in which he now found himself.

Because Giselle *was* perfect. She hadn't an enemy in the world and was adored by everyone who knew her. She was caring, loyal, thoughtful, cheerful and kind. There was absolutely nothing there to dislike. He'd met her, they'd hit it off at once, and the feelings had escalated from there. As their relationship had deepened, he'd assumed they were in love. Because this was how it felt, wasn't it? So when Giselle had started ending their phone calls with a breezy 'Love you!' he had gone along with it because it would be churlish not to. When you looked forward to seeing someone, enjoyed their company in bed and out, and couldn't imagine not wanting to spend time with them in the future . . . well, that meant you loved them, surely?

Or so he'd thought.

Lucas gave his coffee another stir and felt the knot in his chest stealthily tighten like a drawstring around his heart. He and Giselle had been together for six months; they were a recognised couple. But now this thing with Essie was happening, and the way he was starting to feel about her was knocking him for six. He found himself looking forward to her turning up for her shifts far more than he should. Each time she left, he wished she wasn't going. Realistically, though, what could he do? What were his options? He couldn't sack her. He couldn't ask her to leave her job. Nor could *he* leave. But continuing to work here alongside her was going to become increasingly—

'There you are,' said a quiet voice behind him, and Lucas almost dropped his coffee cup.

He turned, and there was Giselle in the doorway, smiling sleepily at him. Her glossy auburn curls fell loose past her shoulders, and she was wearing her grey-and-white stripy nightshirt. Rubbing her eyes, she padded across to join him. 'I woke up and you weren't there.'

'Couldn't sleep,' said Lucas. 'Thought a nightcap might help.'

'Coffee's just going to keep you awake.' She leaned against him, resting her head on his shoulder and placing a hand on his exposed upper chest. 'It's chilly down here. How can you be so warm?'

He flexed a bicep. 'I'm just so manly.'

Giselle laughed. 'Why couldn't you sleep?'

'No idea, just one of those things.' Lucas reached for his coffee cup and downed the contents. 'Let's give it another try, shall we? Sorry if I woke you.'

She shivered. 'I'm freezing now. You'll have to warm me up.'

But it was OK, she didn't mean it in a wild-sex way. Last night she'd finished a late shift and in a few short hours would be starting an early one. Sliding down from his high stool, Lucas put his arm around her and they prepared to leave the bar.

Just before he switched off the lights, Giselle pointed to his photograph on the wall. 'Who's that guy over there? He's pretty good-looking. I could go for someone like him.'

If you knew what was going through his head right now, you wouldn't be so keen.

'He comes in here quite often. I'll get his number for you,' Lucas said aloud.

Chapter 23

It was Friday evening at last; this week it had taken far longer than it usually did for Friday to come around. Next time, Conor vowed, when he asked a woman out on a date and she seemed every bit as keen as he was, he would just say, 'How about tomorrow?' instead.

Anyway, he was here now, approaching Belinda's address in Pucklechurch and wondering if she was as nervous as he was.

Finally, following the sat nav's instructions, he turned into Limes Avenue and pulled up outside number 36. Before he even had time to switch off the car's engine, the front door to number 38 flew open and Caz appeared in the brightly lit doorway.

Great, just what you need on the brink of your first date.

But when he climbed out of the car and Caz briskly beckoned him over, Conor wondered if she was about to tell him the date had been cancelled.

'OK, two things,' Caz announced when only a chain-link fence separated them.

'And they are?' said Conor.

'If you break Belinda's heart, you'll have me to answer to.'

'Excuse me?'

'You heard. She deserves to be happy. Be nice to her. Don't be a bastard.'

'What makes you think I would be?'

'Most men are bastards.'

'You were the one who set us up in the first place.'

'I know. And that's one more reason to do as you're told and not let me down.'

'Listen, it's one dinner, that's all. I seriously doubt any hearts will be broken.' Conor straightened. 'OK if I go now?'

'No. I said there were two things.'

He sighed. 'What's the second?'

Caz smirked. 'Well, I was going to tell you you've got a black smudge on your cheek, but maybe I won't bother after all.'

Oh God, he'd stopped on the way over to fill up with petrol, and there'd been an oily residue on the pump handle. He patted his jacket pockets in search of a handkerchief, without success.

'Come here.' Caz produced a Kleenex and pulled him forward by his lapels in order to briskly scrub the offending smudge from his cheek. For a moment he'd thought she might spit on the tissue first. 'There, done. Now off you go and have a nice evening.'

Conor gave the side of his face a wipe and reluctantly said, 'Thanks.'

'She's my friend. I'm on your side.' Caz fixed him with a stern gaze. 'Just make sure you don't spoil it.'

Evie, as any self-respecting teenager would be, was sitting

cross-legged in front of the TV in the living room, simultaneously painting her nails purple and checking texts on her mobile phone.

'Hi,' she said when Belinda had introduced Conor. 'You're keen!'

'Sorry?' Was 'keen' one of those recently refurbished words he no longer entirely understood, like 'bad' and 'wicked' and 'sick'?

'Early,' Evie explained. 'It's only five to eight.'

'Ah, yes. Sorry. The sat nav was a bit overefficient. I would have waited in the car,' said Conor, 'but your neighbour wanted a word with me.'

'I'll just get my shoes on,' said Belinda. 'Won't be a minute.'

When she'd left them alone together, Evie said, 'So where are we going?'

For the second time, Conor heard himself saying, 'Sorry?'

'You're taking us out to dinner. I just wondered which restaurant we're off to?'

'Er . . . Giorgio's in Bath.' Could he just turn up and ask them to change it to a booking for three? Would that be possible on a Friday evening, or—

'Kidding.' Evie grinned.

'Oh.' Phew.

'Just testing you.'

'Right.'

'You passed, though. So that's good news.'

'Thanks. You can join us if you'd like to.'

'Nah, you're all right. I've got Netflix here and Caz is coming over later with home-made burgers. You two lovebirds go off and have fun.'

'Hey, you. Stop being embarrassing.' Belinda, returning

with her shoes and coat on, dropped a kiss on Evie's blonde head. 'Right, we're off. See you later.'

'Bye.' Evie waggled her wet purple nails at them. 'Be good!'

The evening was going well. In the light from the candle flickering on the table between them, Belinda's face glowed. She was wearing a petrol-blue jersey dress and a coral necklace, and had visibly relaxed as dinner progressed.

Now she said in confiding tones, 'This is nice. Thank you for inviting me. Are you having a good time?'

'I am.' Conor had overcome his own first-date nerves. 'Apart from one thing. Does this mean I'm going to have to be grateful to Caz?'

'Looks like it.' Belinda's eyes danced. 'Sorry about that.'

'She won't let me forget it for a moment.'

'I promise you, Caz isn't as bad as you think she is. And Evie loves her to bits.'

'Ah well, she can't be all bad then.' *Just bossy and opinionated. And loud.* 'So how does Evie usually get along with your boyfriends? Pretty well?' Because he knew that some children made it their mission in life to kick up a fuss when their single or divorced parents brought home potential new partners. Was being a guardian rather than a parent any different?

'OK, don't be scared,' said Belinda, 'but you're the first.'

Conor did a double take. 'What? I'm your first date? You mean, *ever?*'

'Not ever. Since Evie came to live with me. So that's four years now.'

'Wow.' It made him like her more. 'Because you didn't want her to feel insecure. That's impressive.'

'It was only for that reason for the first couple of years.' Belinda spoke drily. 'I did think I was doing the right thing, until one day Evie asked me why I wasn't going out with men any more and had I decided to become a lesbian?'

'And had you?'

'No. Actually, she was a bit disappointed. One of her friends has two mums and Evie thought it might be fun to be like her.' Belinda shook back her hair. 'Anyway, she told me I really should get out there and find myself a boyfriend. So I thought, OK, I'll do that!' She pulled a face. 'Except it turned out to be not quite as easy as I'd thought.'

'Ah.' Conor nodded sympathetically. 'What happened?'

'Well, I suppose I'd got pickier. Now that I had Evie, my standards had to be higher. There couldn't be any wild one-night stands – not that I was ever really a one-night-stand kind of person, but up until then, there'd always been the option. And there was the other side of it too. If you meet some random stranger at a party and happen to mention that you're responsible for a fourteen-year-old who lives with you, it puts a lot of men off. They're not interested in getting to know someone like me because I come as a package deal and they just can't be doing with the hassle. Why go out with me with all my baggage when there are plenty more out there who are young, free and single?'

'Their loss,' said Conor, because the last few years must have been incredibly hard for her.

'That's what I used to tell myself.' Belinda shrugged. 'Although sometimes all I wanted to do was tip their pints over their heads. So anyway,' she concluded with a wry smile, 'thanks for asking me out. I know you might decide not to see me again after tonight, but at least you've broken my duck. I finally met someone nice and he didn't run a mile, so cheers for that.'

Conor said, 'I already know I'd like to see you again. If you'd like to see me.'

'Really?' Belinda's eyes sparkled. 'I would. Very much.'

'How about tomorrow?'

'Yes please.'

'Great.' Feeling ridiculously pleased with himself, he lifted his glass and clinked it against hers. 'That's a date, then. Cheers.'

By the time they left the restaurant, well wrapped up against the cold, it was gone eleven. High above the city, the stars were out.

'I've lost one of my gloves. That's crazy,' Belinda exclaimed, patting her pockets. 'How can I have lost one of my gloves?'

Glad of the excuse, Conor said, 'Here, hold onto my hand,' and extended his arm. His warm fingers closed around her cold ones and he experienced the zing that accompanied the right kind of physical contact.

'You make an excellent glove.' She swung his hand as they made their way along York Street.

'Thanks. You make an excellent compliment.' He smiled, because he'd just caught a glimpse of the two of them reflected in the shop window opposite, and they looked like an actual couple.

Belinda said, 'Uh oh, noisy people. Shall we cross over?'

There was a small crowd ahead of them, a mixed group of people yelling and laughing as they spilled out of a pub onto the pavement. One swung around a lamp post; another leapt up, trying to grab his hat back from his friend. A girl was trying to juggle with plastic cups, letting out a wail of frustration as they fell to the ground then almost toppling over as she attempted to scoop them up. The next moment her face was caught in the headlights of a passing van and Conor recognised her.

A moment later the van drove past Belinda and himself and his own face was similarly revealed.

'I don't believe it,' shouted Scarlett, pointing at him. 'That's my husband over there! Conor, what's going on? Who's that with you, and why aren't you at home looking after our kids?'

'She thinks she's being funny,' Conor murmured as Scarlett cracked up laughing and everyone turned to look at them.

'Is that . . . Does she have purple hair?'

'Yes.'

'Is she drunk?'

'I have no idea.'

Belinda sounded alarmed. 'Is she an ex-girlfriend of yours?'

Scarlett, still grinning, gave them a farewell wave before disappearing along with the rest of her rowdy friends around the corner. Conor exhaled with relief. 'Absolutely not.'

They walked back to his car. As they reached it, Belinda squeezed his hand. 'It's been such a lovely evening. I know it sounds mad, but I keep wishing I could tell Jess about all this. I want her to know that you saw me in the street and thought I was her. I think she'd be glad it happened. Because now we've got to know each other and it kind of feels like fate, doesn't it?'

She was right. Conor nodded. 'It does.'

'Almost as if she made it happen.' Belinda smiled up at him. 'Honestly, she'd be so thrilled we met.'

Chapter 24

The entrance doors were unlocked when Essie arrived at the Red House the next morning, but the bar area was deserted. The fresh smell of furniture polish hung in the air, indicating that Maeve the cleaner had finished and left, and the faint sound of clanking metal barrels being moved around let her know that Lucas was busy in the cellar.

Although he was also here on the wall, in his white open-necked shirt and black trousers, gazing down at her. Giving her that look and that mesmerising half-smile.

Who could have imagined that an inanimate photograph could prove to be so compelling and such a distraction? OK, everyone looked at it and commented on how striking it was, but she was finding it almost impossible to *stop* glancing over at it whilst she was working.

Which was frankly embarrassing. Essie knew she needed to stop doing it before other people started to notice.

There, see? I'm doing it again now.

She took a steadying breath; the answer, clearly, was to get it out of her system. Like when you fell in love with the brilliant new single by your favourite band and kept playing it over and over again because you couldn't bear to stop. But over time the level of entrancement died down and your brain grew tired of the track, until it no longer took over your life and eventually you just didn't want to hear it any more.

Overexposure, that was definitely what she needed. And by great good luck, there was no one else around. Moving closer to the framed portrait on the wall, Essie reached for her phone and held it up. She took a couple of photos with the flash off, then another two with it on. Whenever she had a spare minute she was going to stare and keep on staring at the portrait of Lucas until the urge to look at it was completely out of her system. OK, one last close-up of his face, that beautiful face with those incredible cheekbones and—

'Ooh, flash flash flash, it's like having the paparazzi in here! Hello, my love, what're you up to? Taking pictures of the boss? He looks like one of those Hollywood actors in that photo, doesn't he!'

Maeve had popped her head up over the back of the crimson velvet sofa and Essie had never been more mortified. She clapped the phone to her chest. 'God, you gave a fright. I thought you'd finished and gone home.'

'No, love. Just been dusting these skirting boards and getting a mark off the floor down here! Stubborn little bugger, red wine I reckon.' Maeve merrily waved her can of stain remover and microfibre cleaning cloth as proof. 'You know I don't like to leave a job until it's properly finished! Why were you taking photos of that photograph, love?'

'I . . . um . . .' Oh God, why indeed? Essie's mind had

gone blank and she couldn't for the life of her think of a plausible reason.

'What phone is it you're using? Let's have a look.' Having emerged from behind the sofa, Maeve came bustling over and peered at it. 'Oh, that's OK, I know how to work those. Would you like me to take one of you standing beside the photo?'

What? 'No, no thanks, it's fine!'

'Come on, don't be shy, it'll be like a proper selfie except you won't have to take it yourself!' Reaching for Essie's phone, Maeve made shooing movements with her free arm. 'Get yourself over there against that wall, there's a good girl, and squeeze up right next to him—'

This was the moment, *of course it was*, that Lucas closed the cellar door behind him and said, 'Am I allowed to ask what's going on here?'

Sadly it was a rhetorical question and saying no simply wouldn't have done the trick.

Maeve said, 'I'm just taking a nice photo of Essie standing next to your picture!'

Lucas raised an eyebrow. 'And you're doing that because . . . ?'

'Because it's what she wanted me to do,' said Maeve.

'I didn't,' Essie blurted out. 'Really I didn't.' She looked at Maeve. 'It was your idea.'

'Ah well, same difference,' Maeve said comfortably. 'I saw her taking loads of photos of your photo so I just thought I'd offer. Everyone likes to be in their own pictures, don't they? I was doing her a favour.'

Oh God . . .

'You're a good woman.' Lucas managed to keep a straight face. 'Go ahead.'

Maeve was visibly struck by inspiration. 'Oh, but why make do with a photo when you've got the real deal here? The very man himself! You wouldn't mind, Lucas, would you? Just go over there and stand next to Essie, it won't take a moment—'

'No need,' Essie squeaked. 'It's fine. I really have to start work now.'

'But—'

'And you should be off too, Maeve.' Lucas pointed to the clock on the wall. 'Look at the time.'

Once Maeve had left, they worked together in silence to ready the bar for opening. Finally, as she'd known he would, Lucas said, 'I'm still intrigued.'

'Right.' Essie was preparing to fill the ice bucket.

'You didn't think I was just going to leave it, did you? I have to ask.'

Her cheeks burned as the torrent of cubes came clattering out of the ice maker. 'I was chatting to Scarlett on the phone this morning. She wanted to know what the portrait was like.'

'Oh.'

'That's all. No big deal.'

'OK.'

'Why are you looking at me like that?'

'No reason,' said Lucas. 'Except Scarlett dropped by last night. She's already seen it.'

The next day, the doorbell went just as Essie was putting the finishing touches to her make-up, in preparation for her afternoon shift at the Red House.

To save Zillah the trouble of going to the front door, she

ran downstairs to open it herself. The first thing she saw was a huge bunch of multicoloured tulips, and her breath caught in her throat because multicoloured tulips were her favourite flowers and the only person who knew that was Paul. She'd loved the way he'd always taken such pleasure in surprising her with flowers . . .

Then her eyes adjusted to the bringer of the tulips and she saw that it was Tamsyn, Barry's wife.

OK, it really was time to stop thinking about Paul.

'I brought them for Zillah, to thank her for arranging Barry's wish,' Tamsyn explained. 'Is she in?'

It wasn't until the three of them were gathered in Zillah's kitchen that Tamsyn said, 'Barry died yesterday morning.'

'Oh no. Oh, my darling girl.' Zillah shook her head in dismay. 'I'm so sorry.'

'He wasn't in any pain at the end, which was a relief.' Tamsyn was dry-eyed, pale but composed. 'That was always something he was worried about. And we've known it was going to happen for such a long time. I just wanted to say thank you for making our last week together so special. You gave us the most perfect day and we'll never forget it.'

Zillah was clearly moved. 'We're just so glad we were able to do something to help.'

'You definitely did. The girls couldn't stop talking about it. Here, they made you this.'

Tamsyn opened her bag and took out an envelope. Inside was a hand-drawn card, carefully coloured in with bright felt tips, depicting the family's visit to the dogs' home. Everyone was smiling and waving, surrounded by rainbows and waggy-tailed dogs.

'That's so gorgeous,' said Essie.

193

'They have wonderful memories now of their last outing with their dad, and we can't thank you enough. Anyway, I left them with my parents for an hour so I could come over. But now I need to get back.' Tamsyn gave Essie then Zillah a warm hug. 'There's lots to do, so much to organise. I need to make sure I get it all right. Mustn't let Barry down.'

'You won't. Barry told us how proud he was of you,' said Zillah. 'He said you were the best wife he could ever have wished for. Didn't he?' She turned to Essie for confirmation.

Essie wanted to speak but there was a lump the size of a golf ball in her throat, because how could Tamsyn be so brave when the love of her life had just died?

She nodded instead, and Tamsyn said simply, 'Oh, I was the lucky one, believe me. I got to be Barry's wife.'

Chapter 25

'Hey,' said Lucas when they found themselves alone together for the second time in two days. 'How are you doing? Everything OK?'

It was almost midnight, and they were finishing clearing up after a busy Sunday evening. Jude had left ten minutes ago. Essie had worked non-stop and put on a cheerful front for the customers, but inside she was a tightening mass of contradictory emotions.

Which hardly anyone else would notice, but Lucas had.

Of course he would; he had extra-sensory perception or something surreal like that. Now he lowered his voice, sounding concerned. 'Anything you want to talk about?'

Essie swallowed. Oh, and her period was due, which meant her hormones were going haywire and making her feel that much worse.

She probably wouldn't mention that.

'Come on. Something's happened to upset you.' He patted the stool next to him and leaned against the bar. 'Is it your brother?'

'No.' Essie sat down and tried not to breathe in the havoc-making scent of his aftershave. 'Not this time.'

'Have you heard from the ex-boyfriend?'

Paul. She shook her head.

'Tell me, then.'

'It's just . . . I don't understand how life can be like it is.' OK, here came the pent-up emotions, on the brink of tumbling out. 'Because there are so many awful people in the world, but nothing bad ever seems to happen to them . . . they just carry on being awful and getting away with it. And then there are the really good people who never do anything bad, but something terrible comes along and blows their lives apart. They don't deserve it, but it happens anyway, and it's just so *unfair*.'

Lucas's expression changed. 'What's happened? Essie, tell me. Is this you we're talking about?'

'It's not me.' Essie shook her head despairingly. 'Someone I met the other day. She married her first love and they were so happy together, and their children are just the best, but yesterday her husband died. She's only the same age as me. And she's being so brave, but what has she done to deserve it? Nothing, nothing at all.' To her horror, she realised tears were sliding down her cheeks. 'It breaks my heart and it makes me so angry, because what's the point of trying to be a good person if you're still going to be punished like that?'

'Life isn't fair. You know it isn't,' said Lucas.

'I *do* know that, but it's still not fair that it isn't fair.' Great, and now she was burbling rubbish, because there was so much else she couldn't say. When Tamsyn had arrived on the doorstep with those tulips, she had thought for a split second that they were from Paul. But, being completely honest, had she ever loved Paul as much as Tamsyn and Barry had loved each other? No, she was pretty sure she hadn't.

Plus there were now the feelings she was incubating for Lucas, which were so inappropriate she couldn't reveal them to a soul, let alone the soul who was the cause of them. Because other girls might enjoy the challenge of breaking up a happy relationship, but they were bad people who didn't care how much pain they inflicted on others. And she absolutely *wasn't* that kind of person.

OK, and she was still leaking tears at a rate of knots, which was embarrassing. She rubbed both hands impatiently across her cheeks; she'd never been one to cry, especially not in public, but the thought of Tamsyn and those two young girls of hers having to cope with the loss of Barry was just unbearable.

'Here.' Lucas passed her a red paper napkin and his hand brushed against hers as she reached for it. The physical contact only added to the current confusion in her brain, and she flinched and said, 'Oh, sorry,' before wiping her eyes again. 'Have I got mascara everywhere? I bet I look a fright.'

'Well,' said Lucas, 'you know kiss . . . ?'

Essie looked at him, utterly baffled. What could he possibly mean by that? Was he saying he wanted to kiss her so thoroughly that he smudged her mascara? Because that just sounded bizarre. But he was looking at her mouth as if he *wanted* to kiss it . . .

Aloud she murmured, 'Sorry?'

'You know.' Lucas made up-and-down zigzag gestures beneath his own eyes. 'The band Kiss. Lead singer Gene Simmons. Black make-up all over the shop.'

Ergh, how could she have got it so wrong? How mortifying. And now he was reaching for another napkin.

'Here, let me do it.' He moved closer. 'You've even managed to get mascara on your chin, and that's quite an achievement. Stay still.'

Essie couldn't meet his gaze; she closed her sore eyes and held her breath as Lucas gently wiped the affected parts of her face. Her skin felt as if it were on fire. Could he tell how fast her heart was beating? Did he have *any* idea how much of an effect his proximity was having on her body?

The front door had opened silently; it wasn't until she felt the colder air from outside on her cheek that Essie opened her eyes and saw Giselle heading towards them.

Oh God, what on earth must she be thinking right now?

'Essie! Oh no, what's happened? Lucas, this had better not be your fault!' Giselle dropped her overnight bag to the floor, knelt and pulled out a pack of make-up wipes, then took the mascara-streaked napkin out of Lucas's hand. 'Come on, let's do this properly. He hasn't been horrible to you, has he?'

'Hey, I'm never horrible,' said Lucas.

'It wasn't him.' Essie looked at Giselle as, with nurse-like efficiency and compassion, she took over the task in hand. 'I heard today that someone lovely had just died. And I always wear waterproof mascara, except this morning I accidentally bought a new one in Boots that wasn't waterproof. But I thought it'd be fine because it's not as if I ever cry.'

'You poor thing. And how typical, isn't it always the way? I bet that horrible feeling's been stuck inside your chest all evening, building up and up like a pressure cooker until you just couldn't hold it in any longer and out it all came.'

Essie nodded gratefully. 'That's exactly how it felt.'

'Oh, I know, it happens to us at work all the time. Sometimes a patient really gets to you, you build up a real bond . . . then they die, and of course we're upset. You'd have to have a heart of stone not to be. There, all done now.' She stepped back, task completed. 'You still look lovely. Don't you have gorgeous skin? I'd kill for your colouring.'

Essie slid down from the stool. 'Thanks so much.' She indicated Giselle's riotous auburn curls. 'I've always wished I could have hair like yours.'

'Ah well, I suppose we all want what we can't have,' said Giselle with a warm smile.

It wasn't until Essie was making her way back home across the icy square that it occurred to her to wonder guiltily if it had just been a figure of speech, or whether Giselle somehow knew how she'd begun to feel about Lucas. Had she sensed the longing within her? Had that last statement been Giselle's way of gently reminding her that Lucas was already taken, that he belonged to someone else?

With a shiver, she wondered if the two of them were completely aware of her growing attraction to him. Did they lie in bed together discussing it? Did Giselle tease Lucas about it? Did he laugh?

And would he tell Giselle about her reaction when he'd mentioned the band Kiss and she'd misunderstood?

Because if he did, *oh God* . . .

More guilt.

Up early for the arrival of the delivery from the brewery, Lucas made himself a strong coffee and waited on the top step for the lorry to pull up outside.

From here he could look across the frosty square and see the windows of Essie's second-floor flat. Last night he'd wanted to kiss her so badly it had taken all his self-control not to. It had felt like being a teenager again, when the fact that you were already seeing one girl didn't stop you from being attracted to the next one who came along. Back then, he'd enjoyed being the centre of female attention; relationships hadn't been intended to last or to become serious. And he'd taken advantage of the offers, gaining something of a reputation for himself, because that was what being a teenager was all about, wasn't it? Having fun and not taking life too seriously, because there was plenty of time for that later when you were grown up.

As time went by, he'd realised that playing with girls' emotions wasn't anything to be proud of. Getting to know someone and genuinely enjoying spending time with them was so much more rewarding than just mindlessly sleeping with virtual strangers, then having to fend them off afterwards.

It was one of those life lessons that came to most people eventually. Maybe his own less-than-happy home life had helped him to see it sooner than some of his friends had. Putting the meaningless one-night stands behind him, Lucas had vowed never to cheat on a girl again. It wasn't worth the emotional hassle. From now on he would always remain faithful, be a better person and a nicer one. Plus, his conscience would be clear.

There was a lot to be said for that.

And until now, he'd found it easy to stick to. Which was why this situation with Essie had caught him so completely unawares. He was shocked by the intensity of his feelings for her. Worst of all, he'd known yesterday evening that

Giselle was on her way over to spend the night with him, but while he'd been listening to Essie and wiping her tear-stained face, he'd still wanted more than anything to take her in his arms and kiss her.

Lucas exhaled, shifted from one foot to the other and wondered what was happening to him. This wasn't the person he wanted to be.

Across the square, the front door of number 23 opened and his pulse speeded up. But it wasn't Essie. Zillah emerged wearing a smart navy coat, a fuchsia-pink fedora and a matching scarf. Spotting him, she waved, and Lucas raised his hand in return. Then she climbed into her Mercedes and drove off, and the next moment the lorry from the brewery came rattling around the corner with the delivery he'd been waiting for.

Fifty minutes later, Lucas carried a mug of freshly ground coffee and a bacon sandwich upstairs and let himself into the bedroom.

'Hey. Brought you breakfast.' He sat down on the bed, and Giselle smiled up at him.

'What's brought this on?'

Guilt was the answer. Lucas said, 'Does there have to be a reason?'

'Where's your sandwich?'

'Already ate mine while I was making yours. And no, I didn't forget,' he added as she lifted the upper slice of bread. 'One side ketchup, one side brown sauce.'

'You're a magnificent sandwich maker. And I hardly deserve it after last night.' She gave him a playful nudge with her bare foot. 'Sorry about falling asleep like that. I went out like a light.'

'I noticed.' He'd actually been glad of the reprieve; while he was feeling so confused, it would be wrong to sleep with her in that sense.

'I was shattered.' Giselle yawned and wriggled down beneath the duvet. 'Mm, cosy. Couldn't get me a glass of water, could you?'

'Your coffee's here.'

'I know. Water first.'

There were glasses in the bathroom. As he filled one with cold water, Lucas called out, 'What time are you and Kelly heading off?' Kelly, Giselle's friend and fellow nurse, was picking her up to go shopping in the Mall at Cribbs Causeway, on the outskirts of Bristol.

He returned from the bathroom with her water, and Giselle wrinkled her nose. 'I might text her and cancel. Don't think I fancy shopping today. How about you, what're you doing?'

'Meeting with the accountant, then over to the garage to get the car MOT'd. Jude's in charge here until I get back around two.' Lucas checked his watch. 'In fact I need to get the paperwork together and leave soon.'

'OK, you do that. I'm going to stay here and be lazy, maybe have another little doze.' Giselle held her arms out to him. 'See you later.'

Lucas bent to give her a kiss. 'Bye then. Don't let your coffee go cold.'

By the time he returned at one thirty, Giselle had gone, heading off to the hospital to begin her afternoon shift. She'd left the bed semi-made, which always amused him; at work it was all geometric hospital corners and immaculately smooth covers, but outside of work the duvet was flung across any old how. On the bedside table stood her empty coffee mug, the water glass and the plate strewn with crumbs.

She had also turned the heating up after he'd left, which meant the temperature in the room was stifling. Lucas crossed to the sash window and hauled it open to let in some much-needed cold air. That was the moment he glanced out and saw something on the roof of the property that backed onto the Red House.

He stopped dead in his tracks.

Really?

He looked again. OK, this was a mystery.

It made absolutely no sense at all.

Chapter 26

The next morning, Lucas was up early again. Giselle had stayed over, and he left her dozing in bed once more in order to supervise the day's deliveries.

Once everything was sorted downstairs, he took her up a coffee. 'Want me to make you a bacon sandwich?'

Giselle shook her head. 'No thanks. Not hungry.'

Five minutes later he said, 'Aren't you going to drink that coffee?'

She thought about it. 'You know, I don't really fancy coffee just now. It tastes a bit weird.'

That was the moment Lucas knew for sure. He also realised that Giselle didn't know.

'You're looking a bit pale,' he said, although this wasn't true. 'Are you feeling OK?'

'Oh, there's a bit of a bug going around at work.' Giselle pulled a face. 'A couple of people were off sick yesterday. It's OK, I'll be fine.'

Lucas mentally braced himself; time felt as if it was slowing down. He could have asked her yesterday but had held off, keeping the question to himself until he was sure.

Now he said, 'There was a splash of coffee on the side of the sink in the bathroom yesterday. Did you tip away the one I made for you before I left?'

Giselle laughed out loud. 'Ha, caught out. Well done, Sherlock Holmes! But it's that new kind you've started using. I told you, it tastes weird.'

It was the exact same coffee he'd always bought. And still she had absolutely no idea. Lucas said, 'You didn't eat your bacon sandwich either.'

This time she blushed. 'How do you know that?'

He indicated the window. 'I looked out and saw it on the roof over there.'

'Oh, I'm sorry!' Shamefaced and laughing again, Giselle said, 'I just didn't feel like eating it, but you'd gone to so much trouble and I couldn't think how else to get rid of it. Except the plan was to throw it into the yard below. I couldn't believe I managed to get it stuck on that stupid roof! I just prayed a bird would fly down and make off with the whole thing before you came back and spotted it.'

'Hey, don't worry, not a problem.' Lucas smiled briefly, whilst inside his heart began to race. 'I just wondered why you'd done it. Bacon sandwiches are your favourite.'

Giselle spread her hands. 'I know, I couldn't understand it either! But then I heard about the bug going around, so I realised it must be that.'

She was a fully qualified state registered nurse, yet it genuinely hadn't occurred to her. Lucas sat down on the side of the bed and reached for her hand. 'Look, I don't want to scare you, but do you think there could be another reason?'

Giselle stared at him. Then she froze in disbelief, and this time he saw the colour physically drain from her already pale face. For a moment, as her hand went to her mouth, he thought she might actually be about to throw up.

'Oh my God . . .'

'Is your period late?'

'I don't know.' And now she was flushing, her breathing fast and ragged. 'I can't tell. You know what my periods are like. Oh Lucas, do you think I could be . . . Oh my *God*.'

'Right, calm down. Have a think. When was the last one?'

'End of December? Um . . . Oh help, I can't concentrate.' She flapped her hands, panicking. 'Or maybe a bit before that, before I went home for Christmas . . .'

He saw the fear in her eyes. 'More than six weeks ago?'

'But that's not unusual for me!' Giselle clutched his arm. 'Oh now I really do feel sick . . . I can't even think straight. This is awful . . . I can't cope with this . . .'

She was completely poleaxed, trembling all over and in a state of shock. And understandably so. Apart from anything else, what effect might it have on her career? Lucas took control and spoke reassuringly. 'Look, the first thing we need to do is find out for sure.'

There was still a faint chance, after all, that she'd caught the bug from one of her colleagues at the hospital.

Please God.

Giselle's eyes were huge. 'Will you go out and buy a test?'

'Well, one of us needs to.'

'You'd be quicker.'

This was true. 'OK, I'll go. You'll need to pee on a stick, right?'

She nodded, still trembling.

Lucas said, 'In that case, make sure you stay away from the bathroom until I get back.'

Outside, he headed for the nearest small chemist, then promptly left again when he saw one of his regular customers browsing.

In the second place he tried, he spotted Essie's friend Scarlett buying herself a hairbrush.

In the third pharmacy, Lucas managed to buy two pregnancy testing kits without bumping into or being spotted by anyone he knew.

Never had he felt more like a secret agent, except not in a good way. In all honesty, Giselle wasn't the only one feeling a bit sick. In theory, of course, he'd always wanted to experience fatherhood one day, but at some time in the future rather than this year. Then again, there was no way he'd dream of telling Giselle this. She was his girlfriend, after all. They were a couple. If they were having a baby together . . . well, he couldn't possibly abandon her to go it alone. If it was happening, he'd put on a brave face and make the best of it. And hopefully everything would work out OK once the baby arrived and they fell in love with it, as they surely would.

Oh, but the timing really couldn't have been worse if it tried. Just when he'd been starting to realise that . . . No, don't think it. Don't even go there.

As he left the pharmacy, he almost leapt a mile when a heavy hand clapped him on the back and a voice bellowed, 'Whoa, bit jumpy! What have you been buying in there, eh? Something embarrassing? Picking up your next month's supply of Viagra, is that what it is? Ha ha HA!'

The owner of the loud voice and the heavy hand was a

customer called Brendan Banks, who thought he was the life and soul of every social gathering but who was in fact disliked by pretty much everyone. Lucas managed a fleeting smile. 'Just painkillers. Bit of a heavy night last night.'

'Ah, know the feeling well! Sore head, eh?' Brendan gave him another jovial thump on the shoulder. 'What you need is hair of the dog, that'll see you right!'

If only it could. And fate hadn't finished with him yet. Relieved to have escaped, Lucas reached Percival Square. As he made his way past number 23, he glanced up at the second floor just as a window was being closed and caught a glimpse of Essie's blonde hair and red jacket.

The next moment, the front door was pulled open and Zillah appeared, as stylish as ever in a silver-grey cloche-style hat and a long pale-blue jacket and trousers. Turning, she called up the staircase, 'Come on, darling, let's go!'

Lucas heard the thud of footsteps on the stairs, then Essie joined Zillah on the pavement.

'Morning!' Diamonds flashed in the icy sunlight as Zillah waggled her fingers at him and said brightly, 'Don't worry, I'm not taking her away from you. She'll be back in time for work. We're just popping out to the shops for a couple of hours.'

'No worries.' Lucas forced himself to sound as happy and relaxed as Zillah did. 'See you later.'

Had he managed it? God, he could barely bring himself to look Essie in the eye. If anything was going to take her away from him it would be the two small packets currently hidden inside his jacket pocket.

Five minutes from now, they'd know.

It took less time than that. Giselle, her bladder evidently

close to bursting point, cried, 'Oh, thank God, you've been *ages*,' and grabbed the packets from his hand.

'You need to read the instruct—'

'Are you kidding? You pee on a stick, it's not rocket science.'

'Which one are you going to use first?'

Giselle stared at him in muscle-clenched disbelief. 'Lucas, it's called multitasking, I'll pee on both of them at once.'

He stood outside the bathroom while she did the deed. When she emerged, they waited in silence for the seconds to tick by.

And there it was – one extra blue line and one brief statement in pink lettering: PREGNANT.

He'd hoped it wasn't true but deep down he had guessed it would be.

'Oh Lucas.' Giselle's voice was unsteady. 'I don't know what to say.'

'It's OK.'

'We were always so careful.'

'I know. I guess these things happen.'

She fell into his arms and Lucas held her close, because it wasn't her fault any more than it was his. These things *did* occasionally happen; you just really hoped they wouldn't.

'I'm sorry.' Her voice wobbled and broke as she fought back tears.

'Don't say that. It's fine. We'll get through this,' he murmured, stroking her curly hair, because what other response could there be?

'I can't stop shaking. I can't believe that an hour ago everything was normal . . . and now *this* is happening. We're going to have an actual baby.'

Were they? He held Giselle and gazed past her, saying nothing. But she sensed the change in his breathing and pulled back to look him in the eye. 'I couldn't not have it, Lucas. God knows, we didn't plan for this to happen . . . but I can't do that. Please don't ask me to.'

'I wouldn't. Of course not.' He shook his head and wiped away a tear that was rolling down the side of her nose.

'It would be easier, I know that. But I just couldn't go through with it.'

'It's OK, don't worry.'

'How about us? You and me?' Giselle searched his face. 'I mean, we've been together for six months and everything's been great, hasn't it? We get on so well together . . . I love you, and you told me you loved me too. Unless you were just humouring me.'

'Of course I wasn't just humouring you.' It had seemed like the right thing to say at the time.

'So . . . if you meant it, maybe this needn't be such a disaster after all. My mum's friend got pregnant the first time she slept with this guy she met. They'd only known each other eight weeks when they found out. And that was thirty years ago,' said Giselle. 'They've been happily married ever since!'

Lucas nodded. He needed to support her, to be on her side. She was right: sometimes these things happened and everything turned out for the best. They knew each other well. Everyone loved Giselle. He'd thought he loved her too, until very recently, when Essie had come into his life and his emotions had been whipped up into a maelstrom of uncertainty and confusion.

But now this had happened and any idea that he might have had a choice had been blown away.

Giselle was pregnant with his child.

And Essie wasn't.

Time to man up and accept that life was about to change. In pretty dramatic fashion.

'Is everything going to be OK?' Giselle touched his face and he saw the fear in her eyes. It was his job to reassure her.

He kissed her. 'Of course it is.'

Chapter 27

When you had limited resources and a building full of deserving cases, how on earth did you choose the most deserving?

Zillah, arriving at St Mark's Hospice, saw Elspeth in the otherwise deserted morning room, vigorously polishing the French windows that overlooked the terrace and the frost-gilded garden.

'Hello, darling, I got your text.'

Elspeth hopped down from the chair. Since the staff here had looked after her husband during his last months a decade before, she had worked as an enthusiastic volunteer, helping out wherever she might be needed. Naturally chatty and empathetic, she was also an excellent listener.

'Morning, Zillah! It's the lady in room eight; her name's Barbara.'

'How long has she been here?'

'Almost three weeks now. Such a lovely lady.' Elspeth lowered her voice. 'The thing is, it wasn't until I got talking to her sister yesterday that I discovered Barbara had raised her daughter, Gail, on her own. Then last year . . . Hang on, let me just close the door . . .'

Once she'd heard the story, Zillah knocked on the open door of room 8 and introduced herself to Barbara. She explained about the small wishes she tried to grant and said, 'Elspeth told me about the situation with your daughter. It must be so hard for you.'

'It is, but it can't be helped.' Barbara pointed to two photographs in plain silver frames on the windowsill. 'There she is, my beautiful girl. The one on the left was taken on her wedding day. And the other one's the most recent . . . Oh, my heart just wants to burst when I look at her. She's my whole world . . . always has been, since the day she was born.'

Zillah studied the photos. Gail had wavy fair hair, laughing eyes and pink cheeks. In the second photo she was visibly pregnant.

'That was taken two months ago,' Barbara explained. 'Just before my relapse.'

'You didn't tell her straight away?'

'I couldn't bring myself to do it. Poor Gail, she'd have insisted on flying home, and I couldn't put her through that, not in her condition.' Barbara paused. 'I'd been completely well for over two years when her husband was offered the job in Sydney. We thought the cancer was a thing of the past. And the doctors always warned her she'd have difficulty conceiving, so she was over the moon when she found out she was expecting. The plan was for me to fly over to Australia for a long holiday as soon as the baby arrived.' She sighed. 'But fate had other ideas.'

'She knows now, though,' said Zillah.

'Oh yes, of course. But by the time she found out, it was too late. She's at thirty-eight weeks now. No airline would allow her to fly home.'

In order to keep them safe, Barbara had effectively given up her last chance of holding her daughter and grandchild. And now her condition was worsening by the day.

Zillah said, 'Oh darling, aren't you lucky to have had each other for as long as you have?'

'I am,' Barbara replied. 'I wish it could have been longer, but there you go. I couldn't have asked for a better daughter, I do know that.'

'And I wish I could wave a magic wand that would make everything better, but I can't.' Zillah paused. 'Do you remember Elspeth asking you yesterday about the happiest day of your life?'

'I do.' Barbara was smiling. 'And there was only one answer.' She looked up at Zillah. 'She's already told you, hasn't she? I can tell. Is that why you're here?'

'Like I said, I can't produce a miracle.' Zillah perched on the chair next to the bed. 'But let's just say I happen to know the place you mentioned to Elspeth, and I do have the beginnings of a plan.'

Outside the Frog and Ferret in Pucklechurch on Thursday night it was cold, miserable and raining cats and dogs.

Inside, it was raining men.

Conor shook his head with amusement as the multicoloured lights around the stage flashed in time with the music blaring out of the speakers and Caz, wielding her microphone with panache, gave the song her all.

Next to him, Belinda was clapping along and joining in with the chorus, as was everyone else in the pub. Of course 'It's Raining Men' was Caz's signature song; she was never going to be the 'Ave Maria' type. She was also wearing an eye-poppingly low-cut silver-and-white jumpsuit reminiscent of Elvis in his later years. But even Conor had to admit that she didn't have a bad voice. She could hold a tune and entertain an audience. They were loving every minute.

And it was her birthday, so Conor had vowed to be nice to her for the entire evening. Which might be a stretch, but he was going to give it his best shot.

The song finally ended, to wild applause, and even Conor clapped. See? He could be nice. Up on the stage, Caz chose this moment to thank everyone for coming along tonight to help her celebrate and for letting her hog the karaoke.

'. . . Still, if you can't have everything your own way on your birthday, what's the point of it all, eh?' Her spiked-up hair quivered as she laughed. 'Anyway, just to say thanks again to all of you, and here's to the next year. Cheers!'

'Cheers,' echoed her captive audience, raising their glasses.

'And while I'm up here, can I also say how brilliant it is to have my friend Belinda here tonight looking so happy. All thanks to me for finding her that guy over there with her. Give us a wave, Conor, so everyone can see you!'

'No,' said Conor to general laughter. 'Stop trying to show me up.'

'Ha, but it's *fun*.' She turned back to address her audience. 'It's OK, Conor doesn't like me much and he gets right on my nerves, but that doesn't matter because he and Belinda like each other a lot. And I'm just glad she's found someone after all this time. Evie, do you like him? What's your verdict, babe?'

Evie, allowed to join them because it was a special occasion, gave a thumbs-up. 'I approve! He helped me with my maths homework last night, so he's definitely all right with me.'

Which was embarrassing but also kind of nice at the same time, because Evie leaned over and gave him a kiss on the cheek. Everyone in the pub said, '*Ahhh*,' and Belinda whispered, 'Caz wouldn't be doing all this if you got on her nerves. She loves you really.' After a pause, she added, 'And she's not the only one.'

Which startled Conor until he saw her incline her head to the left and realised she meant Evie.

Someone else took to the stage and began belting out 'Bat Out of Hell', and Caz danced with Evie in front of the speakers. As he sat there watching them, his fingers entwined with Belinda's, Conor realised that this was what it must be like to be a Z-list celebrity; despite never having met most of the other people here tonight, he was aware that they were watching him and talking about him.

Well, looked like he and Belinda were now officially a couple.

And really, who would have thought it? But then you never did know, did you, until it happened to you?

It still seemed impossible to believe that just two weeks ago, they hadn't even been on their first date. Belinda's endearing openness that evening had enabled them to admit that the attraction between them was mutual. The second date had taken place the next night, swiftly followed by date three the night after that. And now here they were, a recognised two-for-one item. Apart from the times spent working and sleeping, they'd scarcely been apart since.

It was a happy situation to be in. Belinda was great and so was her niece; getting along with Evie had been easy and a definite bonus. Although as Belinda had already told him, it was just as well. There was no way she'd be interested in a relationship with someone who wasn't prepared to love Evie too.

Smiling to himself, Conor watched as Evie and Caz stomped their way around the dance floor Meatloaf-style while the music blared out. His phone began vibrating against his chest and he took it out of his shirt pocket. When Zillah's name flashed up on the screen, he showed it to Belinda and mouthed over the blare of the karaoke machine: *I'll take it outside*.

The music was still so loud in the corridor that Conor needed to step into the adjacent deserted skittle alley to escape it.

He pressed Answer and heard Zillah say, 'Hello there, stranger! How are you?'

'Everything's great.' He'd barely seen her this week, what with getting home so late each night and leaving early for work the next morning. 'All going well.'

'Well that's good news. You deserve to be happy,' Zillah said warmly. 'Now, I'm just putting together another wish. How are you fixed for this Sunday afternoon – would you be free then, or is that no good for you?'

'Sunday afternoon . . .' Conor hesitated, his heart sinking at the timing. Sunday was Valentine's Day. Furthermore, Belinda's cousin had called earlier to invite them to lunch on that day. But if this was the date Zillah was suggesting,

217

it meant she'd already organised the hire of the private ambulance.

'You're busy, I can tell. Darling, don't worry about it, not a problem. Scarlett's here with Essie and she says she'd be more than happy to step in and take the photos.'

'Oh would she?' Honestly, what was that girl like? 'I had no idea she was a professional photographer.'

Too late he recognised the faint tinny echo at the other end of the line and realised Zillah had him on speakerphone. There was a rustling sound, followed by Scarlett retorting indignantly in his ear, 'You aren't a professional either. But my uncle was, and he taught me loads. I'm good at it!'

'I thought you had a stall at the vintage market on Sundays,' said Conor.

'I'll get my mum to run it for me. She enjoys helping out.'

'What kind of camera do you have?'

'Well, Zillah said you probably wouldn't mind lending me one of yours.'

Conor exhaled; the last time he'd seen Scarlett, she'd been unsuccessfully juggling in the street, surrounded by dropped plastic cups. No way was he going to entrust her with his precious Nikon.

'I'll do it,' he said.

Scarlett said hopefully, 'You'll lend me a camera?'

'No.' Conor was firm. 'I'll be there on Sunday to take the photographs.'

He could practically hear her eyes rolling in disgust. 'Why? Because you don't trust me?'

Exactly that. But seeing as he was still on speakerphone he said, 'I do trust you, but these are important moments

218

and if anything goes wrong it's not as if the photos can be taken again. Everything has to be perfect.'

'And you're saying I can't manage that?' She was feigning indignation now.

'I just don't want any mistakes.'

'I could go off you, you know,' said Scarlett.

God, thought Conor, *I wish you would.*

Chapter 28

Conor put away his phone and prepared to head back to the main bar. As he was about to open the door of the skittle alley, he became aware of voices in the corridor outside.

When he heard his name mentioned, he paused to listen.

'Where's Conor gone?' That was Evie asking the question.

'He went to take a call, must be outside. Well I'm not getting my hair wrecked. You go back to Belinda and I'll wait here for him. He won't be out there for long, not in that rain.'

'OK,' said Evie. 'But be subtle about it.'

Caz cackled with laughter. 'Me? I always am. Subtle's my middle name!'

Conor heard Evie's footsteps recede. He listened to Caz quietly singing 'It's Raining Men' to herself. Finally he opened the door and feigned surprise at seeing her there. 'Oh, hello. I was just on the phone.'

Caz said, 'That room's usually locked when they're not using it.' Her eyes were narrowed with suspicion.

'Is it? Well it wasn't tonight.'

She pushed past him and peered inside, looking left and right.

'What are you doing?' said Conor.

'Just checking you weren't getting up to no good in there with someone else.'

'Excuse me? Are you *serious*?'

Caz shrugged. 'If you *were* up to no good, you wouldn't be the first. And you're my responsibility, don't forget. I found you, I matched you up with Belinda. I'm the reason you're here now.'

'And I've already told her, I'm not the getting-up-to-no-good type. I've never cheated on a girlfriend in my life.'

'That's what they all say, isn't it.' She paused. 'Anyway, don't get narky with me. All I'm doing is looking out for my friend.'

'Right.'

'She likes you. I mean, a lot.'

'I like her too.'

'Haven't slept with her yet, though, have you?'

'Oh my God.' Conor stared at Caz. 'Is that *any* of your business?'

'Just wondered if there was a problem, that's all.'

'There is no problem.'

'Sure?' Caz gave him a saucy wink. 'No little quirks or foibles you're worried might scare her off?'

'I'm sure. No little quirks or foibles.' Conor couldn't quite believe he was standing here having this conversation. Actually, it was more like an inquisition.

'So why hasn't anything happened yet?'

Conor had run out of patience. 'Can we please stop this?'

'Is it because of Evie?'

Unable to reply, Conor closed his eyes; of course it was because of Evie. The prospect of spending the night in Belinda's bed while Evie slept in the next room, separated from them by only a thin wall, was too off-putting to contemplate. Yet the alternative – Belinda staying overnight at his flat in Percival Square – was apparently out of the question too. At sixteen, Evie was old enough to be left at home on her own, but Belinda couldn't bring herself to do that to her in case she felt abandoned and insecure as a result. It was, she'd already explained to him, a tricky time emotionally. Evie was a teenager just a few months away from sitting her GCSEs, and she needed to know she had Belinda's full attention. She couldn't risk upsetting her now.

That had been what Belinda had told him anyway. He wasn't accustomed to coping with teenagers, but under the circumstances it made sense.

Meanwhile, Caz was still waiting for an answer. Conor sighed. 'Yes, it's because of Evie.'

'Knew it.' Caz took a pack of chewing gum out of her bra and popped a piece into her mouth. 'Bit of a contraceptive, having her there within earshot. Am I right?'

He nodded.

'So that's why she's sleeping over at my place tonight. It's all arranged. Let's hope you've got your lucky pants on, eh? Because it's all going to happen at last!'

'I . . . you can't . . .' spluttered Conor, lost for words.

'I know, I'm brilliant. First I sorted out your barren wasteland of a love life, and now I'm fixing your sex life too. Just call me your fairy godmother.'

She was a nightmare. But undeniably a practical one. With

reluctance, Conor overcame his dismay and realised he needed to give in with good grace. She'd solved their problem for them and he was going to have to be grateful; it was only fair.

'Thank you,' he said dutifully.

'Thank you, Fairy Godmother,' Caz instructed.

'Thank you, Fairy Godmother.'

'Say: "You're amazing and beautiful and thoughtful and generous."'

He smiled. 'That's stretching it a bit.'

'OK, well give me a kiss then.' Caz leaned forward and tapped the side of her face.

Conor kissed her on the cheek. 'You're not as bad as you like to make out, are you?'

'I'd say I was bloody fantastic, seeing as I've now got the human contraceptive staying at my place.' She shook her head. 'Which means *I* won't be taking anyone home with me tonight. *On my birthday.*'

The rain had stopped, thankfully, by the time they left the pub and made their way back on foot to Limes Avenue. It was almost midnight but that didn't deter Caz from singing 'Single Ladies' and clattering along in her heels, doing her Beyoncé impression.

'Come on.' She grabbed Belinda's hand. 'You're still single too. He hasn't put a ring on it yet.'

As the two of them danced ahead down the road, Evie fell into step beside Conor. 'I'm staying at Caz's tonight, did you know?'

'I think she mentioned it.' Conor nodded casually.

In the glow of an orange street lamp, Evie tilted her head in order to peer up at his expression. 'And was she . . . subtle?'

'Not so you'd notice, no.'

'Oh well. It was nice of her to think of it, though, wasn't it?'

'I . . . suppose so.' Of all the excruciatingly awkward conversations to be having with a sixteen-year-old. Conor moved sideways to avoid a puddle.

'Belinda really likes you. It's been great seeing her this happy these last couple of weeks.'

'Well, that's good.'

'And Caz says even older people like you and Belinda still like to have sex sometimes,' Evie said brightly. 'So that's why I'm staying over at hers.'

In the darkness, the next puddle caught Conor unawares and was deep enough to slosh over the top of his shoe.

The next morning, Conor had set the alarm on his phone to go off at seven. Which was just as well, since at two minutes past, a message arrived on Belinda's phone, accompanied by a blast of Beyoncé.

Belinda's eyes were still closed. 'That's a text from Caz.'

'Who'd have thought?'

'Can you reach my phone?'

It was sitting on the shabby-chic white chest of drawers on his side of the bed. Conor really hadn't meant to look at the text, but the words on the lit-up screen kind of jumped out at him:

Morning! Marks out of ten?? Hope he doesn't have a teeny weeny peeny! Xx

'What's wrong?' said Belinda when he spluttered with indignation.

'I can't believe you're friends with her.' He angled the

screen so she could read the text. 'If you don't mind, I'll reply to this one.'

He typed:

Best ever. 20/10. Quite the opposite of teeny.

'I'm not sure I agree,' said Belinda as he pressed Send.

'You don't?'

'I don't.' She curled her arm around his neck and brushed a kiss against his mouth. 'Twenty-five out of ten, at least. Maybe even thirty.'

He laughed and drew her warm naked body closer. In no time, the phone lit up once more:

Ha, let me guess. Conor wrote that.

'What did I tell you?' said Belinda. 'She's always right.'

Forty minutes later, he was ready to leave the house. Belinda clung to him. 'I wish you didn't have to go. If only we could both take the day off work and just stay here together.'

'But sadly we have jobs,' Conor reminded her.

'I know. And at least it's Friday, so we've got the weekend ahead. I can't wait for you to meet Annette and Bill on Sunday – you're going to love them!'

Ah. He'd got distracted last night by Caz's interrogation in the skittle alley, and then by the subsequent arrangements for the rest of the night. 'Damn, I forgot to tell you. That call I had to take yesterday at the pub was from Zillah. I'm not going to be able to make it on Sunday after all – she needs me to help her that afternoon.'

'Oh no!' Belinda looked dismayed. 'Seriously? But it's all been arranged – I can't cancel the visit now. They're really looking forward to meeting you!'

'Look, I'm so sorry, but you don't have to cancel because

of me. You and Evie can still go along, and I'll meet them some other time.'

'But it's Valentine's Day, and I wanted to show you off! Can't you tell Zillah you're busy?'

Conor shook his head. 'She's organising one of her wishes.'

'Oh. But it's only photos. Couldn't she get someone else to take them?'

'No.' Conor stood his ground. 'I want to do them, and I'm not going to let her down.'

Chapter 29

Was everything OK between Lucas and Giselle? There'd definitely been a change in him this week, an almost indiscernible distance and air of distraction.

Not that anyone else appeared to have noticed it, but Essie had. Then again, the chances were that none of the other staff and regulars had a stonking great crush on Lucas, so they tended not to pay him quite as much attention as she did.

Discreetly observing him now, on Friday evening, Essie saw that the distance was still there. But he was evidently keeping the cause of it to himself. During a quiet period earlier, she'd asked him if he was all right, and for a brief moment it had seemed he was on the brink of saying something, as if he were tempted to tell her what was on his mind. But then he'd shaken his head and said, 'I'm fine,' before turning away and busying himself sorting out the float for the till.

He wasn't fine, though. Something was up, and even though Essie hated herself for thinking it, a problem with his relationship with Giselle could maybe . . . hopefully . . . *eventually* . . . mean good news for her.

God, I'm such a horrible person.

Oh, but if they could both just realise they weren't as perfectly matched as everyone thought, and have one of those amicable, pain-free break-ups, wouldn't that be the best possible answer to her dreams?

'Essie . . .'

'Yes?' Oh help, and now he was standing right behind her, hopefully not reading her mind. Essie half turned, her skin tingling at the unexpected proximity of their bodies behind the narrow bar. Honestly, this must be what it was like appearing on *Strictly*; with all that physical contact, was it any wonder emotions ran high?

'I need to pick up some more limes,' Lucas said, rather more prosaically. 'After that tequila party this afternoon we're almost out. I won't be long, but if Giselle turns up before I get back, can you tell her to head on up to the flat?'

'OK, no problem. Unless you'd prefer me to go out and buy the limes?'

Lucas shook his head. 'It's fine, I'll get them. I'll be twenty minutes, max.'

Fifteen minutes later, the door swung open and Giselle appeared, wrapped up in a burnt-orange coat and matching knitted scarf. With her auburn hair, she looked adorable.

'Here she is then!' Brendan Banks, in his usual position propping up the bar, beckoned to Giselle to join him. 'My favourite girl! Come here, come here. When it's all over between you and Lucas, I'm next in line, eh? Don't you forget that.' He beamed at Essie and said loudly, 'Isn't she a cracker?'

One of the downsides of working in a bar was having to smile politely and tolerate the inane comments made by customers who thought they were both irresistible and hilarious. As the girlfriend of the owner of the bar, Giselle was in much the same position. She and Essie exchanged a mutually supportive glance and Giselle said, 'Hi, Brendan, how are you? All good?'

'Never better, lovely lady! Come and sit by me, here you go, have a seat.' He appropriated a high stool and gave it an enticing pat.

'Actually, I'm fine standing.' Rather than take the offered seat adjacent to the coffee machine, Giselle moved over to the right and looked around. 'Where's Lucas?'

'Oh you don't want to worry about him, he's sloped off to meet up with one of his other girlfriends. You stay here with me, I'll look after you.'

Giselle grinned at Essie and, out of Brendan's angle of vision, did a good-natured eye roll.

'We ran out of limes, so Lucas popped out to pick up some more,' Essie explained. 'He said for you to go on up to the flat.'

'Actually, I'll wait down here for a bit. I fancy something to drink.' Giselle reached into her suede shoulder bag. 'Essie, could I have—'

'No you don't! Put your purse away.' Brendan made outraged chivvying gestures with his big hands. 'Let me get this. Essie, she'll have a large glass of Merlot.'

Giselle shook her head. 'No, honestly—'

'Don't offend me, now. I insist. All I'm doing is buying you a drink.'

'I know.' Giselle's tone was placating. 'And it's really kind of you. But not Merlot. Actually, I fancy an apple juice.'

'No no no,' Brendan blustered, appalled. 'What are you

talking about? It's Friday night, girl! Get a glass of wine down you!'

'Honestly,' said Giselle, 'I'd rather have apple juice.'

Brendan gave a snort of disgust. 'I don't know why you'd want one of those. What are you, pregnant?'

It was one of those chance moments when one person's off-the-cuff question coincides with a distinct lull in the general hubbub of conversation. At any other time it would have passed unnoticed, but not on this occasion. To be fair, Brendan always did sound as if he was bellowing through a loudhailer.

But as heads swivelled in their direction, it was Giselle's reaction that gave her away. If she'd laughed it off, dismissing the remark as the joke it was clearly meant to be, everyone else would have gone back to their own conversations and it would have been forgotten in moments.

Instead, her ultra-fair Celtic complexion turned pink, then pinker, then an unquestionable shade of puce.

A classic example of the more you realise you're starting to blush, the more impossible it becomes to stop it.

The colour clashed dreadfully with her burnt-orange coat and scarf.

And now everyone in the pub was staring at her. Including Brendan, who boomed into the silence, 'Bloody hell, you really *are* pregnant!'

Then the door swung open and Lucas appeared, framed in the doorway. All the heads, including Giselle's, now turned in his direction.

It was all very *Gunfight at the OK Corral*.

Lucas, who was carrying a bag of limes, said, 'What's going on?' and for a split second Essie thought this was news to him too. Then she saw the look Giselle gave him and the reason for his recent air of preoccupation became clear. Of course he knew.

'I asked for a soft drink instead of a glass of wine and Brendan made a joke about it,' Giselle told him. 'Then I went bright red and completely gave the game away.' She smiled and crossed the room to slide her arm around Lucas's waist, then turned and addressed everyone in the bar. 'Well, we were going to try and keep it to ourselves for a bit longer than this, but . . . seeing as the secret's out . . . Lucas and I are expecting a baby and we couldn't be happier!'

The whole bar erupted into cheers and applause. Lucas hugged Giselle, and Brendan yelled, 'Looks like the drinks are on you! Just so long as you don't try to fob the rest of us off with bloody apple juice!'

Lucas said, 'You're absolutely right. Now that everyone knows, we can celebrate. Jude, can you get the Moët out of the fridge? And we're going to need some extra glasses . . .'

Essie, on autopilot, busied herself collecting the slender champagne flutes and lining them up in rows along the highly polished bar. So much for secret dreams. It was the end, the definitive end of the fantasy she'd been harbouring, the one where Lucas and Giselle had their completely amicable parting of the ways.

Because there was no way that was going to happen now. They weren't just a couple, they were on course to becoming a family.

And now everyone was moving closer, gathering around the semicircular bar in order to congratulate the parents-to-be and join in with the celebrations. Jude had produced the bottles of champagne, Lucas was expertly uncorking them and Giselle was being told how wonderful she looked.

Essie, clearing away abandoned empty glasses, concentrated on telling herself that nothing had changed. She hadn't lost Lucas because he'd never been hers in the first place. He and Giselle were having a baby; all she could do was be happy for them and wish them well. Moments later, belatedly realising that Giselle still didn't have a drink, she poured her an apple juice. 'Here you go. And congratulations.'

Giselle took the drink with relief. 'Ah, thanks so much. Everyone's being so kind. It's ironic really,' she confided. 'Everybody's saying how well I'm looking, but when Brendan tried to sit me down next to the coffee machine, the smell made me feel as sick as a dog. Do I really look OK?'

Her huge amber eyes were clear, her Celtic skin was flawless. Essie said truthfully, 'You look amazing,' and in return Giselle gave her a hug.

'Thank you. You're so lovely. I still can't believe this is all happening. Obviously it wasn't planned, but it kind of feels so right. And we're both thrilled . . . I can't tell you how happy it's made us . . .' As her words trailed away, Essie turned to see Lucas beckoning for Giselle to rejoin him.

Once the glasses of Moët had been passed around to everyone present, Lucas, with Giselle back at his side, raised his glass. 'This is a special day. Thanks to all of you for being here to share it with us. Here's to Gi and me, and to our baby.'

'To Lucas, Gi and the baby,' everyone chorused, clinking their glasses together. 'Cheers!'

And Essie, belatedly grabbing a glass of her own, saw tears of joy swimming in Giselle's beautiful amber eyes.

Chapter 30

'This place is stunning,' Essie marvelled.

They'd reached the village of Colworth and turned in through the stone-pillared entrance gates, making their way along the narrow road that ran adjacent to a reed-lined river before driving over an ancient humpback bridge and approaching the ivy-clad hotel itself.

Colworth Manor Hotel was one of the gems of the Cotswolds. The manageress, whose name was Daisy, had evidently spotted them pulling up outside and was now coming over to greet them. Tall, dark-haired and with a beaming smile, she shook hands with Essie and Conor, then gave Zillah a big hug. 'Hello, how lovely to see you again. It's been ages! And look at you, as glamorous as ever. I have to tell you, your email made me cry.'

'As soon as I heard she wanted to come to Colworth, I knew everything would be all right. You wouldn't let me down. How's Hector?'

'I'm fantastic,' announced the distinguished-looking man who had to be Daisy's father, emerging from the hotel with two small dogs dancing around his highly polished shoes.

'Calm down, you two. This is Clive and this one's Clarissa,' he explained to the assembled party, before greeting Zillah with an affectionate kiss on each cheek. 'Darling, remind me again why we never married?'

Zillah laughed and tweaked the rose-gold silk tie he was wearing with his beautifully cut dark suit. 'I think it's because you were far too busy having a secret love affair with your future wife.'

'Ah yes, that was it.' Hector's gaze shifted past her, to the private ambulance currently crossing the stone bridge behind them. 'And here's your lady now. Daisy, is everything ready?'

Daisy bent to scoop up the smaller of the two dogs. 'Dad, have I ever been inefficient? Everything's perfect.'

By the time Barbara had been unloaded and reintroduced to Daisy and Hector, Essie had the Skype connection set up and running. As they entered the hotel, she placed the iPad in Barbara's hands. 'Here you are.'

'Mum, hello!' On the iPad's screen, all the way from Sydney, Australia, Gail was waving and showing off the bump beneath her yellow sundress. 'Look, I've got even bigger! I'm *huge*!'

'Oh darling, we're here! At Colworth Manor!'

'I can see exactly where you are,' Gail exclaimed as the stretcher was wheeled through the oak-panelled hallway with the open fire burning merrily in the fireplace. 'I can practically smell the woodsmoke. Is Aunt Peggy there with you?'

'Hang on, this nice young man is taking lots of photos to remind us of today. Peggy isn't here yet,' Barbara explained to her daughter. 'There are roadworks on the M4 and she's held up in traffic, but she'll be here soon.'

'Pretty brave of them to set up roadworks when Aunt Peggy needs to use the motorway,' said Gail.

They paused at the entrance to the ballroom.

'It's almost exactly the same,' Gail exclaimed. 'You didn't do this just for us!'

'No,' said Hector. 'There's an evening wedding reception taking place here at six o'clock. But if there hadn't been,' he added gallantly, 'of course we would have done it just for you.'

'He's such a charmer.' Zillah gave him an affectionate nudge.

The ballroom was bathed in golden light from the two overhead chandeliers, each of the circular tables was dressed in white and silver, and there were groups of candles, fairy lights in bottles, and posies of white flowers tied with gauzy bows.

Barbara's eyes were alight with joy. 'Oh darling, it's just like your wedding day all over again.'

'You were wearing that gorgeous pink dress,' Gail reminded her. 'You'll never know how proud of you I was when you stood up and gave that speech—'

'I'm here, I'm here, sorry I'm late! Those damn roadworks are an abomination.'

Essie looked up as Barbara's older sister Peggy came rushing into the ballroom. In her early sixties, she had shoulder-length mid-brown hair and was wearing a loose faded blue sweatshirt over pale jeans. She gave Barbara a kiss on the forehead. 'Barb, how are you doing? What's it like being back here?'

'Wonderful.' Barbara touched her sister's face with genuine affection. 'If I could get up off this contraption, I'd be dancing.'

Hector said, 'And I'd be dancing with you.'

Essie realised that Conor was no longer taking photos. He was standing back from the rest of the group, behind Hector and Peggy, staring down at the tiny screen on his camera. And he'd been frozen in that position for several seconds.

As the others continued to chatter away, Essie reached across to touch his forearm. 'Are you OK?'

Conor was barely aware of Essie's hand on his arm. He managed to nod and mouth, *I'm fine* at her, but the rest of his brain was in overdrive.

As yet, Barbara's sister hadn't so much as glanced in his direction. Understandably enough, all her attention was focused on Barbara. But when she did eventually look over at him, she was going to get a shock.

Oh, but look at her. The transformation was incredible. Who could have imagined that the woman standing in front of him now was the boss whose law firm he'd walked out of?

Because Barbara's sister Peggy was Margaret Kale, and while he'd been working for her, Conor genuinely couldn't recall ever having seen her smile. At work, she'd always had her hair pulled back in a tight bun, and had worn dark grey suits. Her manner had invariably been brusque and ruthlessly efficient. Beneath the lapels of her jacket had been a heart of solid ice.

Yet now here she was, informally dressed and looking ten years younger, laughing as she exchanged a joke with her niece in Australia and stroked her dying sister's hand.

Having collected himself and resumed taking photographs,

Conor managed to capture the exact moment she noticed him for the first time. Her smile slipped as her eyes widened in recognition.

He smiled slightly. 'Hello, Margaret.'

'Hello, Conor.'

Zillah looked surprised. 'Do you two know each other?'

After a moment's hesitation, Margaret said, 'Conor used to work for me.'

And Zillah, swiftly putting two and two together, said, 'Ah, I see.'

But now wasn't the time for awkward words of explanation, so Conor simply said, 'It's nice to see you again. Now, shall we take some more photos?'

And on the screen of the iPad, Gail said, 'Ooh, the baby's kicking! Mum, look, can you see? That's a foot!'

Twenty minutes later, a visibly tiring Barbara was wheeled off to the bathroom by the paramedics, prior to being taken back to the hospice. Margaret signalled discreetly to Conor. 'Could we have a quick chat? Would that be OK?'

He followed her outside and they sat together on a wooden bench in front of a stone fountain.

'I'm sorry.' Margaret wasted no time. 'I really am. And you might not believe me, but I've been close to contacting you so many times over the last couple of years.'

This was the last thing Conor had expected to hear. 'Why?'

'Because I wanted to thank you for making me rethink my life. You were the catalyst. I was blind, driven, self-centred. Nothing else mattered, only work. And winning, at any cost.'

Conor nodded. Well, that had been true enough.

'After you left the firm, I assumed I'd forget what had happened. But it wouldn't go away. Then Barbara became

237

ill, and all of a sudden I realised that being alive was more important than being successful. That was the other half of the wake-up call. Once Barbara was better, I knew I needed to change my life. I went part-time at the practice, and I took up yoga. I also have dogs now,' Margaret went on. 'And I love them to bits. After all those decades, I've finally learned to relax.'

Conor couldn't resist it. 'Apart from where roadworks are concerned.'

'OK, I'm still learning.' She smiled briefly. 'Maybe one day getting stuck in traffic won't drive me to distraction. But as yet, I haven't turned into a saint. I'm not Maria von Trapp.'

'So you wanted to write to me,' said Conor, 'but you didn't. Why not?'

'I wasn't sure you'd want to hear from me. Besides, you'd put your old life behind you. I googled you, found your website, saw that you were doing what you wanted to do.'

'I was.' Conor nodded, moved by her admission. 'I still am.'

'Do you earn less money now?'

Amused, he said, 'A lot less.'

'And you do this, too.' She gestured to his camera. 'It's wonderful! I had no idea.'

'I love doing it. Zillah's the driving force, though. She's the one who funds and arranges everything. I just turn up and take the photos.'

'And how about the rest of your life? Are you married? Do you have children?'

'Not yet.'

'Are you seeing anyone?'

'I am.' It was so weird, being asked these questions by Margaret Kale of all people.

'And is it serious?'

'We haven't been together for long. But it's going . . . pretty well.' Did he want to tell her about Belinda and Evie, to explain the fateful connection between the four of them? He hesitated, because it was that connection that had seemed to convince everyone else that the relationship was meant to be. As if, having found each other, he and Belinda couldn't possibly break up.

He was saved from having to make the decision by the metallic rattle of wheels as the doors opened and the stretcher was guided down the ramp.

'Well anyway, thank you.' Margaret rose to her feet. 'I'm glad you're happy now. And I'm extremely glad you made me stop and rethink my own life.'

The next couple of minutes passed in a flurry of farewells as Barbara was made comfortable. Finally, once Daisy and Hector had returned to the hotel and while Zillah and Essie were heading back to the car, Conor said, 'Margaret?'

'Yes?' She turned, and he experienced a pang of affection he'd never imagined feeling for his ruthless ex-boss.

'Thanks for telling me.' He broke into a smile. 'I'm glad too.'

Picking up his phone on Monday, Lucas mentally prepared himself to make the call. How could you love someone, yet dread the prospect of speaking to them? You'd think, after so many years, that he'd be used to it by now. But the sensation of impending doom or unease never went away.

Five minutes later, it was over. He'd spoken to his mother

and now his duty was done for another couple of weeks. She hadn't yelled and she hadn't wept, which was a bonus. She'd sounded OK, but as distant as ever. He always got the impression that she'd rather be doing anything else rather than having to speak to him. Well, the odds were that this was true. She was probably checking her watch the whole time, mentally willing him to get off the phone so she could get on with doing the only thing she really enjoyed doing . . .

Bloody hell, what a way to live, what a mess.

'Did you call her?' Giselle emerged from the bathroom wearing his too-big dressing gown and towel-drying her wet hair.

'Yes.'

'What was she like?'

'OK.' What else was there to say?

'Have you told her?'

'No.'

'She's your mother. She's going to need to know at some stage.'

'I know, but not yet. There's still plenty of time.'

Giselle nodded. She hadn't told her own parents yet, either. As she'd already said, it still seemed weird to both of them. The idea that they were having a baby was bound to take some getting used to.

'How are you feeling?' said Lucas, because she was looking pale and distracted.

'Still not great. A bit sick. It's like having the worst kind of exam nerves the whole time.'

'Come here.' He put his arms around her, breathed in the scent of her shampoo. 'Don't worry, the sickness won't last. You're going to be a fantastic mum.'

'Am I? God,' she exhaled, 'I hope so. It's nerve-racking, isn't it?'

Lucas could feel the tension in her neck and shoulders. Everything was about to change; of course it was a nerve-racking experience. He stroked her tangled wet hair. 'Just a bit,' he agreed.

Chapter 31

It was the very end of February and the snow was back, tumbling like fat feathers from an off-white sky. Conor had been working to clear the garden of a house in Monkton Combe. The owners, desperate to sell the property, had put it on the market a few days ago. Having been advised that it might help matters if their garden were less of an overgrown jungle, they had hired him to make it look better in the space of a single day.

Well, he'd given it his best shot in the few hours available, but it would be getting dark soon and enough was enough. Conor filled the last wheelbarrow with tangled dried shrubs and branches and ran it along the narrow path that led from the back of the house to the road at the front, where his van was parked.

He stopped dead when he saw who was standing on the pavement right next to it.

'It *is* you!' Scarlett, wearing a purple gilet and pink jeans, spread her arms wide with delight. 'I thought I recognised your van!'

'Hi.' Pushing the wheelbarrow up the lengths of board

he'd propped up to create a makeshift ramp, Conor emptied the garden waste into the back of the van. 'What are you doing here?'

'Nearly freezing,' said Scarlett.

'That's probably because you aren't wearing a coat.'

'It was sunny this morning! I came over here to help my friend out. She needed someone to look after her kids while she took her grandad to the hospital.' Her face lit up as she saw him throw the boards into the van and close the rear doors. 'Then she came home and I thought I'd be in time to catch the bus back into town but I just missed it and the next one isn't due for another two hours, so now I'm walking. That's if I don't collapse in the snow and die of hypothermia first.'

'Poor you,' said Conor.

Scarlett hugged herself and shivered dramatically. 'You wouldn't be heading into town, would you?'

'No.'

'Don't look at me like that, it's only a lift I'm after.' She rolled her eyes. 'I'm not planning to ravish you.'

As if he'd be scared. Conor relented. 'OK, I'll give you a lift.'

She beamed. 'You're my hero.'

He pulled open the passenger door of the van and hastily cleared the remnants of his packed lunch off the seat. 'Hop in, then.'

'I can smell mustard.' Having settled herself, Scarlett wrinkled her nose. 'Ew, there's an open sachet . . . How can you like that stuff? It's gross!'

Conor said steadily, 'Or you could always walk.'

Three minutes later, as they were driving up a hill, a small tabby cat darted out into the road ahead of them. A lorry coming in the opposite direction tooted its horn but only succeeded in confusing the animal, which scooted to the left then at the last moment darted back to the right.

As it disappeared from view beneath the oncoming vehicle's wheels, Scarlett screamed, '*Noooooo!*'

With a lurch of nausea, Conor braked hard. The lorry driver, clearly assuming he'd managed to avoid hitting the cat, grinned and shook his head, miming relief as he passed the van and carried on down the hill. Within seconds he was out of sight, on his way to wherever he was going.

Conor pulled into a gateway. 'You stay here,' he told Scarlett. 'I'll go.' There was a small unmoving mound visible in the gutter on the other side of the road and he feared the worst.

But Scarlett threw open the passenger door. 'No way!' She jumped down, almost losing her footing on the uneven snowy ground, and together they raced across the road.

The second before they reached the bundle of fur, it moved, jerked, then the cat's eyelids opened and it let out a shriek of pain. It struggled to its feet and stood there staring at them in terror, dazed and clearly traumatised.

'Well, he's alive,' said Conor. That was something at least.

'But there's blood . . . Where's it coming from?' Kneeling on the pavement as the cat let out another yowl, Scarlett breathed, 'Oh be careful . . .'

'I'm *being* careful.' Slowly approaching it, Conor wondered what the next move should be. 'We need something to wrap it in. There's a bit of sacking in the footwell of the van; could you go and fetch it?'

'I already saw it. You can't use that – it's dirty.' Scarlett slid her arms out of her purple gilet. 'Here, wrap him up in this.'

But as they closed in on the cat, it panicked and skittered between them, launching itself across the pavement and disappearing beneath a gap in the fence into dense undergrowth on the other side.

Conor swore under his breath.

'You were too slow.' As Scarlett spoke, they both heard the cat give another mew of pain.

'We can't leave it there.' Conor shook his head.

Scarlett gave him an are-you-mad? look. 'I *know* we can't leave it.' She scrambled to her feet, abandoning the gilet on the pavement behind her.

'You can't crawl under that fence,' said Conor. 'There's no room.'

'Don't be such a defeatist. Maybe not enough room for you. I can do it, though.' There were snowflakes in her hair and on the shoulders of her thin blue long-sleeved top. Ignoring his half-outstretched hand, she threw herself down, flattened herself out and crawled like a ninja through the narrow gap between the fence and the stony ground.

It was a long, high fence but Conor followed it until he reached the entrance to the overgrown area of woodland. By the time Scarlett eventually emerged from the tangle of dense undergrowth, he was waiting for her, holding the gilet.

'I can still hear him,' she panted as he reached out to help her up. She was covered in mud, twigs and dead leaves. 'He's over there to the left.'

'Let me try—' began Conor, but it was too late, she'd already plunged back into the undergrowth while the snow continued to fall steadily around them. Say what you like about the girl – and he frequently had – when she set her mind to something, Scarlett was unstoppable.

'Hello baby,' came her voice from somewhere in the bushes. 'It's OK, I'm not going to hurt you, just stay there . . . Oh!'

There was a sudden loud rustling of vegetation followed by a high-pitched yowl and a small splash.

The next moment, Conor heard Scarlett mutter, 'Oh shit,' followed by a gasp of frustration and a bigger splash.

OK, he had to find out what was going on. Following the sounds, he forced his way through the dense mesh of interwoven twigs and branches. Seconds later, he reached the pond, which must have been undetectable beneath a thick layer of leaves. The cat, he realised, had fallen into the water and Scarlett had launched herself in after it. Now, having scooped it up into her arms, she was struggling to climb out.

The sodden animal glared at Conor as he attempted to take it from her. It writhed and hissed when he wrapped it in her gilet. Having hauled herself onto dry land, Scarlett held out her hands. 'Let me have him. I don't think he likes you very much.'

Back in the van, Conor helped Scarlett into the passenger seat, then took off her sodden trainers and socks and dried her ice-cold feet with the not-very-clean towel he kept in the footwell. Then he took the spare pair of wellington boots out of the back of the van. 'You'll have to wear these.'

'What size are they?'

'Twelve.'

'And I'm a size five.' Scarlett's teeth were chattering like castanets and flakes of snow were sliding down her face.

He held out the first boot. 'Can't afford to be fussy, Cinderella. Now the other one, that's it. OK, let's go.'

They reached the nearest vet's surgery ten minutes later, by which time blood from the injured cat's stomach wound was starting to seep through the gilet and over Scarlett's pink jeans.

Forty minutes later, they were done. The vet had scanned the cat and found the contact details of its owners via the implanted microchip. Within twenty minutes of him calling them, they'd arrived in a flurry of panic while the vet finished cleaning and suturing the wounds. The elderly couple, utterly devoted to their six-year-old tabby, whose name was Barnum, had thanked Scarlett and Conor over and over again.

'You saved his life.' The little old lady clutched at Conor's sleeve. 'Thank you so much.'

'It was Scarlett who managed to catch him,' said Conor. 'She's the one who did all the hard work.'

'Well, you're angels, both of you. We're so grateful.' She turned to Scarlett. 'And to think, if I'd seen you in the street, I'd have been terrified out of my wits by the sight of you!'

Scarlett was taken aback. 'Oh . . .'

'You punk-rock types, that's what I mean. With your strange hair and those scary eyes and . . . you know, the outfits you wear.' The old lady gestured at her apologetically. 'We've always been frightened of you punk rockers, haven't we, Melvin? But now we know we were wrong. Underneath it all, you're just the same as normal people . . . Here, please let me give you something to thank you.' Her quavering fingers delved into her purse and she drew out a crumpled five-pound note.

'Oh no, please don't,' Scarlett protested. 'You don't have to do that!'

'But we want to, dear,' the little old lady insisted, 'because you rescued Barnum for us, and we love him so much. Please take it.' She pressed the note into Scarlett's hand. 'Just promise me you won't spend it all on drugs.'

Back in the safety of the van, Conor finally allowed himself to burst out laughing.

'You could have told me,' Scarlett grumbled, angling the rear-view mirror so she could see her reflection. Flinching at the sight of herself, she wailed, 'Oh God, no wonder she thought I was a drug-addicted punk.'

'It genuinely didn't occur to me,' said Conor. 'I knew what you'd been through, so I just didn't think how you'd look to them.'

It was the truth. There were still twigs and dead leaves caught up in Scarlett's spiky purple hair, and the snow had melted her mascara pretty dramatically around her eyes. There were fronds of pondweed stuck to the knees of her muddy, blood-stained pink jeans, and the filthy, far-too-big wellies provided the finishing touch.

Scarlett said, 'Well that makes you a moron, then. Oh, don't you *dare* . . .' Having spotted the phone in his hand, she held up her arm to warn him off.

'Just one photo,' said Conor.

'Looking like this? No way!'

'Looking like someone who searched for an injured cat and managed to rescue it. If you hadn't, it might have bled to death by now.'

'I'm amazed it didn't take one look at me and drop dead

with fright. Oh you bastard!' Scarlett had dropped her arm, and he'd taken a quick snap.

'Now smile,' said Conor. 'Without pouting.'

Despite her best efforts, she broke into a reluctant grin and raised her middle finger as the shutter clicked again.

'Perfect,' said Conor.

'You can go off people, you know,' Scarlett told him.

His phone rang and he answered it. 'Hi, you'll never guess—'

'For goodness' sake, where *are* you?' Belinda sounded aggrieved. 'You promised you'd be here by five o'clock. You're *late*.'

Chapter 32

'Beetroot.'

'Beetroot,' echoed Lucas. 'I didn't know you liked beetroot.'

'I don't.' Sitting up in bed, Giselle pulled a face. 'I mean, I didn't before. But I want some now, more than anything. Out of a jar. And it has to be the crinkle-cut slices in sweet vinegar.'

Lucas nodded. 'OK.'

'And piccalilli. The kind with the big crunchy bits of vegetable.'

'Fine. And is there anything you want to eat it with?'

He'd meant crusty white bread, or even chips. Giselle nodded vigorously. 'A spoon.'

'This is so weird,' said Lucas.

'I know!'

'Will it make you feel better?'

'I have no idea, I just know I have to eat it now.' She shrugged helplessly. 'Then I'll probably be sick afterwards. But that's just how it goes. If you're too busy to get them, it's fine, I'll go to the shop myself—'

'I'll get them, I'll get them now,' Lucas said hastily, because Giselle was throwing back the duvet, her eyes suddenly swimming.

'Sorry.' She pulled the covers back over her and soaked up the unshed tears with a tissue. 'I'm driving you nuts, aren't I? I'm driving *myself* nuts. Please don't hate me.'

'I don't hate you. It's just your hormones.' She'd reached the three-month stage now, and over the space of the last few weeks, her anxieties and mood swings had taken them both by surprise. But that was apparently par for the course and would settle down in time, along with the bizarre pregnancy cravings.

'I love you.' She gazed up at him.

'I love you too.' If he said it often enough, it would become true.

'And some Marmite crisps,' she called after him as he left the flat. 'And don't forget to phone your mother.'

'Right.' His heart sank further still at the reminder.

'And a coffee doughnut,' bellowed Giselle.

Outside, Lucas decided to get the call out of the way. It was almost midday, which he'd learned from long experience was about the best time to do the deed. Not that any time could be called good, but it was one of those things that had to be done, even if she never seemed to want to hear from him.

The sun was out and the square was relatively empty. Sitting down on an unoccupied bench, he dialled his mother's number and waited for her to pick up. As it rang, he imagined the scene at the other end and, as always, braced himself for the worst.

'Hello?'

'Mum? Hi. How are you?'

He heard the inevitable intake of breath, as if the sound of his voice had caught her off guard.

'Lucas, hello. I'm very well, thank you. Everything OK with you?'

'All fine. We're both fine, me and Giselle. She'd like to meet you, Mum. We were thinking of coming up to see you next weekend, or whenever would suit you . . .' He could sense the increasing tension at the other end of the phone, knew already what the answer would be.

'Oh Lucas, I don't think so. I mean, I'm sure she's a lovely girl, but she doesn't need to meet me. Maybe another time . . . not just now, though. I'm not up to having visitors . . . sorry!'

'You'd like her, Mum.'

'I know I would. And I'll meet her one day, I promise. But not yet.'

'Why not?'

'You know why not. Don't be cross with me, Lucas. I can't help it.'

All the old emotions were bubbling up. 'I know. I do know. I'm not cross, I just want to see you. How about if I come up on my own?'

'I'm fine, Lucas, but don't pressure me. I can't see you, I'm sorry. I just need more time.'

'But—'

'If you come to the house, I won't let you in.' The panic was rising in her voice, as it always did. 'Please don't do that, Lucas.'

'OK, calm down, I won't. I just want to know that you're . . . all right.'

252

Well, as *all right* as she could ever be.

'You deserve so much better than me.' Her voice grew husky, thick with tears. 'I've been a terrible mother. I do love you, Lucas. I love you so much. I'm s-sorry . . .'

'Mum, I—'

Too late. She'd already hung up.

This was how his calls to her always ended. Lucas sat back and pictured his beautiful, damaged, chaotic mother, who would now undoubtedly be sobbing in earnest. His heart ached for her as, for the second time in ten minutes, he said, 'I love you too.'

A hefty slap on the back almost knocked him off the bench.

'Blimey, fella,' boomed Brendan Banks, on his way over to the Red House for his first drink of the day. 'Don't let that lovely young lady of yours hear you say that!'

Since this was how rumours started, Lucas said firmly, 'I was talking to my mother.'

'Ha, course you were!' Tapping the side of his red nose, Brendan bellowed, 'No worries, I won't say anything. Mum's the word!'

'You don't have to stay and watch, you know,' said Giselle. 'It's pretty weird for me too.'

Lucas couldn't *not* look, though; it was like feeling compelled to view one of those David Attenborough wildlife documentaries where repulsive things were happening. Only instead of a gang of hyenas ripping an impala to shreds, he was having to witness his pregnant girlfriend eating her way through a bowl of hot piccalilli as if it were ice cream. And she'd been trying to hide it from him, but he'd spotted her cramming liquorice allsorts into her mouth too.

And to think people thought pregnant women eating lumps of coal was strange.

'Go,' said Giselle, waving her spoon at him. 'I know it's gross, but I can't help it. Go on downstairs and leave me to be disgusting in peace.'

Downstairs, Jude and one of the new barmen were busy serving a sizeable influx of German tourists. Joining them behind the bar to help out, Lucas did his best to ignore Brendan, who was sitting on his usual stool quoting what he thought were hilarious jokes from *Fawlty Towers*.

Finally, Lucas caught the eye of the customer standing patiently behind Brendan. 'Hi, what can I get you?'

'Well, I just have a question, if that's OK. Is . . . umm, Essie Phillips working here today?'

Lucas knew at once who he was. It was the air of hesitation that gave the game away; this was no casual friend dropping by on the off chance. 'No, she isn't. Sorry.'

'Ah. But does she work here?'

'Luckily for us,' declared Brendan, twisting round to view the man who'd asked the question. 'Brightened this place up a bit, I can tell you, since she's been here. Why, got your eye on her, have you?' He gave the newcomer a jovial nudge. 'Join the queue!'

'I'm an old friend.' The newcomer looked faintly horrified. 'I was hoping to see her today.'

'Sorry,' said Lucas. 'She won't be in.'

'But she might be at home.' For all his laddish banter, it was apparent that Brendan did actually realise he didn't stand a chance with Essie. Helpfully, he announced, 'She lives right here on the square. You could go over there now and see if she's in.'

Surprised, the man said, 'Really? Whereabouts?'

Lucas began, 'I don't think you should tell—'

But it was already too late; Brendan was off his stool and leading the stranger over to the door. Pulling it open, he pointed diagonally across the square. 'See the one with the purple front door and the Merc parked outside? That's the place. Just ring the doorbell and ask for her – she's got the flat on the second floor.'

'Thanks,' said the man. 'I will.'

When Brendan had returned to the bar, Lucas said, 'How do you even know which one is Essie's flat?'

'I was walking past the other week and spotted her.' Brendan looked smug. 'I waved up to her and she waved back.'

And for a ridiculous moment, Lucas experienced a pang of completely irrational jealousy, because Essie had waved to Brendan but she'd never waved at *him*.

Oh God, what's happening to me?

Essie, back from a trip to the shops, was just trying on the stripy trousers she'd picked up in Oxfam when the doorbell rang. Which meant she didn't have a moment to lose, because the bulky jacket she'd bought on eBay would be whisked away by the impatient courier if she didn't answer the door in three seconds flat.

Ah, shame the trousers were too small. But never mind . . .

Before the dreaded sorry-you-were-out card could be shoved through the letter box, she yanked open the front door and stopped dead in her tracks.

Stopped breathing, almost.

'Hello, Essie,' said Paul.

Chapter 33

Lost for words, Essie stared at Paul. How many times had she fantasised about this happening? Maybe on fewer occasions in the last week or so, but still more often than she would willingly admit to a living soul.

Except in her fantasies she hadn't been wearing stripy red-and-black trousers that were too small to fasten at the waist and too short to reach her ankles. It wasn't the most flattering look.

She saw his gaze slip, his attention inexorably drawn to the unfortunate trousers. Tugging the hem of her sweatshirt over the gaping zip, she said, 'Paul, what are you doing here?'

'I came to see you.'

'Why?'

'Can I come in?'

She had no clue why he was paying her a visit. The shock of seeing him again had caught her completely off guard. She hesitated for a second, weighing up the options. 'OK then. My flat's on the second floor. You can go first.'

Because the thought of him following her up the stairs while she was wearing these trousers was too much to bear.

'Right, wait here,' she instructed when they reached the landing. Closing the door on him, she rapidly wriggled out of the terrible trousers – with the big £3 price tag dangling from the waistband – and back into her jeans. Then she opened the door. 'Now you can come in.'

Once inside, he seized her by the shoulders, pulled her against him and kissed her, hard.

Crikey.

It was so unexpected, Essie didn't even have time to respond, either to protest or to kiss him back.

Finally releasing her, he held her face in his hands, which were on the chilly side, and gazed into her eyes. 'I've wanted to do that for weeks. Essie, I've missed you so much.'

It was still like one of those daydreams you never imagine actually coming true. In a state of disbelief, Essie realised her knees were trembling. 'Can we sit down?' she asked.

She stepped back, then perched on one end of the pale-blue sofa, facing Paul as he took a seat at the other end. His face was just as she remembered it, handsome and contained. He'd had a haircut within the last week or so. His grey cashmere Hugo Boss jacket looked immaculate, as always, and he was wearing a sage-green shirt she hadn't seen before. His cologne was the Tom Ford one she'd bought him for his birthday; it had been eye-wateringly expensive, but as he'd explained beforehand, rather one cologne you really liked than half a dozen cheap ones you wouldn't be caught dead wearing.

Grey Vetiver, that was the name of it. She couldn't say she loved it herself, but it definitely smelled expensive.

The highly polished shoes were new too. Essie glanced down at her own bobbly tartan socks and tucked them out of sight beneath her.

'What are you doing?' Paul glanced down.

'Hiding my bobbly socks.' It was a purely Pavlovian reaction; they'd always been one of his pet hates.

He exhaled. 'Essie, I don't care about your socks.'

OK, what?

'I care about you,' Paul continued. 'I tried not to, but I just couldn't do it. I wasn't able to stop thinking about you. Christmas was miserable. I kept wondering if you were missing me. Then I kept trying to call your number and realised you'd blocked me. That was like a punch in the stomach, I can tell you.' He stopped speaking and studied her intently, searching her face for an answer.

Essie swallowed. 'It was Scarlett's idea, she said it'd be easier. I was jumping a mile every time my phone rang, thinking it could be you. Once you were blocked and couldn't leave messages, I didn't have to think about that any more.'

'I didn't know where you were,' said Paul. 'It was a horrible feeling.'

'We're only in Bath. It's hardly New York City. You could have found out if you'd wanted to.' Essie remembered how she'd felt racing downstairs to answer the doorbell on Christmas morning, wondering if it was him and finding Lucas on the doorstep instead.

Back when Lucas had been her *least* favourite person . . .

'I know.' Paul shrugged. 'But I was pretty torn at first. You'd written that thing, humiliated my family. I missed you, but I told myself I needed to get over it, put you out of my mind. And that's what I've been trying to do ever since.' He sat back. 'Except it didn't happen. Here we are in the middle of March and . . . Well, here I am. I had to come and see you.' He spread his hands. 'Turns out I couldn't stay away.'

Essie pictured the look of disapproval on Marcia Jessop's bony face. 'And how does your mother feel about it?'

'It's my decision, not hers.'

This was fighting talk. 'Have you told her yet?'

'No. But I will.'

'Is she still angry with me?'

'That's irrelevant,' said Paul.

Of course his mother was still angry with her. So many questions. Essie said, 'Out of interest, how *did* you find me?'

'Giles from the office told me you were working at the Red House. I went over there just now and this guy told me where you were living.' Paul nodded approvingly as he took in his surroundings. 'Nice place. How much rent are you paying?'

Essie ignored the question. 'How's Ursula?'

'She misses you too.'

Ursula the crow-catching cat? Essie raised an eyebrow; this was highly unlikely to be true.

Paul said, 'OK, maybe not as much as me.' He leaned across, reaching for her hand. 'How about you, Ess? Have you missed me?'

It was weird enough just seeing him again, let alone hearing him speaking to her like this. Prevaricating, she said, 'We broke up three months ago. What makes you think I haven't found someone else?'

Paul frowned. 'Have you?'

'Maybe.'

'Ess, tell me. Is there someone else?'

Essie felt her pulse quicken. She conjured up an image

259

in her mind of Lucas, dark eyes glittering as he met her gaze while that irresistible half-smile lifted the corners of his beautiful mouth. The next moment, as he stood in front of her, he was joined by Giselle. And now the two of them, Lucas and Giselle, were holding hands, turning to look at each other, Giselle's baby bump clearly visible beneath her favourite blue paisley-patterned shirt.

Stop it. Essie deleted the mental image. Yes, she'd met someone else, but he wasn't hers and she couldn't have him, even if he was interested in her in return, which he probably wasn't. In an attempt to get over Lucas, she'd been spending the last few weeks on a concentrated mission to find someone else she could like instead, but it hadn't happened and it wasn't the kind of thing you could magic out of thin air. It was probably just too soon to be interested in someone new.

But this wouldn't be someone new, would it? Her mouth dry, Essie considered her options. It was someone old, someone she was already completely familiar with. It was Paul, and they'd spent practically the whole of the last year together, would still be together now if only she hadn't written that awful round robin. It had been her own fault and she didn't blame him one bit for reacting as he had.

That he was here now, prepared to forgive her and put the unfortunate incident behind them was . . . well, quite moving actually.

He must really love her.

And getting back together with him would definitely take her mind off Lucas.

'Well?' Paul was still waiting.

'There's no one else,' said Essie.

He nodded. 'Good.'

'How about you?'

'No one for me either.' He paused. 'So that makes both of us single.'

'Looks like it,' said Essie.

'What d'you think, then? Should we give things another go?'

A quiver of anticipation ricocheted down her back. 'Maybe we should.'

'Sure about that?' Paul broke into a smile and moved up the sofa towards her. 'You don't exactly sound overjoyed.'

'I think I'm still in a daze. You knew you were coming over here to say this today,' Essie babbled. 'But for me it's all been a complete surprise. I wasn't expecting any of this to happen.'

'You won't need much time to get used to the idea. Let me give you a reminder of what we've both been missing.'

And this time when he took her in his arms, the kiss was slow and leisurely and romantic, and it felt reassuringly familiar, as if she were coming home.

Speaking of which . . .

Downstairs, the front door had opened and been closed again, and Essie heard the double thud that meant Zillah was kicking off her high heels. The next moment, from the foot of the stairs, she called, 'Essie, are you up there?'

'Won't be a second,' Essie told Paul. She jumped up from the sofa, opened the door and leaned over the polished mahogany banister to wave at Zillah. 'Yes, I'm here!'

'Oh hooray.' Zillah was wearing a zebra-print coat and a huge emerald necklace over a slim-fitting black wool dress. 'Darling, my book group's arriving at three and I haven't had time to get the food in. Could you be an angel and pop down to Waitrose for me? I just need you to pick up four boxes of mixed hors d'oeuvres and a couple of bottles of that nice Prosecco, you know the one I mean. Ooh, and a decent-sized chocolate cake too.'

'No problem. I'll head down there in five minutes.'

When Essie had closed the door, Paul said, 'Why do you have to do that?'

'What d'you mean?'

He was frowning. 'She clicks her fingers and you rush off to do her shopping for her?'

'This is Zillah's house. She's eighty-three.'

'That's no reason for her to take advantage of you.'

'She isn't taking advantage,' said Essie. 'I help her out in exchange for paying less rent. Otherwise I couldn't afford to live here.'

'Ah right, that explains it. I did wonder, when that guy told me you had a place on Percival Square.'

That guy. Had it been Lucas?

OK, stop thinking about Lucas. Essie reached for her coat and bag. 'I'll introduce you to Zillah. She's amazing, you'll love her.'

'Give me another kiss first, Cinderella.' Paul grinned. 'And don't worry, you won't have to be a skivvy for much longer. Now we're together again, you'll be leaving this place and moving back in with me.'

Chapter 34

'Well?' said Essie a week later as they sat around the table in Zillah's kitchen. 'Am I brilliant or what?'

Conor put down Zillah's iPad and heaved a sigh. 'Look at your eager little face. You make me feel like Simon Cowell about to tell some deluded girl she's tone deaf.' He pointed to the screen. 'Essie, I'm sorry, but these really aren't great.'

'How can you even think that? Oh!' Leaning across, she seized the iPad. 'Those were the wrong ones. Hang on, sorry about that, they're the rubbish ones. *These* are the good photos . . .'

Rolling his eyes good-naturedly, Conor took the tablet back from her. 'And that's the kind of mistake you should never make.'

Essie watched him gleefully as he began scrolling through the second set of photographs. She saw him slow down and look more closely. On Sunday evening, over at the Red House, she'd told him she was going to take some photos of him so he could see if she was up to the task if ever he was unable to be there during one of the wishes. Ha, but what he didn't know was that Scarlett had also been taking surreptitious photos on her phone during the course of the evening . . .

'No, sorry.' Conor shook his head. 'These aren't good enough, either.'

'What? Are you crazy?' Scarlett had taken such care, editing and adjusting her very best photos. Essie stared at him in disbelief. 'They're fantastic.'

'You think so?'

Outraged, she said, 'Anyone can see they are!'

'Just teasing,' said Conor. 'They're great. I'm impressed.' He nodded at her. 'Well done.'

'Thank you! So does this mean I'm good enough to stand in for you if there's ever a time when you can't make it?' Essie was triumphant; she couldn't wait to tell him that—

'Well,' Conor tapped the screen of the iPad, 'it'd make more sense for Scarlett to do the job, seeing as she was the one who took these.'

Zillah burst out laughing and Essie rocked back in her chair. 'I don't believe it! How did you *know* that? How could you possibly tell?'

'I caught her taking sneaky photos of me. Twice.' Conor looked amused. 'Which was probably the first clue. After that, it didn't take a genius to work out what was going on. I did almost say something at the time, then thought it'd be more fun to pretend I hadn't noticed and see how you two decided to play it out.'

'So annoying. We thought you hadn't spotted a thing. But it's worked, hasn't it?' Essie beamed at him. 'I'm so glad! And Scarlett will be thrilled.'

'Does she even know how to use a proper camera?'

'Yes, she does. Her uncle spent ages a couple of years ago teaching her all about lenses and light meters and shutter speeds. She knows her stuff, I promise.'

Zillah pointed to one of Scarlett's photos on the iPad. 'This is my favourite of all of them. How brilliant is that? Your face!'

Together they leaned over to study the photo of Conor and Zillah standing together watching as, across the room, Caz said something outrageous to Belinda. Caz was making some over-the-top gesture with her arms, her head thrown back as she shrieked with laughter. Next to her, Belinda was grinning at whatever it was she'd just come out with. But it was the expression on Conor's face, in the foreground, that really spoke volumes.

'Look at you,' Zillah exclaimed. 'Talk about a picture painting a thousand words. This one's certainly telling us how you feel about Caz!'

'Don't worry, she's never going to see it,' Essie reassured him. 'You can delete the photo. Poor Caz, I know she drives you nuts, but she means well. She's just a bit loud and excitable.'

'A *bit*?' Zillah feigned horror. 'I thought I was going to have to pop back here and pick up some earplugs. She's no shrinking snowflake, that's for sure!'

The doorbell shrilled and Conor let out a groan. 'Oh God, don't tell me that's her, come to give me grief.'

Essie jumped up. 'It's OK, you're safe, it's only Paul.'

'Oh dear, *only Paul*,' Zillah said teasingly. 'Don't let him hear you say that.'

Essie opened the door and gave him a hug. 'Come on through, we're in the kitchen. Conor's just agreed that Scarlett can stand in for him if he can't be there to take the photos. Isn't that great?'

'If you say so, it's definitely great.' Paul gave her a kiss and followed her through to the kitchen, greeting Conor and Zillah with a polite smile and refusing Zillah's offer of a drink because he was driving.

'And I've had to park on yellow lines, so we need to make a move,' he told Essie. 'Table's booked for eight and we don't want to be late.'

He was taking her to a new French restaurant and looking handsome in a cream linen jacket and dark trousers. Essie said, 'I'm all ready,' and was glad she'd worn her best navy dress.

'You both look very smart,' said Zillah, and Essie felt a squiggle of pride. It had been a week since Paul had appeared on her doorstep, and she was still getting used to the fresh turn her life had taken. But things were going well, considering. Tonight would be the third date of their renewed relationship, and Paul was still being wonderfully attentive. She hadn't asked Zillah outright what she thought of him, but there was no need. As far as boyfriends went, Paul ticked all the boxes. He was perfect.

And his phone was ringing. He took it out of his pocket, then hesitated. Essie glimpsed the caller's name as it flashed up on the screen. 'Oh, it's your mum, you can't not answer it!'

See? I'm on my best behaviour too.

Paul looked at her and Essie pointed encouragingly to the still-ringing phone. 'Speak to her!'

He exhaled and pressed Accept.

'Hi, Mum. Yes, everything's fine. No, no problems. It's OK, I've done that. Yes, and they've all been taken care of too. I haven't forgotten anything.' He paused and listened, then said, 'You don't have to worry, all under control. How are things with you?' Another long pause while he listened, then, 'Well that's good. Yes, I will. No, don't you worry. OK, bye now. Speak soon. Bye.'

The call ended. Paul looked relieved. 'There, done. Shall we go now?'

Once they were outside, Essie said, 'You said you'd told her about me and she was OK with us being back together. But you haven't told her, have you?'

Another pause. 'What makes you think that?'

'Because neither of you mentioned me. And listening to your side of the call sounded a lot like the last time she went away and left you to look after her house.' Essie eyed him steadily. 'So, where is she this time?'

Paul shrugged, caught out. 'Machu Picchu.'

'Excuse me? Was that a sneeze?'

'Peru.'

'Right, of course she's in Peru. How long for?'

'Three weeks,' he conceded with reluctance. 'She's walking the Inca trail.'

'And she doesn't know about me,' said Essie. 'How soon after she left did you come and see me?'

'OK, listen.' Paul exhaled heavily. 'I've missed you. I wanted us to get back together. And this last week has been great, it's all going really well, but that wasn't guaranteed to happen, was it? Things might not have worked out. So why would I want to upset Mum if there's no need for her to know until we're sure? I can't tell her now, because that would just ruin her holiday. But if we're still going strong when she gets back, I'll tell her then.' He shook his head as if she were doubting him. 'Of course I will!'

267

'You should have been honest with me.' Essie sighed. 'You told me everything was OK and I believed you.'

'Oh you mean like you pretended you liked my mother, when all the time you couldn't stand her? And I only found out how you really felt when I read that letter you wrote after you'd sent it to everyone you knew? Is that the kind of honesty you're talking about?'

Ah. *Bum*.

'Look,' Paul went on, 'I know what Mum can be like sometimes, but she's still my mother. I was devastated when you wrote that letter, you know I was. But eventually we're all going to be able to put the awkwardness behind us and be happy again.'

Was he right? Essie had been taken aback by his white lie, but it did make sense when you thought it through.

Plus, of course, Paul's white lie had been relatively minor. What she'd done had been so much worse.

'So, are we going out for dinner,' he said, 'or have you decided you hate me too much?'

A flicker of humour; that was a good sign. He'd explained why he'd done what he had, and she was able to admit he had a point: they did need to be sure the relationship still worked before breaking the news to his terrifying mother.

Even the thought of it made Essie feel a bit queasy. Still, it would be worth it.

Was she happier with Paul than without him, and was he making it easier for her to get over the embarrassing fantasy crush on Lucas?

He had to be making it easier, surely?

'I'm starving,' Essie said with a smile. 'Let's eat.'

Chapter 35

Essie had just emerged from Bath Guildhall Market with three multicoloured helium balloons bobbing above her head when she spotted Giselle across the road and called out to attract her attention.

But Giselle didn't hear her. She was leaning on the carved stone balustrade just along from Pulteney Bridge, gazing down into the frothing waters of the famous weir below. Her auburn hair was whipping around her head in the lively spring breeze, her hands were clasped in front of her and she was clearly lost in thought.

Just as Essie was wondering whether to cross Grand Parade and say hello, she saw Giselle straighten up, turn away from the balustrade and pause, staring into the middle distance. The next moment she checked her watch, turned again and without any warning stepped off the pavement into the road just as a—

'Fucking idiot,' bellowed the cyclist, swerving wildly to avoid her as Giselle gave a yelp of alarm and stumbled backwards, tripping over the kerb in her haste to reach the pavement. She lost her balance and landed clumsily on her side as the disgusted cyclist rode off, yelling over his shoulder, 'Serves you right, stupid bint!'

Her heart hammering, Essie raced across the road and knelt beside Giselle, who was white-faced and trembling with shock. 'Oh God, are you OK?'

Giselle took a couple of steadying breaths and manoeuvred herself into a sitting position. 'I think so. What an idiot.'

'He just rode off, the bastard! If we call the police, they'll be able to catch him on CCTV.'

'Not him.' Giselle shook her head. 'I meant me. It was completely my fault, I just wasn't concentrating.' She managed a smile. 'Lucky it was only a bike and not a bus. I'm fine, really.'

'Look, Daddy, balloons!' A small boy further along the pavement was pointing above his head, and Essie followed his gaze. 'Damn,' she muttered as she saw her three balloons sailing up into the sky.

'Oh no, were they yours?' Giselle was dismayed. 'I'm so sorry. I'll buy you new ones!'

'Let's not worry about the balloons,' said Essie. 'I'd rather make sure you're all right.'

Once she was back on her feet, Giselle said, 'Honestly, I'm not hurt at all.'

'Are you sure you shouldn't get yourself checked over?'

'There's no need. I didn't even crash to the ground, it was just a stumble. I should have been looking where I was going.'

'I called out to you before it happened, but you didn't hear me,' said Essie.

'Sorry, I was miles away.'

Essie studied her more closely. 'Is everything all right?'

Beneath the determinedly bright smile, there was a hint of tension.

'With me? Everything's fine!'

But the underlying anxiety was still there. Concerned, Essie lowered her voice. 'Are you sure?'

Apart from the traffic swishing past them, there was silence. For a couple of seconds Giselle gazed past her at the weir beyond the balustrade. Finally she said, 'It's just life, I suppose. Stuff happens out of the blue and it knocks you for six. All of a sudden everything's different and your whole future's veering off piste. Well, you know how that feels, don't you? It happened to you too.'

'I think sooner or later it happens to us all.' Essie's heart went out to her. 'But it's bound to be scary, having a baby when you hadn't planned for it to happen. I mean, it's a whole human being and you're responsible for it!'

'I know, I know. It is scary.' Giselle nodded and mustered another smile.

'You'll be a brilliant mum.'

'I hope so. Look, d'you fancy going for a coffee and something to eat? I mean, if you're not busy . . .'

'Oh, I can't.' Essie pulled a regretful face. 'I have to get back. I need to take some stuff home to Zillah, then my shift starts at six.' Sensing that Giselle was wanting to offload her anxieties about the baby, she added, 'But I'm free for lunch tomorrow, if you are? We could go to Aqua, my treat. Then we'll have time for a proper chat . . .'

But Giselle was already shaking her head. 'I'm working tomorrow. Oh well, never mind.'

'We'll do it some other day, definitely. Any time you like,' Essie assured her. 'Just say the word.'

'I will. Go on, you'd better get back to Zillah.' Giselle gave her a hug. 'Thanks for coming to help. And I'm sorry about the balloons. Will you at least let me give you some money for them?'

'Don't worry.' Essie waved away the offer. 'Lucas asked me to pick them up for Maeve's birthday tomorrow and gave me twice as much cash as I needed. I'll just go and buy some more. And you look after yourself,' she added.

'I will.'

'Be careful crossing the road, too.' Essie was struck by another idea. 'Ooh, we could meet for lunch on Saturday if you like? I'm free then.'

'Thanks, I'd love that.' Giselle smiled. 'I'll check my shifts and let you know.'

When Conor had made his promise to Scarlett, he hadn't expected that she would ever actually need to take his place. But that was fate for you: sometimes it seemed as if it had a sense of humour all of its own.

He'd only said it on Tuesday. Now here they were, just four days later on the morning of the next wish, and Zillah was regarding him like a stern – yet still glamorous – headmistress.

'You can't do it.' She shook her head. 'How would you feel if it was your germs that finished him off?'

Conor's shoulders slumped in defeat. He'd woken up with a high temperature, a banging headache, a sore throat and one of those irritating coughs that announce to the world that you couldn't be more infectious if you tried. If he'd been due to work today he would have gritted his teeth and got on with it. He was also completely capable of taking photos. But when the recipient of the wish was so danger-ously weakened by his own illness, the prospect of passing on an active virus was a risk they simply couldn't afford to take.

That would practically be murder.

'OK.' He nodded, because he didn't want to be a murderer. 'You're right.'

Essie said eagerly, 'Do you want me to tell Scarlett she's doing it?'

'We don't know yet that she can. She might be working.'

'It's Saturday. She'll be free.' Essie took out her phone.

Conor said, 'You'd better let me speak to her, then. She's going to need to borrow my camera.'

Essie called Scarlett's number and handed the phone over to him as it began to ring. 'Mind your ears, she might scream. This is going to be like the understudy in the West End musical discovering that the star of the show's just broken her leg.'

Oh joy. Conor coughed, then braced himself for Scarlett's reaction.

But when she picked up on the fifth ring, he didn't even get the chance to draw breath and speak.

'Morning!' she chirruped. 'Let me guess, you're calling your lonely single friend to boast about your amazing sex life, am I right? Well you can just shut up, because it's been so long since I saw a man naked, I can't even remember what they look like. In fact it's been so long since I last had sex, I'm seriously thinking of taking Danny up on his offer. I mean, would that really be such a terrible idea? What d'you reckon, Ess? Do you think I should?'

It was struggling not to laugh that set off Conor's explosive bout of coughing, causing Scarlett to give a yelp of alarm. 'Oh my God, what's *wrong* with you, have you gone down with Ebola? You sound like an elephant seal!'

Essie, needless to say, was listening in and doubled up laughing.

Conor managed to stop coughing and said, 'Actually, it's me. Essie lent me her phone. And yes, I do think it would be a terrible idea to take Danny up on his offer.'

'People shouldn't be allowed to use other people's phones,' Scarlett wailed. 'It goes against the Trade Descriptions Act. You should be arrested for *fraud*.'

Amused, Conor said, 'Who's Danny?'

'One of my exes. We broke up two years ago.'

'Why?'

'Because he cheated on me.'

'And now?'

'He's single, I'm single, he keeps trying to persuade me we should be friends with benefits.'

Conor already disliked him. 'And are you tempted?'

'Honestly? Most of the time, no, but every now and again I kind of think it might be nice.'

'Is *he* nice?'

'Danny? Not really.' Scarlett sighed. 'He's a bit of a prat. But you know how it is, sometimes you get lonely. Well, not you, obviously, because you've got Belinda now. But I do. Anyway, enough about that. I'm sure you didn't call me to discuss my non-existent love life.'

'Are you free this afternoon?' said Conor.

'Why?' she said playfully. 'Are you offering to be my friend with benefits?'

He smiled; she was incorrigible. 'Listen, you heard me

coughing. I've picked up a virus, which means I can't take the photos this afternoon—'

'Really? Oh thank you! I'll do it, I'll do such a good job.' Scarlett gave a little whoop of delight. 'I won't let you down, I promise!'

Chapter 36

'This is where I was standing when I first saw her.'

Zillah followed the direction of Jerry's bony finger, pointing over to the undulating gallops beyond the stables.

'She was wearing a red shirt and black jodhpurs,' Jerry continued, 'and her hair was flying out behind her as she raced down the hill. Later, when she led the horse back into the yard, I saw her close up. And that was all it took. One look, and I knew she was the girl for me.'

'How wonderful. Go on,' prompted Zillah.

'A fortnight later, she came into my office and said, "Have you ever wondered what it'd be like to kiss me?" And I said, "Why?" And she said, "Because I've been wondering what it'd be like to kiss you." Those were her exact words.' Jerry broke into a smile. 'And that's how it happened. She was the best girl I ever kissed and the last girl I ever kissed. We were married for thirty-three years.'

'Happily married,' Zillah reminded him.

'Oh yes. It's been ten long years since she died and I've missed her like crazy every single day. I can't wait to see my beautiful girl again.'

The bay mare in the stable behind them let out a whinny, and Jerry turned his head to greet her. 'Hello there, gorgeous.' Reaching up to stroke her velvet-soft muzzle, he murmured, 'Fresh straw and warm horse. Isn't that the best smell in the world?'

In response, the mare rested her cheek against the side of his face.

Zillah watched as Scarlett took more of the photos that would bring comfort to Jerry's two sons, currently serving overseas, and to his extended family spread across the world. Jerry's simple comment about looking forward to seeing his wife again continued to echo in her mind. Would it happen when her own turn came . . . would her beloved William be there, ready to greet her? Would he be cross that she'd kept him waiting for so long? Worst of all, would he make fun of her appearance because time had marched on and left its marks on her face but not on his? Or would she magically become younger again, so that they were still a perfect match?

'Excuse me . . . I'll be back in just a moment.' Battling with her emotions, Zillah retreated and headed for the parking area, where she'd left the car. In her haste, and whilst she was busy searching her bag for tissues, she didn't look where she was going until she hit an uneven patch of ground and felt her ankle go over.

Ow. Stumbling and wincing as a red-hot pain shot up her leg, she only just managed not to fall to the ground. Reaching out, she rested her hands on the car's bonnet and caught her breath, allowing the waves of pain to expand and worsen before they receded.

Please don't let anyone have noticed. Because if they had, she already knew what they were going to say.

Still breathing through the onslaught of pain, for a couple of seconds Zillah thought she'd got away with it. Then came the sound of footsteps racing across the yard in her direction.

'I saw you slip,' Scarlett panted, skidding to a halt. 'Are you OK? Give me the keys so I can open the door, then you can sit in the car.'

'I'm fine.' The silver lining was that twisting her ankle had effectively banished the incipient tears that had brought her over here in the first place. 'It's nothing to worry about,' she insisted. 'You know what these little sprains are like – hurts like crazy for a minute, then the pain goes away. It's getting better already, I can feel it.'

This was true, but sadly it didn't prevent Scarlett from looking askance at Zillah's midnight-blue patent stilettos. 'Are these the new shoes Essie was telling me about, from L. K. Bennett?'

'Maybe.'

'I think she warned you they were too high, didn't she?'

'I'm used to heels,' Zillah protested. 'I've worn them all my life.' She adored stilettos; they made her feel better about herself.

'I know, I know.' Scarlett was sympathetic. 'But these are higher than you usually wear.'

'And don't they look gorgeous? Don't nag, darling. Flat shoes just aren't me. There, all better now.' The pain had lessened enough for her to waggle her ankle. She gingerly put some weight on it and struck a pose. 'Ta-daaaa! See?'

'OK, you win. If you're sure you're all right,' said Scarlett.

When they returned, Jerry was greeting the rest of the horses in the yard. Scarlett was taking yet more photos when her phone rang – not for the first time that afternoon – and she rolled her eyes. 'It's him again. Shall I answer it this time?'

'Go on.' Zillah could only imagine Conor's frustration. 'Put him out of his misery, the poor boy.'

'Hi, Conor,' Scarlett said happily into the phone. 'I haven't dropped your camera yet! And I've taken some great pictures. Jerry keeps telling everyone he's so glad he got me instead of you.'

Zillah listened as they went on to exchange technical talk about apertures and light meters. Then Scarlett hung up, sent several of the uploaded photos over to Conor and waited until her mobile rang again.

This time she put it on speakerphone.

'They're good.' Conor's tone was grudging.

'They're better than good.' Scarlett did a little air-punch. 'They're magnificent.'

'You did a great job. I was worried you wouldn't,' said Conor, 'but you did.'

'See? You didn't need to worry.'

'I know that now. You have talent.'

'Oh, I have *many* talents.' Scarlett grinned mischievously. 'I promise you, I'm full of surprises.'

At the other end of the phone, Conor sneezed and Zillah called out, 'Bless you!'

'Thanks.' Conor paused, then said, 'Scarlett, could you take me off speakerphone now?'

Scarlett did so, then listened to him for a few seconds. Zillah watched with interest as a flush of pink coloured her cheeks before she smiled slightly at whatever Conor had just said, and murmured, 'No, you're right.' Then, having listened some more, she said, 'I promise.'

Finally she ended the call and put her phone away.

'Before we go,' said Jerry, 'can we take a look at that sculpture we passed on the way in?'

He said his goodbyes to the horses, then together they wheeled him down the driveway to the racing yard's main entrance, where a life-sized sculpture of a leaping stallion occupied pride of place on a central plinth. The stallion had been constructed from galvanised steel wire that gleamed silver in the afternoon sunlight. The owner of the stables joined them. 'Pretty spectacular, eh?'

Jerry nodded. 'Amazing. Who's the artist?'

'His name's Johnny LaVenture. He lives over in Channing's Hill,' said the owner. 'I saw an exhibition of his work a couple of years back and knew we had to commission one of his pieces for this place. Everyone loves it.'

Jerry reached over and ran his thin fingers over the steel wire flank of the stallion. 'Take a photo of me, Scarlett.'

Scarlett already had her camera at the ready. As she moved around him, snapping away, Jerry said, 'You're a lovely girl, you know. Got a boyfriend at the moment?'

'Me? Nooo, I'm a sad singleton!' Scarlett pulled a comical face. 'It's a tragedy; no one I fancy ever fancies me.'

'Well, more fool them. That's what I say.' He beckoned her towards him. 'Come on, let's have a selfie of you and me together. Just use your phone. You can send it to that guy who keeps ringing you up. You never know, maybe seeing you with a handsome older man will bring him to his senses.'

Laughing, Scarlett duly took a photo on her phone. Whilst she was busy sending it to Conor, Jerry caught Zillah's eye and winked. And that was the moment Zillah realised she hadn't been the only one to notice the earlier flush in Scarlett's cheeks.

Conor was lying across his sofa half watching *The Great Escape* on TV but mainly wondering what the bloody hell was happening to him. When his phone beeped again, he opened the latest message from Scarlett and saw the photo she'd sent him. It was a selfie this time, of her and Jerry. Beneath it, she'd written:

Jerry says he's glad you were ill so he could meet me instead. PS He's wonderful. Thanks so much for trusting me to do this today. PPS I still promise.

Conor studied the photo, an impromptu unedited snap of a desperately ill man in his sixties and a sparky, vivacious girl in her twenties with purple hair and an infectious smile. For once, she wasn't doing that annoying pout.

What *was* going on, though? Why had Scarlett's story about having been offered no-strings sex by an ex-boyfriend bothered him so much, to the extent that he'd needed to tell her again not to do it? Had felt *compelled* to say it, in fact . . . God knows what kind of a lunatic she must think he was, seeing as it was precisely none of his business in the first place.

OK, stop this. He put the phone down.

At least he could pretend it was simply good old-fashioned advice on the basis of taking the moral high ground.

Even if, deep down, he knew that wasn't the real reason at all.

As he exhaled and shifted position in an effort to ease the ache in his shoulders, he felt the phone slide off the sofa cushion onto the floor. On the TV screen, Charles Bronson was grimly digging away at the escape tunnel, living in terror of the roof collapsing on top of him. Down on the rug, Conor's phone beeped to signal the arrival of yet another text.

More photos from Scarlett, sent to playfully taunt him about the brilliant job she'd done this afternoon? He rolled over to retrieve the phone and saw that this one wasn't from her. It was a message from Evie:

OMG, have you seen what Caz has put up on Facebook now? She's outrageous! Brace yourself!

Conor's heart sank. Caz was an enthusiastic user of Facebook. He'd never been a great one for it himself; it was handy for keeping up with old school friends and seeing photos of their families, but that was enough as far as he was concerned.

Whereas Caz liked to post stuff every day. Quite often, more stuff than any normal person needed to post. He knew this because she'd persuaded him in a moment of weakness a fortnight ago to accept her friend request, and now every time he ventured onto the site he saw all the rubbish she'd put up there, an endless stream of jokes, cartoons, memes and typically outspoken comments about any subject that happened to enter her head.

Dreading what he was about to unveil, Conor opened Facebook and saw that he'd been tagged in one of Caz's status updates. Clicking on it, he saw that she'd posted a video of a bride and groom making their way up the aisle of a church. The music playing was the Wedding March and the faces of the couple had been digitally altered, replaced by those of Belinda and himself. Similarly, the two brides-maids in turquoise taffeta were now Evie and Caz. And Caz had written: *Here's something that needs to happen! Come on, Conor, we all know you two are a match made in heaven, so when are you going to make an honest woman of Belinda and pop the question?? You know you want to! And guess what, I bumped into our local vicar this morning and he told me they've had a cancellation at the church, which means the first Saturday in July is now FREE! So what are you waiting for? You need to book it now! What does everyone think? Should he do it??? Let's make this a wedding to remember!!!*

Predictably, in the comments below, dozens of people had left messages to the effect that yes, he should definitely do it, and they couldn't wait to receive their invitations to the wedding of the year.

Conor heaved a sigh of irritation. To think that everyone had assured him Caz was a good person who meant well and he'd grow to like her over time.

Seriously, that was never going to happen. And yes, this Facebook malarkey might only be a joke, but it was a passive-aggressive kind of joke. If he complained about it, he would be accused of sense-of-humour failure. If, on the other hand, he let it go, the teasing comments and heavy hints would keep on coming.

It was a lose-lose situation.

His phone rang and he answered it.

'Have you seen what Caz did?' said Evie.

'I have.'

'Look, I know she can be embarrassing sometimes, but it's only a bit of fun. Are you cross with her?'

'Could you ask her to delete it?' See? He already felt like a miserable killjoy. 'I know it's only a joke, but it feels a tad . . . inappropriate.'

283

'OK.'

'Belinda and I met each other in January. It's only been two months.' He felt the need to explain.

'I know. But I thought everything was going really well between the two of you.'

'It is,' Conor protested. 'The thing is, most people like to leave it a bit longer before they make that kind of decision.'

'Yes, but Caz reckons Belinda deserves to be happy and when you meet the right person there's no need to wait.' Evie sounded frustrated. 'All I'm saying is, everyone wants you and Belinda to be happy.'

'I know they do. It's too soon, that's all.'

'But maybe in a few months from now?' Frustration turned to hope.

Conor was beginning to feel trapped once more. 'Maybe.'

'I wouldn't be a nuisance, if that's what bothering you,' Evie suddenly blurted out. 'I promise!'

'What?' He was taken aback. 'That isn't bothering me. You aren't a nuisance.'

'OK, well that's good.' He could hear the relief in her voice. 'I thought I should say it, just in case.'

'No need.'

'And just so you know, no pressure or anything, but if you'd been wondering how I'd feel about you and Belinda getting married or whatnot . . . well, I'd be all in favour.'

Moved, Conor said, 'Thanks.'

'You wouldn't have to be, like, a stepfathery kind of person if you didn't want to. Just a friendly grown-up, that'd be fine.'

'Right.'

'And I wouldn't mind if you had babies either. That'd be cool.'

'Well, that's jumping ahead . . .'

'Yes, I know, I'm just putting it out there. Plus, she's not getting any younger. You don't want to wait too long, do you?'

'OK, enough for now.' Conor was smiling, because he might have problems in his life, but Evie wasn't one of them. 'Will you have a quiet word with Caz?'

'If I have a quiet word, chances are she won't hear it.' Evie laughed. 'No worries. I'll be firm with her, make sure she deletes it.'

Chapter 37

Lucas knew he had to tell Essie the truth when she arrived early for work on Monday morning waving a bag and calling out, 'Hi! Is Giselle here?'

'Sorry, she isn't.' He felt simultaneously sick and energised, because the need to talk to someone about the situation was becoming overwhelming. Whether it was better or worse for that someone to be Essie, he had no idea.

'Oh, let me show you what I picked up for her yesterday. Have a look at this, isn't it just perfect?' Excited by her find, Essie opened the bag and, with a flourish, pulled out a lavender velvet skirt with a bias-cut swishy hemline. 'I spotted it on one of the vintage stalls at the market and knew Giselle would love it. And look, it has an elasticated panel at the front because it's an actual maternity skirt!' She held it up against herself and gave a shimmy to demonstrate the swinginess of the material. 'Room for growth!'

'It's . . . great.' Lucas paused; he needed to say it. 'Giselle's gone. She's left Bath and I don't even know why.'

Silence. Essie's green eyes widened with shock. Finally she said, 'Oh God. Did she tell you she was going?'

'Not face to face. I got a text saying she was sorry, but she needed time away from here, time to think. I don't know what she needs to think about. I have no idea what any of it means . . . I just know I can't stay here any longer doing nothing.' Lucas shook his head. 'I have to talk to her, find out what's going on.'

'You mean it hasn't just happened? When did she leave?'

'Saturday.'

'Two days ago? Oh Lucas.' Essie's hands flew to her mouth. His stomach churned. 'You're the first person I've told.'

Her look of sympathy was almost worse than the dismay. 'Do you have any idea where she is?'

'Pretty sure she's gone home. I'd added her to my phone-finder app because she kept losing hers. When I checked it, the signal was coming from just north of Glasgow. On the train, I'm guessing. But then she must have switched the phone off. There's been no signal since.' He raked his fingers through his hair. 'It's the not knowing that's killing me. I mean, this is *Giselle*. Why would she *do* this?'

Essie was torn between being lost for words and brimming with questions. The questions were so sensitive, she couldn't bring herself to ask them. As Lucas had just said, this was Giselle they were talking about. She simply wasn't the type to do something so dramatic without explanation. She was straightforward and sensible and just . . . open. Yet clearly something *had* been troubling her . . .

'What?' Lucas was watching her closely.

'I don't know, I'm just trying to think. When I bumped into her last week, she seemed a bit distracted.' Essie struggled to recall the details. 'She asked me to go for a coffee with her but I couldn't because I had to start my shift here. So we arranged to meet up for lunch on Saturday, but then on Friday night she messaged to say she couldn't make it. I just assumed it was to do with work. But now . . . Well, it did seem as if maybe there was something she wanted to talk to me about—'

'Morning!' The door swung open and Jude arrived, ready to start her shift. When she saw them, she stopped in her tracks. 'What's up?'

Lucas didn't *look* dreadful because he was simply too physically attractive, but there were dark shadows beneath his eyes and the palpable tension around him made it clear that something was very wrong.

Essie made coffee for them while Lucas told Jude everything he knew. When he'd finished, he said, 'I'm going up to see her. I have to.'

Jude nodded. 'I think you should. How will you get there?'

'I'll drive. I've already checked the trains. They're no good.'

'Is that wise?' Jude looked pointedly at Lucas as his coffee cup rattled in its saucer.

He shook his head. 'There are track repairs and rail replacement buses. I can't cope with that.'

'OK, but you need to take someone with you. You can't drive all the way to Skye on your own.'

'I've already thought of that.' Lucas dismissed the order. 'There isn't anyone I could ask. Everyone has jobs they can't leave at short notice.'

'One of us could do it,' said Jude. She raised her eyebrows at Essie. 'How about you?'

Essie experienced a jolt of alarm. 'Me? What about my shifts?'

'OK, is your friend Scarlett free?'

This was an even more alarming prospect. 'Scarlett can't drive – she doesn't even have a provisional licence!'

'I meant she could take your place here.'

'Or *you* could go with Lucas,' said Essie.

'I would, but it's my niece's school concert tomorrow and I promised I'd go. I can't miss it.' Jude shook her head. 'How about Billy?'

Young Billy, who was busy getting the bar ready for opening time, looked utterly terrified. 'Not me, no way, my mum says I'm a liability on the road. And I've never driven on a motorway neither.' He turned to Lucas. 'There must be someone else who can drive you up to Scotland . . . Honestly, anyone would be better than me.'

'Hey hey, what's all this about?' The booming voice behind her made Essie jump a mile. 'Someone in need of a chauffeur? Beautiful place, Scotland – I'd be up for a jaunt!'

Oh God, not Brendan. *Really, no.*

Now it was Lucas's turn to look appalled. Jude, leaping into the breach, said firmly, 'Brendan, it's really kind of you to offer, but Essie's going to do it.'

Essie's heart broke into a Grand National gallop.

Nodding with evident relief, Lucas looked at her. 'Thanks.'

Back at the house, Essie threw clothes and toiletries into a small case and went downstairs to tell Zillah what was happening.

'Are you sure you'll be OK? Is there anything you need doing before I go?'

'Well if you could just wallpaper the drawing room and give the house a spring clean, that'd be great.' Having applied a second coat of her favourite Ruby Woo lipstick, Zillah snapped shut the mirrored compact in her left hand, adjusted the angle of her new ivory hat and flashed a brilliant smile. 'Darling, believe it or not, I'm perfectly capable of surviving without you for a couple of days. I'm really not that decrepit! Off you go now, and give my love to Lucas. He must be worried sick.'

Essie nodded. 'He is.'

'Well, whatever happens, I hope everything works out for the best for him and Giselle.'

Essie stood on the doorstep and waved as Zillah drove off. Less than two minutes later, Lucas pulled up in his own car. He swung her small case into the boot, then stood and faced her.

'Look, I'm sorry about this. I know it isn't ideal.' His expression was taut. 'You don't have to come. I can go on my own.'

'Would you prefer to be on your own?'

His dark eyes were haunted. 'No.'

'Well then. You've got me to keep you company and share the driving. Otherwise it's Brendan.'

A flicker of a smile. 'I'd rather it was you.'

'Come on, let's go.' Essie jumped into the passenger seat. 'And don't worry about Giselle doing something stupid. She just wouldn't, OK? She's too sensible for that.'

As they pulled away, Lucas said soberly, 'I never thought she'd disappear, either.'

Chapter 38

Zillah had been invited along to St Mark's to help celebrate Elspeth's seventy-fifth birthday. She had bought her a peony-pink pashmina and a matching Chanel lipstick, because Elspeth had confided the other week that the only lipstick she possessed, made by Rimmel and won in a raffle five years ago, had almost run out.

Zillah, who owned dozens of lipsticks – OK, probably hundreds – had loved visiting Jolly's and choosing a shade of pink that would suit Elspeth's English-rose colouring, rather than the deep red one she'd been enthusiastically applying on special occasions for as long as they'd known each other.

Everyone had gathered in the sunny conservatory for the little party. 'Happy Birthday' was sung with gusto, tea and home-made cakes were passed around and Elspeth opened the many cards and presents she'd been given. She then shed a little tear as she thanked everyone for their kindness to her over the years since the loss of her husband.

'I love it here,' she told them. 'It's my favourite place to be. Keeping myself busy and helping other people . . . it just means the world to me. Thank you so much for letting me work here and giving me my life back.'

Then one of the doctors presented her with a bouquet of roses and told her that they couldn't imagine the place without her; she was one of the family. More hugs ensued. Zillah, her own eyes suddenly brimming, dabbed at them discreetly with a tissue and wondered what it must be like to be as truly good and selfless a person as Elspeth.

The next moment, her attention was caught by the sight of a patient being wheeled past the conservatory. A red blanket had slipped from her shoulders and got caught under a wheel, and as the nurse paused to disentangle it, the woman turned her head to look directly through the full-length windows at the party inside.

Zillah froze. It had been over fifty years since they'd last seen each other, yet she recognised the woman's face instantly.

And it was even more extraordinary that she was able to, when you considered how ill the woman must be. But there was no question, no shadow of a doubt that it was Alice.

A maelstrom of memories swirled around inside Zillah's head. It had actually been fifty-eight years since their last encounter. Alice and Matthew had been so happy together until she'd barged in and stolen him from her. It continued to be the aspect of her life of which she was most bitterly ashamed.

And now here was Alice once more, in her eighties and clearly very unwell . . . Oh God, she couldn't face her; apart from anything else, what good would it do poor Alice? No, she would just have to slip out and stay away from the hospice for the next couple of weeks, or for however long Alice was in residence.

Turning to leave, Zillah found her getaway thwarted by Elspeth, tipsy on half a glass of Prosecco and so grateful for her scarf and lipstick you'd think she'd been given a diamond watch from Cartier. By the time she managed to extricate herself and slip out of the conservatory, it was too late: the nurse was pushing Alice's wheelchair directly past the main entrance.

'And here she is now,' the nurse exclaimed cheerfully. 'Speak of the devil – we were just talking about you! Zillah, this is Alice, our newest lady. I was showing her around the garden before settling her back into her room.'

Alice's once-blonde hair was now white, her eyes were rimmed with grey and she looked as fragile as tissue paper, but her gaze was direct as she studied the woman who'd stolen her fiancé. 'Not many people with that name. I wondered if it was you.' She turned her head slightly to address the nurse. 'Zillah and I know each other.'

'You do? Well, how wonderful! Isn't that just lovely?' The nurse beamed. 'So you already know what a special person she is.'

'Special,' Alice echoed, her expression giving nothing away. 'Oh yes.'

If only she could have escaped. Zillah checked her watch. 'Well, I should be off—'

'Oh don't go,' Alice interrupted. 'Stay for a bit. After all, we've so much catching up to do.'

Minutes later, Zillah found herself sitting opposite Alice in a sheltered corner of the garden beneath the newly leafed branches of a lilac tree. There was no one else within earshot.

'I'm so sorry.' Zillah's scalp prickled with mortification. 'For everything.'

Alice nodded. Silence. Finally she cleared her throat. 'Well I'm glad to hear that.'

Zillah felt herself flush. 'I've felt guilty ever since.'

There was another excruciating pause, then Alice said, 'All those years ago, after it happened, I used to have long imaginary conversations with you. I did it all the time. I'd throw insults at you and tell you how much you'd hurt me.'

'You had every reason to. You still do.' Zillah spread her hands. 'Say it, it's what I deserve. Say it all.'

'Oh please. That was a lifetime ago. And now my lifetime's very nearly over. I'm not going to spend the last few weeks being bitter and snide,' said Alice. 'That would just be a waste. Anyway, it's all behind us now. How are you?' She smiled suddenly and her face softened. 'As soon as the nurse mentioned a visitor called Zillah, I asked her what you looked like. When she said unbelievably stylish and glamorous, I knew at once it had to be you. And my goodness, she was right. You put the rest of us to shame.'

It was hardly fair for Alice to compare herself with someone who wasn't terminally ill. Zillah said, 'It's only make-up. If I took it all off, you'd get a shock.'

'Not true. You always were the most beautiful girl I'd ever seen. No wonder Matthew fell under your spell.'

'I'm sorry.'

Alice waved away the apology. 'Don't keep saying it. So tell me, how long were the two of you happy together?'

Zillah took a tissue from her bag and pressed it between her damp palms. 'Not for long, I'm afraid.'

'I did hear about the divorce. He went on to marry again, I gather.'

'He did. And stayed married. How about you?'

'Just the one husband for me. He was a good man, died twenty-two years ago. We were a decent team. And you?'

'I lost my third husband ten years ago. I miss him every day,' said Zillah, 'more than anyone will ever know. He was the one who made everything worthwhile.'

'Was he more dynamic than Matthew?' Alice raised her eyebrows. 'More exciting?'

'Honestly? Yes.' Zillah nodded.

'I knew it. I knew Matthew would never be enough for you.'

'After William died, I thought it was my punishment for doing what I'd done to you.'

'And when I was miserable and lonely,' Alice confided, 'I used to hope you were miserable and lonely too.'

It was almost a relief to hear it. 'Of course you did,' Zillah said. 'You're only human.'

'Not for much longer,' Alice replied with a wry smile.

Chapter 39

Essie's phone buzzed yet again to let her know the calls were still coming in. Once they'd passed Birmingham, she and Lucas had switched seats and she'd taken over behind the wheel. Luckily the motorway was clear and conditions were good, ensuring a smooth journey. It was actually quite thrilling to be driving such a fantastic car. She had the radio on low and a guilty sensation lurking inside her chest because this expedition, despite being potentially one of the most traumatic events of Lucas's life, was secretly turning out to be rather enjoyable.

Not that she'd ever admit it to another living soul.

Well, apart from Scarlett maybe.

Checking on Lucas, Essie saw that he was still out for the count. Practically the moment he'd moved into the passenger seat, forty-eight hours of stress and exhaustion had caught up with him. She'd only glanced sideways briefly and occasionally, but each time had confirmed that he looked absolutely beautiful when he was asleep. And yes, of course it was wrong to be thinking this right now, but it was true.

He didn't snore either.

Well, you couldn't help noticing that, could you? Always good to know.

But the buzzing phone was starting to get annoying now, and they were only a mile from the next services. When she reached them a minute later, Essie found a space in the car park and climbed out of the BMW as quietly as possible. Stepping away from the car, she looked at her phone and called Paul.

'*Finally*. Do you have any idea how many messages I've left for you?' He sounded like an angry wasp.

'Eleven,' said Essie. 'And three texts.'

'So why haven't you answered any of them? Where *are* you?'

'Somewhere near Manchester.'

'*What?*'

'I didn't have time to let you know. Giselle's disappeared and I'm with Lucas. We need to track her down and find out what's going on.'

After a stunned silence, Paul said, 'And Lucas couldn't go on his own?'

'I'm driving, he's catching up on some sleep. Look, this is serious, he's worried sick about Giselle. It's completely out of character for her to do something like this.'

'Why you, though? Why not someone else?'

'Because it made the most sense for it to be me. I'll be away for a couple of days,' she added.

'But I booked tickets for the Pinter play at the theatre tonight. They weren't cheap, you know.'

He was definitely annoyed. The good news was that being taken to see Pinter plays at the theatre was one of her least favourite things to do. 'Well I'm sorry about that, but you can still see it. You'll have more room to stretch out. OK, I have to go now, bye!'

When she turned back, Lucas was out of the car, watching her. He raised an eyebrow. 'That was Paul. Is he mad at you?'

He had evidently been listening too. Essie said, 'How do you know it was Paul?'

'You always sound different when you're speaking to him. Out of ten, how mad is he?'

'Six, maybe seven.'

'I'm sorry. I don't want to cause trouble between you.'

If he only knew how much trouble he'd caused. Essie smiled. 'Don't worry, you aren't.'

At least not the kind of trouble that was bothering her.

Back at the house, Zillah made herself a cup of coffee. Then she threw it away and poured a large glass of whisky instead.

Sometimes you just needed one.

Oh God, though, that had to count as one of the most mortifying experiences of her life. And the fact that Alice had been so nice about it only made her feel that much worse.

Maybe this was the punishment she'd always deserved.

The photographs were stored in boxes on top of the wardrobe in her bedroom. She'd scanned all the important ones onto her iPad, but there were many hundreds more that hadn't made the cut, including plenty taken all those years ago when she'd been in her twenties. If memory served, there was one particularly lovely one taken at a party, of Alice and Matthew together back when they'd been a happy couple.

Would it be a nice gesture, or unbelievably crass, to pass

the photograph on to Alice? Crass probably, but she'd find it first, then decide. And there were other less contentious group photos too, of the friends they'd all socialised with during that time – Alice might enjoy seeing them.

Zillah kicked off her shoes and dragged the chair over from the dressing table. It was a stretch, but she'd done it many times before. She even knew which of the boxes to reach for; it was the black-and-white one on the left . . .

Reaching up on tiptoe, she felt a sharp jab of pain in her ankle, a remnant of her stumble at the racing stables. It wasn't excruciating but it was enough to tip her off balance just as she'd managed to grab the box. In the split second that followed, a torrent of thoughts zipped through Zillah's brain . . . She was falling, and the landing wasn't going to be a comfortable one onto the soft mattress of her bed . . . No, sadly she was several feet short of that happening and the best she could hope for was the carpeted floor, whereas the *worst* she could hope for was hitting the corner of the carved oak frame at the foot of the bed. She closed her eyes and fell backwards through the air, bracing herself for whatever hideous pain was about to ensue . . .

When it happened, the almighty crack made her cry out, because the right side of her head had indeed made contact with the wooden bed frame. God, *ow*.

She landed in a heap on the floor. For several seconds, she concentrated on her breathing. Dazed, she cautiously checked each part of her body in turn. It was a miracle, and everything hurt, but no actual limbs appeared to be broken.

Oh, but the bruises would be spectacular.

She'd brought the box down with her too; the lid had come off and photos had tumbled out like oversized confetti.

Still catching her breath and waiting for the pain above her right ear to subside, she found one of them resting on her chest. Without moving, she lifted the photograph and held it above her head. When her eyes finally brought it into focus, she saw that it was one of herself and Matthew, taken a year or so after their wedding.

She looked at her younger self, outwardly smiling, slender and gorgeous, and knew that the realisation of what she'd done back then had already taken root in her brain. At the age of twenty-seven, she'd made her bed and was being forced, night after night, to lie in it.

She let go of the photo and allowed it to flutter to the floor beside her; she didn't care if she never saw it again.

Oh yes, this was definitely karma.

The pain in her head wasn't lessening at all.

Lancaster. Kendal. Penrith. Carlisle.

Lucas had taken his turn driving; now Essie was back behind the wheel and he was dozing once more. The further north they went, the more spectacular the scenery became. They were ahead of schedule too, having made only one fleeting pit stop for a bathroom break and to pick up fresh cups of coffee.

Essie helped herself to another mint toffee from the bag in her lap. They were approaching Glasgow now; she'd never driven this kind of distance before. What if they reached Kinlara on Skye only to discover that Giselle wasn't there?

What if she was there but flatly refused to see or speak to Lucas?

And why, *why* had she done this?

300

It was an endless loop of unanswerable questions, and if it was bothering her, Essie could only imagine the effect it must be having on Lucas.

The sun was low in the sky. They'd set off at eleven thirty and it was now half past six in the evening. According to the sat nav they were on course to reach Kinlara by ten forty-five.

'Where are we?' Lucas had woken up.

'Glasgow.'

'My turn.'

'OK, when we reach the next services.' Essie's back was starting to ache a bit. Since it hadn't been mentioned yet, she said, 'Any idea where we might stay when we get there?'

He rubbed his hands over his face. 'God, sorry. Hadn't even thought about it.'

'It's fine, it doesn't—'

'Of course it matters.' Lucas took out his phone. 'I'll sort somewhere now.'

By the time they reached the next service station, he'd booked them into a hotel online.

'There, done.'

'Can I see?' said Essie.

He passed her his mobile and she studied the photos of the small family-run hotel situated on Main Street with views over the harbour and the sea beyond.

'It looks nice. Did you get two rooms?' The moment the words were out, she regretted them.

Lucas said evenly, 'I'm on my way to see my pregnant girlfriend. Of course I booked two rooms.'

'I just meant did they *have* two rooms?' Flustered, Essie found herself babbling. 'What with it being such short notice, that's all. But they did, so that's good . . . I wasn't meaning anything else . . .'

'Two rooms. No need to panic. Believe it or not, I wasn't planning on seducing you tonight.'

She bit back a retort, because he was under a huge amount of pressure and now wasn't the time. They opened the car doors and swapped seats in silence. Essie fastened her seat belt and closed her eyes, tilting her head away from him.

Not that she'd be able to sleep.

Five minutes later, as they sped along the M8, she heard Lucas say, 'Ess? I'm sorry.'

'It's OK. Don't worry.'

'It's just this is killing me. The not having a clue what's going on.'

Essie's heart went out to him; it was the most unbearable situation. She opened her eyes and turned to look at him. 'I know.'

Chapter 40

It was dark outside, which meant it must be night-time. Zillah gazed out through the window and saw the misty amber glow from the street lamp. For some reason she couldn't bring the lamp itself into focus, but never mind.

Her head still hurt, but it was a degree of pain she was able to cope with. She had managed to get herself off the floor as well, thank goodness; had made her way to the bathroom, then back again and into bed. She'd been dozing intermittently since then, and had sipped water from the bottle on the bedside table. Her mobile phone was some-where, but she couldn't remember quite where. Anyway, calling someone and telling them about the fall would only earn her a lecture about how she shouldn't have been standing on a chair in the first place. Then there'd be another boring lecture about how she'd brought it on herself through wearing high heels. Nag nag nag. God it was tedious.

Easier to stay here in bed and let this ridiculous headache run its course. It was like a bad bout of flu; you just had to take things easy and wait for it to pass.

Rest, relax, recuperate.

And no need to worry. Either Conor or Essie would be back soon.

The sunset hours earlier had been spectacular, flooding the sky with vibrant shades of crocus yellow, orange and purple streaked with pink. Then darkness had fallen as they'd continued their journey northwards. Glencoe, Fort William, Invergarry were all behind them now, and they'd crossed the Skye Bridge. In the distance, you could just about make out the ghostly snow-topped mountains beneath the milky glow of the moon. It was ten fifteen and Kinlara was up ahead, mere minutes away.

As they rounded the final bend in the road, there it was, a crescent of buildings lit up along the waterfront, their lights reflected in the inky sea.

Having googled the place earlier, Essie knew that in daylight the buildings were painted in pastel shades of amber, violet, pink and green. Kinlara was famed for its beauty and charm, and was a magnet for visitors, one of the Highlands' most popular tourist destinations. Which was why she'd asked Lucas if he'd managed to book two rooms, not because she wanted to spend the night in bed with him, for crying out loud . . .

Essie didn't cry out loud. She said, 'It looks amazing.'

Lucas nodded briefly, his knuckles white as he gripped the steering wheel. 'It does.'

Five minutes later, they reached the hotel and he pulled into the car park.

'What happens now?' said Essie as they hauled their cases out of the boot. It was twenty past ten; was it too late for Lucas to go looking for Giselle?

'I need to find her.'

'Would it make more sense to wait till morning?'

'No.' He shook his head. 'I can't.'

'OK. But she might not be here.'

'I think she is.'

'She might refuse to see you.'

'I know. But I have to try.'

Essie could only imagine how he was feeling. If it had been anyone else she would have hugged them, but it was Lucas so she couldn't. 'Right, you go. I'll take your case and get you checked in. I hope you find Giselle and I hope she speaks to you.'

The door at the side entrance to the hotel creaked as it opened a bit further and a figure stepped out of the shadows.

'It's OK,' Giselle said quietly. 'I will.'

Lucas opened the door to the room he'd booked for himself, and Giselle went in ahead of him. He put his case down in a corner and turned to look at her. She was pale but clearly prepared.

'You were waiting for me.'

Giselle shrugged. 'This is Kinlara. As soon as Molly took the booking and saw that the name on the credit card was Lucas Brook, she called me. You messaged her to let her know you wouldn't be here until after ten o'clock. I just came over and waited in the bar until I heard your car pulling into the car park. Lucas, I'm so *sorry* . . .'

'Are you . . . all right?'

She nodded. 'Yes.'

'I have to know what's going on.'

There was a tartan-covered sofa on one side of the empty

fireplace, a matching chair on the other side. Giselle took the chair and indicated that he should occupy the sofa, so they were separated by a wooden coffee table artfully strewn with glossy magazines and a tin of shortbread.

'You're not going to like it.' Her voice quavered. 'I didn't mean for any of this to happen, I promise you. But it has. And I'm sorry. I was so confused, I didn't know what to do. But now I do know, and I can't live a lie. The baby isn't yours . . . you aren't the father.' She stopped abruptly and covered her mouth with one hand, her eyes wide with anguish. 'I can't believe this is happening. I can't believe I've actually said it.'

Silence filled the room like fog.

It wasn't until Lucas exhaled that he realised he'd been holding his breath for a good thirty seconds. 'You said it.' He sat forward. 'Is it true?'

Slowly Giselle nodded once more. Tears filled her eyes and her hands trembled as she wiped them away. 'Yes, it's true.'

It was the possibility he had never even considered. Not seriously, at least. Some people you could imagine being unfaithful – with some, you almost expected it – but Giselle simply wasn't one of them.

'Who is he?' said Lucas. 'Someone I know?'

'No. You've never met him. It didn't happen in Bath,' she explained. 'He lives here.'

She was having a baby, but it was no longer *their* baby. His foreseeable future had just taken a pretty definitive U-turn. And Giselle had known the truth all along.

Wow.

'Tell me everything,' said Lucas.

So she did.

'His name's Gregor McTavish. We were at school together. We've known each other since my family came to live here when I was ten.' Giselle's fingers were twisting together in her lap. 'When we were sixteen, we started seeing each other, but our parents both thought we were too young, so there was pressure not to get serious. Which made us that much more determined not to split up, of course, and we carried on being a couple until we were eighteen. Then I moved away and started my nursing training, and a girl named Claudine arrived here to work as an apprentice chef at the Castle Hotel . . . Anyway, long story short, Claudine set her sights on Gregor and eventually he gave in, because it wasn't easy keeping a relationship going with me when I was hundreds of miles away. So we broke up. And it was a pretty rough time, but I got over it in the end, because these things happen and that's what we all do, isn't it?'

'Keep going,' prompted Lucas.

'They moved to Italy to work together in a hotel in Florence, and eventually they broke up too. Then Gregor headed off to New Zealand . . . but six months ago his dad was taken ill and he moved back here to Kinlara. Which meant that when I came up for Christmas I saw him again for the first time in ten years.'

'And you took one look at him and knew you still loved him.'

'No!' Giselle looked at him in anguish. 'I loved you! It was great to see him, like catching up with an old friend . . . and there were a couple of other people from school, Jen and Jamie . . . it was just natural for the four of us to meet up and socialise together. Then on Christmas Eve,

Gregor invited us over to his cottage for dinner, but Jen and Jamie had to cancel at the last minute when Jen's gran was rushed into hospital. So I went on my own, and that was when it, you know . . . happened.'

'You slept with him.'

Giselle flinched. 'The snow was getting worse . . . Gregor's cottage is a couple of miles outside Kinlara and Mum had given me a lift there. At ten o'clock she called and said she wasn't going to be able to pick me up. Basically, I ended up having too much to drink with the boy who'd been my first love . . . and he told me how much he'd missed me and how he wished we'd never broken up, and it felt like I was finally hearing everything I'd always wanted to hear, and somehow . . . well, you already know the rest. It just . . . happened.'

Lucas shook his head in amazement. 'How many times did you sleep with him?'

'Just the once. When we woke up the next morning, I told him it must never happen again. I couldn't believe we'd done it. I couldn't believe I'd been unfaithful to you.' She was looking pleadingly at him, willing him to understand. 'It was the biggest mistake I'd ever made, the worst thing I'd ever done in my life. So we decided to put it behind us, pretend it had never happened.'

'But it didn't occur to you that you could be pregnant?' said Lucas.

Giselle flushed. 'My period had only finished the day before. I thought it would be completely safe . . . It *should* have been safe. I just convinced myself everything would be fine. Then I came back down to Bath, and to you, and it seemed as if none of it had ever happened. I'd never thought

I was the kind of person who could do something like that, but . . .'

'It turned out you could,' said Lucas when her voice trailed away.

She nodded resignedly. 'Well, yes.'

It certainly explained why their sex life had gone out of the window after her return. At the time, the excuses had seemed plausible – she'd either been exhausted or feeling off colour or needing to get up very early for work.

Now he understood the real reason why.

He also understood why she'd seemed so distracted once the pregnancy had been confirmed.

'And the plan was to carry on letting me think the baby was mine?' This was the hardest part to come to terms with.

'I didn't know *what* to do. I was so shocked and ashamed.' Giselle sat back and let out a groan of self-loathing. 'You were right there when I did the test . . . I didn't have time to get everything straight in my head. If I hadn't loved you, it would have been easier . . . but I did love you.'

Lucas noted the use of the past tense. 'Enough to pass off another man's child as mine.'

'I panicked and I'm sorry. The longer it went on, the more impossible it became to tell you the truth. And inside my head, everything was just getting more and more tangled up.' Fresh tears of anguish were sliding down her cheeks. 'I thought I was going to go mad. My whole life I've been a good person and everyone liked me, then all of a sudden I'd turned into a bad person who'd done this terrible thing . . . and now here I was doing something even *more* terrible.' Giselle's voice cracked and she wrapped her arms tightly around her own ribcage. 'By Friday I knew I had to sort it out one way or another, but I needed to do it myself, without you being there. And I had to tell Gregor, too. Whatever else happened, he deserved to know. So I managed to book a week off work and came up here.'

'You've told him?'

'Yes.'

'Was he shocked?'

'That's an understatement.'

'Are you going to be . . . keeping the baby?'

Giselle looked at him steadily. 'Oh yes.'

Lucas nodded. A lot of girls in Giselle's situation might have taken the decision not to continue with the pregnancy. In a way, you had to admire her for choosing to carry on.

'We've done a lot of talking,' she went on, 'me and Gregor. This afternoon he said we should give our relationship another go, see if we can get back what we used to have. For the sake of the baby.'

'Do you think it'll work?'

'I have no idea. But it makes sense to try. I'll need to work out my notice at the hospital, then I'm going to move up here and we'll give it our best shot.' Giselle wiped her eyes with the sleeve of her blue-and-white stripy sweater. 'I know it sounds old-fashioned, but Kinlara hasn't shifted into the twenty-first century quite yet; it's what our parents would expect us to do. I also realise it doesn't sound very romantic, but what other choice do we have? I messed up big-time and now I have to live with the consequences.'

'You never know, it might all work out OK,' said Lucas.

'That's such a nice thing to say. And after everything I did to you.' The tears flowed faster, dripping off her chin.

'You and me, we were so happy together, weren't we? I've managed to ruin the best relationship of my life.'

He shook his head. 'No you haven't. The best relationship of your life is going to be with that baby of yours, and that's all that matters right now. You need to look after yourself.'

'It'd almost be easier if you yelled at me,' said Giselle.

He managed a brief smile. 'Well I'm not going to.'

'I deserve it.'

'But it wouldn't change anything,' said Lucas. 'Would it?'

Chapter 41

All was quiet outside the hotel. Essie was in her room, curled up on the broad window seat with her feet tucked beneath her, gazing out at the lights reflected on the water across the main street. Sleep was out of the question. It had been over an hour now since she'd left Lucas and Giselle to talk things through, and she still had absolutely no idea what was going on.

Were they still talking, or had it all been sorted? Had Giselle suffered a hormonal wobble that had caused her to panic and flee, and had Lucas reassured her that everything would be fine, that he loved her more than anything and together they'd get through this? Were they at this moment indulging in passionate make-up sex . . . ?

Not wanting to dwell on that last thought, Essie told herself that whatever her own squashed-down feelings for Lucas, it would undeniably be the best outcome. Because this wasn't simply a case of two people deciding whether to remain a couple, was it? There was a baby involved.

Her phone rang. Paul again. Oh God, this time he was FaceTiming her.

Tempting though it was to ignore the call, Essie answered it. Paul's handsome, unamused face filled the screen and he said without preamble, 'Where are you?'

'In my hotel room.'

'And where's Lucas?'

'In his hotel room, talking to his girlfriend.'

'Show me your room,' Paul instructed.

'Seriously? Why, do you think Lucas might be hiding under the bed?'

'I don't know, do I? That's why I'm asking.'

At that moment, a switch flipped in Essie's head. She looked at the man she'd tried so hard to be happy about being back together with, and knew it was never going to work. She said evenly, 'Shall I tell you something? If I wanted to spend a night in a hotel with Lucas, I wouldn't drive five hundred and seventy miles to do it. We'd probably settle for somewhere just outside Bath.'

He visibly bristled. 'Listen to yourself. You've changed.'

'I have.' Essie nodded. 'And you still haven't told your mother that you've been seeing me again.'

'That's because—'

'It's OK, doesn't matter any more. You don't need to tell her.'

Paul gestured with irritation. 'What are you talking about?'

'Well, it's not working out, is it? You don't trust me. And your mum's never going to stop hating me. We gave it a trial run, but I think our relationship's pretty much died a death, don't you?' With every word, Essie felt herself growing lighter; it really was the most incredible sensation. Unable to prevent a smile spreading across her face, she said joyfully, 'We may as well call it a day.'

'But . . . but . . .'

She ended the call, leaving Paul gaping like a fish on the screen. Phew, that was one job she could now tick off her to-do list. Although it really should have been done before. And there was no need to feel sorry for Paul; his pride might be bruised, but he'd recover in no time at all. Deep down, he knew as well as she did that resurrecting their relationship would never work.

Downstairs, a door opened and closed. Essie leaned forward, resting her face against the cold glass, and saw someone leaving the hotel. Her heart did a dolphin leap when she realised it was Giselle, walking alone down the street with her long auburn ringlets bouncing around her shoulders and her hands plunged into the pockets of her favourite purple coat.

What had happened? It was impossible to tell. Within half a minute, Giselle had turned left down a side street and disappeared from view.

Essie looked at her phone. She could call or text Lucas. But he knew she was here and he knew she'd be waiting to discover the outcome of the meeting. Far better to leave it up to him.

Twenty minutes later, there had still been no word. While she was in the en suite bathroom brushing her teeth, Essie heard the same sound of the door opening and closing downstairs and instantly pictured Giselle running back into the hotel to throw herself into Lucas's arms . . .

It was the not knowing that was the unbearable part. Skidding out of the bathroom and across the bedroom, she flung herself onto the window seat, almost knocking out her front teeth as the handle of the toothbrush went *clonk* against the glass. OK, if there was no one outside, that meant it could be Giselle returning . . .

But there was someone out there, and it was Lucas, instantly recognisable in his navy polo shirt and jeans. She watched him rake his fingers through his dark hair as he stood and surveyed first the street, then the sea.

Was he about to go after Giselle? Essie held her breath and waited, but it didn't happen. Instead he turned right, crossed the street and strode along until he reached the stone jetty. Toothpaste dribbled down her chin as she pressed against the glass; what was he *doing* out there?

The next moment, he jumped off the jetty and disappeared from view.

Oh God, *God no* . . .

'You aren't being very kind to me,' said Zillah.

'Oh, I thought you needed looking after,' Alice retorted. 'I didn't realise I had to be kind too.'

Zillah had never felt worse. Here she was, stuck in bed and feeling dreadful, and there was Alice, looking incredibly young and glamorous, serving her the most horrible food imaginable. There was mouldy bread on the tray she'd just brought into the bedroom, a glass of milk that had separated and gone lumpy, and a bowl of soup that had ominous objects floating about in it.

'What are those?' She pointed weakly at the bowl.

'Slugs. I found them in the garden,' Alice said with satisfaction.

'Oh no, please, you can't make me eat slugs . . .'

Smirking, Alice mimicked her wail of despair. 'Oh yes, I think you'll find I can.'

Zillah opened her eyes and almost sobbed with relief to find the bedroom empty. Yet another terrible dream; that was all it had been. And it was still dark outside, but at some stage she'd managed to knock her alarm clock off the bedside table so it was no longer possible to tell the time. Her head was still hurting too, a crushing ache that showed no sign of abating. Which didn't help.

She vaguely wondered if it might be an idea to call someone and tell them about her headache. Then she remembered that she'd mislaid her phone, had put it somewhere safe and not been able to find it since. Oh well, better not to make a fuss anyway . . . it was only a headache. God knows, it was people complaining about things that weren't serious that had got the NHS into the state it was in.

Sleep, that was all she needed to get through this, and luckily she was feeling sleepy all the time now.

Oh but please, no more dreams like the one with Alice and the slugs.

'What's happened?' said Lucas, looking up at her.

What's happened? Was he seriously asking her that question?

Essie couldn't catch her breath enough to speak; she had hurtled out of the hotel and along the main street, fully expecting to find him in the cold black sea.

But he wasn't; he was casually sitting on the stone slipway that sloped down into the water on the other side of the jetty.

She gathered herself with difficulty; the feeling that her lungs might burst was heightened by the iciness of the peppermint toothpaste in her mouth and throat. She waited until the gulps for air became less gulpy and said, 'I thought you'd . . . fallen into . . . the sea.'

'You were watching from the hotel?'

Essie nodded; if she hadn't been watching him, why would she have raced down here? *Duh.*

'Did you think I'd fallen? Or that I'd jumped?'

'I didn't know, OK?'

'Sorry.' He smiled slightly, his white teeth visible in the light from the street lamp behind them. He patted the section of slipway beside him. 'Come and join me. It's OK, it's dry.'

'Why are you sitting out here?'

'I saw them when I came out for some fresh air.'

Essie blinked. 'You've lost me. Saw who?'

'You haven't noticed them yet?' Lucas pointed to the lower end of the slipway, where the stone met the gently lapping waves and clumps of seaweed bobbed on the surface of the water.

'Oh!' As Essie concentrated and gave her eyes time to adjust, she realised they weren't clumps of seaweed. The dark blobs were the heads of seals, black eyes gleaming as they floated in the sea. And there were a couple more, too, lying at the bottom of the slipway, calmly surveying their night-time visitors.

'See them now?' murmured Lucas.

'Yes! They know we're here, but they're not scared at all.'

'They don't need to be scared. No one harms them here. Giselle told me about them, ages ago.'

Essie didn't say anything; it was up to him to tell her what had happened between him and Giselle. She sat breathing in the salty night air, and waited.

'I'm not going to be a father,' Lucas said finally.

317

Her heart went out to him. 'Oh no. She lost the baby?'

He shook his head. 'The baby's fine. It just isn't mine.'

'*What?*' Shock made Essie say it louder than she'd planned. The bobbing heads in the water turned to look at her, askance.

'I know. Unexpected twist.'

'I can't believe it!' *Giselle, of all people?* 'I'm so sorry.'

'No need to apologise. You aren't the one who slept with your old boyfriend.'

Well, technically she *was*, but that wasn't what Lucas meant. And now wasn't the time to announce that she'd just finished with Paul.

'You don't have to tell me what happened,' she said.

'Except you might combust with curiosity if I don't. And I did drag you all this way up here.'

Essie nodded. 'True.'

They sat there together, watched by the enigmatic seals, and Lucas told her everything. He didn't slag off Giselle; merely explained what had happened. And when he'd finished, all he did was shake his head and say, 'So that's it, the whole story.'

He sounded calm, but he had to be in a state of shock.

'How are you feeling?' Essie ventured.

'Mixed up. Confused. Relieved. Having a baby wasn't something we'd planned. But for the last few weeks, thinking it was going to happen . . . Well, I'd kind of got used to the idea. Which is what's making all of this so . . . so . . .'

'I know.' Essie's breath caught in her throat as he turned his head to look directly at her. The expression on his face was completely unreadable but at the same time was managing to unleash a torrent of adrenalin that was causing her to tremble uncontrollably.

'Everything's changed,' Lucas murmured. 'In the space of an hour. My whole life . . . I thought I knew how it was going to play out, and now none of that's going to happen.'

'You need time to get used to it.'

But Lucas was looking at her again, intently. After a long pause, he said, 'Do I?'

And now it was as if there were two unspoken conversations going on, inside their heads. Because Essie knew only too well how she felt about Lucas, and right now it seemed almost as if he might feel the same way about her.

Except what if he didn't? What if she was just imagining it because she so badly wanted it to be true? And no way in the world could she take the risk of making the first move or saying the wrong thing . . . not ever, but *especially* not tonight . . .

'You're shivering,' said Lucas, his gaze still fixed unwaveringly on her face.

'I'm cold,' Essie lied.

'And you smell all minty.'

See? That wasn't remotely romantic. She said, 'That'll be the toothpaste.' Which wasn't romantic either.

'We should go inside.' He rose to his feet and held out a hand to help her up, but she pretended not to see it and stood up by herself.

They headed back to the hotel and encountered the manageress still sitting behind the reception desk, busily tidying brochures.

Even though it was past midnight.

'Seen the seals, have you?' She flashed them a professional smile.

'We have. Is the bar still open?' said Lucas.

'I'm afraid not.'

'Right, so can I order room service?'

'Room service? Oh Mr Brook, this isn't the London Ritz, you know!'

Lucas managed a polite smile. 'Could I buy a bottle of wine, then? Or just take one upstairs and replace it in the morning?'

'Sorry, Mr Brook.' Unmoved by the request, the manageress shook her head. 'Time for everyone to go to bed now. Your room is up there,' she reminded him, indicating the narrow staircase to the left. 'And yours is over there,' she told Essie, nodding pointedly at the other staircase on the right.

Which, if the situation had been different, might have been entertaining and an invitation to break the rules.

But under the circumstances, maybe it was just as well.

'I'll see you in the morning,' Essie told Lucas.

He exhaled, then nodded. 'Yes.'

The hotel manageress beamed at them both and brought out a fresh batch of brochures. 'Goodnight. Sleep well. If you really do want a drink . . .'

'Yes?' Lucas paused halfway up his staircase.

'There's a kettle in your room. You can always make yourself a nice cup of tea.'

Chapter 42

At seven thirty the next morning, they checked out of the hotel and climbed into Lucas's car.

Essie said, 'Did you get any sleep?'

'I did. Unexpectedly.' He took his sunglasses out of the glove compartment and put them on to shield his eyes from the low sun. Then he pulled out of the car park and turned right, ready to begin the long journey home.

'You don't want to see Giselle again before we leave?' She felt compelled to give him the option.

'No point. It's over. Look how stunning this place is,' said Lucas. 'I don't suppose I'll ever see it again.'

He was right; it was beautiful. The multicoloured shops and houses lining the main street glowed like sugared almonds in the early-morning sunlight. Ahead of them, a man in his late twenties emerged from the village shop with a baguette and a carton of milk, and Lucas slowed to let him cross the road. But when the customer glanced over at the car, he did a perceptible double-take and nearly dropped his baguette.

'It's almost as if he recognises me from Facebook or somewhere,' Lucas murmured.

When he'd told her the full name of the new man in Giselle's life, Essie had looked him up; unsurprisingly, there was only one Gregor McTavish living in Kinlara. For a second, all three of them stared at each other. Then Gregor turned and opened the door of his grey Peugeot. With a cheerful nod, Lucas raised his hand in acknowledgement and carried on down the road.

Essie said, 'Were you tempted to run him over? Just for a second?'

'I've had time to get over the shock now.' Lucas broke into a crooked smile. 'You know what? I reckon he did me a pretty big favour.'

Essie nodded with relief and thought: *Good.*

The notebook and pen had rolled off the bed, torn-out pages crackling beneath her as Zillah clumsily pushed back the covers. It had taken a long time and involved a considerable amount of leaning against walls, but she'd managed to reach the bathroom. Bladder emptied, she now flushed the loo and washed her hands, then peered at her reflection in the mirror above the sink.

What a shocking sight. She'd never looked more dreadful. Oh, but there was her mobile phone on the window ledge. She was pretty sure someone had been calling her earlier . . . Hadn't she heard it ringing while she'd been asleep?

Anyway, found it now. Through the fog of her brain, it occurred to her that it might be an idea to call someone and tell them about the pain in her head. Because it wasn't getting any better and Alice had told her to stop complaining, but sometimes you really needed to let people know how much it hurt . . .

Still clutching the edge of the sink, she leaned across and reached for the phone, but her hand shook and she misjudged the distance. The various bottles of mouthwash, shampoo and Elnett hairspray toppled like dominoes and clattered to the floor, and the phone flew off the window ledge along with them. There was a splash as it landed in the just-flushed loo.

A fresh wave of pain and exhaustion swept over her, followed by weary fatalistic acceptance. Oh well, never mind. Alice probably wouldn't have let her phone for help anyway; she was still being so unkind . . .

Actually, no, must stop thinking that . . . The thing with Alice hadn't been real, it had just been a horrible dream . . .

There was a glass still left intact on the shelf. Zillah filled it from the tap and gulped down water, then mentally prepared herself for the arduous journey back to the bedroom.

No, it was too far, she couldn't do it; all the strength had gone out of her now.

Slowly, very slowly, she lowered herself to the bathroom floor and pulled the soft white towels down from the towel rail. She made one into a kind of pillow and carefully rested her aching head on it, then did her best to cover herself with the other.

Not as comfortable as her bed, but she was here now.

It would do.

She pushed the fallen cans and bottles out of the way and closed her eyes.

Lucas was single again. He wasn't going to be a father. He was driving south with Essie at his side, and if she only knew what had been going through his head last night . . . well, it was just as well she didn't.

The hotel manageress who had ordered them up to their separate rooms might have been doing it for her own puritanical reasons, but he was grateful to her all the same. Any attempt to reveal his true feelings towards Essie would have been the worst thing he could have done. She'd have been appalled, and rightly so. Only a complete idiot would have attempted it.

Because he knew how he felt about Essie, but she didn't have any idea. And making a move at this stage would be unbelievably crass. He needed to take his time and find out if she felt even a fraction of the same attraction towards him.

And that was the problem, because he couldn't tell, not for sure. Nor could he take the risk. Sometimes the strength of his emotions towards her was so tangible he thought she must be feeling it too.

But just because he longed for it to happen didn't necessarily make the feelings mutual.

Anyway. Nothing *had* happened last night, and that was a good thing.

The bad thing was that she was still seeing Paul.

Oh well, they had time on their side. So long as Essie didn't suddenly announce that now *she* was pregnant . . .

'Carlisle,' Essie exclaimed, pointing to the big blue sign looming ahead of them. 'You were asleep when we drove past it on the way up. Our geography teacher at school was from Carlisle and he was forever forcing us to learn fascinating facts about the place. Go on, ask me for a fascinating fact.'

Amused by her enthusiasm, Lucas said, 'I'm agog. Give me three.'

'OK, brace yourself. Carlisle was part of Scotland until

324

1092. Carlisle Castle was originally built in 1093. I know, I did warn you these facts were fascinating.' Holding up the third finger, she said, 'And the name of Carlisle United's football stadium is Brinton Park.'

'Brunton Park,' Lucas corrected her automatically.

She frowned. 'I think you're wrong.'

'I know I'm right.'

'You don't even like football.'

'True. But I've visited Carlisle a few times.'

'Oh well, that's just cheating. I didn't know you knew the place. Fine, you win,' she said cheerfully. 'So what brought you up here?'

He hadn't meant to say it. Almost of their own volition, the words spilled out of his mouth. 'It's where my mum lives.'

She turned to look at him. 'Really?'

'Well, yes.' It was hardly the kind of thing you'd lie about.

'But . . . we're practically there,' Essie exclaimed. 'You must call in and see her!'

'No, it's OK.' His stomach muscles had tightened up. He was already regretting saying it.

'Lucas, you should,' Essie pleaded. 'You said you hadn't seen her for a while, and we're only a few miles from Carlisle. It's crazy not to! And I don't mind, honestly I don't.'

'Still not happening.'

'Is it because I'm with you? You don't want her to meet me? That's not a problem either,' she babbled on. 'You can drop me in the middle of Carlisle for a few hours, pick me up later.'

Lucas was feeling sick now. Why in God's name had he told her in the first place? He tightened his grip on the steering wheel and realised he needed to explain some of it, at least.

After several seconds of silence, he said slowly, 'It's more a matter of not wanting *you* to meet *her.*'

Essie looked blank. 'I don't understand.'

'She wouldn't want to see me either.'

'But . . . why not?'

'Because she never does want to see me. And when I do turn up, she can't get rid of me fast enough.'

'Why?' Essie's voice had softened, and Lucas knew he was going to have to tell her everything.

He kept his eyes firmly fixed on the road ahead as he spoke. 'Mum's an alcoholic. She can't cope with the world and all she cares about is her next drink. She never got over losing Dad, and alcohol became her way of getting through it. And she knows I hate seeing what she's done to herself, which is why she'd rather not see me at all. The last time I drove up, she locked herself inside the house and refused to open the door. And yes, I've tried everything I could, for years. But the fact that I wanted her to get help didn't do any good.' His voice cracked with emotion, which was the last thing he wanted to happen while they were travelling down the motorway. 'Because it's not my feelings that count. It has to come from her. She has to *want* to do it, but she just can't. It's been going on for too long now. To be honest, it's a miracle she's still alive.'

Chapter 43

'OK, get off the motorway,' Essie ordered. 'Let me take over.'

The slip road was up ahead. Once Lucas had pulled into a lay-by, they switched seats. Essie then deliberately turned off the engine and faced him. 'I'm sorry, I didn't mean to upset you.'

'Believe me, you aren't the reason I got upset.' Lucas uncapped his bottle of water and took a long swallow, then looked at her. 'So anyway, that's it. Now you know.'

'Do you wish you hadn't told me?'

'No, I'm glad I have.' It was true; he already felt less burdened.

'So it was both of them, your mum and your uncle Max.'

'He was first. For the first couple of years, he was the one drinking his way through what had happened, and the ironic thing was, Mum hated it. She couldn't bear to see what he was doing to himself. She despised him for it, told him he was being selfish and weak. Then she started drinking too. Like it was some kind of competition. When I asked her why she was doing it, she said it helped her to stop thinking and remembering. She said it was a distraction and helped with the pain.'

'Do you speak to her on the phone?' said Essie.

Lucas nodded. 'I do. I call her every week, and every week she gets upset and apologises, and tells me she can't see me.'

'Is she always drunk when you call?'

'I've learned the best time to do it. Well, I've had plenty of practice. Around midday, she's had a couple of drinks to get the shakes under control, but not so many that she can't hold a conversation. So that's when we talk. As soon as I put the phone down, I know she'll make a start on the gin. And it won't stop until . . . well, until she's completely paralytic.'

'What's her liver like?'

Lucas grimaced. 'It's not something she ever discusses with me, but I imagine it's like a football about to explode.'

'She could die,' said Essie.

He took another gulp of cold water. 'Yes.'

'It's only one o'clock.'

'Are you about to start nagging me?'

'Of course I am.' Essie pointed to the road sign ahead of them. 'We're here. I think you should at least try to see her, even if it's just for a few minutes.'

'She'll push me away.'

'She might not.'

Lucas held out his hand. 'Will you give me the key?'

'No.'

'Why are you doing this?'

'Because she's your mum,' said Essie. 'And she might be dead soon.'

Lucas made a gesture of defeat. 'Fine, but she doesn't want

to see me. Fifteen minutes from now, I'll be saying "I told you so".'

It didn't take long to reach the small estate on the outskirts of Carlisle. Lucas directed Essie and she drove, reassuring him and telling him he was doing the right thing. He knew better, but never mind; now that he'd told her the whole story, her eventual reaction was no longer his problem.

'OK, take the next left,' he said as they approached Pargeter Close. 'The house is down here on the right, past that blue van. Now pull up . . . that's it—' His words abruptly died in his throat as they passed the van and he saw his mother out in the front garden, throwing something into the recycling bin.

Bottles, probably.

'There she is. You stay here.' He hopped out of the car, called, 'Hi, Mum,' and raised a hand in greeting, as casually as if they saw each other every day.

His mother turned and covered her mouth in shock. 'Oh my God, Lucas! What are you doing here?'

At least she wasn't slurring and staggering; he'd caught her at just the right time. But her hands were trembling, which was something he'd grown used to over the years. And the tears were already spilling from her eyes.

'I was just passing, Mum. Thought I'd pop in and see how you're doing.' Having caught her off guard, he gave her a quick hug and for a moment she clung to him. He breathed in the smell of her just-washed hair and rose-scented shower gel, felt the suppressed emotions shaking her thin ribcage. And then she was letting go, stepping back and saying helplessly, 'Lucas, I'm sorry, it's good to see you but you shouldn't be here . . . You can't come in . . . You didn't tell me you were going to do this.'

She was backing away, glancing wildly around, clearly on the verge of a panic attack. Lucas said, 'What's wrong? It's OK; if you don't want me to come inside, we can just stay out here.'

'No! No, you have to leave!'

'Are you worried about the neighbours seeing me, is that it?'

'What?' She looked desperate. 'No . . . I mean yes! Lucas, *please* go! I'll speak to you next week.'

'Mum—'

But it was too late; his mother had darted to the front door, run inside and slammed it shut. He heard her call out in a panic, 'Go home, please. I love you, but you have to leave now. I can't *do* this.'

Back in the car, Lucas said bluntly, 'See what I mean?'

'God, I'm so sorry.' Essie had been watching and listening through the open driver's window. 'It's just awful for you. And for her, too.'

'Something's up, though. She was different this time.' Lucas frowned. 'She was agitated, but it was a different kind of agitated.'

'In what way?'

'I can't work it out.' He attempted to pinpoint what was puzzling him. 'It was like she was a not very good drugs mule trying to smuggle a caseful of heroin through customs. There was definitely something she was hiding from me . . . and it felt as if she was panicking because she didn't want anyone seeing me with her.'

'Or there was something she didn't want *you* to see,' said Essie. 'Or someone.'

Lucas looked at her, running through the likely options. 'You're right. That's what it was.' Had his mum fallen out so badly with the neighbours that she'd been terrified they might come storming out of their houses to tell him he had to sort her out? Had things spiralled completely out of control? Were the police involved?

But actually, she'd been glancing most often down the road, rather than at the other houses whose front doors might be about to fly open. He said to Essie, 'She'll be panicking now because the car hasn't moved. Come on, let's get out of here.'

Essie restarted the engine, did a three-point turn and drove out of the quiet cul-de-sac. A hundred metres down the main road, they came to a small convenience store. Lucas said, 'Can we stop here for a minute?'

It was a typical corner shop selling newspapers and magazines, cigarettes, groceries and – of course – drinks. Picking up a carton of milk and a packet of chewing gum, he took them to the counter and said easily, 'Hi, I'm Paula Brook's son, just popping by for a visit. Has she been in today?'

The man behind the counter said, 'Paula's son? Nice to meet you. No, I haven't seen her today, but her friend should be calling in soon.'

Bingo. 'Ah yes, I've been hearing all about her friend,' Lucas said casually. 'I've forgotten her name . . .'

'No, no, this one isn't a lady.' The shop owner shook his head. 'I meant her gentleman friend . . . He seems like a good man. My wife and I, we're pleased she's found him. Is the milk for your mother?'

'Uh . . . yes.'

'She prefers semi-skimmed.'

'OK. Thanks.' Lucas swapped the carton and paid. Risking it, he said, 'Well, I'm certainly looking forward to meeting him!'

'I think he finishes work at one o'clock; he usually drops in here around this time on his way over to Paula's.'

'Great. And it's been very nice to meet you too,' said Lucas. 'Can you do me a favour? If he does call in, don't mention that I'm here with Mum, OK? It'll be more fun if it's a surprise.'

Forty minutes later, they were still waiting in the car.

'Sorry about this,' said Lucas.

'It's fine.' Essie brushed aside the apology. 'Of course you want to see him.'

'If he's ever going to turn up.' So far, only two women with toddlers in pushchairs had disappeared into the cul-de-sac.

'It's like we're a couple of private detectives on a stake-out.' Essie sat up like a meerkat. 'Ooh, *car* . . .'

But it was an elderly woman behind the wheel of a beige Ford Focus.

Ten minutes later, Essie said casually, 'When private detectives are on a stake-out, what happens when they need the loo?'

Lucas smiled briefly. 'They do it in a plastic bottle.'

She winced. 'Well I'm not doing that.'

Lucas wondered if his mother had phoned her male friend in a panic and told him to stay away, even though she couldn't

332

know they were still here. 'Five more minutes, then we'll go.'

Two minutes later, he saw the man walking down the road towards them and said in a voice that didn't sound like his own, 'Here he is now.'

'What?' Sitting up and leaning across to catch a glimpse, Essie said, 'How do you know that's him?'

A muscle jumped in Lucas's jaw as he watched the man approach them. 'It's Uncle Max.'

Essie stared at Lucas. All the colour had drained from his face. And the middle-aged man currently just a few metres away from the car was Max, his father's brother.

The next moment, he'd veered to the right and disappeared into the corner shop. Lucas exhaled.

'What now?' said Essie.

'The last time I saw him, he was too drunk to stand,' said Lucas. 'He turned up at my eighteenth birthday and threw up all over the table with the cake on it. Which was . . . nice.'

'Shall we drive off before he comes out?'

'No way.' Lucas opened the door and stepped out of the car.

Less than a minute later, Max emerged from the shop carrying a magazine and a bag of doughnuts. He almost dropped them when he saw Lucas waiting for him.

'Hello, Max,' said Lucas.

'Lucas.' Max looked dumbstruck. 'It's . . . good to see you again.'

'What's going on? What are you doing here?'

'Your mum said you'd been to see her. She told me you'd left.'

'Well we didn't.' Lucas indicated Essie, still in the car. 'Because we wanted to know what she was hiding.'

The silence stretched between them. Finally Max nodded. 'Of course you did. And I told her she should tell you. Come on,' he said, 'let's get this done now.'

'I'll wait here.' Essie shrank into her seat because he was beckoning to her.

'No you won't.' Lucas opened the car and reached for her hand. 'I want you with me. We're going to get this thing sorted out, once and for all.'

They left the car where it was and entered the cul-de-sac on foot. Max double-rang the doorbell and Lucas's mother pulled open the door. When she saw who was with him, she clutched the side of the door for support and whispered, 'Oh God . . .'

Essie made coffees that no one really wanted, and listened to the story unfold.

'We met up again at a friend's funeral in Manchester, just under a year ago,' said Paula Brook, 'after not seeing each other for . . . well, so many years. And after the service, we ended up having a massive row.'

'What about?' said Lucas.

She shrugged. 'God knows what started it off. We certainly can't remember. The usual, I imagine. But it was the first time he'd seen me in that state and he told me I looked a bloody mess.'

'And she told me I was a bigger mess,' said Max. 'We spent a while slinging insults at each other, drinking everything we could lay our hands on, each of us sneering at how pathetic the other one was.'

Lucas briefly closed his eyes. 'Were you still at the funeral while this was going on?'

'No, thank God.' Paula shuddered. 'We'd left as soon as they stopped serving us drinks. Ended up in some awful back-street pub. And when they kicked us out at closing time, we slept under a bridge.'

Essie marvelled at her calm tone and matter-of-fact retelling of that night's events.

'And when I woke up the next morning,' said Max, 'the first thing I did was ask the homeless guy next to us if he could lend us a tenner so we could go and buy a drink.'

'And he did.' Paula joined in. 'So we spent the money on cider, and sat there drinking it, and people were walking past us on their way to work . . .' She paused, dry-eyed. 'That was when I saw a man stop to look at me.' She turned to Lucas. 'Just for a second, I thought it was your father, come back to see what I'd made of my life. And that was my rock-bottom moment. I just knew I couldn't do this any more, because if it had been your father, he would have been *so* appalled . . .'

Her voice trailed away, and Max took over. 'She was inconsolable. She told me she needed help, she wanted to stop drinking and start living again, and I could see she meant it. It really got to me, like . . . here.' He pressed his hand to his chest. 'I said I couldn't do it, but good luck to her and I hoped she could.'

'And I said we should both go for it,' Paula chimed in, 'because if we did it together, maybe we could help each other through it.'

'So that's what we did,' said Max. 'I still had some money left from selling my place in Spain.'

'And I took out a loan against this house,' said Paula.

'We went into rehab and stuck it out for six weeks. And the amazing thing was, it wasn't even as hellish as we'd thought it would be, because nothing was as bad as the hell we'd been living through for the last few years.'

'We saw a counsellor, too.' Paula was still gazing at Lucas, tears brimming in her eyes. 'He told us it wasn't anyone's fault that your dad had died. I mean, so many people had told us that, but for the first time we realised it was true. It was an accident and we didn't need to punish ourselves . . . we didn't have to feel guilty any more.'

'Because killing ourselves wasn't going to help anyone,' said Max.

Lucas was shaking his head in disbelief. 'And this happened a year ago? You've been through rehab, but it didn't even occur to you to tell me?'

'Leaving rehab was harder than being in there,' said Paula. 'We struggled when we came out. But we're battling through, supporting each other, going to AA meetings every day.'

'And still you didn't mention any of it to me.'

'Oh Lucas, don't be cross. I've wanted to, so much. Every time you rang me.' Paula pleaded with him to understand. 'But I was terrified of letting you down, of telling you I wasn't drinking any more, then hitting a bad patch and starting again. I needed to prove to myself that I really could do it. And we have, we've *been* doing it, taking it one day at a time. I made a promise to myself that once the year was up, I'd tell you. Because then I thought I could trust myself to keep going, and you'd trust me too . . . and I wanted you to believe, *really* believe, that I could carry on not drinking. And I am, I'm doing it . . . we're both doing it. One day at a time.' Her shoulders straightened and she said with pride, 'OK, it hasn't been a year, but I didn't know you were going to turn up like this, so I'll say it anyway. It's ten months and twenty-six days since my last drink.'

The room was silent. Outside in the garden, birds were darting around a bird feeder that hung from a spindly cherry tree.

Finally Lucas swallowed. 'Oh Mum, I love you so much. This is what I've been waiting for.' He rose to his feet and crossed the room, holding out his arms and wrapping them around his mother. 'It's all I've ever wanted.'

'I know, darling, I know.' The words caught in Paula's throat as she clung to him. 'And I'm so sorry it took me this long to do something about it. I've been the *worst* mother . . .'

'No you haven't. You were ill, and it wasn't your fault.' Lucas's dark eyes glittered as he hugged her, years of suppressed emotion rising to the surface. Max was watching them with love and empathy, as affected as they were. Essie's heart went out to him too; he'd lost not only his beloved brother but almost twenty years of his own life.

The next moment, releasing his hold on his mother, Lucas turned and said with raw honesty, 'Max, I've missed you. I'm so glad you and Mum found each other again.'

The two men embraced, and now the tears were flowing freely down Paula's thin cheeks. Then she blurted out, 'There's something else you have to know. Max and I, we aren't just friends. It's more than that.'

'OK,' said Lucas. 'That's great.'

Paula shook her head in utter disbelief. 'I thought you'd be horrified. I was dreading you finding out.'

'Mum, all I've ever wanted is for you to be happy again.

For both of you to be happy. If you're happy, then I am too.' Lucas's smile was miraculous to behold as he addressed them both. 'In fact, this is the best day of my life.'

They left Carlisle at seven that evening. Following the joyous reunion, the four of them had settled down and continued to talk over cups of tea and toasted sandwiches. Lucas told his mum and Max that his relationship with Giselle was over, without mentioning the awkward issue of the pregnancy, because there was no longer any need for them to know about it. Max paid a second visit to the corner shop in order to buy more doughnuts.

When Paula asked, 'So are you two together now?' Lucas said instantly, 'No, no, Essie has a boyfriend. We're friends, that's all.' Then it was time for Paula and Max to set off for their AA meeting in the centre of Carlisle, and for Lucas and Essie to head home.

'Well,' said Lucas once they'd hit the motorway, 'I suppose some road trips are just that bit more eventful than others.'

It had been an incredible afternoon. Essie said, 'Seeing your mum and Max like that . . . well, it's made *my* year. I can't begin to imagine how it's made you feel.'

'It's just indescribable.' He kept his attention fixed on the road ahead. 'I wasn't kidding when I said this was the best day of my life.'

And guess what. It isn't over yet.

Essie kept this renegade thought to herself. Watching him, she felt all lit up inside, simply because his joy was so infectious. His whole demeanour had changed, his body was palpably relaxed and he couldn't control the smile that was lifting the corners of his mouth.

Oh that mouth, that beautiful mouth. If he only knew how desperately she longed to cover it in kisses and—

'You're looking at me,' said Lucas.

'I'm just so happy for you.'

He exhaled. 'I think I've been weighed down for so long, I'd forgotten it was possible to feel like this.'

'You look different,' said Essie.

'And it's all down to you, for making me call in and see her. If you hadn't, we wouldn't have known.'

'You'd have found out eventually. Once the year was up.'

'But it's even better knowing it now.' He reached across and gave her arm a brief squeeze. 'Thank you.'

'My pleasure.' The sensation of his warm fingers touching her forearm was electrifying; it took all her self-control not to jump.

'I'm glad you were with me,' said Lucas.

Essie's mouth was dry. 'I'm glad too.'

Really glad.

'Then again, if you hadn't made me stop, we wouldn't still have a five-hour journey ahead of us.' His tone was wry. 'We'd have been home by now.'

'It's fine.'

'Was Paul expecting to see you this evening? If it helps, I could drop you at his place on the way back.'

'No need,' Essie said casually.

'He hasn't called you today.'

Time to come clean. 'That's because we aren't seeing each other any more.'

'Seriously?' Lucas sounded outraged. 'Just because you came up here with me? He finished with you because of *that*?'

339

Cheek.

'Thanks for making that assumption.' Essie shook her head. 'If you weren't driving, I'd push you out of the car. Actually, I was the one who finished with him.'

Silence.

Then Lucas said slowly, 'Because he wasn't happy about you coming here with me?'

'That was one reason. But it wasn't the only one.' Essie knew she had to tread with care. 'It wasn't working anyway. The last few months have made me realise . . . well, certain things. Quite a few things, really. We should never have got back together.'

'So you're not upset?'

'Absolutely not.'

'Well, that's good.'

Essie nodded. 'Yes, it is.'

'And you're sure you're OK?'

'Completely sure. Completely OK. Relieved it's over.' As she said it, Essie remembered he'd said the same about Giselle. She glanced sideways at him, wondering if he'd noticed, just as he looked over at her. For a moment their eyes met and it felt like stars colliding.

This time the silence seemed turbo-charged and the unspoken message in his gaze was enough to send adrenalin rocketing through her bloodstream.

If he only knew what she was thinking.

If only she knew what *he* was thinking.

Oh God, this was intense.

Then the smile returned, that irresistible, magical smile, and Lucas said, 'We'll be home by midnight.'

Chapter 44

Well that just about put the tin lid on it.

Conor searched through the rest of his overnight case, but the phone charger wasn't there, either in the side pocket where he'd left it or anywhere else in the case.

'I don't believe it.' He gestured with exasperation. 'I told her to put it back afterwards, and she couldn't even be bothered to do that.'

'Who?' said Belinda. 'Evie?'

'Not Evie. Caz.' *Who else?* 'She asked to borrow my charger yesterday afternoon because she'd broken hers, and I made sure she understood that I needed to bring it away with me. So she told me to chill out, of course she'd put it back. And guess what? Didn't happen. I *knew* it.'

'If you knew,' Belinda told him, 'you should have checked it was back in your case before we left.'

'I should have done. I forgot.'

'And Caz forgot too. It's easily done,' Belinda protested. 'It's not as if she did it on purpose!'

Conor sighed, because any criticism of Caz never went down well, but surely he was allowed to be annoyed? His phone was out of battery and now he had no way of charging it. God knows, he hadn't even wanted to come down here to Winchester, but Belinda had insisted.

'It's been six weeks since the last time we were meant to see Annette and Bill,' she chided. 'They've started calling you the invisible man. And it's their wedding anniversary . . . Oh please, we have to go!'

So he'd relented and they'd driven down yesterday morning, and as Belinda had promised, Annette and Bill were lovely people. Although he wished they weren't quite so enthusiastic about his relationship with Belinda.

To hear them talk, you'd think the wedding invitations had already been sent out.

'Come on, don't be so grumpy,' Belinda said now. Up in the attic bedroom, she took Conor's dead phone out of his hand. 'We're having a great time, aren't we? And now we're all going out to dinner, so why would you even need your phone anyway? It'll do you good to give it a rest for one night and manage without it.'

Hmm.

Almost home, almost home.

As they crested the hill that would lead them down into Bath, the lights of the city glittered like a constellation of stars and Essie's stomach tightened with anticipation, because some of those lights emanated from Percival Square and within minutes that was where they would be too.

And then what?

'Nearly there,' murmured Lucas.

'Nearly.' Aargh, she sounded like a parrot, but she couldn't help herself. Her heart was galloping away too. If they were to be flagged down now by a police car and ordered to open the window, would the police officers be able to tell how she was feeling? Would they know at once that here was a girl whose hormones were on the rampage?

'Are you tired?'

'No. Why?' The little hairs were quivering on the back of Essie's neck; sleep was currently the very last thing on her mind.

'Me neither.' Lucas glanced at her. 'I was just thinking, I could do with a drink once we're out of this car. If you want to join me.'

If I want to . . .

It was five minutes past midnight and the Red House would be closed. They would have the place to themselves, with no risk of being disturbed. The sexual tension between them had been building steadily throughout the journey home, all the more powerful and exhilarating for having remained unspoken. As if by mutual agreement, they'd talked about everything else other than their own feelings and emotions.

The degree of heightened anticipation was beyond anything Essie had experienced before. 'I think we deserve a drink, don't we?' she said. 'It's been quite a day.'

And although Lucas didn't reply, the look in his dark eyes and the slant of his eyebrows seemed to hint that it could go on to be quite a night.

But when he eventually swung the car into Percival Square, Essie said, 'Actually, could you drop me here?' as he was about to drive past Zillah's house.

Lucas frowned, but did as she asked.

'I'd just rather, you know, change out of this top . . .

freshen up a bit.' Hastily she added, 'Give me ten minutes and I'll be over.'

His expression cleared. 'Right, of course. Good idea. I might do that too.' He broke into a smile of what looked like relief and Essie thought he might be about to lean across and kiss her. But they'd waited this long; they might as well wait that little bit longer.

She opened the passenger door. 'Don't fall asleep before I get there.'

And Lucas, his irresistible smile broadening, put the car back into gear. 'See you in ten.'

There were no lights on in Zillah's flat, which meant she must be out. Letting herself into the house, Essie raced up the staircase to her own flat. She might have mentioned casually changing her shirt and freshening up a bit, but what this really meant was taking a lightning-fast shower, brushing her teeth, finding a whole new set of clothes and spraying herself with scent.

As she stepped under the stream of hot water, she thought she heard a noise like someone crying out. She stuck her head out of the shower and listened, but it didn't happen again. Probably a vixen outside in the square, yowling for a mate.

Ha, I know the feeling.

Seven minutes later, having thrown on a blue-and-white polka-dotted jersey dress and blue ballet flats, she grabbed her shoulder bag and raced back down the stairs. OK, her hair was still wet, but that didn't matter. If Lucas had jumped into the shower, his hair would be wet too, it was—

She screeched to a halt in the hallway, jolted out of her happy fantasy as she spotted what she hadn't noticed before.

There were half a dozen envelopes scattered over the mat

by the front door. They'd been there for over twelve hours. Which must mean that neither Conor nor Zillah was here.

But Zillah hadn't mentioned anything about going away.

Essie stared at the post on the floor, then at the locked door to Zillah's apartment. If Zillah was asleep in bed, she wouldn't appreciate being woken up by someone bellowing her name. But if she *were* here, why hadn't she picked up the letters?

Essie kept a key to Zillah's apartment on her key ring. She found it now and fitted it into the lock, opening the door as quietly as possible.

The living room was empty and in darkness.

As was the kitchen.

The door to the bedroom was half open. Her heart thudding, Essie peered inside and saw the empty king-sized bed, the tipped-over chair, the old black-and-white photographs scattered across the carpet.

Oh God, what's happened? Where is she?

'Zillah?' Her voice rose. 'Zillah!'

And then she heard the eerie cry again, less distant this time. Swinging round, she realised it was coming from the bathroom, and her blood ran cold.

Zillah was lying on her side on the black-and-white tiled floor, fully dressed and half covered with a bath towel. Her face was deathly pale, there were smears of dried blood on her temple and her eyes were closed. Her breathing was shallow and irregular, and as Essie knelt beside her, she gave a groan of pain.

'Zillah, can you hear me?'

No response.

Essie's hands shook as she dialled 999.

345

Chapter 45

The ticking of the clock up on the pale-grey wall was the only sound in the hospital waiting room, until the door opened and a doctor came in.

Except he wasn't a doctor, he was a surgeon; the neuro-surgeon who had, in the small hours of the morning, carried out the emergency operation on Zillah's brain.

On her *actual brain*.

'Well, it's done,' he told them as Lucas reached for Essie's hand. 'She's come through the surgery, but now we just have to wait and see how she gets on from here.'

'Did it go well?' said Lucas. 'As far as you can tell?'

'The procedure was straightforward, that's all I can say for now. We won't know if there are likely to be any residual problems until she wakes up, and that isn't going to happen for a while.'

Essie nodded helplessly. The operation had been explained to them beforehand. Basically, the dried blood on Zillah's temple had been the least of her worries. The head injury had caused a slow intracranial leakage of blood, known as a subacute subdural haematoma, which had collected beneath the meninges, which in turn covered and protected the surface of the brain.

As a consequence of the bleed, the build-up of pressure within the skull would have caused headaches, drowsiness and increasing confusion, which apparently explained why Zillah hadn't called 999 herself.

'I think the best thing you can do is go home and catch up on some sleep,' the surgeon told them now.

For the millionth time, Essie wondered how long Zillah had lain there helplessly, in pain and alone. She shook her head. 'No, I can't do that. I'm staying here.'

Ninety miles away in Winchester, Conor got up early and drove into the centre of town. He bought himself a new charger and took it back to Annette and Bill's house.

'You're obsessed.' Belinda rolled her eyes as he plugged in his phone. 'We're driving home this evening; can you really not wait until then?'

'I have a business to run. It's unprofessional not to reply to messages.'

'You mean emergency gardening questions? Help, help!' Belinda waved her hands in mock panic. 'My dahlias have gone droopy and I don't know what to *dooooo*!'

Conor didn't respond to the jibe. Nor did he point out that Belinda had earlier spent twenty minutes chatting happily on her own phone to Caz and to Evie, who was staying with her.

Ten minutes later, he saw the messages pinging up one after the other.

'What do you mean, we have to go? We're not leaving until this evening,' Belinda protested. 'Look, it's a gorgeous sunny day. We're going on a tour of Winchester Cathedral!'

Unbelievable.

Conor said, 'If it was Evie in hospital, would you go home early?'

'Of course I would. But that's because it's Evie. She's only sixteen and I'm her guardian!'

'Zillah's in the neurosurgical unit at Southmead Hospital. She's had emergency brain surgery,' Conor repeated.

'I know, and I get that you like her, but what is she to you?' Belinda spread her arms in disbelief. 'I mean, all you are is one of her tenants, and she's your landlady.'

Conor looked at her. During dinner last night, there'd been casual mentions of where they might spend next Christmas, and how a trip to Tenerife might be nice. He'd silently marvelled at Belinda's certainty that they'd still be a couple then.

And now he realised it wasn't going to happen.

'OK. I know you've been looking forward to visiting the cathedral,' he said slowly.

'I *have*.' Belinda nodded, evidently pleased that he'd come to his senses.

'So you should stay. But I'm leaving now.'

Her blue eyes widened. 'Are you serious? How am I meant to get home?'

As clear as day, Conor heard Scarlett's voice in his head, saying innocently, 'Maybe on your broomstick?'

But that would be wrong and deeply inappropriate. In lots of ways, Belinda was a kind and thoughtful person, not witchy at all.

Aloud he said, 'Don't worry, I'll pay for you to get the train.'

★   ★   ★

348

'She could have *died*,' Essie told Conor yet again. It was two days later and he was probably fed up with hearing it, but she couldn't help herself. Every time she said the words, or even thought them, her skin crawled with shame. 'And it would have been all my fault. I should have been there.'

What she hadn't admitted to him was just how close she'd come to missing the clues, skipping out of the house and leaving Zillah there on the bathroom floor, simply because the need to be across the square and back with Lucas in his flat had been uppermost in her mind. Imagine if that had happened, and one thing had led to another and she hadn't returned to Zillah's house until the following morning . . .

Because by then the very worst thing imaginable would have happened. Zillah would have been dead.

The horrifying thought of it was still replaying in Essie's mind.

'But she didn't die,' said Conor. 'And none of this was your fault anyway. You have to stop blaming yourself.'

Of course he felt this way. Because he didn't know. He had no idea.

'I feel so responsible. When she didn't reply to my texts, I just thought it was because she'd left her phone switched off in the bottom of her handbag, because that's what she does. But she's eighty-three,' Essie wailed, 'and I shouldn't have assumed that was the reason. I should have got someone to check up on her, make sure she was OK.'

'Hey, this is Zillah. Being nursemaided isn't her style. She'd have hated that.'

'Well she's going to have to get used to it from now on,' said Essie grimly.

'And someone has to tell her her days of climbing up on chairs are over too.'

It was all right for Conor; he didn't have a reason to feel guilty. Essie said, 'She won't take any notice of us. We'll have to get someone really terrifying to do it.'

Conor pulled a face. 'That'd be Caz.'

The neurosurgeon, wearing a paisley bow tie, emerged from the ward. When he saw them waiting in the corridor, he said, 'You can go in now. I've finished examining her.'

'How's she doing?' Essie held her breath.

'Astonishingly well, considering her age.' The surgeon's smile was dry. 'And if she heard me say that, she'd give me short shrift. No, she's making an excellent recovery. We're very happy with her progress. At this rate, you'll be able to take her home with you in the next two or three days.'

'We're calling her Superwoman,' one of the ward nurses chimed in, beaming as she passed them in the corridor.

'See?' Conor gave Essie a reassuring nudge. 'No need to feel bad.'

But Essie still did.

Zillah was out of bed, wrapped in her red silk dressing gown, and sitting like a queen in the high-backed chair beside it. Her glossy black hair was carefully combed over the site of the burr hole in her skull through which the subdural haematoma had been extracted. Her dark eyes were kohl-lined and as bright as they'd ever been, her skin was velvety and her mouth was its customary shade of glossy scarlet.

'Hang on, you asked me to bring your make-up in for you!' Essie held up the bag containing everything that had been on Zillah's dressing table at home. Indignantly, she

350

pointed to the expensive cosmetics clustered together on the bedside locker. 'Where did you get all *that*?'

'Oh I couldn't bear to wait.' Zillah reached up and kissed her on each cheek. 'Ordered it online with same-day delivery. Isn't technology marvellous?'

'You look great,' said Conor. 'And you're sounding better too. Your speech is back to normal.'

'I know. Thank goodness!' Zillah pulled a face. 'I could hear myself slurring like a drunk before. All the side effects but none of the fun of actually getting to enjoy a few cocktails.'

Conor's eyes were twinkling. 'Your surgeon tells us you could be coming home in a few days. You'll need to take things easy for a while. Concentrate on getting your strength back.'

'Taking things easy is boring. Anyway, enough about me. How are you two getting on?' Zillah observed them with avid interest; since hearing that their respective relationships with Paul and Belinda had broken up, her keenness for Essie and Conor to get together had resurfaced with a vengeance.

'Me and Ess?' said Conor. 'We're getting married.'

'*Really?*'

'No,' Essie said firmly. 'We aren't.'

'Well thanks for getting my hopes up,' Zillah told Conor. 'All I'm trying to do is sort out the failed love lives of two sad, lonely singletons. Could you consider it, at least?'

Essie rolled her eyes with amusement, because Zillah took directness to the next level. 'Sorry, not going to happen.'

Later, when Conor had left them to go downstairs for a coffee, Zillah said, 'You aren't yourself, darling. Something's wrong. Are you upset about Paul?'

351

How, *how* was she able to detect these things? Was it some kind of extrasensory radar? Essie could have sworn she was managing to keep her true feelings under wraps.

With a dismissive shrug, she said, 'No, I'm really not. And I know you weren't that keen on him either, so you don't have to be polite.'

'Oh darling, it's not that I wasn't keen. I'm sure he's a nice enough person. I just didn't think he was right for *you*.'

'Well he's gone now. *Anyway*.' Changing the subject, Essie delved into her shoulder bag. 'While Conor's downstairs, I wanted to ask you about these.'

'What are they?' Zillah leaned forward to see the contents of the envelope.

'I tidied up your bedroom, put all the photos back in the box. But there were these sheets of paper too, torn out of a notebook and scattered over the bed. You'd been trying to write a letter. Do you remember doing that?'

'I'm not sure.' Zillah frowned. 'It's all a bit hazy. I couldn't work out what was really happening and what was a dream.'

'Well look, I wasn't trying to be nosy but I couldn't help noticing the name. It kind of jumped out at me. I don't know why,' said Essie, 'but you were writing to Alice.'

'Oh . . .' Zillah took the sheaf of torn-out pages and nodded slowly. 'That's it, I remember now. Alice was there with me. Except I suppose she wasn't, because how would she have got into the house? So that means it was a dream, but it felt real. And she was so . . . angry with me. And I couldn't make her understand how sorry I was . . . I kept trying to tell her, but she wouldn't listen . . .'

'Don't cry,' Essie blurted out, because tears were running down Zillah's immaculately powdered cheeks and crying surely couldn't be good for someone who'd just had a bleed in their brain. What if it caused the mended blood vessel to explode? 'You mustn't cry! It wasn't real, it didn't happen!'

'Let me read it, I want to see what I wrote.' Wiping her eyes, Zillah reached for her reading glasses.

Essie watched her. She'd tried to put the pages in order, but the sentences had been disjointed, little more than random thoughts that Zillah had scribbled down as and when they'd occurred to her in her confused state. Clearly haunted by the past, she had been overcome with remorse and had felt the need to apologise:

All these years I've hated myself . . . You were so good and kind . . . and I was selfish . . .

Oh I'm so thirsty . . . Alice, you can shout at me, I deserve it. I'm a horrible person and I should die first . . . Please no slugs . . . And now I think I am dying . . . my head hurts so much. But I found the photo of you and . . .

Those were the last words Zillah had scrawled and it still turned Essie's stomach over to think they could have been her last words ever.

'That's it.' Zillah nodded. 'I was looking for the photograph of Alice and Matthew together when I fell. I found it, too.'

'It nearly killed you.'

'I really did think I was going to die.' Zillah fiddled with the piped edging of her silk robe. 'And I thought I deserved to, as well.'

'Well you didn't,' Essie said with feeling. 'Thank goodness. What were you even doing, looking for some old photo of Alice and Matthew?'

'I saw her,' said Zillah. 'On Monday. She spoke to me.'

Essie was gripped with fear; did this mean Zillah was still

a bit confused after all? Gently she said, 'No, that was in the dream, after you'd fallen down and hit your head.'

'I know you think I've gone doolally, but I haven't. I saw her on Monday afternoon,' insisted Zillah. 'She'd just been admitted to the hospice.'

Well *phew*.

'Really?' Essie was simultaneously shocked and relieved. 'Oh God, how *awful*. Did she shout at you? Was there an embarrassing scene?'

'You watch too much *EastEnders*.' Zillah plucked a fresh tissue from the box beside her and dabbed carefully beneath her eyes. 'No, it was far worse than that. She was *nice*.'

It was as if a heavy metal door had clanged shut in his face, and Lucas knew exactly when it had happened. Of course, in that hospital waiting room, while Zillah was being operated on, he'd understood that Essie had been beside herself with anxiety and too on edge to speak.

Then the surgeon had come to tell them that the operation was over, and Lucas had taken hold of Essie's hand, purely in order to support her.

But she'd withdrawn her hand from his as if it were contaminated and there had been no physical contact between the two of them since. That moment had also marked the end of any emotional connection; it was as if Essie had come crashing back to her senses and realised she'd been on the verge of making the most terrible mistake of her life.

It had become brutally apparent that she was relieved nothing had had the chance to happen. The chemistry had evaporated; the whole sense of attraction had closed down so completely that it was as if it had never existed in the first place, to the extent that Lucas now found himself wondering if he'd only imagined it to be mutual.

Because the feelings still existed on his side – oh God, if anything they'd only intensified – but Essie was making it blindingly obvious that she was no longer remotely interested in him.

Lucas mentally braced himself, because he was about to attempt to get to the bottom of the situation. Scarlett had continued covering for Essie here at the Red House, but her work as a tour guide at lunchtime, followed by a trip to Bristol, meant Essie had been forced to come in and work today's shift. It had been like those weeks when she'd first been working here: in front of customers she had been outwardly polite to him, whilst managing not to look at him directly once.

But now the shift was over and she was about to leave. Returning from the coat rack with her yellow jacket slung over her arm, she was moving fast towards the exit.

Moving faster, Lucas cut her off. 'Look, could we have a chat? Can we go upstairs? We need to—'

'I can't.' And still she was avoiding his gaze, angling herself away from him, almost as if his proximity was too much to tolerate. 'Sorry, I have to go.'

'Essie, please . . .'

'No, don't do this; there is nothing to talk about.' She was shaking her head, emphasising her determination to make the point. 'I mean it . . . There isn't anything to say, and I really have to go.'

Lucas stood aside, because you couldn't get clearer than that. And no way was he going to beg. He still couldn't believe he'd misread the earlier signs so badly, but obviously he had. What had felt so important and inevitable had been no more than a moment of weakness for her, much like Giselle's on Christmas Eve, when she'd spent the evening with her first love and ended up pregnant as a result.

A cautionary tale if ever there was one.

OK, time to get over what he'd got so wrong. Lucas watched as Essie left the Red House without so much as a backward glance. He needed to put the whole non-relationship behind him and let it go for good.

His chest tightened as he turned away. Oh, it was hard to let someone go when you'd never had them in the first place.

But he had to, so he would.

Chapter 46

Five days after the surgery, and having been given the all-clear by her consultant, Zillah was allowed to leave the hospital.

'Oh, it's good to be home.' She sighed with relief as Conor helped her out of the car and Essie greeted her on the doorstep with a hug.

'Come on in,' said Essie. 'Everyone's missed you so much.'

'It smells like a florist's shop,' Zillah marvelled.

'Wait till you see what it looks like.' Grinning, Essie opened the door to Zillah's apartment and led her inside.

'Oh my word.' Zillah blinked in amazement, because there were arrangements of flowers everywhere, as well as gift boxes of toiletries and chocolates, and metallic helium balloons swaying in the air.

'People have been delivering things all day. Everyone's longing to see you. We're going to have to make an appointment system, otherwise you'll be exhausted.'

'I love having visitors.'

'We know you do,' said Essie. 'But you know what the doctor said about taking things easy.'

Taking things easy was unbelievably tedious and Zillah had no intention of doing it, but she nodded and said, 'Of course I will. Oh look, how gorgeous! Where did you get those?' Because pinned up around the kitchen at eye level were lengths of bunting, thick paper triangles in ice-cream shades of pink and green, decorated with fine squiggly patterns and strung on yellow ribbon. She clapped her hands in delight. 'Isn't that just beautiful?'

'Move closer,' Conor prompted, passing over her reading glasses. 'Put these on and take another look.'

Mystified, Zillah obeyed him. Slowly she realised that the patterns weren't just random squiggles; they were written words. Then she saw what the words were saying, each triangle bearing a different message with a name beneath it:

Dearest Zillah, we're missing you so much – this place isn't the same without you! Penny at number 38.

Get well very soon, lovely lady – big hug from Philippa at the bridge club.

Very best wishes to the kindest lady I know. Terence x (postman)

To the old lady with the butiful smile and red lipstik. Sorry your poorley! Love from Ben (6) and Snowy (woof) xxxxx

To darling Zillah, our Queen of the Square! Make a speedy recovery please – we all love and miss you dreadfully. Jude and all at the Red House. XXX

Sending love and good wishes to the cheerful, stylish lady who just happens to be our favourite customer. From all the staff at Kaye's Cake Shop.

There were many, many more messages but Zillah could no longer read them; her vision was too blurred with tears. Choked with emotion, she said, 'But . . . how?'

Essie found her a tissue and gave her a hug. 'Once word

358

got out that you were in hospital, it just spread like wildfire. Everywhere we went, people were asking after you and telling us how wonderful you are. And I thought, everyone loves you but I don't think you have any idea how much, or what a difference you make to their lives. So I started asking them to write little messages to you on my Facebook and Twitter pages . . . and it was like setting off an avalanche. These are only some of the messages, by the way.' She gestured to the lengths of bunting with her free hand. 'If I'd used all of them, we'd have had enough to decorate the whole of Percival Square.'

Zillah shook her head, touched beyond belief, both by the messages themselves and by Essie's thoughtfulness. She was so used to presenting her smiling, perfectly made-up face to the world that scarcely anyone was aware of the feelings of not being a good enough person that lurked beneath.

But Essie knew.

'The make-up girls at the shop where you buy your lipsticks sent you those.' Essie pointed to a vase of appropriately striking crimson roses.

'And the freesias are from one of the most annoying humans on the planet,' said Conor. 'But when I saw what he'd written on the card, I nearly cried.'

'Who?' Zillah dabbed at her eyes and he handed her the card: *Dearest Zillah, I still have the beautiful letter you wrote to me after my mum died and will never forget your kind words. You're a truly wonderful person. Please get well very soon. Brendan Banks.*

Poor Brendan. He *was* incredibly annoying but he didn't mean to be. Zillah remembered the afternoon last spring when she'd been sitting on one of the benches in the square and he had joined her, wondering if he was ever going to find himself a girlfriend. She'd assured him that it would happen when it was meant to happen, and then he'd talked a bit more about how much he was still missing his mum . . . Well, she'd tried her best to cheer him up, but another year had passed and the poor man still hadn't managed to find a girl to share his life.

'And this basket of flowers is from everyone at the hospice,' Essie continued. 'Elspeth dropped them off this morning. She said to tell you that they all send their love – well of course they do! – and they hope they'll see you back there as soon as you're fit and well again.'

Zillah glanced up once more at the pastel-shaded bunting fluttering gently in the breeze from the open window. *Queen of the Square* . . . How she'd always glowed with happiness when people had teasingly called her that. So many messages, so many kind words; it was just the most extraordinary feeling. If she were to die now, she would die happy.

It was as if she'd been magically granted her very own last wish.

Except she wasn't about to die, which was even better.

She gave Essie's arm a squeeze. 'Oh I'll definitely be seeing them again soon. I can't wait to go back.'

Chapter 47

Well this was nice, being allowed to leave the house un-accompanied. Zillah smiled to herself; it was like being let out on parole.

Not currently allowed to drive, she had insisted on calling a taxi to take her to St Mark's.

'But I can take you there,' Essie had protested. 'I won't get in your way, I promise. I'll just wait in the car, then drive you home again afterwards.'

Zillah, busy spraying her neck and wrists with scent, had said, 'Darling, you have to stop worrying about me. I'll be *fine*.'

'But what if you're not? What if you're taken ill?'

'You mean while I'm at the hospice?' Amused, she'd spread her hands. 'What better place for it to happen?'

An hour later, having been enthusiastically welcomed back by both the staff and those residents who were in the sitting room, Zillah went to seek out Alice. She knocked gently on her door and said, 'Hello, it's me. Are you up for a visitor?'

'I am. Come on in. Goodness, what a sight for sore eyes.'

Echoing what so many others had already told her, Alice said, 'You look so well.'

'Thanks. I was very lucky.' Almost a fortnight had passed since she'd last been here. Outside the window, spring had truly sprung; green shoots had pushed their way up through the earth and the grounds were now bursting with colour and new life.

Whereas in this room, the change in Alice was equally noticeable, but in the other direction. She was thinner, greyer, visibly more exhausted. Zillah bent over the bed to greet her with a kiss on the cheek. 'And thank you for the card. It was beautiful.'

'I'm glad you've made such a good recovery.' Alice's pale eyes crinkled at the corners. 'If you'd died before me, I think I'd have felt quite guilty, as if I'd somehow caused it to happen.'

And she didn't even know. She had no idea. Disarmed by her honesty, Zillah said, 'You almost did. The reason I fell off the chair was because I was looking for this to give to you.' She took the photo out of her handbag and passed it to Alice, who looked stunned.

'Really?'

'Really. I thought you might like it.'

Alice studied the photograph for several seconds, nodding as the memory of the night it had been taken came back to her.

'I do, very much.' She looked amused. 'Not at the expense of your life, though.'

'I know. Although I did think I probably deserved it. But of course it was just one of those random things.' Zillah shrugged. 'Every action has a consequence, and all that.'

'Well, I'm glad you're still alive. I'd have felt bad if I'd killed you.'

'See? And this is why you're still one of the nicest people I've ever known.' Zillah pulled up a chair and sat down. 'Now, did Elspeth tell you why I come and spend time here?'

'She did. She told me about the wishes.' Alice coughed weakly, then nodded as she lay back against her pillows. 'Such a lovely thing to do.'

'I'd like to arrange one for you,' said Zillah.

'Me? Oh . . . that's so kind.' Alice paused. 'But I can't think of anything to wish for. Well, nothing that's physically possible,' she amended. 'I think I've left it a bit late to take up skateboarding.'

'OK, take your time. What was the happiest time of your life? Where was your favourite place? What did you most love doing when you were younger?' These were the questions Zillah always asked, designed to trigger memories and ideas. 'Is there one occasion that stands out?'

Alice's face softened as she gazed into the distance.

'Tell me what you're thinking right now,' Zillah prompted gently.

'Nothing.' Alice summoned an apologetic smile. 'Well, not nothing, but it's way beyond anything I could manage.'

'Tell me anyway.' From experience, Zillah knew that recalling happy memories brought its own kind of joy.

'The ballet,' Alice said simply. 'Matthew took me to Covent Garden for my birthday. He'd bought tickets for us to see the Royal Ballet perform *Swan Lake*, and it was just the most magical experience of my life . . .' Her thin fingers fluttered in an attempt to signify how perfect it had been.

'I had no idea . . . I'd never been to the ballet before. And that was the night I fell in love with it. The music, the dancers, the *feel* of it . . . oh, it was all so stunningly beautiful, I thought I was in heaven.' The corners of her mouth lifted once more at the memory. 'And that was the start of my lifelong passion.'

Zillah's eyebrows went up. 'You *danced*?'

'Oh gosh, no.' Alice's smile broadened. 'I was just the biggest fan. Every opportunity I had, I'd go to the ballet. Nowadays I watch it on TV.' She pointed behind Zillah, to the DVD player and the piles of DVDs lined up beside it. 'Not the same, of course, but better than nothing. Have you ever been to the Royal Opera House?'

Zillah shook her head. Ballet had never particularly appealed to her. Matthew had once asked her if she'd like him to buy tickets for some production or other, but she'd said no. Back then, visiting Soho jazz clubs had been far more her idea of fun.

'Matthew used to enjoy the ballet.' Alice glanced fondly at the black-and-white photo. 'Oh, bless him. I'm so glad he was happy at the end. How long ago did he die, do you know?'

Zillah did a double-take. 'Matthew? He didn't die. He's still alive.'

'*Is* he?' Alice was visibly stunned. 'Oh my God . . .'

'Why did you think he was dead?'

'I was sent one of those round-robin things in a Christmas card a couple of years back. From Jessica Hurd-Stockton, do you remember her? She was always one of those types who kept in touch with everyone. Anyway, she mentioned it, said how sad she'd been to hear that Matthew Carter had died. I mean, it was a bit of an odd letter, to be honest, quite a lot of talk about pigeons, but I didn't have any reason not to believe her.' Alice was still looking incredulous. 'Are you absolutely sure he's alive?'

Zillah took out her phone. 'Well, it'd be weird if he wasn't, because he sent me the most amazing arrangement of tropical lilies yesterday.'

'Oh.' Overwhelmed, Alice's thin fingers fluttered to her chest. 'Why would Jessica have said that if it wasn't true?'

Having googled the name, Zillah pulled a face. 'Ah. It says here that Jessica Hurd-Stockton died last year.' She scanned the obituary notice rapidly. 'She'd been suffering from dementia.'

Alice nodded. 'Poor woman. That explains the pigeons. Goodness, I can't believe Matthew's still alive. Where does he live?'

'Berkshire. He's turned into quite the golf fiend in recent years. From the sound of things, he practically lives at his local club. But it keeps him active, so why not, if that's what he enjoys.' A glimmer of an idea was forming in her brain now, prompted by the look in Alice's eyes. Casually, Zillah said, 'You know, if I told him you were here, I bet he'd love to come and see you.'

Alice stared at her. 'Oh, surely not. He wouldn't want to. I mean, why *would* he?'

'I wouldn't say it if I didn't mean it. And trust me,' said Zillah, 'he definitely would. We were chatting a few years ago and he was wondering how your life had gone. He loved you, Alice. I know he broke your heart, but he never stopped caring about you. And he's such a lovely man . . .'

They sat in silence for several seconds. Alice rolled the

edge of the sheet between her fingers as she gave the matter some thought. Finally she said, 'Well, I might not be able to get to the ballet, but I can manage sitting up in bed to receive a visitor. And if I'm being granted a wish, I can't think of anything I'd love more than seeing Matthew again. It'd just be the most perfect present . . . if you really and truly think he wouldn't mind.'

'He'd be delighted,' Zillah reassured her. 'He'll be out on the golf course now, but I'm going to call him tonight. You just leave everything to me.'

Chapter 48

It was Sunday night at the Red House. A man had just come up to Conor and thanked him for changing his life for the better.

'Really?' Conor was intrigued. 'How did I manage that?'

'My wife left me six months ago. I was so down, I couldn't see any point in carrying on.' The man, in his forties, was large and shaven-headed, with multiple tattoos. 'I came in here one night and saw one of the photos you'd taken. It was over there.' He pointed to a spot on the wall beside the fireplace. 'It was a photo of a bloke in Victoria Park, rolling on the ground with his dog, and there were autumn leaves all over the grass and the bloke and his dog just looked so *happy* together . . . Swear to God, I couldn't take my eyes off them. Reckon I must've stared at them for a good couple of hours.'

'I remember it.' Conor nodded; of course he remembered the photo. Everyone had been charmed by the evident bond between the man and his beloved pet.

'So the next day I went up the dogs' home and found Bertie.' The man indicated the small, bright-eyed black mongrel sitting at his feet. 'And it's all thanks to you that I did. He's the best thing that could have happened to me and he's made life worth living again. I couldn't be without him now . . . well, we wouldn't want to be without each other. So we just wanted to come and say thank you.'

Conor was touched beyond belief. 'That's fantastic, I'm so pleased. And now I need to take some photos of the two of you. Who knows, maybe someone else will see them and be inspired to get a dog as well.'

The man lifted Bertie into his arms, beaming with love and pride as the dog licked his tattooed ear, and Conor took a dozen or so shots. As he was finishing, the back of his neck began to prickle and he sensed he was being watched.

When the man had left, Conor turned and saw Caz leaning against the bar, wearing her turquoise snakeskin-print jacket and more mascara than all the Kardashians put together.

And crimson over-the-knee stiletto-heeled boots.

Oh God, what was about to happen? If she was here to have a furious row with him for finishing with Belinda, how should he handle it?

He mentally braced himself. This could be embarrassing. No one enjoyed a shouty showdown more than Caz.

'I need to speak to you,' she said evenly. 'Shall we go outside?'

Which instantly made him think going outside could be a bad idea.

'We can talk in here.' Hopefully this would give him the upper hand. Scarlett, who was still working behind the bar so that Essie could stay at home with Zillah, was observing the exchange with interest. Putting his camera down on the bar, Conor said, 'What's this about?'

As if he didn't know.

Caz lifted her chin. 'I want to know what happened between you and Belinda.'

'I don't think that's any of your business, is it?'

She bristled visibly. 'I think it is. Belinda's my *friend*.'

'I don't care.' Conor spread his hands. 'It's private, between *us*.'

'Is it, though?'

Oh God, talk about persistent. 'What's that supposed to mean?'

'I'm here to ask you why you finished with her,' Caz said tightly, 'and I need to know the truth. Was it because of me?'

Bloody hell, *what*? Conor stared at her in disbelief. If she seriously thought he'd ended his relationship with Belinda because he secretly wanted to be with *her* . . .

'Tell me the truth, please.' Caz was insistent. 'If I'm the reason you broke up with her, we can sort this out.'

Now he was even more confused. 'I'm not sure what you mean.'

Scarlett, who'd been listening, suddenly blurted out, 'OK, can I just explain? Caz doesn't think you're madly in love with her. She's asking you if the reason you and Belinda broke up is because you can't stand *her*.' She pulled an apologetic face at Caz. 'Sorry, but we both know it's true.'

'Of course it's true!' It was Caz's turn to be stunned. She jabbed a finger at Conor. 'You seriously thought I was here because I thought you fancied me? Ha, are you *nuts*? I wouldn't think that! I know you can't stand me!'

'That's why I was so confused.' Conor was indignant.

'OK, at least now we're on the same page.' Caz drew a deep breath. 'So let me ask you again. Am I the reason you finished with Belinda? Because if I am, I'll step aside. I won't be her best friend any more; you'll never have to put up with me again. And I mean it, OK? If you and Belinda walk into the pub and I'm there, I'll leave, because all I want is for her to be happy, and I couldn't bear to be the person getting in the way of that.'

'Whoa.' Conor held up his hand to stop her. 'It's not you. You're not the reason.'

'But you hate me.'

'I don't *hate* you. You're loud and annoying, and sometimes your voice is like nails being scraped down a blackboard, but I don't hate you. And I promise you now, you weren't the reason the relationship didn't work out.'

Caz narrowed her eyes, clearly not convinced. 'But you were so happy together. The only thing you weren't happy about was me.'

Conor was unexpectedly moved. As Belinda had always reminded him, Caz was a loyal friend with a good heart. She was essentially a kind, well-meaning person. Maybe he did need to explain.

'We were happy to begin with. But after a while it began to feel like everyone was so enthralled by the story of how we met that we had to stay together just so they could get their happy-ever-after.'

'That makes sense.' Caz nodded slowly. 'You mean you felt pressured.'

'I did. And Evie's such a fantastic kid . . . that was another pressure. But sometimes it just takes a while to realise you aren't as good a match as you hoped you would be. Which was what happened to me,' said Conor. 'These things don't always work out. I didn't want to hurt Belinda, but you can't just stay with someone to avoid upsetting them, can you? That wouldn't be fair to her or to me.'

Caz looked at him. 'It wouldn't.'

'Thank you. Finally we agree on something.'

'And it absolutely definitely wasn't because of me?'

'Absolutely definitely,' said Conor, relieved that there hadn't been an almighty showdown. 'And to prove it, I'm going to buy you a drink.'

This perked Caz right up. 'Ah, cheers. I'll have a large voddy-tonic!'

If only she knew how much the way she said 'voddy-tonic' set his teeth on edge.

Then a heavy hand clapped Conor on the back and a voice bellowed, 'Getting a round in, are we? Ha ha, looks like I timed that well!'

Oh joy, it was Brendan, with his uncanny knack of attaching himself to people who'd rather he kept his distance. Conor opened his mouth to explain that actually they were having a private conversation, but Brendan was already gazing with open admiration at Caz.

'I say, you're a veritable vision! Are you Conor's new lady friend? Hello, I'm Brendan, how delightful to meet you!'

'Are you out of your mind? Me and Conor? Hahahahaha.' Caz let out an ear-splitting parrot screech of laughter. 'As if! He can't stand me!'

'Oh now, I don't believe that,' Brendan protested.

'It's true,' said Conor. 'And pretty much mutual.'

'Pint of Heineken for me, Scarlett. Well that's just crazy.' Brendan turned back to Caz. 'Look at you – you're a goddess! What's the matter with the chap?'

Conor blinked; Brendan appeared to mean it.

'I tell you what, I'd be too much for him to handle.' Caz was both smirking and eyeing Brendan with interest. 'I prefer a bigger man, someone who knows how to look after a woman, know what I mean?'

Urgh, *urgh*, and now she was winking at him, with her giant spidery lashes and lascivious grin. On the brink of retorting that he was perfectly capable of looking after a woman, Conor caught Scarlett's eye and realised that this definitely wasn't the occasion to be defending himself.

What was more, Brendan had got his wallet out and was saying excitedly, 'Let me get these! I like a lady who knows what she wants. And I don't even know your name yet!'

'It's Caz.' As she said it, Caz was squashing her arms at her sides to push her boobs up and out.

'Caz, it's a pleasure to meet you. Short for Caroline, am I right?'

'You are.' She beamed at him as if he'd just got a brilliant answer on *Pointless*.

At once, Brendan burst into song at maximum volume: 'SWEET CAROLINE . . . BAM, BAM, BAMMM!'

Caz screamed with delight. 'That's one of my favourite karaoke songs!'

'Mine too.' His face red and shiny and suffused with joy, Brendan grabbed her hand and pressed it to his own ample chest. 'Can you feel my heart? It's going like the clappers. You're the one making it do that!'

'You just wait,' Caz promised with a filthy cackle. 'I can make all sorts happen when I set my mind to it.'

★   ★   ★

372

'Well, well,' Conor marvelled three hours later as Brendan and Caz left the Red House arm in arm. 'I think that's what you call a turn-up for the books.'

Time had been called at the bar. Jude was clearing tables and Scarlett was stacking glasses in the washer behind the bar. She looked up at him. 'Like my nan always used to tell us, there's a lid for every pot.'

'My grandfather used to say there was a shoe for every foot.' Conor was struck by the coincidence. 'When we're old, d'you suppose we'll start spouting stuff like that?'

Scarlett used her forearm to push her hair out of her eyes. 'To be fair, you're already pretty old.'

He shook his head sorrowfully. 'You've changed. Remember when you couldn't stop flirting with me? You used to tell everyone how much you liked me.'

'Liked. I did like you back then. Past tense.'

'Oh?' Half-jokingly, Conor said, 'So you went off me, did you? What did I do wrong?'

Scarlett wiped dry a couple of trays and gave him an are-you-kidding look. 'You mean apart from not being remotely interested in me and going out with Belinda instead? OK, I know I'm hopeless in lots of ways, but one thing I've learned to do over the years is train myself not to waste my time mooning over men who don't fancy me back. Because it doesn't help, it just makes everything worse. God knows, I've made a prat of myself often enough without adding that to the list. Finished with that glass, have you?'

'Not quite,' said Conor, because she was holding out her hand like a teacher about to confiscate a phone.

Behind him, the door opened and a male voice called

out, 'Scarlett! Don't be long, OK? I'm on double yellows and there's a police car doing the rounds.'

Conor twisted sideways on his stool and saw a good-looking guy with damp blonde hair standing in the doorway.

'Five minutes,' Scarlett called back.

The man disappeared and Conor said, 'Who's that?'

'Danny.'

'Danny the ex?' He raised an eyebrow. 'The guy who cheated on you, then tried to persuade you to sleep with him anyway?'

Energetically she wiped down the brass-topped bar. 'That's the one.'

'And now he's waiting outside for you?' Conor felt as if a nest of snakes had taken up residence in his gut.

'Hear that?' Scarlett pointed to the nearest window, which sounded as if it was having handfuls of gravel flung at it from outside. 'It's tipping down. Danny offered to give me a lift home. What am I going to say to him, "Ooh, no thanks, I'd rather walk"?'

'So does that mean you're back sleeping with him now?' The words had spilled out without warning, prompting Scarlett to give him a pointed look.

'And what business is that of yours?' She tilted her head to one side. 'Oh yes, that's it, none at all.'

Since there was no answer to this, Conor finished his drink and handed her the empty glass.

Go away, snakes.

Aloud he said, 'You still shouldn't do it.'

Chapter 49

They'd arranged to meet at St Mark's at two o'clock, but when Zillah arrived early in her cab, she saw that Matthew was already there in the car park, waiting for her.

She smiled to herself; his excessive punctuality had always driven her mad.

Ah well. It had taken five days to make all the arrangements, but now it was about to happen. At least the weather was perfect. Fingers crossed everything else went according to plan.

As she emerged from the taxi into the sunshine, a warm breeze loosened the blossom from the cherry trees, showering her with baby-pink petals.

'Zillah.' Greeting her with an affectionate kiss on each cheek, Matthew smiled and carefully removed a couple of the fallen petals from her hair. 'You look like a bride, if that isn't an inappropriate thing to say to one's ex-wife.'

One's ex-wife. His turn of phrase still entertained her.

'I'm eighty-three.' She patted his arm. 'I think that ship has well and truly sailed. Anyway, thanks for doing this.'

'No need to thank me. I'd have done it anyway.' He studied her face. 'You're looking well. How are you feeling?'

'Pretty good, considering. Still get a bit tired. But I was lucky.' She changed the subject. 'And you look very healthy too.'

'Thanks to the golf. It's a wonderful game. You really should come up to my club sometime, give it a try—'

'Not in a million years,' Zillah said bluntly, before he could launch into yet another version of the spiel he'd subjected her to on the phone the other night. 'I'm not a tartan-trousers kind of person.'

'You don't *have* to wear—'

'And the green-keepers get cross if you play golf in high heels. Anyway, you're dressed very smartly. Nice suit.' She dusted a speck of lint from the lapel of the jacket. 'Alice is in her room. She can't wait to see you.'

Matthew collected a basket of flowers from the boot of his extremely clean Peugeot and followed her into the building. She had forewarned him about Alice's frailty, so that he wouldn't be visibly shocked.

When they reached the room, she tapped on the closed door. 'Alice? It's me.'

The ensuing silence was long enough to make her wonder if Alice had fallen asleep. Or died, which would be just unbearable.

Oh God . . .

Then she heard Alice say, 'Come in.'

Phew, not dead.

Zillah signalled to Matthew to wait outside and opened the door with considerable relief. Alice was sitting up in bed, wearing her best peach silk bed jacket. Her fine white hair was brushed back from her thin face and the parchment pallor of her skin had been softened with a touch of powder and blusher. By the look of it, she'd also just applied a dab of apricot lipstick.

She said, 'Is he here?'

'Oh yes.' Zillah nodded. 'He can't wait to see you.'

'He's going to get a fright when he does.'

'Rubbish. You look fine.'

'Could you do me a favour? I just tried to get something but couldn't quite reach.'

'Of course.' Zillah went to the bedside cabinet and opened the drawer Alice was pointing to. She passed her the bottle of scent that had rolled to the back, and watched as Alice applied it behind her almost translucent ears.

'Don't worry,' Alice confided. 'I'm not trying to seduce him. I just want to smell nice.'

Then Zillah opened the door to let Matthew into the room, and watched from the doorway as Alice's face lit up.

No digital camera filter could ever mimic that effect.

'Oh . . . you're here, it really is you.' Her voice quavered with emotion as she gazed at him.

'It's really me. Oh Alice, it's so good to see you again.'

'Did Zillah tell you I thought you were dead?'

'I know, but I'm not. And these are for you.' Matthew placed the flowers on the bedside table, then bent to embrace the first love of his life. As he did so, he murmured, 'You're wearing the scent I bought you for your birthday. Guerlain's L'Heure Bleue.'

'It's my favourite,' Alice told him with a shrug. 'I've worn it for the last sixty years.'

Zillah silently withdrew, leaving them alone together. An alternative story flickered through her mind, the life Alice and Matthew could have shared if they'd stayed together: a beautiful home in the country, happy holidays by the sea, adorable children who'd grown up to become loving, responsible adults with children of their own . . .

Except that thanks to me, none of that exists.

Twenty minutes later, Zillah checked her watch and looked at Essie. 'OK, all ready. Time to bring them through.'

The spacious hall had been transformed by Essie and various helpers, and was now almost full. Outside, the sun was still shining, but in here the dark velvet curtains had been drawn. Swathes of midnight-blue netting covered the back of the raised spotlit stage. Rows of chairs were occupied by patients, relatives and staff. Some of the patients were in wheelchairs. In the centre of the front row was space for the most important guests.

'Let's go and get them,' said Essie. 'I can't wait. It's going to be great.'

This time the door to Alice's room stood open. Conor was in there taking photos of Alice and Matthew together.

The smiles on their faces as they sat with their heads tilted together were magical to behold.

'All done?' said Zillah when Conor had finished.

'Oh, do you have to leave now?' Alice looked at Matthew, who smiled and reached into the basket of flowers.

'Not yet. Here, let's just pin this on you.' He produced a small corsage of pink rosebuds and fastened it to her bed jacket.

'Well how lovely,' Alice exclaimed, delighted but mystified. 'You won't remember, but you gave me a corsage once before, the night you took me to the Royal Opera House to see—'

'I remember,' said Matthew. 'And I wish I could have taken you again, but—'

'Oh I know.' Alice nodded. 'But sometimes these things just aren't possible.'

'Hopefully this is the next best thing,' said Zillah. 'We couldn't get you to the ballet, so we thought we'd bring the ballet to you.'

Alice was helped into her padded reclining wheelchair, and everyone applauded as she was wheeled through to the main hall with Matthew at her side.

'Oh my goodness, thank you so much. I can't believe this.' Tears of joy swam in her eyes as she touched Zillah's sleeve. 'I feel as if I'm in a dream . . .'

Conor was leaning against the wall at the side of the hall, ready to take more photos. The main lights went down, the ethereal opening chords of Tchaikovsky's *Swan Lake* filled the air and a spotlight appeared in the centre of the stage. As the first dancers emerged from the wings and the music soared, he kept his gaze fixed on Alice, sitting in the front row between Matthew and Zillah, her face a picture of delight. He watched as Matthew turned to smile at her, then took her hand in his and gave it a gentle squeeze.

He took a couple of photos of them to capture the moment, then turned his attention back to the stage. It wasn't the full ballet being performed, of course; that would have been impractical, both too complex and too long for many in the audience to cope with. But the performance was a carefully curated, edited-highlights version of forty minutes' duration, performed by an adult ballet school from Bristol.

When Zillah had first told him about it, Conor had

envisaged something a bit amateurish and embarrassing. But this wasn't amateurish at all. As Zillah had discovered, the school was attended by dancers who had trained to a high standard at major ballet academies and worked with prestigious companies around the world. They might not currently be working on the professional stage, but they still attended regular classes in order to keep up their skills, and put on performances to raise money for good causes or to entertain those who might not be able to experience the joy of ballet first hand.

And it was a joy, Conor was now realising; the standard was so much higher than he'd expected. The dancers on the stage looked amazing in their gauzy white costumes and matching headdresses. He didn't know the technical terms for much of what they were doing, but they were doing it incredibly well, dancing *en pointe* with their toned legs moving in absolute unison as they leapt and pirouetted across the stage.

He raised his camera, entranced by the elegance of their coordinated arm movements and marvelling at the uniformity of their costumes. Even their make-up was identical, each dancer's eyes heavily outlined beneath the feathered caps covering their hair—

Oh what?

What?

Surely it couldn't be.

Conor froze, staring at the figure currently closest to him on the left-hand side of the stage. It couldn't be, but for a second there he'd been so strongly reminded of Scarlett that he'd thought it was her.

Holding his breath, he watched her face as she executed

a series of swanlike moves. Those eyes . . . the shape of her face . . . the tilt of her chin . . . It really was the most extraordinary thing . . .

The next moment her eyes met his, and with a thud of recognition Conor realised it was indeed Scarlett, up on the stage and dancing like a professional. Furthermore, she'd seen his face but hadn't reacted, had turned away now and was continuing the sequence of moves, stepping and stretching in time with the music and her fellow dancers.

All the complicated emotions he'd been feeling towards Scarlett over the course of the last few weeks came rushing to the fore. Conor felt invigorated, electrified. As the music soared, filling the hall with its timeless magnificence, he realised that Essie had turned her head and was observing him with a tiny smile on her face.

He had so many questions to ask. *So many.* And forty more minutes to go before the performance ended.

OK, time to remember why he was here and take some more photos . . .

Chapter 50

The applause at the final curtain was thunderous. Everyone capable of cheering was doing so. The ten dancers up on the stage curtseyed and beamed and in turn applauded the audience, and fresh tears glistened on Alice's thin cheeks as she clapped her hands together and shook her head in delight.

Then the dancers jumped down from the stage in order to greet her, and Conor took a few informal photos before making his way over to join them.

Essie, who'd beaten him to it, was saying to Scarlett, 'That was brilliant. Everyone loved it.'

'Good.' Still out of breath from her exertions, Scarlett glanced at Conor. 'Although I'm sure there were one or two people in the audience who weren't that impressed.'

It was a dig. Conor ignored it. 'Well they should be impressed. I was. You were amazing.'

She shrugged, bringing her breathing under control. 'Thank you.'

'Why did no one tell me you'd be dancing?'

'Because I didn't want you assuming I wouldn't be good enough,' Scarlett said flatly. 'I was nervous anyway. The last thing I needed was you telling me I'd be a big let-down and ruin the show.'

Conor was taken aback. 'Why would I say something like that?'

'Well you didn't trust me to take those photos at the racing stables, did you? You always expect me to mess things up.'

'But . . . I had no idea you could do this!' He gestured at her costume, at the stage. 'I mean, you were incredible. And you're clearly trained, but no one ever told me . . . neither of you even mentioned it!'

'I did,' said Essie. 'Once. You weren't impressed.'

'What?' Conor turned to stare at her in disbelief. 'That's not true. I've never known that!'

'Yes you have. I *told* you.'

'You didn't.'

'It was around Christmas time. We were in Zillah's kitchen and I mentioned how Scarlett had done some busking last summer, and you pulled a face and said, "What, singing?" and I said no, she was a ballet dancer. And then you pulled another face and did a little oh-my-God laugh, so I gave up and left it there, because you clearly weren't—'

'No, no.' Conor shook his head vigorously, recalling the conversation. 'You said *belly* dancer.'

Essie gave him a look. 'I said ballet. I wouldn't say belly, would I? Because belly dancing isn't what Scarlett does.'

Scarlett removed her white headdress and raked her fingers through her slicked-back purple hair. And Conor, acknowledging his mistake, said, 'Look, I'm sorry. If it sounded like a toss-up between ballet and belly dancing, I must have just assumed you'd been busking as a belly dancer. I had no idea. And you're so *talented*.'

'I was, once.' Scarlett dismissed his praise. 'Ballet was the love of my life. I was awarded a bursary to study at White Lodge. That's the Royal Ballet's lower school,' she explained. 'And I had an audition for the upper school in Covent Garden. I was sixteen and it was all I'd ever dreamed of.'

'What happened?' said Conor, because something clearly had.

'I was crossing the road one morning and got hit by a motorbike that didn't stop. I was left in the gutter with a broken ankle, and that was pretty much it. The dream was over. My ankle mended eventually, but by then it was too late. And it was never as strong as it needed to be, not for the Royal Ballet School. They need you to be one hundred per cent.' She shrugged. 'So now I just do it for fun. I go over to Bristol to do my classes every week and occasionally we put on shows, and it isn't what I'd dreamed of, but that's life, isn't it? At least I'm still here. I could have been killed.'

Her calm acceptance was causing Conor's heart to feel as if it were being squeezed by a giant fist. 'Did they ever catch the motorcyclist?'

'No.'

'It changed your *whole* life.'

'I know, but stuff happens to all of us all the time. You walked out of your job, didn't you? If you hadn't, everything would be different now. You'd still be working as a solicitor, you probably wouldn't be living in Percival Square, you wouldn't have met Essie . . . or me. I mean, imagine how terrible that would have been . . .'

She was joking now, but Conor had never been more serious in his life. 'You—'

'And if Ess hadn't written that round robin, she wouldn't

384

have met Zillah either. Every day we do things that are capable of changing everything, and that's what makes life exciting. When I was busking last summer, I used to fantasise that Steven Spielberg would come to Bath and catch sight of me and be completely *enthralled*, and then he'd beg me to appear in his next film.'

'And did he?'

'No, but it could happen. That's the point. The other week when I was working on my market stall, I sold one of my stained-glass necklaces to a woman, and it turned out she worked as a receptionist at the hotel where Steven Spielberg stayed while he was filming *War Horse* in Castle Combe—' Scarlett stopped abruptly. 'What? Why are you looking at me like that?'

In a rush, the memory had come back to him. Conor said slowly, 'Last Christmas . . . one evening when it was snowing, I saw a guy playing a violin on Milsom Street, and a girl came up and started dancing around him . . . like proper ballet steps . . .'

'Well, you couldn't call them proper,' said Scarlett. 'I was wearing trainers.'

Conor exhaled and spread his hands. 'It was you.'

'It was me.' She nodded with amusement.

'I can't believe it. You were amazing.' He couldn't begin to explain the effect her brief performance had had on him; he'd been completely blown away, both by the magical scene itself and by the idea of a girl who could break into dance like that for the sheer love of it. For weeks afterwards, he hadn't been able to stop thinking about her.

And it had been Scarlett all along. If he'd been able to catch up with her that evening, would she have captured his heart from the word go? Would he have felt about her then the way he felt about her now?

Who knew?

There was nothing else for it: he needed to seize the moment. 'Could we go outside?'

Scarlett's eyebrows went up. 'Why?'

Oh great, and now he appeared to be on the brink of a heart attack. 'Please. We need to talk.'

Out in the garden, Conor found a secluded spot where they wouldn't be overheard, although Scarlett still couldn't work out why he was being so weird.

Carefully arranging the gauzy layers of white tulle that made up her skirt, she seated herself on the wooden bench. 'What's this about, then?'

'You. Me. Me being sorry.' Conor sat down next to her and fiddled distractedly with his shirt collar, as if gearing himself up for some awkward admission. 'Look, I know it's none of my business, but are you seeing anyone else right now?'

Scarlett blinked. 'You mean Danny?'

'Anyone at all.'

'No. No one.' At times like this, she found it helpful to channel cool, in-control women. Surveying him with outward calm, she conjured up her inner Helen Mirren. 'Why?'

'OK, let me just get this out.' He took a deep breath. 'When I met Belinda, I liked her straight away. Then over time I gradually went off her. That's the way it usually goes for me. But when I first met you, I didn't like you at all.'

Charming. 'I noticed.'

386

'The thing is, though, as time went by, how I felt about you kind of . . . began to change. I stopped finding you annoying and started liking you. Just a tiny bit at first, then more and more. And now I really like you,' said Conor. 'I mean, a lot.'

Yee-ha!

'Are you saying I've grown on you? Like ivy?' Scarlett looked mildly amused, Mirren-style.

'I suppose.' He raked his fingers through his already tousled hair. 'Look, it's never happened this way round before. But it has now. And I'm wondering if maybe this is the way to go.'

'How . . . romantic.'

Conor grinned. 'Sorry. I'm just trying to explain how I feel. I wasn't expecting any of this to happen.'

'Except you seem to have forgotten one thing.' *Oh my God, will you listen to me? I'm brilliant at this! Helen Mirren is the best!*

'What have I forgotten?' said Conor.

'I started off *really* liking you. Then you made it very clear that you weren't interested, so I stopped.' Scarlett tipped her head to one side. 'I told you the other night, remember?'

He looked taken aback. 'But now I *am* interested.'

'But it's too late. I switched off that switch, closed that door, deleted that app.'

'Seriously?' said Conor.

'Seriously.'

'Can you not . . . switch it back on?'

Heeee!

Scarlett frowned. 'That's not the way it works for me. Once it's gone, it's gone.'

'Oh.' He looked dismayed.

'Although there might be one thing we can try . . .'

'What's that?'

'Kiss me.' Thrilled by the flare of surprise in his eyes, Scarlett slid across the bench towards him. 'Go on, give it your best shot. Let's see if we can't manage to jump-start this cold, dead heart of mine, bring it back to life.'

And as their lips met, she waved goodbye to Helen Mirren. She had done her job, and done it well. It was no longer necessary to keep up the super-cool facade.

To be honest, even if she'd tried to, the way her entire body was now trembling would have given her away.

Finally they paused for breath. *Phew.* And Conor was smiling down at her.

'Well?' he said. 'Any good?'

Scarlett reached up and rested her fingertips in the little hollow at the base of his throat; how many times had she looked at this hollow and longed to touch it?

She smiled too. 'Not bad. Although we might need a bit more practice.'

'Let me consult my diary. I think we could probably manage that.'

She dropped the facade completely. 'You're gorgeous.'

'Thanks. You have excellent taste.' Conor tucked a wayward strand of purple hair behind her ear. 'Not so bad yourself.'

'I'm free for the rest of the afternoon.' As she said it, Scarlett gazed with longing at his mouth.

'Damn, I wish I was.' He checked his watch. 'But I need to be back in Bath by four thirty. Two-hour job in Albert Street.' He grimaced at the prospect.

'Albert Street? My friend Carrie lives at number twenty-two.'

'My client's Geraldine Marsh at number eighteen.'

The name rang a faint bell. 'Is she the bossy one who complains a lot?'

'The very same.'

'Oh!' Her eyes widened. 'I was at Carrie's party on the night of the storm! A huge tree came down in Geraldine's back garden and someone spent hours with a chainsaw chopping up branches . . .'

'It wasn't the best night of my life.' Conor's tone was rueful.

'I was watching you! Feeling sorry for you! I was going to bring you a hot drink to cheer you up!'

'That would have been brilliant. Why didn't you?'

'I think my favourite music started playing,' said Scarlett, 'so I went back downstairs and had a dance instead.'

'I'll let you off.' He leaned forward and gave her another kiss. 'You didn't know it was me.'

Every single touch of his warm mouth on hers set off a Disney-sized firework display in her chest. 'What's Geraldine's number?' she said.

Conor found it and she held out her hand for his phone.

'Hello?' she said when the call was picked up. 'I'm calling on behalf of Conor McCauley, to let you know that he won't be able to come to you this afternoon. He fell off a ladder earlier and is currently in the A and E department here at the Royal United . . . No, he's hurt his back, but the X-ray was clear. He sends his apologies and says he'll give you a call as soon as he's able to work again . . . Yes, I'll tell him. Bye!'

'Tell me what?' said Conor.

'She said it's very inconvenient because the tulips need digging up.'

'That sounds about right.' He paused. 'And you knew my surname too.'

'That's because I asked Essie what it was, so that I could practise writing my new name if we ever happened to get married.'

He looked amused. 'You see, you come out with things like that and I used to hate it. But now I just think it's funny and honest. Did you really write your name with my surname?'

'Well, not on paper,' said Scarlett. 'But I tried it out in my head. Just a few times.' She grinned, utterly unrepentant. 'Anyway, looks like you've got the rest of the afternoon off now.'

'Looks like I have.' Conor shook his head. 'I wonder what we could possibly find to do?'

Was she dreaming? No she wasn't. After all these months it was finally about to happen. Giddy with adrenalin-fuelled anticipation, Scarlett said, 'No idea, up to you. But we'd better be careful not to damage your bad back.'

Chapter 51

Zillah carried her cup of tea through to the living room, switched on the TV and settled down to watch the last ten minutes of the early-evening news.

It had been quite a day. But a good one. She took a sip of tea and estimated that she had twenty minutes before Essie was back. Honestly, it came to something when you had to invent a shopping list of items you needed purely to get a bit of peace in which to think through what had happened.

Hopefully Alice had enjoyed herself too. Picturing her face, Zillah thought she had, but Alice was so polite she would never dream of saying otherwise.

Had she even fractionally made up, though, for the bad thing she'd done to Alice and Matthew in the first place? Of course not. Poor Alice had lost the love of her life and what could ever compensate for that? Zillah put down her teacup and picked up the TV remote. God, the local news was boring tonight. What she needed was a decent film to distract her from dwelling on her own failings.

'. . . And finally this evening, the Duchess of Cambridge

paid a visit to Bristol Zoo earlier today, to officially open the new meerkat enclosure.' The male TV presenter had adopted his jolly, end-of-the-show voice as footage of the visit appeared on the screen. 'I'm glad to say the meerkats were on their best behaviour for the royal visitor, who was later also introduced to some of the workers at the zoo.' The camera was now panning along a line-up of employees in their bottle-green uniforms, waiting to shake hands with the Duchess. 'At one end of the scale we have Harry Critchley, who has been a keeper here for fifty-one years, which is an amazing achievement, isn't it? Well done, Harry! And at the other end, we have the newest employee, seventeen-year-old Ben Gallagher, who began working here just last week. But something these two do have in common is their passion for animal welfare and their absolute commitment to the work this zoo continues to do . . . so very well done to both of you, and let's hope you'll both continue to work here for many more years to come!'

Zillah covered her mouth, because the look on Ben's thin, happy face as he shook hands with the Duchess was a sight to behold. It was him; he'd achieved his dream to work at the zoo and she couldn't have been prouder of him if he'd been her own great-grandson.

As the presenter wrapped up the piece, then linked to the weather, Zillah reached for a tissue. Thank heavens she hadn't changed the channel; she'd have missed it completely.

How lovely, though, to know that when she'd met Ben and made her impulsive decision, she had done the right thing.

The next morning, whilst Conor was in the shower, Scarlett began leafing idly through the printed-out A4-sized photos he'd taken in the last week. Spreading them out across his desk, she then studied each one in turn, wondering which he'd choose to frame and put on display in the Red House.

Then she noticed something about two of the photos that made her lean in closer and pay extra attention.

Well, well. This *was* fascinating . . .

Five minutes later, Conor emerged from the bathroom with a dark-blue towel fastened around his hips. Moving up behind her, he kissed the nape of her neck. 'I wish I didn't have to go to work.'

'I know. But you do.' The feel of his warm mouth on her neck sent little shivers of pleasure through her; she twisted round and ran her hands over his beautiful broad shoulders. 'We both do.'

'I'll see you this evening, though?'

'I should probably be playing it cool.' Scarlett beamed and stroked his still-damp chest. 'But I can't. Yes please.'

'What have you been doing?' He looked over at the spread-out photos.

'Admiring them. You're pretty good at this, you know.'

Conor winked. 'I'm pretty good at lots of things.'

'Well I've already made that discovery.' Scarlett grinned again, because he didn't even know yet that, thanks to him, she never had succumbed to Danny's suggestion that they should be friends with benefits. But that was completely irrelevant now, because last night and earlier this morning with Conor had been completely out of this world; he'd been worth the wait. She pointed to the photographs. 'But I was wondering if you'd happened to notice something interesting about a couple of these?'

'Which ones?'

'That would be cheating. I'm testing your powers of observation.'

She watched him scan the photos intently. 'I don't know . . . This one's unbalanced . . . the light isn't very flattering in that one . . . and that woman's leg looks weird; I need to crop it out.'

He was all about the technical issues and the composition. He hadn't spotted what she'd spotted. Scarlett said, 'Is it OK if I take two of these away with me?'

'Why?'

She shook her head. 'I won't say, not just yet. I don't think I'm wrong, but I might be.'

'Fine, then. No problem.' Conor reached past her for a folder. 'Put them in there.' He gave her waist a squeeze. 'I'd love to know what you're up to.'

Oh God, he smelled completely delicious, of lemons and limes and sunshine.

'Wait and see.' She kissed him on the mouth once more. 'I'll tell you if I'm right.'

Twenty minutes later, after Conor had reluctantly left for work, she made her way across the square. The Red House wasn't open yet. When Lucas opened the door to her, he took a step back and double-checked his watch.

'It's only ten thirty. You're half an hour early.'

'I know. I want to talk to you.' She followed him inside. 'In private.'

He raised an eyebrow. 'About what?'

'Be patient. Here.' She opened the folder, took out the two photos and laid them side by side on the bar. 'Take a look. Tell me what you see.'

They had been taken here in the bar last Sunday evening.

The first photo was of Brendan and Caz, their heads both thrown back with laughter because Caz had just made a racy comment about a courgette. The second one, featuring the man holding his beloved rescue dog, captured the moment the dog had reached up and enthusiastically licked his ear.

But it wasn't the subjects in the foreground that had caught Scarlett's attention, and she knew at once, discreetly observing Lucas, that he had seen it too. Like her, he'd zoned in on the people in the background.

In the first photo, there he was behind the bar, and there were Essie and Zillah standing several feet away, having dropped in for a quick drink because Zillah had complained that she was going stir crazy at home. Essie was looking at Zillah, whilst Lucas's gaze was fixed on Essie, and the expression on his face was almost heartbreaking in its intensity.

In the second photograph, Lucas was serving one of their regulars and Essie, this time standing alone, was watching him with an almost identical look of longing in her eyes.

It had been two chances in a million, but Conor had unwittingly managed to capture them both.

Was that serendipity, or what?

Because right now, it certainly felt like it.

Scarlett looked at Lucas in his white cotton shirt and black jeans, with his dark hair falling into his eyes and a muscle going in his jaw as he continued to avoid her gaze.

Finally he exhaled. 'What's she told you?'

Which instantly made her want to make up something outrageous and trick him into confessing all. But no, he hadn't denied it, she mustn't do that. Instead, with absolute honesty, she said, 'She's told me nothing at all. Which is what makes it so interesting, because Essie's my best friend and she always tells me everything.'

'Maybe there's nothing to tell.' But this was so clearly a hypothetical suggestion that all Scarlett had to do was glance down at the photos laid out on the bar, then up again at Lucas.

He blinked first.

'So, I'm right. I think you should tell me what's been going on. Were you seeing each other before Scotland?' Surely not, though. 'Or was that when it happened? Oh *wow* . . .'

'Nothing's happened.' Lucas shook his head. 'Before or after Scotland. Look, can we change the subject?'

Was he serious?

'I'm sorry, but we need to talk about this. We have to. You and Giselle broke up, then Essie finished with Paul, which I was delighted about, by the way. So I don't get it.' Scarlett frowned. 'If you two are crazy about each other, which you clearly *are* . . . well, there's no reason why you shouldn't . . . *Aaahh*.' She nodded as light dawned. 'It's to do with Zillah, isn't it? That's why Essie was so guilty . . . I get it now.'

'She felt guilty?' Lucas looked taken aback.

'Hello! Have you not seen what she's been like with Zillah? No, I don't suppose you have.' She pulled a face. 'Honestly, though. She's like a cross between a bodyguard and a baby koala. She feels terrible about not being there when Zillah was ill, and we keep telling her it wasn't her fault, but she still blames herself because she just feels so guilty and ashamed . . . and *that's* why she won't leave Zillah on her own,' Scarlett concluded with a triumphant jab of her finger. 'Which is driving Zillah completely nuts, by the way.'

'Right.' Lucas nodded, just a bit. He was looking pretty stunned.

'Did you really not know?'

'I assumed she'd had second thoughts about me.'

'But she didn't actually tell you that.'

'Well, no, but . . .'

Honestly, some men. 'How much have you two said to each other about this?'

'Nothing,' said Lucas.

Scarlett surveyed him with fascination. 'And how much does she mean to you?'

'Oh God.' He exhaled heavily. 'Everything. And I can't believe I just told you that. This isn't the way things usually are for me.'

She smiled, because Lucas was *so* good-looking and normally *so* confident that discovering his unconfident side was quite the revelation. Practically every female who met him fell under his spell, but only in that fantasy out-of-reach kind of way you'd fancy someone like Hugh Jackman or Chris Hemsworth.

Yet somehow she just knew instinctively that this time he had met his match.

'Time to have that talk with Essie,' she told him kindly. Oh, and she fully intended to take *all* the credit for this, once it was sorted out.

He still looked wary.

'Trust me. I'm not wrong. Why are you so scared?'

Lucas pushed his fingers through his dark hair and said simply, 'Because it matters so much.'

Chapter 52

It was one thing knowing you were going to be seeing Lucas at work and getting yourself mentally prepared beforehand. And quite another opening your front door and finding him, with no prior warning at all, on the doorstep.

Oh God, look at him, look at those eyes . . . except no, don't look at those eyes . . . Her heart racing, Essie blurted out, 'I'm busy.'

'Not a problem.' Lucas surveyed her with an easy smile. 'I've come to collect Zillah.'

'Ah, you're here. Marvellous!' Zillah materialised in the hallway behind Essie, wearing her turquoise turban-style hat and carrying her oversized silver handbag. 'Thanks so much, Lucas.'

Essie stared at her. 'Where are you off to? What's going on? I'm in the middle of cooking dinner.'

'Oh, I just fancied some company and a change of scenery.' Pausing in front of the mirror in the hallway, Zillah produced a lipstick from her pocket and expertly applied it, then smacked her lips together. 'Lucas is walking me over to the Red House.'

'I could have done that,' said Essie. Also, wasn't she company enough?

'Except you need to be here to cook the dinner.' Zillah's dark eyes danced as she took Lucas's arm. 'You just carry on, my darling. I won't be late home, I promise!'

Bizarre. So that was who Zillah had been exchanging texts with when they'd been in the kitchen, catching up on an episode of *Pointless* while Essie put the chicken into the oven to roast and made a start on the vegetables.

She headed back into the kitchen now, slightly miffed that Zillah had chosen to leave her on her own to carry on chopping carrots, simmering the bread sauce and making the stuffing and gravy. Oh well, may as well get on with it.

Last night Zillah had suggested they both drop into the Red House for a couple of drinks, but Essie, knowing Lucas would be there, had persuaded her that they'd be better off staying here, playing Boggle and watching a film. It was still a tiny bit irritating, though, being left here on your own while the person you were supposed to be looking after waltzed off on the arm of someone else.

Someone else who happened to be Lucas.

Five minutes later, as she was peeling apples for the stuffing, the doorbell rang again.

Essie headed out into the hallway, then paused at the door and called out, 'Who is it?'

In case this time it was a burglar.

Well, a polite one.

Then a voice said, 'It's me,' and Essie felt as if she'd touched an electric fence.

It was hard to catch her breath. 'What do you want?'

'Could you open the door?' said Lucas.

'Is Zillah with you?'

'No, I'm alone.'

Essie's heart broke into a panicky gallop. 'I don't understand.'

'Opening the door might help,' said Lucas.

'And what if I don't want to?'

'Well, Zillah did give me her front-door key.'

OK, she needed to get a grip. Essie unlocked the door and opened it. 'Did she forget something?'

'No.'

'Where is she?'

Lucas shrugged easily. 'No idea.'

'You *what*?'

'Joking. She's sitting in state on the red velvet sofa, surrounded by adoring fans.'

'You shouldn't joke,' said Essie.

'And you probably shouldn't answer the door brandishing a knife,' Lucas replied with a faint smile. 'Look, now that I'm here, can I come in?'

Essie stared down at the paring knife in her hand and placed it on the rosewood table beside the door. 'Why?'

'OK, two reasons. One, because you're driving Zillah mad.'

'I am not!'

'You are. Scarlett told me, and now Zillah has too. She's feeling a bit smothered.'

'I'm taking care of her. That's not smothering!' As she said it, a group of people made their way past the house and eyed her with interest. Outraged, Essie hissed, 'Oh God, and now everyone's going to think I'm a murderer . . .'

'Shh, no they won't.' And now he was in the hallway, closing the door behind him.

'Honestly, I can't believe Scarlett. What's she been saying about me? She's got a nerve.'

'Don't be cross. It smells fantastic in here. Oh, I heard all about this.' Lucas paused at the entrance to the kitchen to admire the bunting that was still strung up. 'It looks great.'

'And I still don't know what's going on.' Essie's mouth was dry. It was too much to take in; having practically forced his way in here, Lucas was now telling her that everything she'd done was wrong, and it was confusing enough that he was speaking to her in the confident, cheerful tone he'd always used before Zillah's accident had changed everything.

'Well I think you're cooking a roast chicken, aren't you? That's what it smells like.' Briefly opening the oven door, Lucas said, 'Yes, looks like a chicken to me.'

Essie blinked. 'Why are you doing this?'

'I said there were two reasons. You haven't asked me what the second one is.'

OK, now he was just playing with her, and it was pretty unsettling. As if it wasn't hard enough keeping her true feelings under wraps. Essie said, 'I don't want to know the second reason.'

And now Lucas was smiling at her in that devastating, havoc-making way of his, as if he knew for certain that this wasn't true. Raising an eyebrow, he murmured, 'Really? Are you sure?'

Her throat tightened. 'Will you stop looking at me like that?'

'I can't help it. Scarlett says you're crazy about me and the reason you've been denying it is because you feel so riddled with guilt about Zillah's accident. And that's been a pretty fantastic thing to find out, because for the last couple of weeks I was beginning to think I'd *imagined* all the—'

'Wait! What?' Belatedly Essie blurted out, 'How could *Scarlett* have told you that?'

Lucas shrugged. 'She just did. She knew.'

'But not from me.' Essie shook her head in bewilderment. 'I didn't tell her anything.'

'Scarlett's more observant than you think.' His dark eyes were bright with amusement. 'I know, I was surprised too. She also told me I was crazy about you.' He paused. 'Well, to be fair, I did already know that.'

Essie could hardly breathe. She leaned back against the kitchen worktop, light-headed with shock and fear and experiencing a tsunami of emotions – joy, shame, panic and stunned disbelief. Because what he was telling her was everything she'd longed to hear, but also everything she'd told herself she didn't deserve to hear.

Helplessly she repeated, 'I didn't tell Scarlett.'

Lucas moved towards her. 'That's how she knew.'

'Zillah nearly died.' Essie's voice wavered, her chest aching at the thought of how narrowly that tragedy had been avoided. She still couldn't stop thinking about it.

'But she didn't.' His gaze was steady. 'Believe me, I know how guilt feels, but it wasn't your fault that Zillah fell off the chair. Nor was it your fault that we didn't get home until midnight.'

'I was the one who made you visit your mother.'

'And I'm so glad you did,' said Lucas. 'Because look what happened.'

Essie took a deep, shuddery breath; she'd been bottling up her emotions for so long, she had to confess everything.

'I nearly didn't find Zillah, though. On my way into the house I stepped over the post on the mat without even noticing it was there. I heard someone cry out when I was in the shower, but told myself it was a fox out in the square. All I could think about was getting over to the Red House to see you, and it just makes me feel so sick and *ashamed*.'

'Hey, listen to me.' And now Lucas was standing before her, placing his hands on her shoulders, and her skin felt as if it was on fire. 'You did notice the post on the mat, you found her in time, you *saved* her life. And now she's well again. Thanks to you, she's made a complete recovery.' He nodded. 'Plus, all she could think about tonight was getting over to the Red House—'

'To get away from me,' said Essie with a rueful half-smile.

'No, not that. She wanted to come over because she loves going out and meeting new people and being independent.' As he spoke, Lucas's thumbs were slowly massaging the skin above each of her collarbones, which was proving to be a pretty heavenly experience. 'Also, I was the one who asked her to go over there, so I could come here and speak to you.'

'Oh.' Essie swallowed; the collarbone thing really was incredible.

'You can't keep on punishing yourself for saving someone's life.' Lucas's voice was low, his mouth close to her ear now. 'That just doesn't make any sense.'

'I don't know . . .' It had become Essie's default reaction to tell herself that it did.

'Shh. I'm right and you're wrong.' He drew back a fraction in order to look at her. 'Now tell me, if Zillah hadn't fallen off that chair, what do you think would have happened between us that night we arrived back here in Bath?'

Oh God . . .

Essie whispered, 'I don't know.'

'Really? No idea at all? Completely sure about that?' He gave her an enquiring look. 'Because I know what I was hoping might happen at some stage after you turned up at my place.'

This time he was close enough to feel her body quiver in response to his words. Essie glanced out of the window, up at the starry night sky, and saw a perfect crescent moon over the square. She looked back at Lucas. 'Now you're not being fair.'

'I don't want to be fair. You have no idea how much I've missed you. Just like you have no idea how much I've wanted to kiss you. It's been killing me.' He stroked the side of her face. 'Thinking you really liked me, then thinking you *didn't* like me . . . this last couple of weeks has been pretty hard to handle. If you only knew what you've done to me—'

'Right, that's enough.' Essie, who was only human, wrapped her arms around his neck and kissed him, the whoosh of electricity catching them both by surprise. Oh God, this was heavenly. Lucas was the most sensational kisser, his fingers sliding through her hair and their bodies pressing together . . .

'You're amazing,' he murmured when they finally came up for air.

She took a deep breath. 'There's something I have to tell you.'

'Oh God. Go on, then.' He waited, clearly braced for the worst.

Essie held his gaze. 'I don't feel guilty any more.' It was true; the shame and self-recriminations had melted away.

'You have no idea how happy that makes me. I've never felt this way about anyone before. Do you believe that? Probably not,' said Lucas, 'because I can still hardly believe it myself. But it's true, I swear it is. That very first morning after your brother had sent that round robin . . . my God, I'd never seen anyone so furious, but even then, all I could think while you were yelling at him was how incredible you were. And I know that makes no sense, but it's the truth.'

'I didn't think you were incredible,' Essie told him. 'Not then.'

'I kind of guessed.' Amused, he briefly kissed her again. 'Then when you came to work at the Red House—'

'I didn't think you were incredible then either.' She studied his beautiful face. 'But you grew on me. Once I found out you hadn't sent the email. And once I realised how much nicer you were than I'd thought, you won me over.'

'Thank goodness for that,' said Lucas.

'I'm glad too.' Essie wished he would massage her collar-bones again. 'I can't believe this is happening.'

Then they both jumped as the timer on the oven beeped loudly, bringing them back to earth. Now, of course, dinner was the very last thing on her mind, but Zillah would be expecting to eat when she came home. Essie opened the oven, hastily basted the roast chicken and reset the timer.

'OK, how long do we have?' Lucas slid his arms around her waist.

'Forty minutes.'

His mouth twitched. 'That'll do for a start.'

And Essie, realising that she was about to take him up to

her tiny flat at the top of the stairs, said, 'What if Zillah decides to come back? You've got her key.'

'She'll ring the doorbell.' Lucas pulled a face, indicating that they probably wouldn't want her doing that.

Essie picked up her phone and dialled a number. It was answered on the fifth ring. 'Zillah! Hi, are you having a good time?'

Over the hubbub of background noise at the Red House, Zillah said cheerily, 'I'm having a marvellous time, darling! How about you?'

Very soon, hopefully.

'Great,' said Essie. 'I just wanted to check that everything was, you know, fine with you.'

'If you're wondering what time I'll be home, it won't be for a while yet. Everyone's being so lovely, and Scarlett's just made me the most delicious cocktail, and guess what it's called? A hanky-panky!'

'Sounds . . . interesting.' Essie caught Lucas's eye and tried not to laugh, because he'd grabbed her hand and was edging her out of Zillah's flat into the hallway. 'Well, I just wanted to check in, make sure you're OK . . .'

Above the music and chatter and shrieks of laughter, Zillah said happily, 'Of course I'm OK, my darling girl. I'm being spoiled rotten.'

Essie smiled as Lucas nudged her towards the staircase. Then to Zillah she said, 'That's because you're the Queen of the Square!'